Unmasking Truth

UNMASKING TRUTH

BOOK 2 OF MANTLE OF THE GODS

TRICIA SPARKS

TRINITY GATEWAYS LLC

UNMASKIING TRUTH, Book 2 of *MANTLE OF THE GODS*

This is a work of fiction. All characters and events portrayed are fictional, and any resemblance to real people or incidents is purely coincidental.

Cover Design by Doris Ross

A Trinity Gateways LLC Publication
www.TrinityGateways.net

ISBN: 0988195165
ISBN-13: 978-0-9881951-6-5

DEDICATIONS

To my parents, you've been my life's compass, showing me my true north.

To Mrs. Dent, my high school English teacher, who took an interest in my writing and put the wind in my sails to pursue my dreams.

To Doris Ross, the captain of my ship. You've been behind me every step pushing me to go further and never give up.

To Lisa Gastineau, my creative partner and crew. You're the one that works behind the scenes and keeps my voyage smooth.

To Dustin, my life's partner on this grand adventure, you make each day brighter because you're in it.

Thank you all for helping me to reach this stop in my journey and I hope that you'll sail with me into the future as well.

Sam swore as he raced towards the shore. He was well aware he had to get as much distance between himself and the isle of Atlantis as possible. He shook his head at the thought. It still dumbfounded him that only a few hours earlier he'd stood in the lost city. He looked to his precious cargo and was relieved to see that the lovely Dr. Annalynn Gallagher seemed to be doing fine. Hard to believe; given the fact he'd just rescued her from one of the fallen ones, who had walked the earth since the war in heaven, pretending to be gods.

Gods – it was unbelievable! Sam was not the sort to believe in myth or fairytale; yet he'd seen it with his own eyes. The statues of the ruling deities at Sodom and Gomorrah predated the Greek pantheon that they resembled by over ten centuries. The map of the King of Sodom's domain revealed the locations of the other four plains cities: Gomorrah, Admah, Zeboim and Zoah. Along with the map; there had been half a riddle the second half had waited in Gomorrah; the answer had lead Anna and her team to Atlantis itself.

Atlantis the lost city; which the archeological world had longed to discover had laid waiting beneath the sea, hidden in the Bermuda Triangle. It slumbered undisturbed until Sodom was discovered; then like a beast from the deep it rose. The most unholy place on the face of the earth; the place the Fallen had called home since before man walked the earth. Where the Devil himself had waged bloody war from; with the Creator; until hell was fashioned and the earth flooded. In the confusion of that time his armies were captured or scattered to the four winds but Lucifer escaped. He lay in wait for his time to take his vengeance.

He'd seen his opening with mankind in the garden. Deceiving the woman had been easy and the man had followed right along with her. True it had cost him this treacherous act but he'd stripped them of their dominion of the earth and enslaved them to their carnal desires. His rage unending the Devil had not been satisfied with merely taking the Creator's beloved humans; no he'd waited biding his time.

He found his next opening when the Creator began sending angelic messengers to speak for him to the humans he'd made. Lucifer still the most beautiful of his brethren came to them concealing his identity. He tricked at least ten of them into taking upon themselves mortal flesh in order to make their task easier. Unaware of the danger, inherent, in the act they did so; his advice making sense. Once they were as men, the Devil struck – he set their eyes upon the beauty of woman and caused them to burn with desire.

The ten became his great generals; they took for themselves from the daughters of men as they wished; making the girls into their brides. In exchange for the right to do so they shared with the rulers of men secrets of power never meant to be known. For this they were named gods. They established their kingdom in the cursed city of their prince's rebellion. They ruled mankind from there for centuries; until they were imprisoned within the graven images that lay beneath the city in the throne room of Lucifer.

How did they become trapped? Sam wondered; as he taxied the boat to the slip of the dock. He tied the boat off and helped Anna disembark. He told himself he'd need to thank Catharine for her help and figure out how to repay Lance for his part in getting him to the isle in time to get Anna out of there unscathed.

No, not unscathed; he'd managed to get her out but they'd both suffered a loss as well. Anna had watched a man she once loved Dr. Ian Broody be consumed by the Fallen One known as Hermes, the god of Knowledge. Sam's loss had been his ex-wife, Pamela Walsh, an over ambitious reporter, who when Anna refused to become Hermes bride had been selected in her place. While Sam no longer loved her he did not want to see her enslaved to the Fallen One's will.

Sam cursed again as the two of them made their way down the dock and toward the street. They had failed, their first time out, to prevent the mantle of the god Hermes from finding its way into a mortal's hands and back to the lost city. Anna had declared it earlier. It was a hard pill to swallow but as he'd said before the war wasn't over, there were still eight others to find and find them they would. But their search couldn't start from here. Artemis was still out there somewhere and it wouldn't take her long to find them in Miami.

1

DENVER, COLORADO

Anna sat staring at her fifth book of Scandinavian folklore. Her head was pounding and the letters were beginning to blur together on the page.

"Sam, I've got to stop for a bit, my eyes feel like they're going to bleed," Anna grumbled as she brushed a strand of her unruly blonde hair out of her face. It had managed to work its way out of her neat bun as she worked.

"Yeah, I think a break is in order. Have you had any luck?" Sam asked as he looked up from his own book of German tales. His blue eyes met with her ever changing eyes and he noted they were their normal hazel color. It relieved him. When he'd found her hoursearlier in that god forsaken throne room they'd nearly been black with her fear and pain. He watched as temper flared and the color changed darkening.

"Nothing, I wish I knew where to begin there is so much to go through. I never realized just how many fairytales and myths there were not to mention this mountain of folklore from around the world. We could be at this for years," she said exasperated.

Sam raked a hand through his dark hair and sighed. He hated to admit it but she was right and they didn't have that kind of time here not with Artemis out there hunting for them to say nothing of Kadar's employer, Mr. York. "Yeah, didn't realize how big an undertaking this was going to prove to be."

"When I stop to think that I held one of them in my hands before this whole thing got started and that now it's gone. Stolen right from under the museum's nose it makes me want to scream," Anna groused.

"No sense lamenting something you couldn't have known at the time. Why don't we give Lance a call and see how he's doing with the investigation? Besides I should let him know we're in the clear for now and have him pass on our thanks to Catharine." Sam suggested as he marked his page and closed the book.

"Sounds good to me, don't want them to worry needlessly any longer," Anna replied. She followed his lead marking her place and setting the work aside.

Sam noting the time pulled out some of their provisions handing her a snack before pulling out his cell phone and dialing the detective's number.

2
WASHINGTON DC, VIRGINIA
SUNDAY
5PM

Detective Lance Roman sat behind his beat up oak desk studying the reports on his latest case. He looked at the earthen cup that had until recently been on display at the small auction house for the Smithsonian and groaned. The Crime Scene Unit had found nothing to help him identify the thief. As he stared at the forgery he willed it to grow fingerprints, he could track, with no success.

His gaze moved from the cup to the stack of photos sitting on his desk. They were copies of a similar stack he'd received anonymously at his private residence. The gruesome images were ones he'd hoped to never see again; the fact that he'd spent half his morning discussing them with the chief didn't sit well with him. He didn't want any part of that case again. It had taken quite a bit of dancing on his part to convince the older man that he had no business getting involved in the matter again.

But even that hadn't weighed as heavily on his mind as the major concern hanging over him that day. He'd tried to bury himself in his work to avoid it but nothing had truly been able to distract him for long. His thoughts kept drifting back to his phone call from Sam Abrams late last night.

"We got hit, they got Anna." Sam's words echoed around in his head like a record caught in a loop. Lance had contacted Catharine in LA on Sam's behalf and arrangements had been made to get the former reporter turned MMA fighter out to an undisclosed isle in the Bermuda Triangle – the city of Atlantis.

Lance laughed; the whole thing was insanity, from the place his friend had been headed to the reason for going. Mantle of the gods – nonsense! Sam had finally lost his mind. One too many blows to the head Lance reasoned. Yet he knew for a fact that when Sam called Anna had been in danger of some kind. Sam Abrams wasn't the sort of guy who called in a favor on a whim.

"Where the devil are they? I'd have thought I'd heard something by now," Lance muttered. He contemplated heading home sitting here wasn't doing him any good and he couldn't take much more of the place. Too many reminders of a life, long gone, lingered here today, stirred up by the damn photos.

Lance shoved the photos in the drawer of his desk and picked up the troublesome cup. He had Sam and Anna to thank for that one too, he reminded himself with disgust. He switched off his computer and cup in hand started on his way to the evidence lock up. As he walked his phone rang. Lance took out the offending object which had been unusually quiet and seeing the number on the caller idea felt a giant weight lift from his shoulders.

"Hello Sam," he said as he answered the call.

"Lance, sorry I haven't called sooner. I got Anna out she's safe. Didn't have a lot of time to talk earlier we were on the run…"

"Yeah, I can imagine. Glad to hear you're both safe. I take it you've landed somewhere away from Miami and nowhere near DC or Vegas," Lance said interrupting, the less he knew about their mission the better he'd feel.

"Right, be sure to thank Catharine for us when you talk to her next."

"Will do, don't forget Abrams, you owe me for this one," Lance stated.

"Yeah, more than you know, just let me know where and when and I'm there," Sam assured him.

"I'm going to hold you to that, Sam."

"Lance, I hate to ask for anything else but have you had any luck with the cup?" Sam questioned.

"No, wish I could say otherwise, but no. I'm getting nowhere on the damn thing and fast."

"Sorry to hear it."

"How are things on your end going?"

"About the same, we are buried under a mountain of research," Sam stated with a sigh.

Lance chuckled, "Well, I got to admit I think this whole thing is nuts, but good luck to you."

"Can't say I blame you for that or that I don't understand how you feel about it. Even to me this whole mess seems crazy even after seeing what I have. Thanks for your help and the luck; we'll need it. Good luck to you as well," Sam answered before he hung up.

Lance laughed if he'd been talking to anyone other than Sam

about gods and powerful relics he'd have had them tested for sobriety and quite possibly locked up for insanity. Sam was not your average guy off the street. He knew things – Lance wondered how much Anna really knew about her protector and shrugged. Not his business, he reasoned.

Lance held up the evidence bag holding the cup in question and studied it again. This was a replica of the cup of a god? It seemed rather plain and unimpressive to him, a simple clay chalice. It had no engravings in it, no finery to it at all. It was completely blank – no he was wrong. Lance blinked, clearing his vision, verifying that the faint mark hidden inside the lip of the rim was real. Seeing that it was indeed still there he turned and headed back to his desk.

Pulling out a pair of gloves he opened the bag and with a magnifying glass examined the mark closer. The image depicted was that of a hammer leaning against an anvil with flames rising above it. In front of the image were two small rectangles with a smaller image within them that he couldn't quite make out. Lance smiled; it seemed that the forger couldn't resist signing his work. That had to be a maker's seal. Grabbing his digital camera Lance snapped a couple close-ups of the mark. He'd seen it before somewhere he was sure of it but where escaped him. Brushing the matter aside for later Lance picked up the phone and dialed the number of a local jeweler in the area. He'd used the guy in the past as a contact; he hoped that Frank would be able to identify the brand.

3 ATLANTIS, SOMEWHERE IN THE BERMUDA TRIANGLE

Zaharrah Lynch made her way past security headed in the direction of the city temple. Her brown eyes studied the dig site with disgust. Since Anna left things there had gotten worse. Any hope of trying to get into restricted areas was gone. Dr. Broody had tightened things up for reasons she didn't know. Whatever it was; it had to do with that chamber Anna had discovered beneath the temple.

Something had happened in that throne room early this morning. Zaharrah had felt the earth shift; watched the sky above darken without warning, seen the seas rage and boil as the weather went wild; waging war with an unseen foe. She wondered just what had taken place, in the hours before dawn, as she made her way up the steps of the temple and through its corridors in the direction of the library; where she'd spent more days than she could count reading through old texts.

Zaharrah was by no means a religious zealot she'd walked away from that life long ago but every fiber in her being urged her to abandon her task there and get as far away from the isle as she could. Something dwelled here in the shadows – it seeped out of every nook and cranny of the land and threatened to consume those who it caught off guard – whatever it was; it was evil.

Zaharrah recalled Anna's cryptic words before she left the isle "There are some secrets in this world that are never meant to be discovered." Zaharrah had heard similar words her whole life from her family; she'd never believed them – until now. She'd do as Anna asked of her not because she'd paid her well, though she had, no she'd do it to protect the people she cared about from this cursed place's reach.

As she stepped into the library, Zaharrah was puzzled to find the torches already lit. She cursed as she realized she wasn't alone. A handsome young man with dark hair and blue eyes stood in her corner with a woman she didn't recognize. She had bottle blonde hair and whisky colored eyes. Zaharrah studied the pair with interest wondering who they were and how they'd gotten in here past security.

"Dr. Lynch, I see you don't take the weekends off either," the man said amused. His voice was familiar and yet strange to her.

"With all the added security it's difficult to get any serious work done when the rest of the staff is here," Zaharrah said, her voice cool and crisp, hinting at her anger.

"Yes, I'm sorry of that; but it can't be helped. We don't want another Ithaca on our hands," the man explained with a laugh. Zaharrah blinked with shock; the man before her was Dr. Broody.

"No, we wouldn't, how can I help you Dr. Broody?"

"Zaharrah, please, call me Ian; we're old friends after all. I'd like you to meet my wife, Pamela Walsh. She's fascinated by our work and I was hoping to show her the wonderful candle you found. "

"Hello, Pamela. I'd love to help you Ian, but I'm afraid I shipped the candle back to the Smithsonian. Dr. King requested to see some of the cataloged finds. It should be arriving there later this week."

"Oh, well, don't worry about it. I know how these things are. Zaharrah, I'm going to pull you out of the library on Monday."

"Why?"

"Well, quite frankly, with Anna gone, I need my best archeologist looking for additional artifacts, like the candle, things that will tell us more about the sort of place this is. I can put a grad student or low level researcher in here."

"Okay."

"Why don't you take a look through Anna's notes and see if you can find anything she found out about the candle or other items like it?" Ian stated as he handed her a copy of Anna's research.

Zaharrah nodded. She said a distracted goodbye to the new Mrs. Broody and set off in the direction of her office.

"What is he really up to?" She murmured as she closed herself in her workspace. She checked the room to ensure she was indeed alone; finding no electronic bugs or cameras Zaharrah breathed a sigh of relief before picking up the phone and punching in Anna's number. If anyone could tell her what was going on she was certain Anna could.

4 Denver, Colorado

Anna sat enjoying the warmth of a fire as she finished her simple snack of nuts and fruit. She sighed, relaxed, a break had been just what she'd needed. The headache that had been threatening to come on full force earlier had faded. She contemplated taking a soak in a nice hot tub but before she could consider the idea any further her phone rang.

"So much for that idea," Anna muttered as she pulled the offending object from her coat pocket. Sam looked up from the TV where he sat with question. Seeing the number she shrugged before connecting the call.

"Dr. Gallagher," a familiar voice said by way of greeting.

"Zaharrah, is that you?" Anna questioned surprised by both the call and the unusual greeting.

"Yes, I'm not sure how much time I've got so let me make this quick. Broody pulled me out of the library, asked to see the candle. I told him it was in route to the museum. It should arrive there later this week."

"Thanks for the tip. Why the rush though?"

"Security here has gotten tighter since you left. I've given some serious thought to walking but I can't. He's looking for something in your research pertaining to the candle and any other artifacts they might mention; really closed mouthed about what though."

"I was hoping I'd have a bit more time before that happened."

"You know what he's looking for?"

"Yes, it's connected to the disk I had indirectly."

"Anna, what is this all about?"

"Powerful relics known as the Mantles of the gods, the candle was only one of several. The clues he wants are in my notes; it's not blatantly obvious; but close scrutiny will reveal them. Do me a favor and stall him as long as possible. He can't be allowed to find them."

"Okay, what are they, these mantles, so if I come across them here I can keep them from falling into his hands?"

"The ones still unaccounted for are, the sword of Ares, the bow of Eros, the whip of Helios, the Trident of Poseidon, the gauntlets of Hephaestus, the scroll of Chaos, and the crown of Zeus. I have the horn of Hermes, the candle you had and the cup is here somewhere in the USA, it was stolen recently. I've got a friend tracking it down for me. Zaharrah, if you find one of them don't touch it directly – they're dangerous."

"I'll be careful doctor, I suggest you do so as well," Zaharrah said before she disconnected the call.

"I take it our breaks over," Sam said.

"Yes, afraid so, Zaharrah said Broody came to her asked about the candle. It's apparently in route to the museum. I'll need to contact Dr. King have him keep it hidden upon arrival."

"So that's one that will be safe," Sam stated.

"Right, but Ian's started looking for the other mantles too."

5

Sam prayed for patience, as jealousy woke within him, and his temper flared at Anna's once again referring to the opportunistic doctor as Ian. He drew a breath, looking for calm; reminding himself that there was no reason to be envious.

"He's not Ian anymore Anna, you said it yourself, he's become the Fallen One, Hermes. The man you once loved is no more." The words fell from his lips, despite his best intentions, harsh and cold. He looked on as her hazel eyes darkened with pain and mentally cursed himself for the verbal attack.

"Yes, I know Mr. Abrams. Do you think I could forget? I watched it happen in that godforsaken throne room beneath the earth – he was going to kill me," Anna reminded, her voice as cold as a winter's frost.

Sam swore, she'd not called him Mr. Abrams in days. He shook his head realizing he'd hit a sore spot with his ill-tempered words. As he replayed them in his mind he recalled what he'd read earlier that morning.

"The Power of life and death is in the tongue, Proverbs 18: 21"

In his mind's eye he pictured his words striking her like that of an arrow loosed from a bow. "I'm sorry Anna, I didn't mean that I just…"

"Get jealous where he's concerned; I know and I can understand it but I don't care for your lashing out at me like that," she stated.

Sam was sure she was holding back words of her own that she could say in her anger and felt condemned. She had more reason to attack him than he did, yet she was refraining. Why was this so hard for him? "It wasn't my intent to hurt you Anna, I didn't think I just reacted."

She nodded and Sam watched as she relaxed again. He sighed knowing that she'd let the matter go and they were once more on safe ground. "What do you think Hermes wants with the other mantles anyway? They were made to be given to mortal men loyal to their gods, so what good would they do him?" Sam questioned steering their conversation back to the task at hand.

"I don't know. It does seem odd. Whatever it is I'm sure it can't be good. So, back to the books; we've got to get to those mantles before he can."

6

Detective Lance Roman rubbed tired eyes as the last line of text in the file in front of him began to blur. He glanced at his clock and noted the time. It was a little after nine which meant he'd been sifting through his old B & E cases for four hours now. Searching for any reference to the strange makers mark he'd identified on the forged earthen cup from the museum. At the moment the only thing he had to show for the extra four hours was a stiff neck, the beginnings of a headache and a rotten mood.

Lance cursed. Where was it? He knew he'd seen the image of a hammer leaning against an anvil burning with the two rectangles in front of it before. So, why couldn't he find it? He wasn't going crazy.

Lance raked his fingers through his red spiked hair and turned his head cracking his neck, to relieve the tension. He'd had enough for now. He needed to have a clear head when he met with Frank and pushing further would only sabotage the meet. Closing the file he set it aside and picked up the phone. He dialed the number for Catharine in L.A. Lance reasoned it was time he got back to her and a pleasant chat with the spirited writer might be just what he needed to clear his head.

He listened as the phone rang a number of times and sighed with disappointment when he was directed to her voice mail. It seemed they were going to be playing phone tag. He wasn't fond of the back and forth of voice mail but despite his distaste of speaking with a machine when the message ended he spoke.

"Hi Catharine, its detec…ah – its Lance I got your message earlier and I thought I'd give you a call; see how things are going out there. I guess you're busy or away from the phone. I'll try again later. Bye." Lance groaned inwardly at the message, this was why he didn't speak with machines, he always sounded like an idiot tripping over what to say and how to say it.

Setting the receiver down; Lance glanced at the clock. Noting the time he grabbed the leather jacket from the back of his chair and headed for the door. It was time he got on his way for his meet with Frank.

7 LOS ANGELES, CALIFORNIA

Catharine Nichols sat in a 30 inch tall wooden framed director's chair. A copy of her revised script for Heart of Clay rest on her lap, at her side sat a man with striking blue eyes and shoulder length golden blond hair. The man in his mid-thirties was James Hardagen, a former teen star recently turned director, looking to make his big comeback as the vampire lord Syvarin. Filming for the movie was supposed to have begun two days ago but the process had ground to a halt when their lead actress didn't show.

Catharine's blue eyes closed as she struggled for calm. She'd been watching for hours as various young actresses with blond hair and blue eyes stepped up to the red x on the concrete floor in front of the camera to audition for the vacant role. She heard James thank the latest one and call for another. Catharine opened her eyes and looked at the new comer with the same mild interest she'd given the others before her. She definitely looked the part.

The girl stated her name for the rolling camera and listed a couple of her more noteworthy films before reading the test lines for the casting call. Catharine groaned as yet another Serenity hopeful performed the scene as they interpreted the character.

She was going to scream.

They just didn't get it.

Serenity was not the romantic heroine they all perceived her to be. At this rate they'd be here until midnight and still be looking. None of them could see past the tragedy of what happened to her; to the truth of what lay at the heart of Serenity's character.

It was a shame Kim had vanished on them. She'd been perfect for the role. Playing the exact balance of victim and femme fetal; wielding the power she held upon the men in the narrative like the weapon it was. She had seen Serenity in a way that none of these hopefuls did.

When James had contacted Kim's staff to find out where she was, he'd been informed that no one knew. It seemed the actress hadn't been seen since the premier.

Unbidden the haunting image of the photos Lance had received while she was staying with him flooded her mind. She saw the striking beauty lain out upon the green earth beneath a full moon. Her skin white as snow draped in an airy crimson fabric and pierced by the fangs of golden serpents. Haunting eyes of hazel appeared to cry tears of blood as she stared back at her from a face brimming with pain and fear. Her pose was provocative and suggested that of a woman lost in the throes of passion. The face changed to reflect Kim's and goose bumps rose on Catharine's flesh.

"Stop it girl, you're letting your imagination run away with you again," she muttered as she reminded herself that Kim was notorious for vanishing on a whim. She was probably just out on a vacation somewhere.

Catharine drew her thoughts back to the screen test and called it to a halt. The young actress looked at her with confusion.

"Why'd you stop me I was getting to the best part," the girl said with disappointment.

Catharine cursed, certain she was dealing with yet another crazed Serenity groupie. They really didn't understand the character at all. "Can you tell me in your own words what you think is happening here in the scene?" Catharine asked struggling for patience.

"Well, Serenity is being approached by the vampire lord's advances, terrified she tries to keep him away from her but using his power upon her he seduces her."

"More or less that's right, but under the text we see a change here in Serenity from where she was in Heart of Glass, when the rogue werewolf is pursuing her we saw her flee from him at every opportunity. He'd hunt her and capture her right?"

"Yeah."

"Here there is no running. Serenity is not a frightened victim anymore, she is a woman manipulating a man of power to her own ends. She knows who Lord Syvarin is and is aware of his power. She sees him as an ally to be used against the werewolf who has slain her beloved Davrik."

"Really?"

"Yes, she plays the role that the vampire desires of her, giving her the appearance of both the innocent you want her to be and giving him the illusion that he has the power here as he desires." Catharine explained.

"I don't know that seems awfully calculating. I like her better..."

"Seeing as I'm the one who created her I don't care what way you like to see her; I'm telling you who she is and that is how I want to see her performed," Catharine snapped at her wits end.

Catharine watched as the girls blue eyes lit with insult. She prepared herself for an argument but before the girl could speak James intervened.

"Ladies, please let's not get overly emotional about this, it's been a long day. Corin we'll let you know."

Catharine watched as the young woman walked away and drew a breath, in a bid to prepare for the next actress.

"Catharine, I know how important it is to you that the book be portrayed as it was written but these girls don't know Serenity like you do. I want to see her played as you perceive her, personally I prefer the calculating woman to the helpless weak willed girl that most your readers see her as but attacking the girls won't help matters."

"Your right, I'm sorry it's just I'm really sick of..."

"Tell you what, why don't we take a short break we've been at this for a while," James said his voice was soothing and cooled her growing temper.

Catharine nodded her agreement. As James announced a short break Catharine made her way back to her on set office.

8 ATHENS, GREECE

A formidable figure sat behind his white marble desk. His blue eyes gleamed as he looked over the woman Annalynn Gallagher's notes yet again. Thinking of her name brought her face to his mind, he pictured the golden head and her intelligent hazel eyes lit with discovery, so like those of his first wife.

Hermes felt hunger stir within him and then rage as he reflected on the fact that Anna had refused him. No mortal woman had ever escaped him once he set his gaze upon her. That his host, Ian Broody's pretty fiancé had done so infuriated him. She'd regret her decision, he vowed as he poured over her work; trying to see what it was she had. Hermes sought to unlock the secret of the other mantles, the lost key and his own past.

To his growing frustration Hermes found that his memory had holes. Details were missing from his mind, his power was limited somehow. His ability to see the knowledge he desired was being blocked. It was the Creator's doing, Hermes reasoned and he cursed the maker of all for his interference. Not for the first time, he pondered how he'd come to be trapped, within his graven image, in the temple of the city from where he and his brethren had once ruled the earth. He found no answer.

Looking up from Anna's notes, he studied the work space he'd taken as his own upon possessing Ian Broody's flesh as his own. The office was a circular chamber much like that of the Parthenon where his image had been worshiped in the past. He laughed at the thought as his gaze fell upon the stone images of his winged brethren; surrounding him, forced to look upon him as he worked to ensure they never came back into their own power as he had.

He heard their hissed curses and reveled in their inability to do anything to stop him. His pleasure grew as he thrilled in the fact his dwelling lay in the heart of an isle once dedicated to the worship of Zeus. Feeling pleased with himself Hermes crossed to the silent image of the former king of the gods.

"Once you were mighty oh lord of the heavens, now you are no more. Soon I will have your crown for my own and I will rule this world alone as the new king of the gods," Hermes crowed. His brethren hissed and raged at his declaration but could do no more. They writhed within the confines of their prisons and waited silently for the opportunity to lash out against him.

Hermes crossed back to the desk and picked up the phone dialing the number for Broody's contact at the Smithsonian Museum in the USA. He listened to the sound of the phone ringing, with delight, in the days when he'd roamed the earth communications had been limited. It had taken days to months to pass word from one mortal to another; now in this world of advanced technology people were only a few button presses away. If it had only been so in his time then Rome may not have fallen; he mused. Hermes waited for Dr. Phillip King to pick up the other line. He was pleased he didn't have to wait long.

"Hello," the older man said in greeting.

"Hello Phillip, its Ian." Hermes said his voice taking on the sound of his former host's.

"Ian, how are things going in Israel?" Phillip questioned.

Hermes smiled amused, recalling the older man had no idea that Ian Broody was no longer in Israel or the Jordan and hadn't been for well over a year. "They are going well. Phillip an artifact was shipped to you earlier in the week it should arrive by Friday."

"What is it?"

"A candle, trouble is I wasn't done researching it yet and I need it back. It and the cup that Anna was working on before she was called out here," Hermes stated as the image of the cup surfaced in his mind, a memory from his possessed host.

"I'll be sure the candle gets sent back, unfortunately I can't help you with the cup." Phillip said with a sigh.

"Why not?" Hermes asked trying to remain calm. In the room he heard the spirit within the image of Dionysus laugh.

"I'm afraid it was stolen Ian. Apparently someone had a forgery made and replaced the real one with a copy. I just became aware of it. A police detective by the name of Lance Roman is handling the investigation but there isn't much hope of recovering it." Phillip explained.

"I see, well, here's hoping that this detective will be able to recover it," Hermes stated politely before ending the call. Once the receiver was back in the phone cradle he spun and faced the image of his laughing brother.

"So, you've found a host. It will do you no good. You don't even know where you are. You'll not be able to lead your mortal vessel to you. No one knows where you are." Hermes mocked before flinging his power at the graven image, he delighted when the imprisoned spirit cried out in pain.

Hermes turned away from the image and walked out of his office headed down the hall in search of his lovely new bride.

9 Los Angeles, California

Catharine sat in her office on the movie set in front of her laptop. Her fingers flew over the keys as she worked at typing up the final scene for the Heart of Clay script. If she could just nail down this last bit she'd be free to get back to work on the new book for the publisher. She really wanted a few minutes away from Serenity for a while. The troublesome heroine was starting to get under her skin, all these naive readers that worshiped Serenity were enough to make her sick.

Not for the first time Catharine found herself wishing she'd never written the damn trilogy or at least that she'd given a clear end to the damn character. With a sigh she closed out the script knowing she'd get no further with it now. She was too worked up to focus. Turning her attention to the answering machine she noted she had two new messages. Pressing the play button she sat and listened as the device went through the routine of announcing the day and time of the call as well as the number of the caller before playing back the first message.

"Catharine, it's Bryan I know you're busy out there with screen tests but when you get a few minutes we need to meet..." the message began Catharine hit the fast forward button having no desire to hear any more figuring the message pertained to Dark Heart.

"Hi Catharine, its detec...ah – its Lance I got your message earlier and I thought I'd give you a call; see how things are going out there. I guess you're busy or away from the phone. I'll try again later. Bye."

Catharine giggled at the message for such a confident police man he sure sounded nervous on the phone. She reminded herself that the last time they spoke he'd not been that uneasy. She reasoned he didn't like talking to answering machines and filed that little tidbit away in her mental notes on the handsome detective's character. It was something she might include in her heroes behavior for the new book.

Catharine considered calling the detective back but figured it wasn't the right time for her to talk she was still too wound up about the casting calls, better to wait until she could talk about something more than work. Her mind having shifted gears from the script to her new book, Catharine opened the file with her notes and concepts and typed up the new detail for her detective.

She contemplated the scene in her actual life that had sparked her imagination. Seeing Lance at the edge of the ball room, watching the crowd, intently longing for Anna but resigned to the fact she was beyond his reach. Wondering who he was and what he'd been doing there. Picturing it clearly in her head; she set to the task of typing up her thoughts and ideas on where she wanted to take that moment. It wasn't long before Serenity fell into the shadowed corners of her mind and she found her peace, once more lost in her work.

10 Denver, Colorado

Sam looked up from his book of Russian tales and let his gaze settle upon Anna. Her blonde head was bent over the pages of another book; her hazel eyes skimming over the text. A writing tablet lay on the table to her left with a few scribbled notes. He noted the pen tucked behind her left ear and sighed as he found himself wishing the lovely doctor would give him that kind of undivided attention.

Sam chuckled at the idea of being jealous of a book. Glancing at the clock and noting the time, he decided it was time they called it quits for the day. Dinner was in order and maybe a movie to take their minds off work, but he'd have to draw her out of her book to get either.

"We're getting nowhere with this," he grumbled loud enough to be heard before closing his book.

He watched, pleased as Anna lifted her head, her hazel gaze meeting with his own. He felt that instant pull of desire as their eyes locked and felt the same growing connection between them. He was pleased to find his earlier mistake had been forgiven.

"Yes I know it, we must be missing something but what that is I'm not sure," she admitted with a sigh.

"You're probably right," he agreed. "Why don't we…"

"It must have something to do with what the angel said to us before," Anna interrupted cutting him off. He groaned, it seemed that she wasn't ready to just set the search aside yet. Knowing he'd not be able to dissuade her from the task until she'd satisfied her curiosity, he turned his focus from her to what had been said to them in the throne room at Atlantis by the angel.

"The angel said that the mantles have turned up many times over the years; that they will often appear in tales of myth, legend and folklore. Hence why we are reading all these books."

"Yes, I know but there was more to it. Didn't he say that the mantles often turn up where people would least expect them to? What do you suppose he meant by that exactly?" Anna questioned. She bit her lip as she tried to figure it out.

Sam shut his eyes turning his attention away from her. If he was going to contribute anything to this conversation he couldn't get distracted by her.

"Well, I guess he's referring to preconceived ideas about what the mantles are and who might wield them."

"Okay, so because we know they are evil by nature we're assuming that they'd be evil in the myths, legends and folklore, but what if they don't have to be."

"Just because the item is evil doesn't mean it only calls out to evil men. After all, the key tried to influence you as did Hermes image. You're not evil by nature," Sam stated.

"Right, I've been looking for stories with the villains possessing the objects, limiting who can hold them given the angels words, maybe we should be looking for the hero to be holding them."

"We'll start again then, but after we get a proper meal. All we've done is read and snack on junk. Get dressed we'll go grab a bite in the restaurant downstairs." Sam stated.

Anna nodded then rose from her seat and crossed the main room to her bedroom in the joint suite. Sam got up and crossed to his own room to do the same. He was looking forward to a quiet dinner with no work interrupting it.

11

Lance pulled his squad car up to the curb in front of the small pawnshop owned by Frank Murphy. He shut off the engine and got out of the car. With photos of the makers seal in hand he approached the front door. He noted the sign in the window had been flipped to say closed and figured Frank had probably chased his last patron out of the shop about ten minutes ago.

Before he could knock, an older gentleman with maple brown hair and sharp dark eyes opened it, ushering him in.

"Detective Roman, long time no see. How are things in B&E?" Frank questioned, as he took Lance's hand in his and shook it in greeting.

"Frank, good to see yah man it has been a while. How's the wife? Thing's at work are about the same, you know how it is," Lance replied as he returned the hand shake and gave his friend a bear hug.

"Rita's fine, so what can I do for you tonight?"

Lance handed a copy of the photo of the makers seal to Frank. "Do you recognize this?" he asked hopeful.

Frank studied the image with interest. "Yeah, it's a maker's seal. I've seen it before, but I'm not sure who it belongs to. It's a more obscure signature than I usually see here in the shop. If I were you I'd check into more of the private run, small name, personally operated, jewelry businesses in the area."

"Thanks Frank, I appreciate your time," Lance said taking the image back.

"No problem Detective, always glad to lend a hand. Don't be a stranger now Lance, and stop by if you want, Rita would love to see you she misses you since…"

"I might," Lance said noncommittally, interrupting the other man before he could mention Dana's name. He should have contacted someone else on this one. He'd been foolish to call Dana's father, but he'd been in a rush, wanted the answer right then and knew that Frank wouldn't hesitate to give it.

"It was good to see you again son," Frank said before he let Lance go on his way. Lance made his way back to his cruiser, grateful to Frank for not pushing.

12 Athens, Greece

Hermes stepped into his private chambers. The spacious master suite was furnished with a king size bed, two night tables, one at either side, a pair of elegant oak dressers, an ornate full length mirror, entertainment center with TV and stereo, as well as a book case lined with movies and music, a mini bar, and a huge fireplace.

He made his way past the sleeping quarters of his room towards the bath chamber where he knew he'd find his wife waiting. Opening the door with care, he slipped into the room wanting to catch her off guard.

Hermes found her sitting in front of her vanity. She was wrapped in a vibrant blue plush towel. In her hand was a silver brush that she was busy drawing through her still wet hair. She fussed at getting all the knots out of it and muttered to herself about needing to touch up her roots; before moving her attention to touching up her face.

She was a stunning beauty his Pamela and though a bit older than Anna had been she made up for the age with her various enhancements to improve what she was born with. Hermes felt his flesh stir with hunger and moved closer. His blue eyes gleamed as her every desire washed over him through the bond of their union in the throne room.

Images of their coupling filled his mind and he reveled in the power of it and the thrill of having her with his brethren looking on, hungry to take but unable. No god would ever touch his bride again without his knowledge. His temper flared at the thought, recalling a time when his king had dared to touch what was his in secret and polluted her body filling her womb with one of his many bastard children.

Never again, Hermes vowed.

Pamela was his!

Driven by a duel need to please her and to mark her as hisHermes stopped her ministrations; taking the lipstick from herfingers. "Close your eyes my dear lady, I wish to give you a gift," he murmured. He looked on, pleased as she did his bidding. When her eyes were closed he drew upon his power and with trembling hands reached for her.

Too long – he didn't know how long he'd been a prisoner within cold stone but his newly acquired flesh told him it had been too long. He ached with want of her. Nearly drunk with it, he struggled to keep his touch light upon her so that the gift he desired to bestow her could be given without flaw. He ran his fingers through her damp hair from root to tip caressing each strand.

He delighted in her pleasured moan at his touch, pleased to find that his hold upon her grew with each time they met. Her flesh's senses heightened with each joining. "Shh, not yet my lover, soon," he murmured soothing her as his touch moved from her hair to her face tracing each curve, eliciting a startled yet still pleasured cry as his power seeped into the cells of her skin altering them.

Hermes's fingers unclasped the towel about her and traced over her bare flesh stirring her with desire as his magic did its work. "All right my sweet wife, open your eyes," he murmured before his lips brushed against her ear.

He watched as her whiskey colored pools flew open, pupils wide with her need of him. She gasped then smiled with elation at the sight of herself. Her hair shown bright a beautifully blonde the exact shade she'd always wanted no sign of her brown roots peeked out at her. The few signs of ageing lines in her face were gone. Her nose's shape had changed slightly and her lips were the fuller ones she'd always wanted their color a deep red without a hint of lip stick.

"Do you like it my dear?" Hermes questioned as his hands ran over her flesh, his touch rougher now, possessive where before it had been light and airy.

"Yes, I've always wanted to look like this," she breathed before she turned in his grasp, kissing him hard. He pulled her firmly against him returning the kiss with the all-consuming fierce hunger he felt within him. Hermes lost himself in her embrace letting the fire of their shared passion burn wild between them. He'd come to her with another purpose but it would wait for now. In all his years he'd never possessed a bride so eager or willing to surrender to his lust for her. He was really starting to like this new world he'd awoken to.

13

Catharine saved her notes and the outline for the new book. She was almost ready to start work on fleshing it out. She was looking forward to seeing what it would become, but not yet she had to finish the final scene for the movie script before she got too far into the new book. Closing the file she pulled up the script once more. Her head was clear now and her temper cooled enough that she should be able to finish it now.

She pulled up the last page she'd worked and backed up two scenes re-immersing herself in the story. When she got back to where she left off once more, she found that the words flowed from her mind like water in a river. She typed away lost in the task.

Serenity looked on with pleasure as the vampire Lord Syvarin's sword sliced through the neck of the werewolf Kovrin. His head came away from his shoulders and blood sprayed filling the night air. She thrilled in knowing that the monster; that had savaged her body and murdered her beloved was no more. Her child Rachel would be safe now. No member of the wolf pack would dare to touch her so long as she was under the vampire lord's protection.

Serenity's blue eyes met with Syvarin's red ones and he smiled at her. She looked on with disgust as he licked his rival's blood from his blade. Reminding her of what it was she had allied herself. He was a monster as well, more deadly and powerful than Kovrin had ever been. She'd run to the protection of his territory to escape the advances of a man she'd once loved. Syvarin had been more than willing to shelter her from the rogue wolf provided she agreed to be his.

She watched as his eyes began to glow, as the hunger within

him grew stronger – his need of blood having awakened. The scent of his rival's blood in the air and the small taste he'd allowed himself was but a sample of what he now desired to consume. The vampire lord looked upon her his eyes raking over her from head to toe.

Serenity felt the air in her lungs back up and she swallowed fighting to breathe. She trembled under his gaze aware that her struggle with Kovrin had left her clothes in tatters and her body all but bare for him to see. Her heart now pounded wildly. She could hear it in her own ears and knew that he heard it more clearly than any sound in the surrounding wood around them.

She thought to run but resisted the urge. If she did so the protection she'd gained for her child would be lost. Rachel would suffer at the hand of the pack. Serenity refused to let that happen. Serenity loved Rachel dearly and she would do all that was within her means to protect her.

In order to keep Syvarin's protection for the child Serenity would have no choice but to surrender herself now to the vampire lord's desires. As if he were aware of her thought Syvarin kicked the carcass of the wolf aside and made his way toward her.

"Now my princess you shall be mine," he breathed the words as he drew her to him. Serenity struggled in his embrace as if she meant to flee. It was a token protest, one he desired, that gave him the illusion that he was in control here and she was weak. The vampire lord broke past her feigned attempts at defending herself and she screamed as his fangs sank into her neck.

A pounding broke the silence Serenity blinked…

Catharine cursed as her concentration snapped and the knocking repeated.

"Who is it?" Catharine asked her voice edged with annoyance. She'd been so close. Only a minute or more and she'd have been done with the second script.

"It's Bryan," was the answer that came from the other side of the door and Catharine groaned, aware of the fact that she'd not begetting back to the script anytime soon. Whatever it was he had on his mind he wouldn't let it wait.

"Just a second," she called out to him. Catharine saved the script, closed the file, before rising from her seat, crossing her work space to unlock the door and let him in. "what do you need Bryan,

I'm a bit busy," she stated hoping to avoid dancing around the matter at hand and get it handled.

"We need to talk about the contest. I left you a message earlier…"

"Yeah I got it, sorry I've been working. I'm about done with the second script."

"That's good. How's the casting call going?"

"Not well, these girls don't see who Serenity is," Catharine said with a sigh.

"Why not play the part yourself?"

"Bryan don't even joke, you know how I feel about being in the public eye, and you're one of the few people who knows why. It was bad enough going to that stupid party what if…"

"I'm sure nothing will come of it," Bryan said interrupting her.

"I don't like how much my face has been in the news lately," Catharine said, ill at ease.

"It comes with the territory, if you wanted to stay private you should have been a ghost writer."

"Yeah, I know it. So let's get this contest thing nailed down so I can get busy on the new project."

"Fair enough, we had discussed the possibility of a castle getaway and I was thinking what if we rented like a Hollywood mansion/castle and had some kind of bash there like we held at Caesar'spalace in Vegas. We can hold the drawing about the time of the premier and let the winner attend it."

"Not a bad plan. We can do the place up to fit the motif of the book and provide attire like we did for the Serenity ball. Let the winner meet the cast and such. They'll love it."

"So you're good with that?" Bryan asked.

"Yeah, it'll be great," Catharine replied picturing the winner's excitement at the prize package.

"Great I'll take it to the publishing house and my crew, we'll start putting things together for it. Now about your new project…" Bryan began moving on to the next point of business. But before he could say anything more Catharine cut him off.

"I'm working on it when the script gets stuck. I just finished my outline earlier I can't wait to start fleshing it out," Catharine said excited.

"That's great but you'll have to save it for later."

"What? Why?" Catharine asked confused, she'd told him about her latest idea for the new book and he'd been as excited about it as her.

She watched as Bryan closed the door making the discussion private and felt her stomach tighten with anxiety. "I got word from the publishing house yesterday..." he began and stopped abruptly as if unsure how to say whatever it was that was on his mind.

"Okay," Catharine said prompting him to continue.

"They are only interested in seeing one property from you right now and that is a fourth Dark Heart Novel."

"No!" Catharine's refusal had her turning away from her publicist.

Bryan grabbed her by the shoulders and turned her so that she faced him. She felt his fingers dig into her skin, holding her in place. His gaze locked with her blue eyes she saw no signs of humor in them. He was serious. "If you send them anything else they'll bury it."

"Then I'll take it elsewhere," Catharine snapped, not about to be bullied into writing a book she didn't believe in.

"You could do that but it would be a bad move."

"Why?"

"Per your contract they own all rights to works produced with your name and symbol."

"What?"

"They own you princess."

"Like hell they do!" Catharine shoved herself free of his grasp with disgust wanting to hear no more. "I'll use another name." She said seeing a way out.

"It's an option, again I wouldn't as you are under contract for a title and if you fail to produce they'll have you black listed. You won't be able to find work ghost writing."

"No," the word, parted her lips, heavy with despair, she couldn't believe this was happening.

"Afraid so; my advice, write the damn book and move on." Bryan stated coolly.

"But what if the readers demand more again?" Catharine asked, her voice quivered with fear.

"You'll no longer be under contractual obligation to produce a text, then you can go elsewhere but not with your name."

Catharine nodded. "I'll start looking at it as soon as I've finished the script," she whispered, tears threatening to fall.

"For what it's worth Catharine, I'm sorry about this."

"It's not your fault. This is Tom's doing. I was stupid to let him handle my legal affairs."

"No, just young and in love," Bryan corrected.

"Yeah, and three years later, he's still screwing me after the break up," Catharine said with disgust; she seized hold of the anger she felt for her ex, using it to drive back the tears that threatened to fall, afraid that if she gave into the pain she'd drown in it.

"It'll be okay Catharine, you'll get through it," Bryan assured her, as he drew her into his arms, giving her a bear hug. Catharine leaned against him for a moment, accepting his comfort and then drew back.

"Well, if I'm going to get this damn thing done I better finish up the script and look over Heart of Stone; try to figure out a way to write a book for Serenity."

"Right, I'll let you get to it. Good luck princess," he whispered, before he turned and left. Catharine locked the door behind him and moved back to the desk. Overwhelmed by Bryan's news she buried her face in her hands and cried.

14

WASHINGTON DC, VIRGINIA
SUNDAY
10PM

Lance stepped out of the cool Virginia evening air into the still and quiet of his apartment. After flipping on the main entry light he made his way for the kitchen. He was in need of a drink after talking to Frank. Seeing him again had been harder than Lance had anticipated. Part of him wished he'd let the matter wait until the following morning; when he could have used a different source.

Lance sighed, disgusted with himself. He'd never been one to run away from a problem. So why was he wishing he had this time. Avoiding Dana's family wasn't going to change the reality of what had happened to her. Nothing would. That he was trying to avoid facing the reality of it head on irritated him. He'd been avoiding a lot of things lately where Dana was concerned; Lance admitted. He asked himself why, but found no real answer.

"It doesn't matter," Lance muttered to himself, as he pulled a beer from his fridge. He glanced over at the silent answering machine, before popping the top on his drink. No calls today. The truth of it stung a bit more than he'd expected. He admitted to himself he was disappointed to find Catharine hadn't returned his call. Lance shrugged it off, she was probably just busy. Then again there was always the chance she wanted no more to do with him.

He'd screwed up where she was concerned. First by not telling her about Dana and then again when he didn't explain those photos. He'd told her they weren't meant for her but she'd been spooked anyway. Almost as if she didn't believe him. He should have explained. He'd messed up worse when he'd tried to use her to prevent himself from drowning in his grief. If she was avoiding him it was no wonder. He'd made nothing but bad decisions where she was concerned.

Lance drew a sip from his beer and then groaned. Despite his need to set Dana and the homicide away, it seemed he'd find no reprieve here. His mind was consumed by them both. Giving up the fight he allowed the old case and his own loss to fill his mind.

Lance stuck his key in the lock for the front door, weary from a long day. He turned it and cursed to find the damn thing was stuck again. He made a mental note to replace it as he tried again. This time it worked but when he went to push the door open it resisted. "Oh come on I just want to go to bed," he muttered with irritation. Work had been long and frustrating settling into B & E was harder than he'd figured. It didn't help matters though that he missed Dana. He hadn't seen her in weeks. She was immersed in the Fury Killer case. She'd been pushing too hard when he walked away from it; afraid her obsession would become his own.

He hoped she was doing better. Lance hated that this mess had postponed their wedding but understood. If he'd lost his best friend he reasoned he wouldn't be in the mood to celebrate until the killer was caught either. As the door gave Lance knew instantly someone was there. Drawing his gun he moved through the living room with caution until he spotted her jacket on a chair in the kitchen. Crime scene photos lay scattered on the table.

"Dana?" he called, wondering where she was but no answer came. He made his way down the hall to his room thinking that maybe she'd gotten tired of waiting and gone on to bed. As he stepped in the room the hair on the back of his neck stood on end as his cop instincts roared at him with warning.

Something was very wrong here.

He noted the bathroom door was open and the light on within, gun still ready he moved to the door and peered inside. The room was still with no sign of life. The mirror over the sink broken, the words "I'm sorry," were smeared upon it in red. He reasoned it could be lipstick but his gut told him otherwise, it was blood.

Lance pushed the door open and his weapon fell from his hands at the sight of what lay within in. Dana lay upon the tile floor her body curled in upon itself. Her doe eyes wide with pain and despair. Eight tiny cuts lined her face, under her eye matching the ones the killer had left on her friends face. A pool of blood surrounded her lifeless hands clung to one of the kitchen knives they'd received as awedding present. The blade buried into her left breast had pierced her heart.

"DANA, No!" He shouted with disbelief as he rushed to her side. He reached with trembling fingers to find her pulse willing it to still be there; only to find nothing.

Lance blinked turning his mind from the hated memory, finding it was more than he could bear, as a tidal wave of grief washed over him. Lance drank down his beer in an effort to drive it all back. Splintered images crowded his mind spilling out of the dark corners fighting for a chance to be seen.

He saw in his mind's eye a golden band coiled like a snake. Near the tail was a small indentation. The image grew as he peered through a magnifying glass Dana held out to him and Lance cursed.

"That's where it was," he muttered to himself. Setting down the empty beer can; Lance moved out of the kitchen and straight for his office. Stepping into the room he flipped on the light and walked over to the stack of dusty boxes.

Lance pulled a Swiss Army knife from his pocket and sliced open the tape that had sealed their shared files. He pulled aside the lid tossing it without care. He stared at the folders within with disgust, for a moment, before lifting the first from the box. He flipped over the cover and began the hunt for the enlarged image of the serpent band, if the memory he triggered was right the makers seal was here in this mess tied to his past.

15 DENVER, COLORADO

Anna stepped back into her joint suite with Sam and smiled. He'd been right, a break was just what they needed. She felt much better.

"So, are we going to watch a movie or get back to the grind?" Sam asked as he closed the door behind them.

"I think a movie sounds good. I just need to call Phillip first and let him know about the candle coming his way and Dr. Broody's interest in it."

"All right, what movie do you want to watch?"

"Doesn't matter to me you pick," she replied before stepping into her room. She crossed the carpeted floor to the night table and grabbed her cell phone. Picking it up; she punched in Phillip King's number at the Smithsonian and hoped that her mentor would still be in. Anna listened to the familiar sound of the phone ringing and waited for either the man or his machine to pick up on the other end.

"Hello?"

"Phillip, I'm glad you're still in," Anna said with relief.

"Anna my dear good to hear from you; how are things going with your little project?" Phillip questioned.

"They're okay, I wanted to give you a heads up, there is an artifact coming in on…"

"Friday, yes a candle I believe. Ian called earlier asked for it and the cup. He was not pleased to hear it had been stolen."

"No, I'd imagine not. When that candle arrives please make sure it gets misplaced; I can't let him have it." Anna stated.

"I figured as much. I'll do the best I can."

"Thanks Phillip; I know I've put you in an awkward position with this whole thing. Don't do anything that could get you fired on my account okay."

"Understood, now listen to me as well, don't go taking any foolish chances that could end up getting you killed," Phillip countered.

"Right, I've got to go Phillip; thank you again."

"You're welcome, my dear and good luck." Phillip answered before hanging up.

Anna tucked her cell phone in her pocket and stepped back into the living room where Sam sat at their work space staring at the silver horn they'd recovered at Atlantis.

"All done," Anna stated. She watched as Sam's blue eyes rose from the horn to look at her.

"That's good. So what did he say?"

"That he knew the candle was coming in, Dr. Broody had already contacted him."

"Oh…Anna, why did you take this?" Sam questioned as he picked up the horn to study it. "I mean it has no power left in it."

Anna blinked, surprised by the question. She'd been asking herself the same thing since they escaped from, the lost city, and the newly restored Hermes god of Knowledge. "I don't know – I just felt led to do so the same way I felt led to hide the key. I know its worthless now, but I couldn't let him keep it."

"Why not?"

"I can't explain it but it's better for everyone concerned if we're the ones holding it and not him."

"Fair enough."

"So, are we still going to sit down to a movie or have you changed your mind?" Anna questioned.

Sam set the horn down. "We'll watch a movie," he replied and moved to take a seat in front of the TV. Anna joined him on the couch and as the credits began to role she laughed.

"Man we are over thinking this whole thing," she stated with amusement.

"What do you mean?" Sam questioned with interest.

"We're sifting through all these old folktales and myth and at least one answer is probably right in front of us now. The bow of Eros; I can't think of a more famous bowman than Robin Hood." Anna stated.

Sam shook his head and joined in her laughter; she was right. "In that case I guess a trip to the United Kingdom is in order."

Anna nodded and the pair fell silent as they settled into watch their movie.

16 ATHENS, GREECE

Hermes woke to the sound of Pamela's heartbeat. He lifted his head from the warm cushion of her ample breast and smiled. His blue eyes opened to look upon her newly made face and he kissed her firm, yet plump lips. She stirred beneath him and whisky colored eyes lit with delight.

"Hello again my darling one," he murmured before untangling himself from her. His flesh yearned for more of her like an eager addict but he denied the urge; there would be plenty of time for that later. He couldn't afford to lose track of his task at hand. The cup was missing, his brother Dionysus was moving, now seeking a means to be free and he had to stop it.

"My lord," her words fell from her lips both a protest at his leaving her and a prayer begging for his return. She reached out for him with a desperate need to have him near her, a fear rose in her mind that she had somehow displeased him.

Hermes laughed thrilled by her need of him and the fear that circled her mind. He reached out and caressed her cheek. "Fear not my love, I am not angry, but there are matters that need attending to and I must return to them. I came to you with another purpose in mind but such was my delight at the sight of you; that I got swept away in your embrace."

"What do you wish of me, my husband," she murmured.

"A cup was stolen from the Smithsonian Museum; a detective Roman was put in charge of the investigation. I need you to go back to Washington DC and find out everything you can about the cup and what he is up to. It is imperative that we find it before Dr. Gallagher can." Hermes stated.

"Consider it done my lord," she assured him. Her crimson lips curved into a wicked grin before she brushed a kiss on his lips and moved in the direction of the closet.

Satisfied Hermes turned and strolled out of the room. He walked down the hall, back in the direction of his office. Upon entering the circular chamber he flicked a switch and watched with fascination as the stones within burst into flame as the gas within lit. He manipulated the flames with his power changing the color from a simple orange to a vibrant blue. "Artemis," the name was not uttered aloud but it rippled in the air as if it had been shouted from the highest peak for all to hear.

Hermes looked on with pleasure as a pair of blue eyes more vibrant than any before them appeared in the fire.

"I am here my lord," the reply was soft and respectful, but held a power of its own.

"How goes the hunt oh daughter of the moon?"

"It goes well, I have located the mortals. They hide within the snowy peaks of the American Rockies."

"Excellent."

"My lord, I don't understand why you're so determined to capture this woman. The horn she took holds no power anymore; of what use is it to you now?"

"True my dear, but it's not the horn in her possession that I seek, it is the knowledge she possesses of the other mantles."

"If you have need of it then you will get her, but my lord when you have her do not forget your promise. You said if I aided you in your endeavors to escape your stone prison, that you, in turn would help me, in gaining my vengeance against my nemesis."

"I have not forgotten my vow oh daughter of the hunt. When I have the other mantles I seek, I will bestow upon you the means to avenge your father's death."

"Thank you my liege. Consider the woman Anna as good as captured and in your house," Artemis stated before those blue eyes closed and her power retreated.

Hermes smiled pleased. Things were beginning to fall into place.

17 ATLANTIS, SOMEWHERE IN THE BERMUDA TRIANGLE

Zaharrah sat in silence flipping through Anna's notes on the various dig sites trying to sort through the various parts to see whatever it was Anna had seen and Broody was missing. As she studied the various photos she smiled. There it was at last – in plain sight. The answer was easy to overlook and Zaharrah chuckled to herself understanding that it was just the sort of thing Dr. Broody always over looked.

While pleased with herself for spotting it, Zaharrah admitted that she'd have missed it herself, except she happened to know that Broody was interested in her candle and a cup stolen from the Smithsonian. The ten gods of Sodom and Gomorrah that were now in the throne room each held a different object – the mantles Anna had mentioned.

Grabbing a note pad she scribbled down the list of the ten items and who they were associated with.

1. Crown of Zeus
2. Horn of Hermes
3. Cup of Dionysus – stolen from Smithsonian
4. Sword of Ares
5. Scales of Hades - I found in north eastern palace
6. Whip of Helios
7. Gauntlets of Hephaestus
8. Bow of Eros
9. Trident of Poseidon
10. Scroll of Chaos

Once the list was completed she asked herself, okay if two are real then that would suggest the other eight are as well. That must be what Anna is hunting for now. But how is she hunting for them, where? Zaharrah wondered as she sat considering the matter, her phone rang startling her. She picked up the offending object and pressed the button to connect the call.

"Hello."

"Dr. Lynch I'm afraid I have bad news for you."

"What is it?"

"The package you asked be delivered, the shipment was hit and the package lost."

"What? Any idea who got it?"

"We believe it was Magnus."

"Son of a – is the other item secure?"

"Yes."

"Good, I'm coming in. There have been too many mistakes."

Zaharrah hung up her phone and picked up her notes before departing from her office.

18 Los Angeles, California

Catharine sat with her face buried in her hands, tears ran down her cheeks as she wept bitter tears in silence. She'd not been able to stem her crying since Bryan left. She couldn't believe how naive she'd been to let Tom run the legal side of her career, not reading her own contract. Trusting him that it would serve her best interests.

Catharine groaned in her frustration, she was so stupid when it came to men. Maybe it was for the best she'd had to back away from Lance. Catharine pushed the thought from her mind as soon as it came. She wasn't that same simple girl who'd run from her hometown and fallen for the first guy to cross her path and show her an ounce of kindness; she'd changed – gotten stronger.

As her thoughts began to wander towards her past, a knock sounded, behind her, a moment before the door to her workspace squeaked open.

"CJ?" James Hardagen's voice called.

Catharine cursed herself for forgetting to lock the door before turning off the tears like a faucet. The last thing she needed right now was for James to catch her crying. She'd worked damn hard at not letting others see her that vulnerable. Being seen as weak was a danger, she refused to risk again. Catharine lifted her head and swiped at tear, dampened cheeks.

"What is it Mr. Hardagen?" She asked forcing her voice to be strong.

"We're getting ready to start up the screen tests again in five. You set?"

"Yeah I think so."

"You okay?"

"Fine, just over tired," Catharine replied crisply.

"I know. It's been a rough day. I know your concerns with finding an actress that will portray Serenity as you've envisioned her. You're not alone. I need consistency in the role for the film to come off right. Believe me I have a lot invested in this thing and I want to see it done right."

"Thanks that means a lot to me." Catharine admitted with a genuine smile.

"Tell you what, why don't you come back to my place after we wrap for the day. Emily, is dying to talk with you and we can see about that drink we discussed, chase the long day away with a pleasant night." James suggested.

"Sounds like a wonderful idea." Catharine replied.

"Great. I'll give Emily a call, let her know you're coming and see you out there."

Catharine nodded and once the door was closed picked up her own phone. She punched in Lance's number and listened to it ring.

"Hello?"

"Hello sir knight how are you?" She asked.

"Better now. How are you Catharine?"

"Okay, it's been a long day out here but it's about over. I take it you've had a rough one also?" She asked with concern.

"Nothing major."

"So, is there any chance I'll be seeing you in the not so distant future?" Catharine asked.

"Afraid not I'm buried under this stolen cup case. I found a makers seal on it earlier this evening, it seemed familiar, just placed it from an earlier case but I don't know whose work it is, got to track it down."

"What's the seal look like?" Catharine asked curious.

"It's An Anvil with a hammer leaning against it..."

"Behind it are flames, in front of it two rectangles." Catharine said interrupting him.

"Yeah, how did you know that?" Lance asked baffled.

Catharine giggled. "I know who the maker is. CJ Nichols commissioned the guy to do a jewelry line for her when the Dark Heart Trilogy started to take off. Guy's name is Harold Miller his shop is called The Vulcan Forge and it's located in New York City."

Lance Laughed. It was a deep rumbling sound so different from her own. One which set her blood to humming and made her toes curl. She blinked surprised by the strength of the attraction she felt for the detective.

"Well damn, Catharine you are just something else, thank you. I'll look into it in the morning."

"Glad I could be of help."

"You said it's been a long day for you out there, how so? Can I help?"

"I wish you could. Unfortunately I'm out of time, I've got to get back out to the set, I'll talk to you later though. Good night detective."

"Night Catharine," he answered before she hung up.

19 WASHINGTON DC, VIRGINIA
SUNDAY
12AM

Lance finished writing down the information Catharine had given him about the owner of the makers seal. He then closed out the last of the files he'd pulled on the Furies Killer. As he rose to his feet to stretch out his neck and back he contemplated heading to bed. He'd put it in the longest day he could remember on a case since Dana died.

The doorbell rang.

Lance cursed with disgust. Who the hell was calling on him at midnight and why? He considered ignoring it but a second buzz sounded followed by an insistent pounding. Lance groaned and turned in the direction of the front door, whoever it was they better have a damn good reason for the intrusion.

Lance opened the door a crack, keeping the unknown visitor on his front step and peered out at them. To his surprise it was a woman on his front stoop. She had brown hair and intelligent chocolate eyes. She looked to be in her mid-thirties and wore a sharp black pants suit. Lance eyed her wearily. "Can I help you?"

"Detective Roman?"

Lance swore inwardly, the tone was a professional one. Given her attire she might have been a reporter. He wasn't fond of their kind but something about her told him this was no reporter. "Maybe," Lance answered noncommittally.

"Are you Lance Roman?"

"Depends on who's asking." Lance stated. Whoever she was she was used to being in charge, she didn't like not getting a direct answer. She was no reporter. It was her eyes that gave her away. Those eyes of hers were cool and calculating, sharp, he imagined they caught every detail she looked at – cops' eyes, but the dress was too professional for an average DC detective – Fed maybe.

"Agent Blackwood, F.B.I. Are you detective Lance Roman of the DC police?" She questioned after flashing him her badge.

Lance said nothing, merely nodded. He'd been right she was a Fed but what was she doing on his doorstep at this hour.

"I'm sorry for the lateness of the hour but your captain said you'd still be awake. Normally I'd let this wait until the morning but I don't have that kind of time. I need your help, may I come in?" She asked.

Lance opened the door for her and stepped aside allowing her to enter his home. Something in her tone woke his cop instincts, the urgency she placed on the meeting suggested whatever she was working on held life or death in the balance. It seemed his long day was going to spill into the early hours of the next morning.

Once she was in the door Lance closed it behind her and led her into his dining room. The two of them took a seat at the small square oak table. "How can I help you Miss Blackwood?"

"I'm working a case that you have some knowledge on and could use your assistance with it."

"Which case? Thieves don't usually gain bureau interest."

"It's not a B&E case Detective. As I understand it you used to work Homicide."

"That's correct, however I..."

"Then I believe you'll recognize these," Agent Blackwood said interrupting him as she set down a stack a photos in front of him.

Lance's stomach churned as the frozen images of horror glared at him. Lifeless hazel eyes stared up at him full of accusation. Unable to look away, he studied the grizzly images. "He's gotten worse," the words fell unbidden from his lips.

"What do you mean?" Agent Blackwood questioned.

"This is indeed the work of the Fury Killer, but this is much more elaborate than what I've seen," Lance replied with disgust.

"How so?"

"Look agent Blackwood, you're right I am familiar with the case..."

"Will you help me?"

"No, I left homicide for a reason. While I may have had this damn case thrown back in my face a couple times lately, that doesn't change the fact I want nothing more to do with it. I'll give..."

"What do you mean the case has been thrown in your face recently?"

"Someone left me an envelope full of crime scene photos on the door step last week and the makers seal on the golden snake bands turned up on a forged cup recently."

"Have you identified the craftsman?" she questioned her brown eyes hopeful.

"Yes, I'm going to look into it in the morning. I'll take it you haven't been able to?"

"Not yet."

"As I was saying before I'll give you what I have on the case including the jewelry maker so long as I can speak with him first."

"I think I can arrange that."

"Good, understand this, beyond giving you my notes I'm not going to get involved any further in this matter."

"I understand Lance but I wish you'd reconsider. Your captain says you have quite a gift for this sort of work. I don't get why you walked away from this case given your partners death."

"I lost everything that mattered to me to this damn case Agent Blackwood and...

"Gail"

Lance nodded. "I knew if I let it, the case would consume me as well so I walked away. I won't give it another chance to sink its teeth into me Gail." Lance stated his voice cold as winter's frost. "Now, if you'll wait here I'll get those files for you and we can be on our way. It's pretty damn clear there will be no putting this matter aside tonight."

Lance rose from his seat and made his way back to the office. He tossed his files back into the box, he'd pulled them from earlier and carried them out to the dining room. "Shall we?" He asked indicating the door. Gail nodded and rose from the table without another word the time for talk had come to a close.

20

Anna woke to the sound of her phone ringing and yawned. She lifted her head from Sam's shoulder and found that the movie had ended some time earlier. The DVD was currently set on the menu and waiting for either her or Sam to make a selection. She sighed as she picked up the offending object that had disrupted a pleasant dream and pressed the button to connect the call.

"Hello," she said her voice heavy with sleep. She kept her tone down not wanting to wake Sam.

"Dr. Gallagher I'm sorry for the hour, I hope I haven't woken you, but I have news I fear can't wait."

"Dr. Lynch?" Anna questioned recognizing the voice but surprised by the urgency in it. Zaharrah's feathers rarely got ruffled from Anna's experience and she sounded upset.

"Yes."

"What is it? What's happened?" Anna asked. She winced as Sam stirred beside her drawn from sleep by her raised voice and the worry it held.

"I was just informed by my contacts, moving the candle, that the shipment was hit. It was stolen." Zaharrah explained.

"Stolen?" Anna inquired with disbelief.

"I'm afraid so."

"Broody?"

"It's possible, I'm looking into it now I'll let you know when I know more," Zaharrah stated.

"Thanks."

"You're welcome Dr. Gallagher. Rest assured I will handle this you continue your hunt." Zaharrah said cryptically before she hung up.

Anna set down her phone and rubbed the sleep from her eyes.

"The candle's been stolen," Anna said with disgust.

"Hermes?" Sam questioned.

"Most likely, Zaharrah's looking into."

"We'll get it back Anna," Sam assured her as he turned off the DVD player and switched off the TV. "We'll be on the first flight out to the U.K. in the morning and focus on the bow, for now, but as soon as we hear anything from Zaharrah we'll see to getting back the candle."

Anna smiled and nodded before setting her phone down, sinking back into the couch, to rest her head against his chest. "Thank you, Sam," she murmured. She felt his lips brush her forehead and sighed contented by the contact. Anna lifted her face so that blue met with hazel.

"You're welcome." He answered before his lips met with hers.

The kiss was slow and gentle holding no demand. Anna purred with delight as she melted into it. She felt his fingers sink into her long golden tresses in response to her body's yielding to his advance. She felt the same startling jolt of hunger that had hit her the first time their lips met and wondered at it. Her fingers itched with a need to touch him that frightened and thrilled her all at once. She'd never been one to rush anything but with Sam she felt reckless. Her heart fluttered wildly within her like a caged bird seeking its freedom.

Anna felt the fog around her mind lift and opened her eyes which she'd been unaware of closing. She gasped to find she now lay on the couch, Sam leaned over her his blue eyes stared down at her, studying her waiting for something but what she didn't know. How had she gotten to be here, her head resting on the arm of the sofa staring up at him? She felt herself tremble with a strange mix of anticipation and trepidation. Unsure she was ready for the next step that moments before she'd blindly run toward.

Anna watched as something flickered in his gaze and with care he helped her back up. Sam placed a tender kiss on her brow. "Night," he whispered before he rose from the couch and disappeared into his room.

Anna sat in silence, her heart pounding, dazed and confused. Trying to understand what had just happened. Apparently he'd judged her not ready to leap. Anna blew out a breath and then laughed softly to herself as relief washed over her. She'd moved too fast.

In as long as she'd been with Ian, not once had she been in such a hurry to have him. If anything Ian had complained she was too slow to act on her desire. So, how was it Sam managed to stir her up so quickly? She wondered before switching off the TV. Anna found no answer as she made her way to her own room.

21

Lance stared at the sign hanging above The Vulcan Forge and felt a chill sweep over him. The image below the name was exactly like the makers logo.

"I'd say we're in the right place," Agent Blackwood commented as she studied the two story brick building.

"Yeah, according to the records I pulled up earlier it seems our artist lives in the loft apartment on the second floor," Lance stated. He studied the building with puzzled disbelief. How had he and Dana managed to miss this place when they ran their search three years earlier?

"Shall we go have a word with Mr. Miller?"

Lance nodded. He turned off the engine on his car and the pair got out.

"Relax detective Roman you're not the only one that missed this place during your investigation. So far nothing has brought me into New York for this case. No victims have been discovered here."

"Might be our guy doesn't like to draw attention to his home town," Lance suggested as they crossed the street and started up the steps that lead to the second floor.

"Could be," Gail agreed as she followed after him. Once at the top of the stairs she took the lead knocking on the door.

Lance heard a deep angry bark on the other side of the door followed by the sound of heavy foot falls as the animal within raced to the door. He cursed inwardly Lance hated large dogs they were a distraction and in some cases a threat.

"Who is it?" a man's voice demanded. Lance pictured the man behind the door peering through the peep hole eying them with both suspicion and alarm.

"FBI," Gail answered as she held her badge out for the man to see.

"Just a minute," the voice answered. Lance stood silent and waited as he heard the sounds of the dog being locked up followed by the chain rattling as Harold unlocked the door.

A moment later the door opened to reveal a man in his mid-thirties. Harold had dark hair and dark eyes that studied them both with question.

"Good morning sir, are you Harold Miller?" Gail questioned.

"Yes."

"Are you the owner of the shop below The Vulcan Forge?"

"That's right lady," he answered.

"Is this your seal," Lance asked as he handed him a copy of the makers trade mark taken off the cup.

"It is. What is it you feds want at this hour in the morning?"

"Did you make this?" Lane asked handing him a photo of the cup.

"Yeah."

"Who for?" Lance questioned.

"What is this about?"

"That cup was used to steal an artifact from the Smithsonian recently," Lance stated.

"Shit."

"Yeah now can you help us out or shall we take this elsewhere?" Lance questioned.

"Records are downstairs. We'll talk there, just let me grab my keys," Harold said. Gail nodded and the pair stood in silence as they waited for the craftsman to emerge once more.

The trio made their way down the stairs no one speaking as the morning sun began to rise. Harold unlocked the front door of the shop and led his two unexpected guests into the business office. He pulled out a file containing records of all his recent sales and flipped through it for information on the cup.

"Oh yeah, right, now I remember this one. Guy came in three months ago commissioned the cup. He paid in cash wanted it done in a hurry. Here's his name and contact information."

"Thanks," Lance said pleased.

"Glad to help," Harold stated.

"I'm happy to hear that because I'm going to need more of it. Do you recognize this," Gail questioned holding up an evidence bag with one of the gold serpent's inside it.

"Yeah," Harold answered, eyes wide with worry at the sight of the golden band.

"These have been featured of late in a series of homicides," Agent Blackwood stated.

"Oh hell," Harold muttered uneasy.

"Yeah, what can you tell me about them and who's buying them?" Gail asked as Lance rose from the table. He got what he needed, he wasn't going to stick around and listen to the rest.

He wanted no more to do with the Fury Killer.

"Where's he going?" Lance heard Harold question behind him. He was aware of Gail responding to the question but heard none of her reply as he studied the name and phone number on the card Harold had given him. John Smith – perfect; Lance wondered where the phone number would lead him and hoped it wouldn't be a dead end as well.

22 LOS ANGELES, CALIFORNIA

Catharine stepped out of her cab and walked up the steps to the front door of James Hardagen's home. It seemed larger to her now than it had the night of the party last week. She supposed it was because now it was calm and quiet compared to the loud clamor that had erupted from it during the celebration. Before she could ring the bell, the door was opened and she was drawn into an eager hug from Emily.

"Hello again CJ it's nice to see you again," she gushed.

"Hi Emily, please call me Catharine."

"Okay, Catharine, how are you? Were you able to replace Serenity, James won't tell me anything," Emily said with a pout.

"Em, quit pestering Catharine she's had a long, trying day," James scolded.

"No its okay, yes we did. The new girl's got promise," Catharine answered pleased.

"Oh thank goodness I was worried the project was going to get canceled," Emily confessed.

"Nope we're all set to start filming Monday aren't we Mr. Hardagen," Catharine stated as she stepped in the front door.

"That's right CJ," James answered, as he led both women through the house, out to the pool side.

"Great. I promise not to ask too many questions about the movie but I've got to know; when you wrap everything up in the third movie will Serenity die?" Emily questioned as she handed her guest a margarita.

"I don't know. What makes you ask?" Catharine asked surprised. She took a sip of the drink. James sat down at the bar and listened to the two fascinated.

"There was something in the book – that scene where Rachel

faces her mother and what she's become. I thought you were going to kill her then but you didn't. Why?" Emily inquired as she sank into a lounge chair near the pool.

"I did in the original write up but I got pressure from the house to change it. They felt the readers would revolt. I caved and left her alive." Catharine explained as she took a seat. It felt good to put her feet up and relax after the long day. The alcohol warmed her blood and eased her spirit after the bitter blow Bryan's news had dealt her.

"Really?"

"Yeah, I've given some thought to killing her in the film but at this point I don't know that I'll be given that choice either."

"Why not," Emily questioned.

"I'm being pressed to write a fourth book."

"What? I thought you said there wasn't going to be a fourth that you were working on a new project?" James questioned cutting in.

"There wasn't but I was just informed today by my publicist that the house refuses to look at anything other than a fourth Dark Heart novel and if I fail to provide one I'll be in breach of contract."

"Oh that's terrible." Emily said.

"I figured you'd be happy Emily, you seem like a Serenity fan," Catharine stated.

"I am but it's not right for them to force your hand like that. Do you have any idea what to do for the book?"

"No, I mean, Serenity she's a vampire now, that makes her a villain. How do I write a story where she gets to live happily ever after as it were?" Catharine grumbled before she took another sip of her drink.

"I'm sure you'll figure it out," Emily offered. "Enough business, lets party," she enthused before finishing off her drink. She crossed to the bar and refilled it, as well as Catharine's. "Feel like a swim?"

"Yeah that would be nice, but I didn't bring a suit," Catharine sighed.

"No problem, come on, I'm sure I've got a spare around here somewhere," Emily said with a laugh, before she pulled Catharine out of the chair and led her into the house.

23

Lance made his way up the steps of the police station, his thoughts focused on tracking down the number Mr. Miller had given him. When he reached the door the sound of clicking heels coming up behind him stopped him. He turned half expecting to see Gail again. Instead the woman headed straight for him had flowing blonde hair and whiskey brown eyes. "Good morning Miss Walsh."

"Detective Roman it's nice to see you again. I'm glad I caught you." Pamela said with a bright smile. Lance blinked as she reached his side, something was different about her.

"What can I do for you today?" He asked as he studied her, trying to figure it out. Her blonde locks were brighter, more natural in appearance and seemed to almost glow in the morning light. The lines of age had faded from her face, she looked young and vital like she had when they first met, before she'd married Sam and before Dana, when he'd been young and foolish enough to fall for her himself.

Pamela fluffed her bangs aware of his perusal, she rest a hand on his shoulder trying to connect with him. "I'm looking for Sam do you know where he is?"

Lance blinked startled by the contact, she hadn't touched him like that since He'd fallen for Dana. With the contact he felt an instant sense of connection and memories of a past love affair long forgotten began to stir in his mind. His simple professional glance wandered on. He felt butterflies stir in his stomach as he noted she was wearing the suit he'd always loved on her. He remembered the one night he'd gotten to see the skin it hid beneath it and felt his blood begin to stir. "Afraid not." He said his voice was too thick and he cursed realizing she'd hear it and pounce. Lance watched as she pouted, and sighed. Miss Walsh had always been good at getting what she wanted. It was a good thing for him, in this case, he really didn't know the answer.

"Oh," she sighed disappointed. She drew back a step and he felt his body groan in protest. God, what was wrong with him he hadn't given Pamela another second of his time since Dana, and she hadn't had an eyelash to flutter in his direction since Sam and yet here she was using all her old charms and getting to him.

She turned as if recalling something and smiled. "One more thing, I nearly forgot. I understand that a cup was reported stolen from the Museum. Rumor has it you were placed in charge of the case is that correct?" She asked, her whiskey eyes studied him with interest.

"Yeah," he replied dumbly. He'd never been awkward around her before even when they'd been involved. Why was he now?

He watched with pleasure as she crossed back to his side with her slow sensual and powerful strides. "You look good Lance I think the change from homicide agrees with you," Pamela commented as delicate hands reached out to straighten his shirt collar and tie in a way that put him back nearly ten years.

"You look amazing," the words fell from his lips without his knowledge. She blushed prettily and her red nails combed through his hair. Lance blinked, breaking eye contact with her what the hell was happening between them? Why?

"Have you learned anything about it?"

"About what?" he questioned.

"The cup silly," she teased.

"It was forged by a jewelry maker in New York at a place called the Vulcan Forge for one John Smith," Lance muttered. His eyes snapped open with shock. Good lord, what was the matter with him? He shouldn't have said that.

"Thanks, you've been great detective," she purred before those crimson lips brushed against his cheek. She then turned and walked away; pausing only in her stride to give him a wink over her shoulder.

Lance rubbed his eyes and drew a breath as the attraction he felt faded into the past once more. "Weird," he muttered still a bit shaken that he'd told her any of those things. "Pamela Walsh," he said simply before moving into the station to begin the task of tracking down Mr. Smith's phone number. He hoped it would be a legitimate clue to finding the commissioner of the cup.

24 NOTTINGHAM, ENGLAND

Sam and Anna strolled through a small museum dedicated to the Robin Hood tale; an older woman with salt and pepper hair and kind blue eyes walked ahead of them leading them from one exhibit to the next. The guided tour had cost a little extra than the price of admission but the difference so far seemed to be worth it, as their guide knew a great deal about the legend and seemed to be a fan.

As they came to the last display the woman asked. "Does anyone have any questions?" Sam watched as a few of the younger patrons asked various questions about Robin Hood and his band of Merry Men. Once she was done answering Sam spoke.

"Can we have a few moments of your time Mama?"

"I suppose so, I've not got to start the next tour for a while yet, what can I help you with?" the woman asked.

"Has anyone ever found a bow they claim was Robin Hood's?" Anna asked.

"Aye, there've been many over the years but none have proven to be the real thing."

"Can you tell us what it looked like?" Sam asked.

"There are a lot of different descriptions, some say it was an ordinary bow of ewe others say it was ornate. No one know, as it's been lost for years."

"Lost?"

"The reason we've been certain the bows are fakes, is the true bow vanishes out of the myth, here in the city, after Richards return. No one knows where it is."

"I see." Anna said. Her voice held disappointment and Sam lay an arm over her shoulder for comfort as the bell over the door chimed signaling a new arrival.

"There have been several different versions of the tale over the years; who do the scholars say he was?" Anna asked. Sam glanced to the door as she spoke and his blue eyes studied the new arrival with both fear and disbelief.

"Most agree that he was probably the son of Lord Locksley."

"Thank you for your help," Sam said quickly, cutting off Anna's next question, before dragging her into a corner of the gift shop clear of the door. When she moved to protest the abrupt end of the discussion, he put a finger to his lips requesting quiet.

Anna nodded not sure of the reason for their silence but trusting it was important. Sam watched as the new comer moved towards the ticket booth, then into the museum. Once he was sure they were beyond the first bend he led Anna outside into the evening air.

"What was that about?" Anna asked.

"The last patron to walk in the door was Artemis and I'd assume not be found just yet." Sam replied.

"Right."

"Come on let's get back to the hotel. We'll check with the hall of records tomorrow and see about finding Locksley's land."

"Okay. But how are we going to find something that his people haven't been able to find in all these years?" Anna questioned.

"You found Sodom, I have faith that you'll find the bow," Sam murmured before he brushed a kiss on her cheek. He watched as she blushed prettily and smiled.

"Thanks for the vote of confidence," she whispered and she lay her head on his shoulder as they walked back toward the rental car. Sam helped her get in the passenger seat then slipped behind the wheel of the auto to head back to the hotel.

25

Zaharrah stepped off the chopper that had brought her from the dig at Atlantis to Dr. Broody's home in Athens. She'd never been fond of this place and it seemed less inviting now somehow since the change. She hated that she was here but in order to leave the dig she had to inform him of her departure and the reason for it. He wasn't in Miami or at either site which meant she'd had to seek him out on his own turf. As she made her way up the path from the helipad that led to his home Zaharrah hoped he'd forgive the intrusion.

"Ah Dr. Lynch, what a pleasant surprise what brings you to my home?" Broody questioned as he came down the path to meet her. She noted he seemed pleased and wondered what it meant but brushed such notions aside. She had business to attend to.

"Dr. Broody, please forgive the intrusion but I need to leave the dig site for a few days and have come to request permission," Zaharrah explained.

"No need to apologize for coming here, you are most welcome Zaharrah. Why is it you'll be leaving the dig? I thought you were in it for the long haul," Broody said with disappointment.

"I've had a family emergency come up..."

"Ah I see. Of course you may go, take as much time as you need. Family is indeed precious. I sent my dear lady away on a business matter and I'm missing her already," he said with a hint of regret.

"Thank you Doctor."

"Call me Ian after all we've known each other a long time I'd think we could be friends," he murmured. Zaharrah nodded but gave no reply. What was with him, he was beginning to spook her a bit and she wasn't the type to spook easily. Yes they'd known each other but he was not anyone she counted a friend. When he'd cheated Anna out of her credit for the dig in Ithaca he'd cheated her as well. She'd purposely avoided working his digs since then until now.

"Have you gotten anything out of Anna's notes yet," he asked off handedly, but there was a glimmer in his eye that revealed the apparent lack of interest to be a lie. He wanted to know and he wanted to know badly.

"Not yet, Ian," She replied politely, hiding her distaste at using his first name. She watched as temper flared in his steel colored eyes and for a moment they seemed to glow blue. Whoa what the hell was that?

"No matter, I trust you'll sort it out soon enough," he said with a disarming smile that made her skin crawl.

Zaharrah gave him a quick goodbye. He leaned in and brushed a kiss on both her cheeks that dropped a small ball of ice in the pit of her stomach. The man before her was not Dr. Ian Broody. Zaharrah didn't know who or what he was but she was sure going to talk to Anna about it and soon.

26 NOTTINGHAM, ENGLAND

As Sam drove down the roads of the famous hamlet in the British countryside the sky turned dark and rain began to fall. It pelted the windshield in sheets that the wipers could not keep up with. He watched as Anna jumped in the seat beside him shaken from a rest filled sleep as thunder crashed and lightening split the sky.

"Sam," she cried out in panic.

"Relax Anna we're okay," he assured her recalling her fear of being on the road in a down pour.

"Can we please stop?" She asked sheepishly.

Sam nodded as his thoughts of bed were derailed. He sighed but was relieved to be getting off the road, he could barely see. "Where did this come from?" he muttered with disgust.

"Do you think this is Artemis's doing that, maybe she saw us go in and has realized by now she lost us?" Anna questioned.

"Maybe," Sam replied unsure. "I'm going to pull into the lot here and we can either wait it out here in the car or move into one of the shops."

Anna nodded as he pulled up along the curb. He switched off the engine. The only sound now was the steady patter of rain as it fell on the windshield. Anna unfastened her seat belt and repressed a yawn. Sam turned and looked at her fighting back a yawn of his own.

"Sorry," Anna murmured seeing how tired he was.

"Don't be I needed to stop the wipers, weren't doing much to help," he assured her as he unfastened his seatbelt.

"You look beat," she said with worry.

"I'll be okay I just need a cup of coffee or something," Sam assured her.

"I think there's a book shop out there maybe we can find you a coffee inside," Anna suggested.

"Good idea," Sam commented. Waiting in the car was not a good idea he realized, besides the possibility of falling asleep it left them completely alone together and Sam could already feel her nearness beginning to affect him. Now was not the time to get distracted, if Anna was right about the storm Artemis might be out there even now trying to track them down. Sam got out of the car, drawing his coat over his head, he rounded it and let Anna out under the thin cover the pair made a mad dash to the nearby awning of the book shop and slipped inside.

27 HOLLYWOOD, CALIFORNIA

Catharine lay out on one of the many deck chairs surrounding James Hardagen's luxurious swimming pool under a full moon. On the table next to her sat a half full margarita. She'd had at least three before it and she could feel her body relaxing under the influence of the alcohol. She wondered if maybe she'd had too many as she turned and looked at her hostess. Emily had partied hard since she got there and seemed unaffected by the half dozen drinks she'd had since they stopped talking business.

It had surprised her how insightful Emily was about Serenity and she wondered if the young model might have worked for the role. Then passed on the idea, Emily had gorgeous dark hair which it would have been a shame to hide under a wig or a crime to color. Besides the woman had no acting experience and if she landed the part Hollywood would cry foul.

Unbidden thoughts of the past began to surface, James's place was a lot nicer than Tom's had ever been. Catharine blinked, now she was sure she'd had too much to drink, she'd not thought of him in years. She blamed Bryan for the stray thought; he'd mentioned her ex-husband's name. No doubt that was what had triggered the line of thought. She sat up a little dizzy and noted she was still wearing Emily's sexy blue suit. Where had she left her clothes? Catharine tried to recall but the image was fuzzy.

"Ah so you are awake, we were just debating it," James said amused as he took a seat on the end of her chair.

"Yeah I'm awake. I should probably get back to the hotel," she said moving to get up.

"No way Catharine, you're wasted you have no business driving and you shouldn't go getting into a cab at this hour with a stranger," Emily scolded. "You can stay with us in a guest room," she said with a smile.

"Oh, that's really kind of you but…" Catharine began uneasy she didn't do well in foreign environments and given her state she might just have some nightmare connected to the past and disturb them.

"It'll be fine the guest rooms are on the other side of the house you can blast the radio down there and we won't hear you and you won't hear us either," James assured her with a wink. "Come on I'll show you to a room," he entreated as he offered her his hand. Catharine took it and allowed her host to lead her into his home. Emily followed behind them.

James showed her into a large guest suite that made her hotel room look like one at a budget motel. Emily handed her things to her. "There are clothes in the dresser, help yourself. You should find something that will fit for you to sleep in," Emily informed her, then wished her good night.

"You're sure this is okay?" Catharine asked not wanting to intrude.

"Positive," now go on get some rest we'll see you in the morning," he answered before placing a kiss on her cheek. "Good night CJ and sweet dreams," he murmured before he turned and left.

Catharine closed the door and set her things on a chair. She crossed to the dresser and opened the drawer to see what there was. She blinked at the sight of an assortment of various silky pieces in different colors then reminded herself Emily was a lingerie model and probably got as much of the stuff as she wanted. She pulled out a simple blue silk piece and crossed to the bathroom to change.

Once dressed; she crawled into the bed. As her head hit the pillow her thoughts drifted to Lance. She wondered what he was up to at the moment and for half a second considered calling him. She pushed the impulse away she'd definitely had too much to drink and decisions made when she'd been drinking where men were concerned tended to be bad ones. She wasn't about to add Lance to the list. Her mind made up, Catharine closed her eyes and fell into a dreamless sleep.

28

Lance made his way up the sidewalk to his front step. He was beat and couldn't recall the last time he'd had such a lousy shift. First dealing with shadows from the Fury Killer Case, then having his only lead on the cup turned out to be a bust. Mr. John Smith's phone number had also proved to be a dead end. Worse still, when he'd driven back to New York to speak further with the owner of the Vulcan Forge there had been feds everywhere; they'd seized control of the location and his minor case had been placed on the back burner due to a homicide taking precedents. In short he was screwed. He'd been working the thing now for over 12 hours straight. He was still nowhere, nothing to show for his efforts. It was time to put it to bed.

Stepping inside Lance made his way down the hall to his room and shed his coat and holster, hanging them on his coat hook on the back of the door. He pulled his gun out secured the safety and locked it away in his safe. The next thing to go was his shoes. He felt like he'd walked a hundred miles in them since waking Sunday and it felt good to lose them. His toes sighed with relief before he loosened his tie and tossed it on the bed.

Now a bit more comfortable, he moved back down the hall to the kitchen and checked his messages. He was disappointed to find Catharine had not called again but figured she'd been busy as well. He hoped the rest of her day had gone better than the morning. Tired but restless, Lance knew sleep would not come easy and to help himself along he crossed to the fridge and pulled out a beer. He pulled off the cap and opted to forego the glass tonight.

He took a swig then moved back to the living room and flipped on the T.V. He cruised through the various stations and finding nothing of interest he switched it off again. With a sigh he picked up his copy of Heart of Glass and opened it to the page where he left off. There wasn't much left now, he might be able to finish it tonight before he gave into sleep.

29

James Hardagen stepped into his shared room with Emily and found her already dressed for bed. "So Em, what do you think of our house guest?"

"I think she's amazing, so talented and fun, I wish she could stay with us it would be like having a sister." Emily sighed.

"Do you want her to stay love?"

"Yes very much,"

"Okay then we'll invite her to stay, over breakfast in the morning," James said with a smile.

"I feel sorry for her having to write another book like that, it's just wrong of them," Emily murmured.

"I know but on the other hand think of the attention the film will raise. I mean what if we did the Fourth film at the same time the book comes out. This is a huge opportunity Emily." James breathed excited.

"Yeah I know it. Her fans have been begging for a fourth book since the last one came out." Emily admitted.

"What about you princess, don't you want another book," James questioned as he shed his clothes and joined her in the bed.

"Of course I do, but not if it makes her miserable. She seems like a nice person and the whole thing seems to really upset her."

"It'll be okay pet, I'm sure," James said with a grin. He drew her into his embrace. "Be my Serenity tonight?" he requested.

"Tonight and always," she assured him.

James kissed her greedily more than ready for her. He'd watched her by the pool as she rested, danced and had gotten a thrill while watching her cut through the water alongside CJ. His Emily was a dazzling beauty and he'd wanted her then but had waited for a moment alone having no wish to drive away Miss

Nichols either, there was something about the writer that had sparked his interest.

As he made love to his fiancé James slipped into the role of the vampire lord playing the opposite to her Serenity nipping and biting, tormenting her eager flesh with an overwhelming mix of pleasure and pain. He tore her nightie with a wild sense of urgency a voice within him driving him to take her hard and fast without mercy to make her drunk with want of him. Hands and mouth were everywhere in flaming her until she all but screamed at him to stop teasing her.

When he gave her that which she begged for, it was more than she could bear, she crashed over the edge into ecstasy. He road through the waves of her passion his teeth sinking into her neck drawing blood. Following the desire within him, he drank it as he began to move inside her racing toward his own release. His ruthless pace set her to trembling beneath him again and he waited her out. When she stilled, he began again pressing harder, moving faster, driving deeper. When his body was stated he found she'd lapsed into unconsciousness. He kissed her gently and whispered of his love before rising from the bed.

The act of coupling with her, rather than draining him, had served only to waken him further. He crossed over to his office restless. Taking a cup from its pedestal he pulled out a bottle of red from the mini fridge and poured himself a glass. The taste of it was sweet and inviting he felt a rush of power wash over him and wondered at it.

The cup since he acquired it had been changing. The outer layer of earth was crumbling to reveal gold beneath it with amethyst set in it. He'd believed the cup to be the Holy Grail but now he wasn't so sure. There was something more here, as he considered the matter and how to find out what, he sat in silence and watched the screen in front of him with avid interest.

30 Washington DC, Virginia
Tuesday
5pm

Lance woke groggy. Disoriented. He was aware of the sound of music starting and stopping; only to repeat. Opening his eyes he looked up to see the TV still on. The DVD was set on the menu screen waiting for him to make a choice. A half-finished beer sat on the coffee table in front of him. He blinked as he tried to recall putting on the movie. The last thing he remembered, he'd been reading Catharine's book.

He noted it sat on the couch beside him, closed, bookmark on the table he'd finished it and not having the sequel he'd turned on a movie hoping to distract himself from where the story might lead. He assumed it wasn't good given what Catharine had said about Serenity becoming a vampire at the ball.

Lance cursed as he sat up. He wasn't fond of dozing off on the couch. He always woke with a crick in his neck and sore back. He turned his head cracking the stiff joints; then got to his feet. Glancing at the clock he found 12 hours had passed since he came in. The book stores were still open at this hour, he could go get the other two novels and start reading before his next shift started; Lance reasoned; then growled as he realized Catharine had managed to get him hooked to a damn romance series. If the guys at the station found out, he'd never live it down. No, best to wait until his day off.

Lance groaned as he made his way back to the bathroom. Along with the sore back he had the beginning of a bad headache. He'd dreamed again. Though what exactly even he wasn't sure. There'd been death he was certain of it. It wasn't all that surprising given his unwanted mail a couple nights ago. As he reached the end of the hall Lance looked at the guest room and sighed.

Catharine had only been gone two days. He missed her already.

He'd caught the interview with Miss Walsh the other night. Was glad to see her well, but he couldn't shake the feeling she was in some kind of trouble. Something about the arguments he'd overheard with Bryan bothered him.

Lance opened the door to his room, then crossed through it to the bathroom. He reached in the medicine cabinet and took out a bottle of Ibuprofen. Popping the cap he shook out two then sealed the bottle; sticking it back in the cabinet. He swallowed the pills without water. Closed the cabinet. Lance turned on the tap and cupped his hands in the cool water. He splashed the liquid in his face then looked up at the mirror, to study his reflection. What he saw instead were red letters that chilled his blood.

His mind raced to another day a year earlier when he'd come home to find the mirror broken and written in blood I'm Sorry.

Lance blinked before his mind could bring back the rest and the image receded into the dark corners of his brain. He drew a breath. Read the message aloud. "Expected more of you Detective. My lovely Dana would be disappointed. Catch Me if You can. A." Lance cursed and reached in his pocket for his cell. He punched one on his speed dial. Reporting the break in. He moved back to the living room where he'd left agent Blackwood's card. Lance dialed the number. He waited for Gail to answer.

"Hello."

"Agent Blackwood."

"Detective Roman is that you?"

"Yes."

"I didn't expect to hear from you."

"I wasn't planning on calling. Your friend left me a message," Lance said with disgust.

"What?"

"You heard me. Your killer left me a damn love note. I haven't heard from this guy, in two years, since I walked off the case. You led the sick bastard right to my front door. I don't want any part of that investigation in my life again."

"I'm sorry detective. I'm at the latest crime scene. You have little choice."

"What the hell does that mean?"

"He left you a message here too. Says if you're not back on the case he'll kill one person within 24hrs, until you are."

"Shit."

"I'm sorry Lance I didn't mean to..."

"Where are you?"

"Lurey Caverns you're not going to believe where he left this one."

"I'm on my way. I've got a team coming here to look at the place. I suggest you send one of your team here to take a look as well." Lance said before he hung up. He grabbed his keys, scribbled a quick note for the crime scene team explaining where he'd gone, then left to meet up with Agent Blackwood.

31

Pamela watched with interest as Lance sped away from his home and pulled into traffic a few cars back. Where was he off to in such a hurry? Had he gotten a lead on the cup? As she headed out of DC she had her doubts it had to do with the cup. Lance was driving like the devil was on his tail, red lights flashing but no siren. She hadn't seen him drive like that since he left the homicide beat.

If it wasn't the cup that had him racing out of his front door after only twelve hours down time, not even shaved, then what was it? As he pulled to a stop ahead, the thick group of cop cars and unmarked cars set her blood to humming. Oh yeah this was a lot bigger than a simple theft. Based on the various suits about, Pamela was willing to bet she was looking at feds.

"What have you gotten yourself mixed up in detective Roman?" she murmured as she killed her headlights and pulled into a parking slot; out of his line of sight. She was going to enjoy tailing him more than she'd realized. In her mind she called to her husband and reported all that was going on in the states. He praised her craftiness and bid her stay with the detective.

"Use whatever means necessary in order to obtain the information we need, then come home to me as soon as possible. I miss you my clever wife," Hermes mind whispered and then His spirit joined with her in the car rushing over her teasing her with the promise of pleasure to come when next they met in the flesh.

"It will be done, my lord," she breathed as her eyes fell shut and she joined him, as he'd taught her, in the spirit realm to indulge in their shared desire to please each other.

32

Lance stepped out of his unmarked squad car. He made his way through the crowd of officers and agents securing the crime scene. Lance stared at the yellow crime scene tape, closing the entrance of the hedge maze and sighed. Agent Blackwood was right he didn't believe where the killer had decided to leave his latest victim.

Lance made the necessary preparations to enter the scene before crossing under the yellow crime scene tape. He made his way through the vast maze to the center where a smaller crowd had gathered in the late afternoon heat. He spotted agent Blackwood in the middle speaking with his boss. Lance cursed.

"Bad news travels fast," he muttered as he made his way toward them. He watched as Gail fell silent; turned to look at him. Her brown eyes held both sympathy and apology. Lance drew a breath to steel his nerves before moving his focus to the victim.

She like the others before her was in her late twenties to mid-thirties petite and skinny. Every inch of her 5'3 frame had been covered after death with the same red Grecian style toga as the victims before her. Her left breast lay exposed. A snake of gold, his calling card, was coiled about her beneath the breasts. Its fangs sunk into her heart, a knife wound in the ivory skin where he'd dealt the killing blow. Her death had not come quickly.

Lance remembered from previous victims that this guy tortured and raped his victims before piercing their heart. He moved past the killing blow; forcing himself to take it all in. Dana had died because of her inability to catch him. The fact he was still out there sickened Lance.

The woman's hair was the same stunning red. The front had been shorn short and styled in spikes. The same golden serpents wreathed her head like some twisted crown their fangs sunk into her scalp. Long tresses hung curled in the back. At the sides more snakes hung from the crown by their tails, fangs exposed emerald eyes glaring at him.

Her hazel eyes were open wide, they held, fear pain and rage. Beneath them the skin had been cut from the eye to jaw in jagged lines causing blood to fall from the eyes. They stared up lifelessly at Lance and the others almost a silent accusation of their failure to protect her.

Her ivory skin was bruised. She was battered from the rough treatment of her captor. Another snake was coiled about her throat. Its fangs sunk deep into her jugular. Blood ran down her throat; testifying that the wound had come before death. This one was new. It had been the crown and band at the arm or ankle before.

His killer A. was getting more artistic with his work; a bad sign. On her left arm the flesh was charred. The impression of yet another snake branded deep in the skin. Another change, he was looking for more ways to hurt them, his furies. When had he gotten so blood thirsty?

Six months ago Blackwood had said. Lance wondered why then but set it aside. His gaze moved on. The right arm displayed another brand; this one from her wrist to her elbow. The next mark he found was yet another golden snake wrapped about her waist. Fangs sunk in the navel through the gown.

He found a final branding around her ankle to her calf on the left leg. Parting the splitting of the gown he found a final snake coiled round her thigh on the right leg. The serpent sat poised to strike any who would try to touch her here. It belonged to him. To A. whomever he was he was becoming more possessive of his furies as well. He noted the tattoo of the black hound on her right foot. Figured that her back would be the same as the ones before; cut up the slices looking like wings.

Taking in the whole image Lance felt ill.

In his mind the woman's eyes changed from hazel to blue. Instead of a stranger he saw Catharine. Lance closed his eyes and drew a steadying breath – willing the image away. It wasn't Catharine there. Never would be. He'd have nothing more to do with Miss Nichols until the matter was done.

Lance's glance shifted to the setting, he noted the Angel poised at the top of the wall overlooking the corpse, then he saw the writing above her head on the stone. His blood burned with rage. It was true what Gail said the killer's threat was cold and serious. A warning that the body count would rise each day he refused the case. Starting with an associate of his in B & E. Lance swore. His stomach rolled with disgust. He had little choice and he knew it. Like it or not he was going back to working homicide.

"Detective," Agent Blackwood said by way of greeting.

"Agent Blackwood."

"Glad to have you aboard."

"Wish I could say I was happy to be here," Lance grumbled. "What do we know about her?"

"Not much yet I'm afraid. There was no ID on her. Coroner is enroute," Gail answered.

"Tell the coroner to make sure he cuts that band at the thigh off before beginning his exam." Lance muttered.

"Why?" Gail questioned wondering what he had seen.

"Not sure. Something in the way it's positioned. Like a guard at the gate. Might be dangerous."

"Lance, our team just arrived at your place looks like the message is in blood."

"Is it possible he went straight from the scene here to the detective's place and put up the note in the victim's blood?" Agent Blackwood asked.

"Sounds about right. Oh, he left us a clue to his identity," Lance stated.

"What do you mean?" Gail asked curious.

"He signed his note 'A.' I'm willing to bet it's a clue as to his identity," Lance stated.

"Why now?" Agent Blackwood asked.

"Because now he's got a full team hunting him again," Lance stated.

"Meaning?"

"Your appearance is close to Dana's; same height, weight general appearance. Now Dana, his favorite advisory, is back to working the case with, her partner, Me. He's got his opponent in place. Now he's ready to let the real game begin," Lance said with disgust.

"You mean to tell me what I've been seeing was just a warm up?" Gail asked with disbelief.

"Yeah, that's right this thing is about to get worse," Lance breathed. He looked away from the victim up at the darkening sky. Lightening streaked it. "Storm's coming I suggest we get this place secure before the rain washes away our crime scene."

"Our crime scene?" Gail questioned.

"Yeah, I'm in but I'm going to need a complete update on the case."

"You'll get it." Gail assured him.

"Good let's get started the sooner we catch this sicko the better."

33

Catharine woke well after 2p.m. with the disconcerting feeling of being watched. She cursed as she noted the time she was really late for the second day on set. Why hadn't she gotten her wakeup call? Looking around she groaned. She wasn't at the hotel she was in a guest room at Mr. Hardagen's home. She'd definitely had too much to drink last night.

With a sigh she climbed out of bed and crossed the room to the chair where she'd left her clothes from the night before. To her disquiet they were missing and where they had lain was a note. "Sent your clothes out to be washed; help yourself to anything in the closet. See you downstairs for brunch," Emily.

Catharine crossed to the closet and stepped inside flipping on the light. She looked through the various garments hanging in the closet. She tried on a couple different options and in the end settled on a simple blue sundress that while sexy was not so uncomfortable for her, she'd feel like hiding in her office the rest of the day.

Satisfied with her attire Catharine fixed her hair then moved downstairs to seek out her hostess.

She found Emily and James sitting by the pool where she left them the night before, Emily wore a black slinky dress that hugged all her curves with a matching scarf that made her look stunning she had a small fruit plate with yogurt in front of her. James was dressed in a black suit with red dress shirt. He was chewing on bacon and eggs and looked ready for the set.

"Ah she's alive at last," James teased.

"Sorry I didn't have an…"

"No need to apologize I told the crew you'd be in later after all your consulting not in the film. I hope you rested well."

"Actually I did thank you. I really appreciate you letting me stay."

"Sit eat I'll give you a ride to the set when I go back after lunch," James instructed.

"That's not necessary," Catharine began embarrassed.

"Please, stop I insist. In fact after we tucked you into bed Em and I did some talking and well..." James began.

"We want you to stay here at the house with us while you're in LA," Emily exclaimed excited. "It was so nice having you over last night, like having a sister and I get lonely here when he's working," Emily gushed.

Catharine blinked stunned and a bit uneasy. As she sat down James poured her a glass of juice. "I couldn't..."

"You wouldn't be intruding you'd be doing me a favor," James assured her.

"Please," Emily requested batting her lashes at Catharine.

"Well, okay but if it gets to be any trouble I'll go back to the hotel," Catharine stated.

"Yay!" Emily cheered before she wrapped her arms around Catharine's shoulders in a hug. "I don't believe it CJ Nichols is going to stay as my house guest."

"What do you want to eat?" James asked her.

"Got any bagels?" Catharine questioned with a laugh.

"As it so happens we do. I recalled you'd had one on the set yesterday and sent out for one," James replied. He set a plate with the fresh bagel and flavored cream cheese spread.

"Thanks," Catharine said before she turned her attention to the food.

"When you're done eating we'll swing by the hotel and get your things before heading back to the set," Emily explained and the trio then once more fell into a comfortable silence as they ate their various meals.

34

Anna sat at her workspace flipping through yet another book she'd picked up at the quaint book shop they'd stopped in at to get out of the storm. She'd found an entire section on myths surrounding the Robin Hood legend, tales about Nottingham itself and additional stories pertaining to Sherwood Forest. In addition to the books, she'd also found a display of heraldic mugs and was surprised to find her own. She contemplated picking it up and the one for Locksley but had refrained. Unfortunately there had been no coffee.

They'd left the book shop with an umbrella and moved on to the next shop, it had proved to be a jewelry shop. A set in the display had caught her attention but she'd refrained from going in. the next shop had been a small café where Sam had muttered something about forgetting his wallet and then told her to wait there. She'd ordered them each a coffee and bought a bag for the room.

She was sipping her cup when he came back. When she asked if he found his wallet he said he'd left it on the counter at the book shop. Sam had bought a book on Greek myth. When she asked why he'd muttered something about knowing his enemy. Anna had laughed as it still seemed absurd to her, they were really pitted against a fallen angel, puffed up in the role of a Greek god, in the hunt for a group of mantels; that if they fell in the wrong hands would see the return of his brethren as well.

"Any coffee left?" Anna questioned her roommate.

Sam nodded then rose from his seat to get it for her. He set a cup on the table beside her and when she picked it up she found it was not a hotel disposable one but a ceramic. Turning she was surprised to see a white mug with the Gallagher heraldic crest. The image of a black lion in rampart treading upon a green snake with green clovers surrounding it.

"You didn't have to do that," Anna said with objection.

"Actually I did; I owed you a mug," Sam said sheepishly.

"Why do you owe me a mug?"

"I broke one at your house," Sam confessed.

"When?"

"After Pamela showed up and you ran off; I was mad, shoved it and everything else off the counter."

"Oh, you still didn't have to," Anna assured him.

"I wanted to," Sam stated as he set the other mug next to it.

"Thank you," she murmured.

"How's the reading?"

"Okay though not much that stands out. I've read three different versions of the Robin Hood story now. In one version it was actually Marian who was the archer," Anna commented.

"Interesting."

"How's your book?"

"Boring. I can't get past all the crazy names," Sam admitted.

"Give it here I'll read it for you," Anna said setting her book aside and holding out a hand for his paperback.

Sam handed it over and Anna opened the book and flipped to the front page. Sam sat silent and listened as she read by firelight about the Greek gods and the various heroes of their legends. The sound of her voice was soothing and he found his mind wandering. As in the car earlier he felt her presence pull at him.

Her words were lost to him as he rose from his chair and crossed to her side. Anna looked up from the book as he pulled it from her grasp. "Enough for tonight," he breathed before he leaned down and kissed her. Her mouth came alive under his tasting and teasing as she surrendered to the impulse which had been crowding her since the car.

"Sam," she breathed his name when their lips parted, her hazel eyes were a brilliant blue from the intensity of the emotions running through her.

Sam drew a long breath working to cool himself down, reminding himself that with Miss Gallagher he was not going to rush blindly where his body led him. "Good night Anna," he murmured before he turned and moved off to his room.

Anna blew out a breath that ruffled her hair around her face. "night," she muttered before turning her attention once more back to her books she wouldn't be sleeping anytime soon after that shock to the system.

Lance's eyes felt like they were going to bleed and the edges of a headache began to bloom between them. He'd been reading over reports on the Fury Killer since he and Agent Blackwood got back to his place. It was grim and dark stuff, he'd yet to go through the photos as he kept seeing that girl in the maze change from a stranger to Catharine.

"You okay?" Gail questioned.

Lance wondered if she'd seen something earlier at the crime scene; the moment when he'd gone from cop to survivor – when he'd seen Catharine. "Yeah, just need a break," Lance stated, hoping a few minutes away from it all would help him to get a grip.

"How's your theft case going?"

"It's going nowhere the guy who commissioned the piece left the name John Smith and the phone number turns out to be a blending of said explorers birth date and death date," Lance said with disgust.

"Really?" Gail questioned amused.

"Yeah I got dick," Lance groused.

"No, you got lucky is what you got," Gail corrected.

"How do you figure?"

"I know the guy. He's a thief for hire, worked a case with him about five years ago we popped him for the theft of a priceless gem. He flipped on his employer, guy with mafia ties, for immunity. His calling card was to leave the names of famous explorers at the places he robbed. He's actually local as we relocated him here. If you don't mind a drive we can go pay him a visit now," Agent Blackwood stated.

"Let's go I guess we'll need to call Mr. Miller in as well," Lance said as he grabbed his coat, Gail nodded and the pair set out.

36

Pamela watched as Lance and the brunette from the maze came out of his place and got in the car. They pulled out of the drive and set off across town. Getting on the highway they headed north. She followed at a safe distance knowing if she lost them, any chance of learning what was going on would slip through her fingers as well.

The car stopped in front of a low rent apartment complex. Pamela pulled over near the side of the road out of sight and waited. She watched as the pair moved up the sidewalk and climbed the stairs to the second floor. Pamela pulled out the pair of binoculars she kept tucked in the glove box and watched as the woman banged on the door marked 202a. The pair waited and then she flashed a badge. Pamela grinned she'd been right there had been feds crawling all over the scene at the cavern.

A man with blonde hair and blue eyes stepped outside and the trio spoke briefly before moving back downstairs together and getting in the car. Pamela pulled away from the curb and followed after them wondering just what the ex-homicide detective had gotten tangled up in. Her drive took her back to the police station. She watched as the pair led the other man inside, as she switched on her news band her whiskey colored eyes gleamed with excitement as reports began to come in of a 187 reported in Caverns, speculation circling that the Fury Killer is back making this one victim number 5 locally. Pamela grinned. She checked her makeup in the mirror then lifted her breasts in her hands making sure that enough of them was peeking out of her top. This was one story she wasn't about to walk away from. "Look out detective Roman I've got my eye on you now and soon enough you'll tell me all," she purred with pleasure before slipping out of the car and crossing the street to go after him.

37

Lance led his suspect through the station to the waiting line up. He set him in it and then issued Mr. Miller into the room to identify his Mr. Smith.

"Take your time," Lance instructed.

The shop owner studied the various men and then after a few minutes of scrutiny spoke. "Mr. Smith is number 3."

"Thank you Mr. Miller," Lance said pleased he turned to the black and white in the room with them "Put him in interrogation room A," Lance ordered pointing at number three before he lead the shop owner out to sign the paperwork needed. Once it was done, he turned and with agent Blackwood in tow moved on to talk with his thief. With a little more luck he might just get the cup back for Sam and Anna tonight.

Lance walked into the room and without any preamble asked, "Where's the cup?"

"What cup?"

"Don't play dumb Mr. Smith the shop owner at Vulcan's Forge identified you as being the one who had the fake made. Where is the real one?"

"I don't know what you're talking about," the thief said stubbornly.

"Oh now that's a bad deal for you then Jarod, your agreement with the feds stated you'd be cooperative in any and all investigations pertaining to your past or future thefts so long as you are forthcoming with Intel you stay out of jail," Gail reminded.

"Look it's gone I put it in a safety deposit box and the dude switched me cash for it."

"What dude?"

"I don't know we never exchanged names but he looked kind of familiar."

"Which deposit box?" Lance questioned.

"It wasn't local."

"Okay I want…"

"Detective we got a problem, press got wind of what went down earlier, they're here asking questions. Miss Walsh is out there now talking to your witness she must think he's got something to do with the case." A black and white said as he stuck his head in the room.

"Ah hell, we'll continue this when I get back," Lance said with irritation.

"Can't wait," the thief said with a laugh.

Lance followed the cop back down the hall out into the waiting area, but there was no sign of Pamela or Mr. Miller. Lance cursed. Wherever she was he could bet that it meant trouble.

38 Unknown

HE sat at the small workspace that passed as a table in his temporary lair. HIS latest Fury lay on display under the angel head board. She was a masterpiece the best one thus far. HE hoped Detective Roman and Agent Blackwood would appreciate his art. It was good to have a true opponent in the game again. It had been far too long since HE felt challenged. The feds were about as clueless where HIS craft was concerned. They'd painted HIM as some mad abused child. They were fools all of them, their minds trained to see in the way the rulers of the day desired. It never crossed their minds that a sane man or woman could do the things He had done. Nor could they fathom the truth that HIS Furies were not dead but merely in a pupa stage waiting for the time when they would wake to be more than the mortal women they had believed themselves to be.

"So pretty, each one you've chosen is the embodiment of what they once were, soon they will wake," A woman's voice murmured. HE felt the brush of her pale skin against his face and thrilled in the touch. HE drew in her scent and the voice within his mind warned she could not be trusted. Reminded him of all IT had done for HIM, assured HIM that soon his heart's deepest desire would be HIS. HE need only wait a little longer.

"You're wrong, her gaze has fallen upon another," HE hissed with rage at the voice within HIS mind, recalling the sight of them together. "She always looks elsewhere," HE said with disgust.

"She always gets hurt and in the end she comes back to you," the voice reminded.

"Stop your arguing and come play with me," the woman entreated. HE moved to the bed where she now sat, in her delicate hands she held a stack of photos, she fanned the images out in much the same way a magician does for a card trick. He humored her drawing a picture from the fan. "An excellent choice she'll make a great Fury," the woman said with approval before she set the other photos down in HIS bag.

"Finish the note," the voice within HIM demanded.

"No, play with me," the woman purred.

"Soon," HE promised the voice within HIM before HE turned HIS attention to the woman and joined her once more by the bed. Taking out his knife HE cut his Furies face creating the bloody tears as the woman watched with pleasure, when the task was done she drew HIM against her . HE pressed the bloody blade to her lips and watched as she licked it clean before her mouth met with HIS, forceful and demanding she drew HIM deeper into her web as the voice inside HIS mind raged at HIM telling HIM to send her away she was not HIS beloved.

39

Catharine sat in a director's chair besides James Hardagen with her laptop on her knees, she was busy working on the notes for book four of the Dark Heart Series: she'd given the book a temporary title Heart of Steel but wasn't convinced that was what it would stay. She'd reread the scene between Rachel and Serenity like four times since arriving on the set. She would look down at her screen and mentally cursed, she'd been at this since she got here and all she had to show for her efforts were the basic requirements for the book.

1. Story needed to be focused on Serenity
2. Needed to have a happy ending for her (so fans and publishing house will get off my back)
3. Needed a new romantic lead
4. Burn when completed

Catharine groaned. How am I going to do this? How can I take a character I hate and write an entire novel around her in which she gets her heart's desire? For that matter what was Serenity's heart's desire? How am I supposed to decide where to take my character now, when the last time I saw her she was supposed to just vanish into the sunset so to speak? How am I going to take this Vampire Queen and present her as anything but a monster? Where do I start? What if she walks off to vanish but someone finds her or follows her? Catharine typed under the list of requirements. Why?

The sound of the new actress's voice reading the latest lines penetrated her cocoon of silence and she cursed.

"Cut!" James called annoyed by the break in silence. "What's wrong CJ?"

"She's reading the line wrong," Catharine replied.

"No I'm not," the actress argued.

"Yes you are. You're all breathy and scared but that's not right. See it's in this moment that Serenity begins to change even before Syvarin bites her. She sees a way to escape from Kovrin and without batting an eyelash she takes it. She's not afraid of the vampire lord here, she's using him, manipulating him to her own ends. She gets him to deal with her foe and then walks into the embrace of her love. She never looks back or considers the consequences."

"She doesn't read that way to me," the actress said puzzled.

"Okay, CJ we'll shoot it both ways yours and hers and then decide what works best later," James said.

Catharine nodded her consent. Before turning her focus back to the laptop. Frustrated she closed it up. She watched as the new girl ran through the opening sequence both ways then rubbed her eyes as a headache began to set in. Opening the laptop she went back to her last question. She typed up a couple possible options and then closed the document turning her focus back to the script.

Lance moved back down the hall toward interrogation room A, he pushed the question of where Pamela had vanished to and what she was up to aside. He was about to crack the case of the stolen cup wide open. He needed to focus on finishing out the interview with Miller. Whatever Pamela was after could wait for now, he needed to get his head back in the game, Lance reasoned.

As he stepped back in the room he eyed the thief with interest. "Okay, now let's see where were, we? Oh yeah, I was about to ask you for the location of the safety deposit box, the name of the bank there, the number and the time in which you were there to collect your money."

"The deposit box was in a Bank of America in Las Vegas Nevada. The number was 1191. I was there the weekend…"

"Detective agent Blackwood sorry for the interruption again but we need you immediately."

"Can it wait five minutes?" Lance asked irritated.

"Chief said now."

"Fine, we're on our way I guess we'll wrap this up shortly," Lance said eyeing the thief with warning.

"Look forward to it detective but I figure that cup is long gone from Vegas by now." Mr. Miller answered.

Lance and agent Blackwood made their way out of the interrogation room and followed the black and white to the chief's office.

"This just arrived for the two of you," Lance's superior stated as he handed over a sealed envelope.

Lance swallowed recognizing the grim package from years

earlier when he'd gotten others like it addressed to Dana and himself. He eyed the discolored stamp with disgust knowing that it was wetted not by the killer's saliva or a moist rag but the blood of his latest victim. Lance pulled on a pair of gloves and with a shaking hand took the gruesome package, wondering where they'd be sent by the riddle within to find the latest Fury. He broke the seal and pulled the letter out, with care. Like the others before he found the note to be a typed message of five lines, within whose words were clues to the location where they would find his latest kill.

"In a gilded castle upon hot sand
Not cross the sea on foreign land,
Where cards are turned and men throw dice
She waits having paid the ultimate price,
A star no more she wears my band."

"Okay so let's look at what we've got. Hot sand, sounds like a desert." Gail commented.

"Cards are turned and dice are thrown in Vegas," Lance muttered having just been there not long ago.

"Okay so a casino but which one?" the chief asked.

"Gilded castle could be golden palace. Caesar's Palace could also be found in Rome a foreign land," agent Blackwood stated.

"Yeah that fits," Lance said unnerved by the fact that the cup and the killer may have both been right under his nose while he was in Vegas and he missed both.

"Let's get moving the sooner we find this girl the better." Agent Blackwood said. Lance nodded and together the pair left the station.

41 New York, New York

Pamela slipped out of Harold Miller's bed and padded cross the floor to gather her clothes as she let her thoughts run back to everything she'd learned from him since meeting him at the police station. Harold it seemed had been hired by a man calling himself Mr. Smith to craft the forgery of the cup for the museum heist. He'd been at the police station to identify Mr. Smith who was currently in questioning, Pamela figured as she slipped back into her suit.

Her next stop would be back at the station to speak with the infamous Mr. Smith and find out everything she could about who hired him. With a little luck she just might beat Lance to the cup and manage to get it for Hermes before Lance could recover it for Anna.

As she made her way downstairs Pamela felt the same strange call of power she'd felt stirring here when she first arrived. There was a mantle here. Moving into Harold's work area she moved about with care searching for the source. She found it in the form of a pair of copper gauntlets with amber stones set in them. An intricate design was molded in them. So that when they lay crossed as they did now it depicted the image of an anvil and hammer in front of a fire.

"The Bands of Hephaestus," she whispered with wonder before she tucked them in her purse. Hermes would be pleased. She'd recovered one of the mantels without the other side knowing about it.

Having done everything she could there Pamela slipped out into the night and headed back towards DC to meet the thief of the cup and learn what had become of it.

42 HOLLYWOOD, CALIFORNIA

Catharine sank into the chair in her room at James Hardagen's home and flipped open her laptop, she turned on the computer and waited for it to boot up. She was glad to be away from the set and Serenity if only for a while. She knew she wasn't supposed to be working on anything else but book four for the Dark Heart Series but if she didn't step back from Serenity she knew she'd scream.

When the computer came alive she opened her file on the new project she'd been working on, as well as the notes she'd written on the events at the Serenity ball, she pictured Lance staring at Anna with such longing and sighed. It was an amazing scene but she had nothing to build on it yet. Glancing back at the other file she went over her notes, for the thriller she'd begun, what felt like years ago, before the Serenity thing started.

News articles were stored with her notes on the bizarre series of slayings that had been taking place in DC just before she moved back to New York. The Fury killer. As she read back over the notes, she blinked at the details about the victims deaths. She'd seen those grizzly images herself a few days earlier. They'd fallen from her numb fingers after she saw one come out of a manila envelope addressed to Lance. Why had the killer left them for him? Lance had said they were not for her but him what did that mean? She skimmed over the articles again and looked for the name of the detective in charge of the case. His name was nowhere to be found. The only name mentioned was a Detective Murphy.

Catharine flipped through the article clippings and froze as she found an image of the lead detective. A pretty young brunette with warm, sharp brown eyes, stared back at her. A face she knew all too well. She'd seen it briefly in a dusty picture frame in a box Lance had taken away from her. Who was she to him and why did he refuse to talk about her? Picking up the phone, Catharine dialed the number for the police station in DC. She'd been wanting to speak with Detective Murphy anyway, perhaps it was time she arranged an interview.

Catharine listened to the phone ring and waited for someone to pick up on the other end. She felt a strange pang of apprehension and wondered if she should forget the whole thing after all, she'd promised not to ask about her. Catharine drew a breath and considered hanging up but reasoned she wasn't asking him about her or snooping, this was research for her book.

"DC Police department," a man's voice said.

"Hi I was calling to speak with a Detective Murphy from homicide I was wondering if you could tell me when she would be available to speak."

"Detective Murphy? What is this in regard to?" the voice on the other end questioned with suspicion.

Catharine froze something not right here she realized, something bad even, yet she plunged on. "I'm a writer and the Fury Killer case caught my attention a while back, I wanted to talk to her about it and the investigation as I'm writing a book based loosely on it." Catharine explained.

"I see. And you are?"

"C.J. Nichols," Catharine answered, she felt her throat go dry as she bit her lip something really off here. I shouldn't have called, she told herself as she waited for the voice on the other end to answer her.

"Miss Nichols I'm afraid talking to Dana Murphy will be impossible as she's dead has been for over a year."

"Oh, I'm really sorry," Catharine answered, "Do you know who is in charge of the case now?" She asked.

"No one here I believe it's become a federal case," the police officer answered.

Catharine felt her stomach role, understanding that if he was right, not only was the killer still out there but his kills were no longer restricted to DC. "Thank you." Catharine muttered before she hung up.

In her file she added the note Dana Murphy dead a year and put next to it two questions Why? How? She saved her notes and crawled into bed, her heart heavy with fear of an unknown monster still lose in the country, hurting innocent women and sorrow for Lance's loss. However Dana had died, the one thing she was sure of was that Detective Roman had loved her.

43 WASHINGTON DC, VIRGINIA

Pamela Walsh made her way up the steps of the police precinct and over to the counter, where a rookie black and white, straight out of the academy stood. She watched as his eyes lit up at the sight of her and smiled.

"Hello, ma'am how can I help you?" he questioned brown eyes wide and hopeful much like that of a puppy.

"I'm here to see a friend of mine. Guy in holding by the name of Mr. Smith," She murmured as she batted her long silky lashes at him.

"Mr. Smith," he muttered as he looked over the register list for prisoners in the holding tank. "Yeah he's here, was in interview with Detective Roman but he and agent Blackwood left.

They left interesting, why? "Can I see him?" Pamela asked.

"I think it can be arranged," the rookie replied and he led her down the hall to holding to meet Mr. Smith.

She recognized him on site as the man that Lance had picked up earlier that night and smiled, so this was the thief who had stolen the Cup of Dionysus.

"Smith you have a visitor," the rookie called and then turned to go. Pamela watched as the thief turned to see who was there. He looked up at her and smiled with a wolfish grin as he took in her figure from head to toe.

That's right Mr. Smith soak in the view, her mind purred as she moved closer to the cell.

"Well hello there gorgeous and what can I do for you?" he asked with a wink.

"I understand from our mutual acquaintance Mr. Miller that you had a cup made for someone and took another I was wondering who that cup ended up with?" Pamela questioned.

"Man what's with this cup I was under the impression it was just some replica of the Holy Grail but you and the Detective seem awful interested in it. Maybe it was worth more than I realized." Mr. Smith said amused.

"Believe me it is, if you still have the item, I'd be willing to pay you triple what your employer gave you for it," Pamela murmured.

"Nice offer legs, but I'm afraid it's no longer in my hands. As I told the detective before he left I put it in a safety deposit box in a bank in Vegas."

"Vegas?"

"Yeah he asked me when I was there but then left before I could answer."

"He left?" Interesting what was more important than the cup?

"Yeah some other business I guess, next thing I know I'm being moved back here."

"I see so will you tell me everything you didn't tell the detective?"

"Get me out of here doll face and I'll tell you anything you want," he assured her before he reached through the bars and brushed his thumb over her lower lip.

"Consider it done," she whispered before she turned to go. She felt his eyes on her tight ass as she strutted back toward the front. She sent her thoughts to Hermes for a moment thanking him once more for the gift he'd bestowed upon her and told him she was closing in on his prize.

Within minutes she had paid Mr. Smith's bail and the pair were on the move headed for the airport and Vegas.

44 UNKNOWN

Zaharrah walked through the double doors of the old library, passed the common section to the area designated for employees only. It had been years since she last set foot within the private passages of the ancient library but she'd been careful to protect her people's darkest secret. Not because she cared about that anymore but to ensure the safety of others.

It annoyed her that her access code was still valid given she'd never intended to return. It wasn't as if she'd kept her purpose a secret. Zaharrah told them outright, she was done the day her life changed. She'd severed all her ties and loyalties to the group; even going so far as to declare herself dead to her kin. That she could still come and go as she pleased as though nothing had changed, though it irritated her, she admitted it wasn't all that shocking. She'd taken an oath in her youth. One that made her a staff member at the library for life.

As she passed through the maze of corridors into the heart of the 'Black Hand's' operations she tried not to think about why she'd left; for now all that mattered was why she was back; her brother. Darian Lynch was young and idealistic, he still believed in the oath he'd spoken and aimed to fulfill his sworn duty; a task which had set him in Dr. Ian Broody's path.

Darian didn't understand how dangerous Broody was or what was really happening for that matter, Zaharrah wasn't even sure she really understood what was going on. She just knew down to her bones that he was in over his head. So much so she'd stepped into help him. She wished now that she'd steered clear after all. Weird things were going on around the dig. Whatever Anna and the others had unearthed it was bad and if she wasn't careful it might just end up costing her more than she was willing to pay.

"Ah Zaharrah my darling it's been too long."

"Skip the pleasantries Nassor. I'm not back."

"Yet you stand before me."

"Darian's in trouble. Broody's changed."

"Has he discovered the tablets?"

"As far as I'm aware no. However there is something more going on he's looking for some sort of relic. He's discovered the throne room."

"Has he discovered the key?"

"No. We have it for now."

"Good make sure those tablets are never recovered."

"I want Darian out of there. Broody is dangerous."

"Your brother will finish the task for which he was assigned. When it is done then and only then can he leave. So the sooner you recover those tablets and ensure they vanish the better."

"My task would be easier if you would tell me where they are," Zaharrah snapped annoyed.

"Our records do not tell. My advice, check the temples again."

"If anything happens to him because you sent him into that god forsaken isle, I will kill you and burn this place to the ground before vanishing for good." Zaharrah hissed in warning before she turned and left.

Lance rode silently beside Agent Blackwood trying not to dwell on his destination and the fact he'd been there only a week earlier and quite possibly while the killer was there. It infuriated him that he'd missed both killer and thief by 168 hours or less, in the crime world a few hours meant the difference between life and death, and if the crime was solved or went cold. In this case he hoped the near miss would not lead to either criminal getting away with it.

"You seem agitated detective what's bothering you?" Agent Blackwood questioned.

"I was here at Caesar's Palace a week ago on other business. Both the killer and thief may well have been here and I missed them."

"You didn't know you should be looking for either," Gail argued.

"I know it just rubs me the wrong way that I may have missed them both by mere hours. When we get in let me ask the questions."

"My jurisdiction, I'll ask the questions," Agent's Barnes said coolly from the driver's seat.

"We'll find both," Gail assured him as the local agents black SUV pulled up in front of the famous hotel and casino.

The trio slipped out of the vehicle and made their way to the front desk to speak with the concierge.

"Can I help you?" the man asked eyeing the trio with discomfort.

"Yeah, we were wondering if a blond woman with blue eyes age late twenties to early forties has checked into the hotel recently." Agent Barnes questioned.

"You're kidding right? I mean half my clientele last week

matched that description thanks to the Dark Heart giveaway thing."

Lance groaned he'd already known that answer would be given. Before the other man could speak again he asked. "Have any of them vanished mysteriously or not been answering their pages?"

"Yeah as a matter of fact Miss Frasier vanished on us the day of the ball, she was supposed to make an appearance. The publishing house and Mr. Hardagen were furious that she'd bailed. We figured she'd just taken a personal day like the Hollywood types do."

Lance swallowed at the news, it was worse than he'd figured it was likely the killer had taken Kim Frasier the same night he'd been in the hotel. He wondered now if the killer had seen him that night and that was the reason for the package on his doorstep soon after returning to DC. "We need access to that room."

"Why, what's going on?"

"We received an anonymous tip that we would discover a murder victim here." Agent Blackwood replied discretely.

"Dear God," the concierge exclaimed with alarm. "Of course Miss Frasier is staying in the penthouse suite. Let me just get a keycard and I'll show you up."

Lance waited in silence as the man grabbed a key card and made his way around the front desk. The trio followed after him in silence, careful not to draw unwanted attention to themselves.

When they stepped off the elevator moments later on the penthouse floor the concierge knocked on the door and announced his presence, giving Miss Frasier a chance to respond, before inserting his electronic key in the lock and opening the door.

As the door swung in Lance knew right away they were at the right room. There were signs of a struggle within and the unpleasant stench of death, though masked was faint. Hollywood starlet Kim Frasier was the latest victim of the Fury Killer.

"We need the video feed for this floor and the elevator for the past week; a list of your single male clients in the hotel the night of the ball and a few days prior age 21-37. In addition I want a record of key swipes for this suite and to know when this do-not disturb sign was first noticed. I want it all ASAFP." Lance barked at the concierge before beginning the task of suiting up to enter the suite. He paid no mind as the employee scurried away to speak with his employer and carry out the tasks.

"I thought I told you my town I was in charge." Agent Barnes hissed.

"I knew your line of questioning would go nowhere." Lance snapped.

"How?" Gail questioned curious.

"I was here playing bodyguard for the ball."

"That's convenient," Agent Barnes scoffed.

"No, it's frustrating. If I'd known the guest list, been aware that Miss Frasier was supposed to be there and not, then maybe..."

"You've been off this case for three years now detective don't go there, how would you reason a missing guest tied back to the Fury Killer?" Gail snapped. "This isn't your fault."

"I know you're right but it doesn't change the fact I was in the same building with the sick son of a bitch and didn't have a clue." Lance said with irritation as he finished suiting up. Sure that he couldn't contaminate the crime scene, he stepped into the room.

Though he'd known what to expect he still wasn't prepared for it. Like the others before her Kim Frasier lay dead, her lifeless eyes stared up at him from the bed filled with terror and pain, bloody tears dried to her cheeks. A crown of golden serpents sat upon her brow, fangs dug into her flesh. Her blond hair dyed red; the same Grecian style red gown wrapped around her. Fear cut him to the bone as the lifeless figure changed the face staring back at him, Catharine's. He blinked trying to shake off the morbid fantasy but the image would not abate.

She was right, she fit the killer's profile for victim. Don't, he told himself Catharine Nichols was not going to be targeted by the Fury Killer, this had nothing to do with her.

"Damn," Agent Blackwood muttered as she entered the room startling Lance and drawing him back from his dark musings. "Ah how sweet he left us a love note," Gail said with disgust as she picked up the note pad on the bedside table.

Lance blinked, he'd missed it. Turning his attention to her and the pad, he read the bloody message. "Take two to be set on stage. Try to keep up Detective Roman. A."

"Shit."

"What is it?"

"His next victim is in LA on the set of Heart of Clay," Lance said with dread. "He turned and walked out of the room leaving the scene to Agent Blackwood and Agent Barnes. As soon as he was away from ear shot he pulled out his cell phone and dialed Catharine's number. He listened to it ring impatiently and tried to relax. When it went to her machine he repressed the urge to curse. Hanging up the phone he moved on to the elevator.

When the doors slid open the concierge emerged.

"I've made arrangements to get you everything you requested."

"Great. Um I need one more thing. Can you tell me if you recognize this man?" Lance asked as he pulled out the mug shot of his thief.

"No I don't think so. Why, is he the killer?"

"No. A thief."

"I'll check the video feed for him same time but he's not anyone I'm familiar with."

"Thanks."

"Detective, are you all right?" Gail questioned as she came out of the penthouse.

"Yeah, just want to get moving he's already got a head start on us. Agent Barnes can handle the details here, we should get out to LA."

"What about the thief?"

"The thief hunt can fall to someone local, the homicide takes priority for now."

"For a guy who was ready to walk away from this a few days ago you seem pretty determined to dive in head first now," Gail said with suspicion.

"He's made this personal by targeting me as his adversary. I don't have much choice, keep up or the murders to follow are on me."

"On us," Gail corrected as she joined him in the elevator. She pressed the button to close the door. Moments later they emerged in the lobby and were outside flagging a cab headed back to the airport.

46

Pamela cursed as her phone rang interrupting her discussion with Mr. Smith about the stolen cup. Looking at the offending object she groaned seeing her employer's number. In her haste to get back to the states, she'd forgotten to quit her job at the entertainment gig. She connected the call to rectify the oversight.

"Hello, Mr. Blake…"

"Pamela where are you?"

"Back in Vegas, look I…" she began before being cut off again.

"Perfect .Get your ass over to Caesar's Palace. Whatever you've got can wait. We just got news over the wire that the lead actress playing Serenity in Hardagen's films was found dead recently. There's buzz she was murdered."

"Murdered?" Pamela questioned now all ears. Murder would be far more important to deal with than a thief. Perhaps that was why Lance had run off, but why, he didn't cover homicide any more.

"Yeah get on it."

"Of course," Pamela ensured the man before hanging up. "Driver, change of plans, take us to Caesar's Palace instead.

Mr. Smith looked over at her with questions. "Sorry, something else came up. Need to take a look at it before you fill me in on the cup." Pamela said with a smile. She batted her eyelashes at him and rested her hand on his thigh reassuring him that she was still interested in what he had to say.

As their course changed Pamela sighed, men's egos were so easy to bruise. She reasoned she'd have to make it up to him after she got done at the palace. She just hoped that her need of his assistance would be short lived. Mr. Smith was not the sort she normally made a habit of entertaining.

When her limo pulled up in front of Caesar's Palace she found that something was definitely going on, a number of police cruisers were parked on the strip and a couple, she figured for FBI. Slipping out of the car she instructed her driver to take Mr. Smith to their hotel, she couldn't have him getting busted right now, she still needed his help locating the cup.

"You sure you want to stay here doll face?" Mr. Smith questioned.

"I'm not staying just need to find out what the circus is about. I'll be along later and we'll talk business further then," She assured him before knocking a kiss on his lips, letting him know her interest in him had not waned, she felt his fingers tangle in her hair as he deepened the kiss for his own pleasure.

"Hurry back legs," he breathed before she turned and walked inside.

Pamela followed a couple of local cops up the stairs to the penthouse where a crime scene was clearly being worked. As she approached the door, a man in a suit stopped her.

"Sorry ma'am this floor is closed off to civilians," he stated as he flashed a fed's badge.

"What about the press?" She questioned using all her charms to get on his good side.

"Press as well. Have some respect for the dead," he requested but his demeanor was not cold. She'd gotten to him Pamela thought pleased.

"Of course. I'm sorry, my boss called me out of the blue interrupting a great dream and ordered me to get down here and find out what had happened to Kim Frasier. Rumor on the line is she was murdered. "

"I can't comment," he said with a shrug.

"I'm not asking you to, a friend of mine mentioned her beau was in town and was worried about him when she heard the rumors."

"I see and who was her beau?"

"A detective Roman," Pamela stated playing a hunch.

"Assure your friend her pain in my ass beau is both fine and no longer in Vegas."

"Really, where is he?"

"Off to LA in a big hurry. He drops in on my town unannounced informs me there may be a killer on the loose in my own backyard and then after leaving me with this ungodly mess bolts off as fast as he arrived."

"I'm sorry to hear that," Pamela said with a sympathetic gaze as she touched his arm in a show of support.

"Real piece of work your friend's beau."

"Yeah I told her to forget him," Pamela murmured as she ran her fingers through the man's hair.

"Good advice it's not a good idea to get tangled up with a guy who chases serial killers," the agent muttered more to himself than her.

Pamela's eyes lit with excitement. Lance didn't work homicide anymore but if he was chasing a serial killer then she could think of only one that would have him running across country like a scared rabbit. The Fury Killer was back and Kim Frasier was his latest victim. She'd just fallen into the story of the year.

47 HOLLYWOOD, CALIFORNIA

Catharine sat in front of her laptop at the small desk in the converted dressing room. Her fingers flew over the keys as she worked feverishly on her outline. She'd set her new project aside and was currently busy with a basic write up for the fourth book of the Dark Heart series. She was in the middle of a particularly intense scene when a hand grabbed her shoulder and tore her out of her work.

Catharine gave a startled cry as she turned to see her publicist. "Bryan, damn it you're going to give me a heart attack one of these days, wear a bell." Catharine snapped irritated.

"Well, I wouldn't be dropping in unannounced if you'd stop switching off your phone and stayed where I put you. I went by the hotel this morning and they said you'd checked out."

"Oh, I'm sorry I forgot to call you this morning. James and Emily asked me to stay with them at their home. Since we're all working here together I agreed to it."

"I see, and why aren't you answering your phone?" Bryan questioned.

"I'm working. Take a look," Catharine offered as she showed him her notes for the final Serenity novel which she'd given the working title, Shadowed Heart. She waited silently as he read over her work.

"Looks good so far, different angel than I pictured for this," Bryan commented amused.

"This was the only way I could get back into it. So, what did you need?"

"I have an update about the contest for the Heart of Clay give away."

"And?"

"It's a go," Bryan said with a smile.

"That's great the fans will love it."

"I'm sure they will. I passed the word along to the publishing house on book four."

"Thanks, now if you don't mind I'd like to get back to it," Catharine stated.

"Of course, I'll be checking in later next week."

Catharine nodded before turning her focus back to the laptop. She heard the door close as Bryan left and sighed. Picking up her cell phone she flipped it back on and noted she had three new messages. Pressing the button for voice mail she typed in her passcode and listened. She deleted the first two from Bryan as they no longer were needed.

"Catharine its Lance when you get this, call me, don't worry about the time." Catharine blinked at the urgency in his voice and wondered at it. Something had clearly rattled him since last they spoke. Hanging up the voice mail she dialed his number and groaned when she got his voice mail.

If the time didn't matter then why wasn't he answering she wondered as she broke the call. Finding that the unanswered questions made it hard to think about anything else she saved her work and left the set for Hardagen's house.

48 NOTTINGHAM, ENGLAND

Sam and Anna stood near the edge of a large pond, on the outskirts of Sherwood Forest.

"So this is the land the town records indicate belonged to Lord Locksley?" Sam questioned with doubt.

"Yes."

"Shouldn't we see the remnants of a castle or estate?" Sam asked.

"You would think so, however this is just one border of the land. Perhaps further in the forest we'll find something more," Anna suggested. The pair moved deeper into the woods and soon came upon a small house that sat upon a hill. It was surrounded by several ponds like that of the first one they'd stopped near.

"Not exactly a castle," Sam muttered.

"No, but we're in the right place I can feel it, there's just something we're missing here."

"Shall we take a closer look then?"

Anna nodded, but as she moved on the feeling of being watched weighed heavy upon her but she brushed it aside as nerves. She was aware of Sam at her side; as together the pair stepped inside. Sam lit a torch and filled the dwelling with light. In the main room were the remains of old furniture: a couch, chairs, what was once a fine rug, beautiful tapestries and nice curtains. A fireplace was set in the center of the back wall. Directly in front of them was a door.

When Anna opened it she found a shallow closet. She looked at it puzzled, for it would have been of little use. She wondered what purpose it may have served as she closed it and turned her focus to the fireplace. The mantle of the fireplace was ornately decorated and in the middle of it was an old family seal. She noted it was broken but what was there made her breath hitch. "This is the

Loxley home," she murmured with wonder.

"Where is the rest of it? What is the deal with all the oddly placed items?"

"What do you mean?"

"The small closet, the off center candle holder with the odd décor from the rest of the space."

"What candle holder?"

"That one there, near the closet with the feather etching."

Anna moved to inspect the candle holder and found that it moved. "Weird."

"Yeah," Sam replied amused.

"Were in the right place I'm sure of it now, I can sense that the bow is near, but something is missing here."

"What do you think it might be?" Sam asked.

"I'm not sure I think we need to go into town and see about any local legends pertaining to the Robin Hood tale." Anna stated.

Sam nodded and after he'd blown out the torch the pair turned and walked out of the house.

49

Pamela after her meet with the FBI agent had returned to her prearranged hotel with Mr. Smith and had gathered the rest of the needed information pertaining to the cup. After rewarding him for his help, she'd hopped the first flight to LA. As soon as she set foot off the plane she felt the power within her stir in reaction to the presence of another mantle.

She closed her eyes and focused on the foreign power in a bid to identify it. To her shock she found not one but two distinct powers in play. It seemed that there was more at stake for her now than she'd initially believed. Excited and a bit unnerved Pamela decided her first step was to locate Lance Roman and find out everything she could pertaining to the latest Fury Killing in Vegas.

50

Upon exiting the plane at LAX Lance had wasted little time in locating a cab and getting over to Catharine's hotel. To his disquiet he soon learned that Catharine checked out of the hotel earlier that morning. When he asked about a forwarding location the concierge informed him Miss Nichol's had left no information on an alternate location. He then mentioned that her publicist had been by earlier asking the same questions.

Lance nodded his understanding before turning and walking away. He pulled out his phone and dialed Catharine's number again and prayed that she'd answer. To his relief he got a hello on the third ring.

"Catharine, where are you? Are you okay? I just swung by your hotel and they said you checked out."

"Yeah, I'm fine. I'm staying with Mr. Hardagen and his fiancé at their house."

"Oh. How is the shoot going?"

"Fine now after weeding through a number of hopefuls we finally found a replacement Serenity. What are you doing in LA?"

"I'll fill you in, in person where are you now? Can we meet?"

"I'm at the house. Yeah sure." Catharine replied.

Lance listened carefully as Catharine provided details for getting to James Hardagen's home. He then broke the call and turned his attention to his partner.

"Let's move," he stated simply as he headed for the door.

"Where are we going?" Gail Blackwood asked.

"To the director of the Dark Heart movies home," Lance replied.

"Who is it you're trying to find?"

"The author, CJ Nichols. We met in Vegas she's a friend."

Lance answered before flagging down a cab. Together the pair slid into the back seat and were soon on their way.

51

Catharine disconnected her phone and set it back down on the small table next to her deck chair in front of James Hardagen's pool.

"Who was that?" Emily questioned as she turned to look at her house guest.

"Oh that was my detective friend from DC, Lance." Catharine replied.

"What did he want?"

"Not sure, he didn't say, but it seems he's here in town and was looking for me at the hotel. He's headed this way now to see me."

"Really? Is he cute? How did you meet?"

"Is who cute?" James inquired as he joined them by the pool. He carried with him a pair of freshly made cocktails.

"Her detective friend from DC, Lance," Emily supplied before Catharine could respond.

"We met in Vegas during the Serenity ball. He was there as security for the winner." Catharine explained. "And yes, he is cute," she added.

"I hear a "but" there," Emily stated as she sat up.

"I detect a story; if he was there as security," James said, intrigued as he handed Catharine a drink.

"Um, yes, there is a story and I guess, a "but" as well," Catharine admitted. She bit her lip nervously; being set as the center of attention was a bit overwhelming.

"Oh, a story…dish, CJ," Emily demanded as she took her own drink.

Catharine blushed at Emily's excitement but after a sip of her drink, she told the pair about Anna Gallagher, the contest winner and her troubles with an ex. Sticking to the story she'd been given at the hotel. She then went on to describe the scene that night at the ball when she first spotted Lance and there stolen conversation on the edge of the dance floor before the awards presentation. She ended the story with her request to meet later.

"Did he show up?" Emily questioned.

"Yes."

"He sound's dreamy, so, where does the "but" come in," Emily probed.

"He's sort of emotionally unavailable," Catharine muttered before taking another sip of her drink as her thoughts turned to detective Dana Murphy his dead partner.

"But he's here," Emily argued.

"Not for a romantic interlude," Catharine stated.

"What makes you say that?" James questioned with disbelief. Catharine was an attractive woman, her detective may have an amorous meet in mind, a fact that didn't sit well with her host.

Rather than explain, Catharine put her cell phone on speaker and replayed his message. "Does that sound like he has romance on the brain?" Catharine questioned.

"No. I suppose not. Why don't you relax and I'll let you know when he gets here?" James suggested. Catharine nodded her thanks before finishing off her drink and sinking back in her chair closing her eyes trying to put her questions out of her head. It wasn't long before her thoughts fell silent and she drifted into sleep.

52

Once Catharine was asleep Emily got up from her chair and slipped into the pool.

"James dear, when the detective gets here can we invite him to stay on as Catharine's house guest," Emily questioned over her shoulder. Her green eyes flashed with excitement and mischief.

James smirked, he loved that his lady was so fascinated by their house guest. Adored that she felt a kinship with the writer and wanted to provide her with an opportunity to be alone with the detective that she seemed enamored with. "We'll see," he teased, not giving her what she desired just yet. James shed his shirt before he dove into the pool surfacing in front of her.

"Please," Emily requested again before catching her lower lip between her teeth in a way she knew he loved.

"Maybe," he murmured as he drew her into his arms. "Probably," he amended before he kissed her. Emily melted in his arms as his eyes sparked with an inner fire and lust took hold of him. His mouth was hot and demanding against her own as his hands ran over her; seemingly everywhere at once. As he drew her deeper under his spell his eyes fell shut and as they lost themselves in their passionate act he pictured not his delectable Emily but the dark and brooding Serenity. Her ivory skin glowing in the moon light, golden hair a warm wet curtain surrounding him; her blue eyes nearly black with the famous mix of fear and arousal that made her so appealing.

When Emily trembled in his arms with completion and called his name it was Serenity's voice he heard and it was her name he murmured as he found his own release.

53

Silky lashes the color of gold fluttered delicately as the sleeper began to wake. He watched with delight as the stunning beauty he'd been waiting for began to stir. Long slender, delicate limbs stretched as shocking blue eyes popped open to look around.

She lifted her head from the bed of soft earth where it had lain and looked about puzzled.

Where was she?

To her eyes it appeared she was in a forest of some sort; a river lay but a few feet from her. The air was cool with the touch of night, though the sky was beyond her ability to see through the tree tops.

What was this wood and how had she come to be there?

Where was she going and where had she been coming from?

As she sat up she found she didn't know. Getting to her feet the young woman moved to the river. She knelt at the water's edge and splashed the cool clear liquid in her face both to refresh herself and in a bid to wake herself further from her heavy slumber.

How long had she been resting? She wondered as she studied her appearance on the water's surface. Again she found she wasn't sure.

The face that looked back at her was both familiar and foreign to her. She knew the pale skin and the long blonde hair that swept against the back of her knees though it was not her own. Her own hair was … She paused to draw the correct color and saw a flash of red like flame. Red and cut off at about her shoulder.

A pair of startling blue eyes stared back up at her from the water that she knew were her own and for a moment the image shifted to show a reflection of the woman she knew. Peaches and cream skin was topped by a head of fiery red hair and blue eyes.

The woman wore a beautiful blue blazer with a purple silk blouse and a green pencil skirt with a peacock feather pattern. She blinked and the image returned to the face that was not her own.

But if it wasn't hers then whose was it?

What was happening to her?

As she searched her mind trying to understand she found the answers just out of her reach and came dangerously close to crying.

She froze as a new sensation washed over her one she recognized and hated. While she didn't know what was going on there was one thing she was sure of and that was that where-ever she was it wasn't safe. She felt the press of another's eyes upon her and felt a sudden rush of fear. Someone was out-there watching her.

Unbidden a flash of memory danced before her eyes. She saw herself running into the woods away from the sound of hoof-beats. She cocked her head to the side trying to wrap her mind around the image; horses, it seemed like a poor choice for a chase something inside her said there was a far faster means of pursuit but for the life of her she couldn't seem to recall what. Who-ever was out there watching her was doing much worse they were following her.

Why?

No, that couldn't be right she told herself. If they had been following her as the memory seemed to suggest then how had she managed to fall asleep when it wasn't safe?

As she searched her mind for the answers she found that she'd made the assumption she would be safe. Horse at this hour implied mortal and no human dared enter the wood after sunset. The woman froze on that thought; if it were true then what was she? Even as she asked the question a part of her cried out that the memory was not her own. She was not the one being chased by a man on horseback; none of that was real. It was not her life it belonged to Serenity.

Serenity, at the thought of the name an avalanche of memories crashed in on her. But she knew they were lies. She wasn't Serenity she was... Catharine. As she searched for who exactly Catharine was, the one watching her came out of the shadows in which he had concealed himself.

She gasped startled at the sight of him his pail skin gleamed in the moon light, his blue eyes glowed with the hint of his unearthly power. His blonde hair hung loose dancing in the wind. He looked shockingly like an angel and yet she knew he was not.

"Ah my darling Serenity at last I've found you once more,"

Syvarin murmured as he drew her into his arms and kissed her brow. "I feared that hunter had ended you," he added before his hands sank into her hair, his fingers caressing her cheeks.

Catharine felt something inside her stir at his touch but she pushed him away. "I'm not Serenity, she's not real. My name is Catharine and I'm dreaming," she stated as she looked beyond him to her surroundings. She was in her own book it wasn't the first time such a thing had happened but this one felt oddly more real than the others before it.

Syvarin drew Catharine gently back into his embrace. "AH BUT YOU ARE SERENITY, CATHARINE IS THE LIE YOU'VE CREATED TO ESCAPE FROM WHO YOU REALLY ARE," he whispered.

He brushed the pad of his thumb over her lower lip in a familiar gesture meant to seduce and yet she knew it was foreign. The man before her was not who he appeared to be. As she struggled to maintain her sense of self Catharine wondered how he knew that.

"YOU NEED NOT FEAR ME SERENITY WE ARE ONE AND THE SAME," he breathed before he lowered his head to capture her lips.

She drew back once more as her own thoughts began to rise from the depths of dream fog. "You shouldn't be here I wrote you out of Serenity's life, Rachel killed you," Catharine stated. If he was dead then who was it that had been following her, and why?

Syvarin smiled amused, "AH BUT MY DARLING SERENITY I AM ETERNAL, A MERE CHILD CANNOT KILL ME OR SEPARATE US," he whispered.

"Serenity never loved you. You manipulated and deceived me." She argued.

"YOU WERE DRAWN TO MY POWER SERENITY FROM THE MOMENT WE MET. YOU SAW ME AS A PROTECTOR AGAINST A SHARED FOE. YOU EMBRACED ME WILLINGLY TO BE FREE OF KOVRIN." He reminded her before he kissed her.

Catharine felt her mind begin to slip away once more as his kiss blurred the lines between fantasy and reality. She pushed him away not liking the sensation of loss of self. The need to maintain her own identity weighed heavily upon her mind. She couldn't let herself get lost in this dream; there was a danger here that she couldn't yet define. When she looked about her again she found she was no longer in the forest where they'd begun. The dream had shifted she was now in Syvarin's tower; the room in which he'd imprisoned her and seduced her... no, Serenity into loving him. She was not Serenity.

"YOU WASTE YOUR TIME IN REFUSING ME BECAUSE I KNOW YOUR BODY AS INTIMATELY AS YOU DO." Syvarin told her as his fingers played over her skin in secret places that enticed her to want him.

"No, you don't." Catharine argued as she drew free of his grasp. With the pronouncement of her refusal her image shifted. Blonde hair shortening and returning to her natural red. The Grecian gown changing to her modern street clothes. The tower melted away and once more she was in her work space.

His blue eyes became red with temper and exertion of his power.

"You are not the man you pretend to be you may look like an angel but you aren't one, nor are you Syvarin. He is a monster just as Kovrin was, but you, I do not know; nor do I want to. Be gone from me sir or I shall send you forth in a manner that will prove most unpleasant for you devil." Catharine warned as she sat back down at her computer and returned to work on the scene that had set up this strange dream.

"YOU WILL SURRENDER TO ME IN TIME SERENITY," He assured her before he lifted her head and kissed her. When he felt her begin to melt, he drew back his fanged teeth; nipped at her ear.

"Oh God help me," she breathed startled and with those words, he and the dream faded out to darkness.

54

Lance studied James Hardagen's home with both curiosity and mistrust. He knew the man's history due to Dana's fascination. He wasn't sure how he felt about Catharine's staying there with the former heart throb/ heart breaker. It was possible Mr. Hardagen had designs on wooing the lovely writer.

"Your friend is staying here?" Agent Blackwood questioned.

"I guess." Lance said uneasily as he moved to the door to knock. Lifting his hand the door opened. The actor turned director and his luscious girlfriend stood in the doorframe.

"Good evening, you must be detective Lance Roman, Catharine said you'd be stopping by." James stated as he extended his hand in friendship.

"Where is Catharine, is she okay?"

"She's out on the pool deck asleep, she's fine." Emily said politely. "Who is your friend?"

"This is special agent Gail Blackwood," Lance replied as he followed the pair out to the pool.

"What brings you to LA?" James questioned.

"Business I'm afraid," Lance replied curtly. His eyes fell to Catharine who was indeed sleeping peacefully. He let out a breath; he didn't know he'd been holding.

"You were worried about her," Emily said impressed as she eyed the detective with a renewed sense of interest.

"Yeah, a little."

"What sort of business?" James questioned.

"The kind I'd prefer not to discuss in front of Emily if you don't mind," Gail stated.

James nodded and the trio turned and left Emily on the pool deck by Catharine. Once they were out of ear shot Lance spoke.

"We're here because Kim Frasier was murdered. Her killer left a note indicating his next victim would be found on the set of your new film."

"Oh hell, are you serious?"

"Afraid so."

"We need a list of people with access to the set and for you to increase security on your actresses with blonde hair and hazel eyes." Gail stated coolly.

"Of course you'll have both before tomorrow." James assured them. "Say did you want to stay here with us you could go over to the set with me and Catharine in the morning.

Lance knew it would be better to maintain his distance from James until he was cleared as a suspect but he thought about Catharine laying out by the pool deck and he couldn't shake the feeling she was in danger. "Sound's good."

"I'll pass," Gail muttered she eyed the detective with disapproval but said nothing. She could see why he was uneasy. His friend had an appearance that matched the other Furies upon their transformation. She was a potential target.

"Great I'll have one of the guest rooms set up for you."

"I'll be waiting for that list," Gail reminded before she turned to leave.

"Of course," James said politely before he turned to see to making arrangements for Lance's stay.

"I hope you know what you're doing?" Gail said pointedly.

"I know it's unorthodox but…" He began.

"I can see why you're worried. She's pretty." Gail stated.

"We're friends."

"How'd you meet her?"

"At the Serenity Ball in Vegas, a client was the contest winner and she saw me, walked over, we talked and she followed me back to DC."

"Really?"

"It wasn't like that she wanted to research me for a character in her new book."

"Nice, so how long was she in town to research you?"

"Only a day or so, she had to get out here for the second film script."

"Just be careful," Gail instructed before she turned and left.

"I will," Lance assured her. Once she was gone, he made his way back out to the pool deck where Catharine was resting.

55

Catharine woke from her strange dream to find Lance sitting in the lounge chair besides her own watching her. She smiled at the sight of him. She stretched lazily before sitting up. "Hello detective it's good to see you again," she murmured before she leaned over to him and brushed his lips with a kiss. He responded to the kiss in a way he'd not done so; since Dana. His lips tasting hers hungrily picking up where they left off before she got her call from Bryan.

He felt her melting into the kiss and knew that if he led her further she'd follow. Part of him wanted to; feeling a hunger within that Pamela had stirred up. As he considered the possibilities, he felt the moment end; as she drew away yet again spooked.

"I'm glad you came." She whispered as her cheeks flushed with excitement.

Lance blinked, what had spooked her. He saw in her eyes now clearly that she was looking for an out. Though he didn't want to slow down with her; he did. "I wish I could say I'm here on a social visit just to see you, but I'm not. That old case I mentioned before you left; I'm back on it. The reason Kim Frasier isn't doing the second film isn't a flighty actress thing. She's dead."

"The Fury killer got her," Catharine said with understanding as she sank back in her seat.

"You know about the Fury Killer?" Lance questioned surprised.

"Yeah I lived in DC before New York. I was actually going to write a book about it but then Heart of Glass got picked up for film and any notions of a book went out the window."

"A book?"

"Yeah I don't suppose you could tell me about the case," she asked with a sly smile.

"I'm not ready to talk about this case yet Catharine," Lance said his voice having gone cold.

"When you're ready then," she whispered as James joined them on the deck.

"Your rooms ready, if you'll follow me," James said wondering what he walked in on as they were both clearly upset.

"Thanks."

"You're staying here?" Catharine asked.

Lance nodded before he turned and followed James back in the house. Catharine sighed already regretting having pulled away from him. Part of her wanted him but she was afraid to take the chance on love again, she'd made poor choices in the past and was afraid that he was just another part of a preset pattern. Her dream still fresh in her mind; she sighed. Men had a way of becoming monsters around her and she didn't want to find out that the watchful Lancelot she'd been drawn to from afar was in truth a dragon, she'd have to slay later.

Telling herself she'd made the right choice Catharine wrapped her towel around herself and sank back into her chair.

56

Lance followed his host down the hall of the second floor in relative silence.

"Got a preference on where the room is?" James questioned curious.

"Yeah can you put me some place close to Miss Nichols?" Lance requested.

"Sure. You think she's in danger don't you?" James asked.

"What makes you think that?"

"It's not standard procedure to accept the invite of a man who is not yet ruled out as a potential suspect, add that to the request to have your room close to hers and it's pretty clear you're here to ensure her safety."

"You're pretty sharp Mr. Hardagen," Lance stated impressed.

"Not really just researched a couple of times for cop roles that didn't pan out. Remembered the interview with the homicide detective." James explained with a shrug.

"Of course."

"I'd appreciate it if you didn't say anything to Emily or Catharine about your concerns, I don't want them needlessly scared." James said.

"I think it would be best to have them on guard Mr. Hardagen, the killer I'm after is an opportunist, if he sees an opening to strike he'll take it whether he had intended to or not."

"I'm sure both Emily and Catharine will be more than safe here. My security is top of the line," James boasted with confidence.

"Under the circumstances I'm glad Catharine's here rather than a hotel. As I don't doubt your security will be tighter than theirs, but James if this guy wants in he'll get in. Believe me when I say he is not a person to underestimate."

James nodded his understanding. "Your room detective, Miss Nichol's apartment suite is next door. The rooms are interconnected like in a hotel. This key will give you the ability to pass through if need be."

Lance's host handed him a key and opened the door. Flipping on the light, he issued the detective into the guest room. The space would have been better defined as a guest suite. It had a small kitchenette upon entering, with a small office space across from it, after a short corridor it opened up into a large sitting room. On the back wall directly in front of him was a closed door. He reasoned it would lead to the bedroom and most likely a private bath.

In the left wall beside the entertainment area was a second door with a deadbolt on it. This no doubt was the passage-way that led into Catharine's suite. Lance tightened his grip on the key in his hand, he wasn't sure how he felt about being given direct access to her room without her knowledge. He was less than thrilled to realize his host possessed the same ability, to come and go within her space as he'd pleased. The notion was a little creepy to his way of thinking.

"I'll leave you to get yourself settled in, when you're ready you should join us down by the pool." James suggested before he turned and walked away.

Lance moved into the room and set his bag down on the couch, he'd worry about unpacking later, for now he wanted to secure his weapon and his files; once that was seen too he intended to join Catharine by the pool deck and not let her out of his sight.

57

Catharine still felt the press of Lance's mouth against her own though he' d left her side more than ten minutes ago. Her tongue slid past slightly kissed swollen lips and she bit back a groan as she found she could still taste him there. Her eyes fell shut and the image of what had transpired moments ago; before she'd stepped into the emotional mine field; that surrounded him in regard to Dana Murphy, played over again in her mind.

"Wow now that's what I call a kiss," Emily exclaimed.

Catharine's eyes flew open as her cheeks colored with embarrassment to learn that Emily had been witness to the wild exchange.

"Relax nothing to feel ashamed of. I'm sorry it wasn't private but I've got to know was it as hot as it looked?" Emily asked.

Catharine closed her eyes and pictured the kiss from Emily's vantage point. "It was better than it looked," she replied before she got up out of the chair and slid into the pool to cool off.

"He seemed more than available to me," Emily commented.

"He isn't, you heard him, and he's not ready to discuss the case." Catharine said disappointed.

"So?"

"He's not ready because he lost his partner working that case. A woman he loved…no I'm wrong a woman he's still in love with," Catharine explained.

"He looked like a guy ready to move on, maybe you're reading too much into this," Emily stated.

"I make a living from observing people and reading into their worlds. Believe me he's not ready to move on," Catharine said with a hint of disappointment.

"If you say so, but a girl can dream," Emily teased.

Catharine smiled amused, "indeed," she answered before she closed her eyes and let her thoughts wander back to the kiss allowing the scene to play-out in the way they'd both wanted it too.

She pictured them kissing again, his hands running over her caressing warm peaches and cream colored skin, fingers stroking hidden curves and secret places that made her ache with a need to touch and be touched. She moaned with delight as a rough hand slid under her suit top groping her pert breasts. The other moved south, fingernails clawing at her tight butt.

His lips parted hers, mouth skimming over her jaw and down her neck leaving a fire in its wake. Catharine gasped overwhelmed by the erotic mix of sensations that had an intense fire burning inside her; that made her ache with need of him. She felt her body change preparing itself for him as she lost herself in his ministrations.

Part of her mind reminded her she was not alone here but right then she didn't care. All she knew was she was starving for a man and that only he could satisfy her now. If she didn't have him she'd go mad, he needed to stop teasing her and take her.

As if he'd heard her thoughts his mouth which had been tormenting an ear latched onto a tightening nipple through her suit. Catharine cried out with approval as her fingers fisted in his hair holding him to her. Fingers that had been playing with her backside dipped lower to tease the part of her that desired to feel him most.

Blue eyes flew open to look upon him and she froze as a blond head lifted from her chest. She blinked stunned to find it was not Lance that looked back at her now but Syvarin.

"You are truly a vision in this state my sweet Serenity," he murmured before his mouth latched onto her other breast tormenting it in the same manner as he'd done the first. His fingers combed through rough red curls as he rubbed his palm against the center of her feminine body.

"No, stop I didn't want you," she protested, trying to withdraw from him.

"Ah, but you did, my beauty and more to the point you still do," he boasted and to prove it he played her body like a finely tuned instrument eliciting pleasured sounds and wanton moans from her setting her skin ablaze with a lust so strong she felt drunk with it.

"Surrender to me Serenity and I will give you ease," he whispered.

"God no, I know not what you are spirit but I want no more of this," her mind snapped and when she cried out to her maker for aid the vision shattered.

Catharine felt the cool embrace of water as her mind returned to reality. She was back in the pool leaning against the ledge. Emily studied her with raised eyebrow and she wondered how much of the daydream, vision, nightmare, psychic intrusion, spiritual attack, mental rape, she wasn't sure what to call it, the other woman had been witness to.

"Where were you just now?" Emily asked.

"Lost in a scene," Catharine replied.

"Must have been some vivid fantasy," Emily said with a blush.

"Have you ever played a role for a film and gotten lost in it?"

"Yeah, maybe once. Why do you ask?"

"Well, one minute I was writing a very enjoyable scene in my head and then…"

"What was it about?" Lance questioned from the deck behind her.

Catharine's eyes widened with horror at the realization he was behind her. "How long has he been standing there?" Catharine mouthed to Emily.

"Just walked in," Emily assured her.

Catharine drew a sigh of relief; she was mortified to realize that if he'd not spoken he'd have heard her talking about fantasizing about him. Could things have gotten any more awkward or embarrassing than that? "For the new book," Catharine answered quickly.

"Then what?" Emily questioned.

"She opened her eyes after kissing the hero and instead of him she was faced with Syvarin, and she'd become Serenity," Catharine explained.

"Yikes. That must have been unpleasant." Emily said with sympathy.

"They intruded on the scene?" James questioned.

"Yeah," Catharine admitted.

"Has that ever happened before?" Lance asked curious.

"No."

"What do you think it means?" Emily asked.

"It's probably nothing just got them on the brain what with the script and the fourth book."

"Well, then set the work aside for the moment, let's all sit down to a pleasant meal and an interesting chat as dinner is prepared," James said with a smile as he offered his hand to Emily and helped her out of the pool.

Catharine nodded her agreement and when she was sure she'd found her calm, turned to get out. Lance pulled her to her feet and handed her a towel.

"Are you sure you're okay?" Lance questioned feeling her pulse race under his touch.

"Yeah, I'm fine just hungry," she answered before she set off to join their host and hostess.

58 Nottingham, England

Anna's eyes skimmed over a book of local legends she'd picked up at the bookshop. She read yet another entry on Sherwood Forest and flipped the page with a sigh; ghost stories, Robin Hood what had happened to the damn bow? As her frustration grew she looked over at Sam who lay asleep with his face in a book. She smiled amused.

For a former reporter he sure didn't seem to handle research well. Anna wondered if maybe he'd had an assistant when he worked for the DC paper. She considered setting her book down and suggesting he turn in but brushed such notions aside, she was going to get through the last of her books before she called it quits. In the morning she'd have to see about tracking down local story tellers in the hope of finding an oral tale that was not recorded on paper.

Turning her focus back to the book, she read the title for the next tale and blinked it was one she'd not encountered thus far. "Robin Hood's Treasure" The tale began with a young woman returning from London to the shire to reclaim her family home. The dwelling was a small house that sat upon a hill and was surrounded by several large ponds near Sherwood Forest. Upon entering the home she found a shallow closet along with an ornate fireplace with a broken family seal and an oddly placed candle holder.

Anna's heart pounded at the description, she'd just been in the house described earlier that day with Sam. This was what she was looking for here; a connection to the house. Confirmation that what her instincts had told her, was right, the house was indeed Locksley's.

Anna picked up a pen and paper and scribbled down the

important details of the tale. A second cottage in the area once housed the magistrate. A mysterious lever with an etching that matched the one on the candle holder. It spoke of a hidden passage within the small closet that led down into a vast chamber and another corridor leading down to a treasure room. Mentioned within the treasure chamber was a bow.

She smiled pleased at last, she had what she needed. Pulling out her laptop Anna began a web search for information to locate the second cottage that had once been the housing for the local magistrate and the last piece of the puzzle for finding the bow of Robin Hood.

59

As James and his guests sat down to dinner the doorbell rang.

"Are you expecting anyone?" Lance questioned.

"Oh, yeah I forgot when I saw Bryan earlier I invited him to join us for dinner."

Catharine looked up from her plate at the mention of her publicist's name. "He didn't mention he was coming by when I spoke with him," Catharine stated uneasily. She wasn't fond of mixing business and personal time. Staying at James's home was a recent exception to her rule. She'd made the mistake of mixing the two with Tom and look how that had ended even after the divorce he was still screwing her.

"It probably slipped his mind," James said with a shrug.

Catharine nodded and smiled nervously.

"Are you okay?" Lance questioned noting her mood shift.

"Yeah, I just …" Catharine's reply trailed off as the butler showed Bryan into the room. The new comer walked around the table past Lance and the others without a word.

"Catharine how are you doing?" he questioned as he took the empty seat next to her. His eyes fell on Lance. "Detective. What brings you to LA?" Bryan questioned, his tone was cool and hinted at dislike.

"I'm here on business," Lance stated eyeing the other man with misgivings. There was something about him he just didn't like. Every time they're paths crossed, it seemed the other man crossed some unspoken boundary between professionalism with Catharine and invasion of privacy. Even now it felt as if the man was measuring him as a potential rival for her affections.

"What business would bring a B and E cop out of his jurisdiction?" Bryan questioned with doubt.

Lance hesitated to answer but before he could give an explanation James blurted out in his defense.

"Someone murdered Kim and Detective Roman believes the killer is here in LA."

"What?" Bryan asked shocked. "You told me he was a B and E cop," Bryan stated with accusation as he turned his focus to Catharine.

"I was a homicide cop a while back, an old unsolved landed on my desk again recently," Lance explained.

"I see."

"Lance is staying here with us until his case is solved," Emily said with excitement.

"Why?" Bryan questioned.

"I asked him to," James stated.

"CJ may I have a word please?" Bryan requested politely.

Catharine nodded recognizing the tone as his all business tone. She got up from her seat and followed him out of the dining room away from the others into the secluded hall.

"Catharine I don't think his being here is wise," Bryan stated.

"Why not he's a cop, if there is a killer in the area he's added protection."

"He's a distraction. You need to stay focused on Serenity. You were out in DC observing him for another book, don't let him get you side tracked."

"Relax Bryan I'm not planning on continuing my research just now and he'll hardly have time for me if he's catching a killer." Catharine argued.

"What do you know about this guy? What if he's the killer?" Bryan snapped raising his voice.

"That's crazy," Catharine snapped.

"You're hardly a good judge of character where men are involved and you've been attracted to this guy from the first moment you laid eyes on him. Given your track record don't you think that maybe it's possible I'm right," Bryan shouted.

"Lower your voice do you think I want my private matters aired for them to hear."

"I'm sorry you're right I just don't want to see you get hurt again."

"What I do where detective Roman is concerned is none of your business! But I can assure you I've no intention of getting mixed up with him or any other man right now for that matter."

"So you say, but yet here you are, staying in a house with two strange men."

"Enough! Bryan you're way out of line! I think you should go."

"Fine, but just you be careful," Bryan warned before he turned and left.

Catharine drew a shaky breath and struggled to find her calm. She couldn't believe he'd brought up Tom in mixed company. He knew better. She was really starting to get tired of him, poking his nose into her private business. Once she'd cooled off a little they were going to sit down and have a serious talk about what parts of her life he was allowed to be involved in and what was off limits.

Worn out from the confrontation Catharine headed upstairs to her room having lost her appetite.

60

Lance cursed mentally at the sound of the heated debate coming from the other room and wondered just what Bryan meant by the bad track record remark. It was then it occurred to him he knew next to nothing about the pretty author, while she'd been studying him, she'd managed to reveal very little about herself. He smiled amused by the fete and made a mental note to rectify the error. His good humor faded at Catharine's next comment. As it pricked his ego.

"What I do where detective Roman is concerned is none of your business! But I can assure you I've no intention of getting mixed up with him or any other man right now for that matter."

No intention of getting involved with him, he'd see about that, Lance thought to himself taking her refusal as a personal challenge. The rest of the argument faded into the background as noise while he made mental plans to change the lovely novelist's mind.

"Wow that seemed wildly…" Emily began embarrassed to have overheard the heated debate.

"Inappropriate," Lance provided finishing the remark and stating his own mind. Every time he overheard a meeting between Catharine and her publicist they seemed to be arguing.

"Indeed," James commented.

"I'm glad he left," Emily supplied before taking a sip of her drink. "Do you think Catharine will join us again?"

"Doubtful love, she'll probably want to be alone, aware we overheard part of that." James muttered.

"I'm going to go check on her," Lance stated as he set his napkin on the table. He got to his feet.

"Thank you," Emily said relieved with a bright smile.

Lance turned and walked out of the room. Dinner forgotten.

61

Catharine lay on her bed curled in a tight ball feeling sorry for herself. She fought the urge to cry, Bryan's words having hit there mark well. Though he'd overstepped his bounds his words were truth. She had a poor track record with men and the reminder had been more effective in cooling her blood than the cool water in the pool had.

What was she doing? Though she'd told Bryan she had no intention of getting mixed up with Lance only a few minutes earlier she'd kissed him with a heat so intense it threatened to drive her mad if she didn't have him. When she denied the impulse she'd turned to fantasizing about him. She was already well on the way to doing exactly what she said she wouldn't.

Catharine sighed she needed to get a grip.

A knock sounded at the door and Catharine groaned, it seemed her desire to avoid the fallout of her argument with Bryan was going to go up in smoke; someone had come to check up on her.

"Catharine, are you okay?"

Catharine sat up startled, she'd figured on Emily being out there. She didn't want Lance to see her like this. She rubbed her eyes, making sure there were no tears on her face. Getting up she crossed the room to the door. Opening it, she found him leaning against the door frame. "Yeah I just lost my appetite." She explained.

"Can I come in?" Lance questioned.

Catharine nodded and stepped out of the way. "I'm sure you have questions…"

"They can wait until you're ready to answer them. You've allowed me a certain level of privacy, I'll return the favor." Lance assured her.

"Thank you. If you're not here for answers then why…"Catharine questioned.

"I was worried about you. Your publicist seems to have a temper. Every-time I see you together you're arguing."

"He's over-protective," Catharine said dismissively.

"Seems a little possessive to me," Lance stated.

"There is nothing going on between Bryan and me."

"You know that but I'm not so sure he does."

"Geesh, you sound as paranoid of him as he is of you," Catharine said exasperated.

"Sorry I didn't come here to upset you further," Lance said feeling sheepish.

"You're a cop it's your job to be paranoid, I get that, but believe me Bryan is harmless," Catharine assured him.

Lance nodded allowing the matter to go for now.

"Am I in danger?" she asked her blue eyes held no fear they simply demanded the truth.

"I don't know, Catharine; my gut says you are but I've seen nothing to suggest it at least not yet," he answered.

"You're staying here to protect me then, business, the same as with Anna," she said a hint of disappointment in her voice as she turned away from him.

Lance grabbed Catharine by the arm hating that she was withdrawing from him once more. She said she was fine but he saw now she was lying; what Bryan had said upset her. It got to her. The carefree wild spirit he'd met in Vegas was gone, in her place was a scared and broken woman he didn't recognize.

If he told her, she was right, it was better for her physically. The Fury Killer was an opportunist, if he thought she mattered to Lance he might just lash out at her to strike him. The lie was what was best but he understood that the lie would crush her completely. The truth would draw her back from the brink that Bryan had driven her to, but left her vulnerable. Lance cursed mentally as he turned her to face him. Unsure what he intended to say. As their eyes met he saw she was on the edge of tears and his will was undone.

"No, not business, it should be but it's not. With you it's personal," he murmured before he lowered his head to claim her lips.

Catharine gasped startled by the advance not prepared for it but she melted in his grasp surrendering to his will; losing herself in his kiss.

Lance groaned as her mouth came alive under his own for the

second time that day. He drew her closer to him, so that their bodies touched and laughed as he felt her heart pound against his chest, as her arms wrapped around his neck holding him close.

When his lips parted hers to come up for air, he spoke.

"I thought you said you weren't getting mixed up with me," he teased.

Catharine blushed and temper lit her eyes as the woman he knew returned. "Oh you're shameless," she said as she shoved him away.

Now he did laugh out loud. "There's the untamed woman I met in Vegas," he said pleased. Catharine unable to deny her own enjoyment at the oddity of the moment laughed as well.

"I'm already mixed up with you detective but don't gloat its rude," she said with a hint of irritation.

"Sorry, I couldn't resist. Your comment pricked my ego," he admitted as he drew her back into his arms.

"I think your ego can take it," Catharine teased before she kissed his nose.

Lance blinked having expected her to kiss his lips and his pretty faerie laughed at the expression on his face.

"You're going to pay for that," he warned.

"I look forward to it, but for now detective I'm afraid it will have to wait. I've had enough excitement for one night and I don't care to be the center of further discussion for our hosts," Catharine stated before she moved away from him again.

Lance nodded. "Shall we see about dinner then?"

"Yes. Best get back to the others before Emily has time to speculate about what we're up to in here." Catharine answered.

"After you then," he muttered as he opened the door for her.

When she walked past him he grabbed her by the arm once more and kissed her briefly before stepping out of the room and heading down to the dining hall once more.

62 Unknown

HE smiled as HE worked. A knife in hand HE grabbed a clump of blond hair and sheared off the length. Hazel eyes widened with fear as HE brought the blade to ivory skin and cut the flesh under the eye. HE thrilled in the sound of her pained cry. HIS body stirred with lust as HE fantasized about all the things HE would do to her, but she wasn't ready yet. There was still work to be done before HE took their game to the next level.

HE gloated a bit as HE prepared her. Things were going better than HE dared to hope. Detective Roman was once more on the case and with the recent addition of agent Blackwood to the hunt once more HE had a worthy opponent chasing HIM. The detective was sharp but not as good as HE thought. HIS careful work became violent as HE thought further on the Detective. It seemed that LANCE was HIS lady's newest interest. Before HE finished the game HE'D see to it that the detective suffered greatly for his interference.

63 NOTTINGHAM, ENGLAND

After tracking down the cottage connected with the local legend she discovered, Anna woke Sam and the pair now stood inside the main room inspecting the various wall décor for the lever referred to in the tale.

"Got it," Sam exclaimed as he identified an old chandelier hook with the same feather etching he'd identified on the candle holder back at the house in the woods.

"Great. See if it moves," Anna requested.

Sam nodded and reaching out he tried to turn it or press in on it and found it wouldn't budge. When he gave it a pull it slid down a few inches so that it was even in height with the others. When it moved he heard the faint sound of something mechanical moving. "It's done."

"Okay then, let's get back to the house in the forest and see if there really is a hidden passage," Anna muttered. The pair turned and left. Getting in the car they drove back out to the location of Locksley's land and made the short trek back into the house. Anna pulled the candle holder and it too moved as the lever in the cottage had. The pair watched as the half complete seal over the fireplace changed the missing piece, rising out of the mantle. The floor began to shake beneath their feet.

"Is this supposed to happen?" Sam asked as he braced himself in the doorway.

"Yeah it'll pass soon," Anna assured him. The house itself shuddered and Anna held her breath if there was any truth to the legend the castle had not risen in a long time it may not be sound any more.

Sam drew Anna into the safety of the doorframe with him as rotted bits of ceiling began to crumble away and fall. He held her close to him protecting her from harm as the sounds of the house altering grew louder.

"Thanks." She said appreciatively as the house grew still once more.

"You okay?" Sam asked as he brushed bits of dust from her hair.

Anna nodded unable to find her voice as she became aware of just how close they were. She felt her heart pound a little harder as her thoughts drifted to the memory of Sam taking a paperback away from her and kissing her. As before she felt her body stir with awareness of his proximity but she willed herself to stay calm, and on point they were close to the bow now and something inside her told her that Artemis was nearby.

"Come on the passage should be right through the door," she stated once she found her voice again. She moved out of his arms in the direction of the closet.

Sam nodded disappointed at the loss of contact but aware it was for the best, his instincts told him they weren't as alone as it appeared. He opened the closet and sure enough there was a spiral staircase leading down into blackness. Sam flipped on his flashlight and started down the steps; Anna a few steps behind him.

When they came to the end of the stairs they found themselves in a large old chamber. It was full of candelabras, the floor was marble tiles of various colors from white to black laid in a decorative pattern. On the walls were velvet curtains and beautiful panels of tapestries set up telling the story. In the center of the back wall was a portrait of a man and woman beneath it was a piece of parchment framed.

"What's that written in?" Sam asked curious.

"It's Latin," Anna murmured with wonder.

"Can you read it?" Sam inquired.

Anna nodded already doing so.

"What's it say?"

"It confirms this is the dwelling of Robin of Locksley. It's a letter of marriage for Lord Locksley and Lady Marian," Anna explained.

Sam blinked with amazement. "Do you think the treasure room is real too?"

"Sam everything in here is a treasure," Anna said humbled by the find.

"The bow," Sam reminded.

"Right, there should be another corridor in the far left corner of the chamber." Anna stated and reluctantly she turned away from the portrait and the parchment. Heading on in the direction of the hallway.

"Careful up ahead the tale describes a trap. A pressure switch in the floor; if stepped on the suits of armor will swing their axes to bar the way." Anna warned as they entered the new passageway. As the legend described it was lined with armor and weapons. Anna knelt down and inspected the tiles looking for the trigger and was careful to avoid it.

The pair walked on side by side, at the end of the corridor was a second room; the treasure room. In it was a hoard of gold and various jewels. In the center of the room sat a Grecian column at the top was carved the same family seal. On top of the column sat what they sought. A long bow, the grip was made of copper and encrusted with rubies.

As Anna moved to claim it Artemis emerged from the other side of the chamber. Coming out of a different passage, her blue eyes lit with power and in the time it took Anna to blink she was at the pedestal. The demi goddess picked up the bow and threw it over her shoulder. She drew a sword from a scabbard at her hip and held it out in warning. "Thank you for leading me to it mortal," she murmured with a smug smile.

Sam seeing the weapon reacted. He drew a sword from the wall and then grabbed Anna by the arm dragging her behind him. Protecting her from the perceived threat, "You got what you came for you don't need us."

"You're wrong mortal. I don't need you. However I need her. Hermes needs the knowledge in her head."

"You can't have her," Sam said in defiance. "Anna run," he muttered.

Anna blinked startled by the sudden shift in Sam's demeanor. "Go!" he commanded and though she wanted to protest, something in his voice set her to motion. She started back down the hall in the direction she'd come from. As she went she wondered where Sam had learned to wield a sword.

"You're action, while noble mortal, is foolish. I will cut you down and find her."

"You can try," Sam challenged. He held the blade at the ready and prepared to face the angry goddess.

A blinding light filled the room and Sam turned fleeing back down the corridor toward the stairs and Anna.

Behind him Artemis roared in rage as her path was barred by a warrior of light.

Anna stood next to the candle holder waiting for Sam to emerge as she said a silent prayer for his safety. When he emerged from the depths she returned the candle holder to its original position sealing the passage way behind them.

"Are you crazy you just challenged a goddess," Anna snapped with disbelief.

"You're welcome," he said amused.

"Are you laughing? This isn't funny. You do realize I can't do this without you right?" Anna said exasperated.

"The reverse is true," Sam countered. "Come on I doubt that, that passage way is going to hold her for long," he added before grabbing her by the hand and running out of the house. The pair got in the car and sped away.

64

Pamela cursed as she hung up the phone, she'd contacted every major hotel in LA and could find no trace of Lance Roman after learning CJ Nichols was in town she'd played a hunch and tried to track her down as well. She wasn't sure how the pretty writer was connected to this whole strange mess but she was sure Catharine was. Pamela tracked her as far as the Plaza hotel a few nights ago but she'd since checked out and left no forwarding information.

It seemed the pair had vanished off the radar. How was that possible? It didn't make any sense. CJ was directly connected to the Dark Heart film series, she had to still be in LA somewhere. Pamela tapped into the power Hermes had trusted her with and sought the knowledge she needed but it seemed even his eyes were being blocked somehow. As Pamela fumed over the matter the phone still clutched in her hand rang.

Looking down at the offending object she groaned as she noted the caller ID it seemed that Mr. Blake was tired of waiting for word on her assignment.

"Hello," she said sweetly, hoping to cool the man's temper. She had the story of the year and she wasn't ready to spill the beans just yet to anyone who might try to beat her to the punch.

"Don't hello me Pamela in that sweet innocent tone. Where the hell are you, I asked for information of Kim Frasier hours ago?" Mr. Blake snapped having none of it.

"I'm back in LA following the story. She's dead most likely murdered, I'm looking for confirmation from a source."

"Murdered where did you dig that up? All our rivals have got nothing."

"I ran into a temperamental Fed who was less than pleased with an associate of mine. He let it slip she was murdered."

"A Fed?"

"Yeah my contact he's here in town and if he is, then it's likely Miss Frasier's killer is as well."

"Why do you say that?"

"My friend, he's ex homicide the only case he'd be called back into consult on is a serial killer that began his hunting in DC. If Detective Roman is here then The Fury Killer is here also. Let me track him down and I'll give you everything about Kim Frasier's death."

"Are you telling me a famous starlet is dead and her killer is at large in the city of angels?"

"Yes sir that's what it would seem."

"You have twenty-four hours to confirm that and then I'm running with what you have." Blake stated.

Pamela hung up the phone and made plans to be at the film set in the morning if she was going to track Lance down that was her move.

65

He rode upon a black stallion into an enchanted forest. The moon shone brightly overhead. In the cool night he sought her using the trees to navigate the path ahead. In his mind's eye he pictured his lady; the faerie maiden who'd taken the place of Serenity in his heart. He called to her softly longing for her to appear but it was not her voice that answered. Beneath him his mount had spooked as a murder of crows swooped over them blocking the path driving them deeper into the wood as Serenity called to him.

He caught a glimpse of her ahead in the distance. Blonde and beautiful she stared up at the moonlight. She looked like a goddess that had deemed to wander the earth. Her gaze moved from the heavens above to look at him. Eyes like whiskey met his-own and he felt something inside him stir. Guilt flooded him at the strange response, for though he'd once sought her he now looked for the faerie queen.

The knight called to his lady once more as Serenity breathed his name. He froze, torn, but the trees shifted as before, steering his path away from the golden maiden. He watched as once more the beauty surrendered to the embrace of a shadow. The trees hid the pair from his gaze as he moved on in the direction of his lady.

He found her near a small pool at the foot of a waterfall. Her red hair long and flowing tucked delicately behind her slender pointed ears. Her blue eyes glowed with mirth as she looked upon him. The knight brought his mount to a halt. He slipped down from the saddle and moved to her side. "Now I've found you at last," he breathed as he drew her into his arms.

"I'm glad to see you again sir knight," she said with a laugh that sounded like the tinkling of bells.

"Did you not hear me calling you?" he questioned.

"No, I'm afraid that Serenity's power leaves me unaware of much within my own wood. She spoke to you this night," the faerie said with a hint of fear and disappointment.

"I was not seeking her," the knight assured his lady.

"But you desired her."

"I did," he confessed ashamed.

"Such is her power. You must be careful when entering the wood she has corrupted it and her power grows stronger with each night that passes."

"I don't want to waste our time speaking of her. I wish I could take you with me."

"The spell upon the wood and me prevents me from leaving until it can be broken, I must remain." She said with regret.

"I will free you in time," He murmured before he kissed her. She melted into the kiss surrendering to him. His hands ran over her body reveling in the feel of her and she sighed with pleasure at his touch.

"Your kiss is like fire," she gasped as it tore through her stirring her body with an intense hunger.

"You're magic," he murmured as he caressed her hips.

"Tell me this is truly what you desire," she whispered as she ran her hands down his chest.

"I want this," he assured her before he kissed her again. The pair lost themselves in the others embrace holding each other close as they slept.

✦ ✦ ✦

Lance woke to find himself in Catharine's bed. He was naked under the silk sheets and he reached over to draw Catharine to him but found the bed empty.

"So here you are then," A familiar voice called from the distance.

"Pamela?" he asked confused. Looking up he saw it was indeed her and upon seeing her he felt his body stir with desire. Uncomfortable and embarrassed Lance grabbed his shirt off the night stand and pulled it on.

"Who were you expecting Serenity," she said with amusement as she moved towards him.

"Where's Catharine? How did you get here?"

"She went to the film set due to script changes. Emily let me in."

Lance nodded as he reached for his boxers. Pamela' grabbed his hand stopping him. "Don't bother I've seen you naked before, besides you'd just be taking them off again anyway," she purred as she sat down on the mattress straddling his hips. She pressed the part of her that he now desired to fill against the proof of his desire and laughed as he groaned with pleasure.

"Don't," he muttered weakly.

"Relax, Lance I won't bite," she teased before she kissed him. He moaned as those crimson lips crashed into his demanding he give in to the hunger he felt building inside him. "That's right detective see how quickly you remember the taste of your first passion," she taunted as she bunched her skirt up around her hips preparing herself for him.

Lance cursed startled by just how ready he was to have her and ashamed of it. He'd just been with Catharine a short while before and yet here he was racing towards a quick fuck with Pamela what was wrong with him. "Pamela stop," he said weakly before her hot mouth found his own once more teasing and tempting driving him mad with lust.

He felt that wicked mouth move down his neck and a sharp pain before everything went black.

Lance groaned as he came awake. His head was pounding and he was aware of a dull ache at the back of his scull as he lifted his head from the cold concrete. The darkness about him spun and his stomach churned with nausea as he struggled to get up.

Lifting a shaky hand to the part of his head that throbbed he found it was warm, moist and a bit tacky in places as well. Drawing his fingers away from the scalp he looked at them and drew a sharp intake of breath to see blood. His blood. Thinking back he tried to recall what had happened. How had he hit his head? Where was he? Why couldn't he see anything?

Thinking back he found no answers. As he sat up Lance's fingers brushed against metal.

"Please, let me go, I'm not Serenity," he heard Catharine's voice cry from somewhere ahead of him.

"Oh but you are," a sinister voice hissed. "And Serenity will make my finest Fury yet," he breathed with delight.

Lance felt his heart pound with fear as understanding settled in. The Fury Killer had her. Catharine was about to be the latest victim in the mad man's sick art. Not if he could help it she wouldn't be. If he had any say in the matter the killer would not claim another life again after today.

Lance moved to get up but felt the bite of cold steel drag him back against the stone. "Let her go!" Lance shouted in rage. Over head the spotlights came on blinding him. Lance closed his eyes to protect them. When he opened them again the sight before him nearly had him losing the struggle against his churning stomach.

Catharine was sprawled out upon the stage piece that served as the vampire Lord Syvarin's bed. Lance swallowed noting the pair of figures carved in the head board on the left was the figure of death on the right an angel. This was where the monster would leave her staged for him to find.

Lance could see now that her wrists were bound to the head board and her captor hidden by a dark cloak worked to bind her left leg to the foot board

"Ah detective your timing is perfect. As you can see my lovely Serenity is prepared for the scene now, with you awake the stage is properly set." the man said amused as he crossed the floor to where Lance was. With care the man adjusted his head's position so he could not turn away from the bed.

"All is prepared my lord," the cloaked figure murmured with a bow.

"Well done my dear your loyalty shall be rewarded when Serenity's transformation is complete you shall be granted the right to make the detective your own," he murmured. It was then Lance noticed that the killer's appearance matched that of the vampire lord. Lance's stomach rolled as understanding dawned they weren't furies he was trying to make his victims into Nivali.

The vampire lord lowered the disciple's hood to reveal Pamela. Lance blinked dumbfounded as he recalled the seduction scene in Catharine's room as well as the hunt for the Faerie Queen in the forest, it was then he became aware this was not real but a dream.

The killer or vampire lord at this point, Lance wasn't sure which, brushed a kiss on Pamela's brow. He watched helplessly as the other man approached the bed and willed himself to wake up but found he couldn't.

He watched powerless as the phantom villain raped and tortured Catharine before him unable to stop it. He felt sick as the act went on her, cries of agony driving him to madness. He had to make it stop but he couldn't he needed help.

As he cried out for aid from any that would lend it the dream faded and darkness swallowed him. Catharine cried out for help a final time and Lance raced through the dark to try and reach her even as he felt Pamela's arms wrap around him drawing him back enticing him to stay.

66

Lance woke with a jolt his body wound tight with lust and fear weighing heavily on his mind. He was covered in a thick sheen of sweat and the need to be sick was strong. The strange dreams played over in his mind and he cursed. He'd been foolish to read the book after that heated kiss with Catharine last night but he'd needed a distraction.

His imagination was something he tried to keep in check but as of late it seemed to be on the edge of his control. A fact he didn't like. He swallowed thickly as he tried to sort through the strange mix of emotions running riot through him. What was wrong with him lately? He'd been drawn to Pamela again which made little sense to him and he seemed unable to get a grip on his attraction for Catharine either.

He needed to, after all, somewhere in LA there was a killer. At the thought the last of his dream flitted through his mind and he crossed to the bathroom giving into the need to be ill. The strange blending of real with fantasy unnerved him. He'd read the scene where Syvarin claimed the fully turned Nivali as his bride before drifting into sleep. The dark image it seemed had followed him into his dreams and been twisted into the killer's act of transforming Catharine into a Fury.

That was not going to happen, the killer would never get that close to her but even as he thought it Lance felt his fear grow stronger. He was going to need help, he admitted to himself. Moving back into the room Lance picked up his phone. He punched in Sam's number. He listened to it ring and waited for an answer. When it went to voice mail he cursed mentally. Before leaving a message for Sam to call him back; that done he went back in the bathroom to take a cold shower to cool his raging libido before he got ready to face the day.

67

Artemis stood trapped within the tunnels of the underground chambers of Locksley castle. She roared in rage at the loss of her prey before drawing upon her power. Artemis drew upon the power of the wind. Gathering as much of it together as she could. She turned it and twisted it in her hands churning it into circular motion before blowing a hard fast warm breath into the midst of it, she felt the wind grow faster and smiled.

She repeated the process of breathing upon it a few more times until she was satisfied with the gathered power the orb held. When it was ready she cast it from her hands like a ball thrown by a child and watched with amusement and pleasure as the winds of a hurricane tore through the passageway opening the corridor from the treasure chamber into the portrait room. When she was on the other side she drew the wind once more into her grasp and prepared it for opening the next portion of the passage as the first door-way sealed shut behind her.

As she repeated the process, she cursed the time lost, knowing each moment she was delayed the further the woman and her companion got away from her. When the next leg of the corridor was open Artemis began the chase anew. As she raced up the stairs she felt her power brush the sky above as stone no longer kept her separate from it. Drawing upon the full extent of her power she set a storm in the heavens to slow her targets escape. The man Sam would pay for his interference the demi-goddess vowed as she made her way up the final leg of stairs towards daylight above.

68

Sam cursed as the heavens turned against them. The sky turned black as night and rain began to fall like sheets from the heavens above.

"Not again," he muttered with irritation aware that the goddess they'd left below ground was obviously taking steps to slow their escape.

Having little choice Sam took his foot off the gas pedal and allowed the car to slow down on its own as he switched on his headlights and the windshield wipers.

"I really hate this," Anna muttered from her seat.

"Hang in there we'll get out of it soon," Sam assured her. "We better get out of Nottingham before she can track us down."

Anna nodded her agreement and watched as Sam reached in his pocket uneasy with his casual behavior given the weather. Outside the wind slammed into the rental car with a vengeance trying to push them off the road.

"Damn," Sam snapped as he returned his hand to the steering wheel.

"What's wrong?" Anna questioned alarmed.

"I lost my cell phone."

"We can make arrangements back at the hotel," Anna said with a hint of relief.

"I guess your right but what if someone wants to get a hold of me?"

"They can call my phone for now until we can get you a new one," Anna offered.

Sam nodded and then fell silent as he turned his full attention to keeping them on the road and getting them back to the hotel in one piece.

69

Lance sat in the limo beside Catharine trying to forget his dream but having little luck. It seemed slow to fade from his mind. Their host sat across from them, his blue eyes studied Catharine with curiosity. James's gaze wasn't overly heated but it still hinted at an underlying hunger that an engaged man shouldn't be directing at a woman other than his fiancé. It was not overt, but the way James Hardagen stared, at moments when Catharine wasn't looking in his direction, put Lance's back up.

After a shower and a change of clothes Lance had moved downstairs to the kitchen where he'd found Catharine already in the midst of eating. He'd grabbed himself a little food as his stomach was still upset after the upheaval brought on by the nightmare and despite the cool shower he'd found his body stirring once more in her presence.

Now in the car he seemed to have gotten his lust in check but his temper was another matter. His hosts interest in Catharine wasn't the only roaming eye he'd had set his jealousy off in the last twenty-four hours. Bryan's interest had set him off as well. He really needed to get a grip. There was a killer out there one who just might move against her as well. One he was beginning to suspect he needed help to defeat.

Taking out his cell phone Lance dialed Sam's number for the second time that morning and again he got the other man's voice mail. He left a brief message relating where he was and that they needed to talk before putting the phone away once more.

Catharine looked over at him in question but he ignored her. If he was going to keep her safe he had to keep his distance.

70

Artemis blinked at the sound of the strange electronic chirping behind her and turned back to find the source. Laying on the ground was a small black cell phone. She picked up the object and noted there was a new voice mail. Pressing the keys to unlock the phone she put it on speaker and pressed the button to retrieve the message.

The phone asked for a pass code and drawing upon her power she bypassed the security measure and listened to the incoming message.

"Sam its Lance, I'm out in LA and we need to talk. That favor you owe me, I'm calling it in."

Artemis smiled as she moved up the last of the steps. Moving out into the storm she fashioned she made her way back toward the town. The storm around her did not touch her. She didn't rush aware that now she knew where her prey would go. She just had to go there as well and wait for them to turn up.

71

Sam sat next to the fire in their hotel as he waited for Anna to finish packing her things. He'd just gotten off the phone with the airport, their work there done it was time to head back to the states. Hopefully, lose Artemis's trail and pick up the scent of the next mantle.

"Sam should we be leaving? I mean we lost the bow," Anna said a bit dejected.

"Don't fret over that. We know where it's headed we'll track it down again later for now we need to lose Artemis." Sam assured her.

Anna nodded as she sunk down on the couch next to him. She was still damp from the rain and the fire was chasing away the chill. Sam wrapped an arm around her shoulders and rubbed the skin. In a bid to warm her up, she leaned into his touch drawing comfort from him. "I feel like we're always a few steps behind him," Anna muttered.

"We're mortal he's a fallen one and his gift is knowledge whatever is known he knows as well, Don't be too hard on yourself," Sam whispered before he brushed a kiss on her forehead.

"I know, but that doesn't make it any less frustrating." She explained.

"We'll get the job done Anna," he assured her before he kissed her. Anna melted into his kiss giving him control. Sam felt the same spark of hunger hit him but drove it back, he wasn't looking for more now, and he only wanted the brief moment. When he drew back from the kiss her eyes were still closed and she seemed dazed.

Sam smiled it was nice to know he could affect her as thoroughly as she did him. "Ready to go?" he questioned.

He watched as blonde lashes lifted to reveal hazel eyes that had become a vibrant green with widened pupils. She nodded unable to speak and he brushed another quick kiss on her brow before getting up off the couch. He grabbed his things and was aware she did the same. Together the pair left the hotel headed for the airport.

72

Upon arriving at the film set the trio of passengers filed out of the limo and made their way onto the sound stage. Lance watched as James flipped on the lights. Fear seized him in a vice like grip as his eyes landed upon the stage. Before him was the exact same bed he'd seen in his dream. On it bound and wrapped in red silk was the fury killer's latest victim.

Lance turned his focus to his host studying his reaction. He noted the man appeared genuinely stunned and outraged. Turning to Catharine he placed himself between her and the body. "Don't look," he commanded.

She stepped past him her eyes haunted, terror was etched in her face. "I have to," she said her voice calm and controlled hinting at shock.

"Why?" Lance questioned turning her to face him.

"I need to be sure this isn't about me," she murmured.

"It isn't," Lance snapped willing it to be true. The alternative was too much for him to stomach.

"You may be wrong," she stated with regret.

"James call your people tell them the shoot is canceled for the day then get security over here."

"Right."

"When you've got that handled get her out of here," Lance ordered.

The actor nodded but Catharine glared at him. "You can't shield me from this detective. I need to be sure this has nothing to do with me." Catharine stated stubbornly.

"You're not blonde," Lance argued.

"I was once," Catharine revealed as her nerves began to take hold of her.

Lance blinked his mood darkened at the revelation but he still refused to accept the fact that she was in any way connected to this nightmare.

"Security is on their way." James stated.

"Good, get her out of here," Lance demanded.

"Lance…" Catharine began in protest.

"You can see it when the scene is contained," Lance compromised.

Catharine nodded and allowed their host to lead her out to the limo. Once the pair was gone, he took out his cell phone and dialed agent Blackwood's number.

"Gail, get a hold of the local cops and FBI I've got another body," Lance stated. He rattled off the site location and as security began to arrive, instructed them to maintain the doors from outside to avoid contaminating the scene.

Once he knew the proper channels had been covered, Lance moved outside to join Catharine in the limo. He wanted to take a look himself before the others arrived but he wasn't about to risk being thrown off the case for concerns he was tampering with evidence or contaminating the scene. He didn't have the proper tools to work the scene, for now he'd have to wait until his partner arrived. Lance dialed Sam's number again and when it went to voice mail, decided his next move would be to try Anna's phone. In the meantime he intended to find out just what Catharine had meant by she'd been blonde before.

73

Sam and Anna sat in the gate waiting for their flight to arrive. As they sat Anna's phone rang. She pulled the cell phone out of her purse and pressed the talk button.

"Hello."

"Anna, thank God," Lance exclaimed with relief.

"Lance what's up?"

"I've been trying to reach Sam on and off all morning."

"Have you got a line on the cup?" Anna questioned excited.

"Yes, I found the thief and am in the process of identifying the buyer. Can I speak to Sam?" Lance questioned.

"Of course," Anna replied she handed the phone over to him.

"Who is it?" Sam questioned having missed her end of the conversation.

"Lance," She mouthed as he lifted the phone to his ear.

"Hello."

"Sam why haven't you answered your phone? I've called twice; left messages."

"Sorry I lost my phone earlier during a face-off with Artemis. What do you need?"

"I'm afraid to say that the Fury Killer has resurfaced. He's here in LA and there is a slim chance that he's after C.J."

"Shit."

"I'm calling in that favor you owe me Sam I need help on this one."

"You'll have it. I'm done here I'll be there as soon as I can," Sam assured him.

"Thanks."

"Don't mention it. We owe her too," Sam reminded. "Sit tight we're on the move," he added before he hung up.

"Something going on?" Anna questioned.

"Yeah, Lance has hit some trouble on his end. I owe him a favor so we're changing our destination from Colorado to LA."

Anna nodded her understanding as the staff called for passengers to board their flight. Anna put away her phone and the pair made their way down the boarding passage and set foot on the plane bound for New York.

Lance hung up his phone as relief washed over him. Sam Abrams was a reliable man and a hell of a partner to have under the circumstances. The MMA fighter and former reporter was far more than that. He wondered how much Anna knew about Sam's past. Had she picked up on the fact yet that he had certain abilities that didn't fit with the reporter or the fighter. He supposed it didn't matter. What Sam chose to share with her was none of his concern.

Lance put his cell back in his coat before he climbed into the limo with Catharine and James. Their host seemed preoccupied with additional phone calls, which was just fine with Lance. Catharine seemed lost in her own thoughts but the moment he sat down next to her she turned her focus in his direction aware of the fact that an interrogation was about to take place.

"So, what exactly did you mean by you've been blonde before?" Lance questioned not hesitating for a moment to be polite. If she was worried about being a target then he was going to understand why before Agent Blackwood arrived on scene.

"When I lived in DC before I became famous, I was blonde." Catharine replied as she pulled out her DC driver's license. She handed it to him to study.

Lance took the card and looked at it. The image that stared back at him had his stomach tightening. In it she stared back at him with long blonde hair and spiky bangs much like that of the Furies. He noted the name and blinked. "Jade?" he questioned surprised.

"CJ is a pen name, my name in DC was Jade C. Lawson."

"Lawson is not the name here." Lance stated with irritation.

"Lawson was my maiden name."

"You're married?"

"Divorced," Catharine corrected.

Lance nodded his understanding both relieved and envious. "Who was he?"

"It's not important, he's not your killer," Catharine said with certainty.

"If you think this is about you then I have to go over every angel," Lance argued.

"We'll get into it later," Catharine said her voice was sharp and cold and broached no argument as she glanced in James' direction.

"Fine," Lance handed her ID back to her and the pair fell silent as they waited for the arrival of the authorities.

75

Pamela pulled up to the security gate of the famous movie studio and flashed her press badge.

"Miss Walsh."

"I'm here to speak with Mr. Hardagen, he promised me an interview and said I could drop by. I thought that given the movie's success, I'd conduct it on set."

"It'll have to wait another day Miss Walsh," The security guard said crisply.

"Oh, why is that?"

"The shoot has been canceled for the day."

"Really? Did Mr. Hardagen mention the reason?" Pamela asked.

"Some sort of security problem," the man answered vaguely.

"I see," Pamela murmured as her eyes lit with interest, the sudden notion that the killer had struck again right there on the set filled her mind. "I don't suppose you could let a girl in to take a look around," Pamela questioned as she batted her eyelashes at him.

"Sorry Miss Walsh no unauthorized personnel," he answered stating the company line.

"Couldn't you make an exception for a friend Mack?" She asked as she flashed him a Benjamin.

"I suppose I could turn a blind eye," he replied as he took the bill and opened the gate. Pamela rolled through and drove in the direction of the sound stage designated for Heart of Clay.

76

Lance watched as Agent Blackwood and another man got out of a black sedan. Noting the plates and the guy's suit, He figured that the dark haired man with the sharp brown eyes was the local agent assigned to the case. Drawing a breath he steadied his nerves and slid out of the limo aware that Catharine was directly behind him.

"Detective Lance Roman, this is agent Kessler," Gail stated indicating the other man. Lance nodded.

"Agent Blackwood, Agent Kessler this is Catharine Nichols. She and Mr. Hardagen were with me when the body was discovered. She believes that she may be connected to the case somehow and has requested to see the body."

"That's not wise," Gail stated.

"Normally I would agree but Miss Nichols has shown me an older ID and as much as I hate to admit it, she may have a point," Lance said with regret.

"If you think there is relevance to the claim I'll permit her entrance, once the scene is secure," Agent Kessler stated.

Catharine nodded and moved back to the car to await her chance to enter the sound stage.

"Thank you."

"Okay then let's gear up and get this done," Gail muttered. She crossed to the sedan and opened the trunk, pulling out a silver case, she began the task of preparing to enter the scene. Lance watched as Agent Kessler did the same before he moved to do the same, aware that Catharine studied them all with fascination and morbid curiosity. The writer was hard at work taking notes for her damn book.

He watched as the two agents entered the sound stage ahead of him. He took out the yellow crime scene tape and marked the door as the local CSA team began to arrive on sight along with the LAPD detective assigned to the homicide. All the players were gathered, it was time to face the Fury killer's latest victim.

77

Catharine sat in the limo and watched the activity outside careful to take note of every detail. Few writers ever got to see the police or a feds investigation this up close and personal. She'd wanted a chance to see this case from a bird's eye view years ago and couldn't resist the chance to now but as she did she couldn't help but wonder if all of this was about her.

Had Kurt finally snapped? Was he watching her now waiting for a chance to get his hands on her? He'd told her once if she ever left he'd find her and kill her. Had he grown tired of trying to find her and turned to acting out his threat on others. As she contemplated the matter, her phone rang making her jump.

Catharine drew the phone from her purse and pressed the talk button without checking the caller ID. A fact that proved she was more shaken by what she'd seen that morning than she was letting on. "Hello."

"CJ are you okay, you sound upset?" the familiar voice of her publicist questioned with concern.

"Bryan?" She asked confused as if she were just coming out of a trance.

"Yeah, talk to me CJ, you're scaring me," he answered.

"I'm a little shaken. We walked into a crime scene this morning at the sound stage," Catharine confessed. Saying it made her really face it and she felt her stomach churn and her lungs tighten.

"What? Where are you now?"

"I'm in the limo with James outside the soundstage waiting for L... Detective Roman," she replied.

"Stay put I'm on my way," Bryan commanded before he hung up.

Catharine held her phone against her ear with lifeless hands until it started to make the sound announcing the phone was off the hook. She pressed the button to disconnect and put the phone away.

"You okay?" James questioned.

"I don't know," Catharine admitted before she closed her eyes and gave into fatigue.

78

Pamela rounded the corner on the studio lot that led to the soundstage for the Heart of Clay film shoot and the first thing she noted was that James Hardagen's limo was still on the lot. The second thing she spotted was the yellow crime scene tape across the doorway. Her red lips curved into a wicked smile as her hunch was confirmed. Not only was The Fury Killer in LA he'd now struck on the set of the movie Kim Frasier was staring in. There was some kind of connection linking him to the Dark Heart Series. Something the FEDS and Cops had overlooked.

Pamela took out her cell phone and called Mr. Blake she informed him of the latest development on the Kim Frasier story then told him she was going to try and get a first-hand account of what was inside from Mr. Hardagen before hanging up. She then contacted her assistant and bid her pick up a complete set of the Dark Heart Trilogy and cover any news regarding the series in the publishing world. That done she pulled her car into a side lot and waited for her chance to meet with James Hardagen.

79

Lance stood at the far end of the soundstage watching as Gail, Agent Kessler and the local homicide detective spoke. He understood why Gail had elected to leave him out of the meet. He was too close to this thing. The fact that he'd requested Catharine be granted access to the vic, said it all, as far as agent Blackwood was concerned.

He noted the look the other cop gave him and figured about then, Gail was explaining his connection to the case. A moment later he was given a come on gesture and he breathed a sigh of relief. It seemed his presence there had been accepted.

"I understand you were one of the individuals who discovered the body," the detective stated.

"Yes, I was with Miss Nichols and Mr. Hardagen this morning to ensure that the requests Agent Blackwood made last night were carried out. When we entered the soundstage we saw the victim on the bed. I ordered both Mr. Hardagen and Miss Nichols out of the room, after instructing him to contact both security and his people, to ensure that no one else entered the crime scene."

"Did you leave with them?"

"Not immediately, I awaited security's arrival and ensured they stayed outside, then contacted agent Blackwood to start the ball rolling to get this dealt with properly."

"Did you touch anything other than the door or approach the body?"

"No. I maintained the integrity of the scene." Lance assured the other man.

"Good."

"Did you talk with anyone else?"

"Yes. I contacted an old associate of mine a Mr. Abrams, he

owes me a favor and I want to ensure that Miss Nichol's is safe." Lance explained.

"What is the nature of your relationship with Catharine Nichols?" Agent Kessler asked.

"She's an acquaintance. We met in Vegas while I was on assignment, she followed me back to DC..." Lance began

"Why?" the detective questioned.

"She's a writer wanted to study me for her new book."

"I don't know that I'm comfortable letting a writer of any kind in here with the body," Agent Kessler stated with objection.

"I can understand that but the photo she showed me leads me to believe she may be tied to this mess. The same blond hair even the bangs match the way the killer is cutting the victims." Lance explained.

"Oh hell," Gail muttered with disgust.

"Yeah whether we like it or not there is a strong possibility that CJ Nichols holds the answers to identifying our Fury killer." Lance said with disgust.

"All right then, detective go get Miss Nichols, see to it she's suited up and we'll get this over with as quickly as possible," Agent Kessler said. The detective in charge nodded his agreement.

Lance turned and walked back outside into the daylight. A sense of relief that he'd made it past the gate, settled over him and a weight of dread dropped in the pit of his stomach as he made his way to the limo to get Catharine and lead her into the nightmare, he'd known for so many years.

80

Catharine jolted up in her seat as the door to the limo opened. To her relief it was Lance who leaned against the door frame and looked down at her.

"Come on, they're ready for you," Lance said with a sigh as he took her by the hand and drew her out of the limo. She followed behind him, silent as he led her to the trunk of the black sedan. Opening the silver case he pulled out an assortment of items and lay them on top of the case.

"We've got to get you suited up so you can't contaminate the scene," he explained before he handed her what looked like the blue has-mat suits she'd seen a million times in movies. To her shock rather than talk her through how to put it on he began unfastening Velcro clasps preparing it for her. When he was done he took it back from her and knelt in front of her.

Lance lifted her left foot with care placing it inside the blue suit it felt like a strange blend of plastic and burlap against her skin, cool to the touch and a little itchy. She felt Lance pick up her other foot after setting the first down and place it inside the suit. Velcro tightened as he secured the ankles before he stood up and held the suit open for her to stick her arms in.

He was in the process of zipping it closed when she spotted Bryan and tensed. Lance turned aware of her sudden discomfort and she watched as his back stiffened in front of her.

"What the hell is going on?" Bryan demanded as he approached the pair moving to insinuate himself between her and the detective.

"I'm preparing Miss Nichol's so that she can enter the crime scene Lance stated. He moved back to the contents of the case pulling out the footies that would cover her shoes to prevent her from leaving foot prints.

"What the hell for?" Bryan asked with disgust.

"I need to know this isn't about me," Catharine stated with a measure of strength, she didn't particularly feel at that moment.

"Damn it detective. Couldn't you talk her out of this, she's in shock," Bryan stated with irritation.

"I tried but after she informed me about being blonde before and seeing her photo for DC I am convinced she's right, she does need to see what's inside that room." Lance said with regret as he again knelt in front of her and lifted her foot to secure the booties on her feet.

"I don't like this," Bryan stated in protest.

"You think I do," Lance countered as he got to his feet once more. "Now kindly get out of my way and let me finish prepping her because the sooner she's suited up the sooner I can get her in and out of there," Lance stated a hint of temper entering his voice.

"I'll be okay Bryan," Catharine assured him as she pulled the hood of her suit into place.

Bryan stepped aside reluctantly and allowed detective Roman to finish closing fasteners and securing her hair so it would not escape from the hood. The last thing he did was help her put on a pair of rubber gloves, before he tucked an ear piece in her ear and did the same with his own.

"Can you hear me?" he whispered.

Catharine nodded.

"Good now say something," he directed.

"I'm scared," she confessed.

"I'm right here with you, the moment it's too much, say the word and I'll escort you out," Lance assured her.

"Okay," Catharine said with a shaky smile. She then turned to Bryan. "Thank you for coming but I'm fine," she assured him.

"The hell you are. I know you CJ and fine isn't in your vocabulary." Bryan snapped.

"Bry, please just go, I'll talk to you later," she promised.

"Fine, but Catharine, be careful," he requested before he brushed a kiss on her forehead.

"I will," she assured him and then watched as he left.

"Nothing between you," Lance questioned a hint of disbelief was in his voice and jealousy flashed in the depths of his icy blue eyes.

"We're friend's detective, I've known him a lot of years which is more than I can say for you," she snapped, annoyed he'd question the matter again and at a time like this.

"Point taken, but for the record I don't like how familiar he is with you," Lance muttered. "I'm not so sure he thinks of you as just a friend."

"The record is noted detective, now let's get this thing going," she hissed with a barely contained temper of her own.

"In a minute," he snarled. Catharine blinked unnerved by his sudden mood shift; it felt vaguely familiar and made her stomach clench. She watched as he snapped the lid in place on the case and slammed the trunk. She jumped involuntarily and hoped he wouldn't notice. She was frightened now, not just of what she was about to face, but him as well and demons from her past.

She watched as he took a deep breath before he turned to face her once more. He looked beyond her; why she wasn't sure, before he lowered his head and his mouth took possession of hers.Catharine melted into him and his kiss, lost in the storm of emotions rolling between them.

When he let her go the hostility between them had fizzled out. "I don't want you to see this," he breathed.

"I know. I'm sorry to put you in this position. It must be awkward," she stated with understanding.

"Come on let's get this over with," he said and again he turned his back to her and led her from the parking lot in the direction of the crime scene tape

81

Pamela watched the bizarre exchange between the writer, her publicist, and the cop that ended with the heated kiss. She chuckled to herself as she speculated why Lance would be leading Miss Nichol's into the crime scene. Once the pair had vanished she slipped out of her car and crossed to the limo. Opening the door she slipped inside.

James Hardagen looked up from his copy of a script and his eyes gleamed with recognition.

"Miss Walsh to what do I owe the pleasure of your visit?" he questioned exuding a level of charm she'd never been privileged to witness first hand. She felt a jolt of power and gasped as her whiskey eyes glowed with power.

"I heard your shoot was canceled James and I wanted to know if the reason was a murder."

"News travels fast then, I take it." James said amused as he poured himself a glass of red wine. "Care for a drink?"

"I'll indulge a little, if you'll comment on what you saw this morning," she purred allowing her power to wash over him and draw him under her spell.

"CUTE. DO YOU REALLY THINK SUCH A PARLOR TRICK WORKS ON ME? I INVENTED IT. HOWEVER I'LL GIVE YOU WHAT YOU ASK IN EXCHANGE FOR INFORMATION WHICH YOUR LORD CAN GET ME," he murmured.

"Such as?"

"WHY CJ NICHOLS WOULD THINK THE FURY KILLER IS AFTER HER?" James replied as he took another sip from his cup.

"I'll see what I can find out," Pamela assured him before she took the cup and had a sip herself. The alcohol hit her system like a freight-train. She felt drunk with the first taste and despite her intent to only have a taste she tipped the cup back and gulped it down greedily.

As the crimson liquid ran down her throat some slipped out of the cup to dribble down her chin and drip into her cleavage. Where it touched her skin her body burned with a need to be touched.

"You promised," she protested referring to the Intel she'd requested.

"AFTER," he assured her before his mouth fell upon hers tasting the heady mix of the wine and aroused woman. He took greedily aware that she was already marked by Hermes but not caring, knowing that she could give him all he sought and more. The taste of his own wine intoxicating to him against her skin he sank his teeth in her throat the bite was such that it drew blood. James growled as the wild taste of wine, woman and blood laced with the power of a god hit his system. This was what he needed now, he drank deeply until he'd got his fill before giving her that which she craved, like a drug, filling her body with his own and satisfying her lust.

82

Lance approached the bed which he'd seen earlier from a distance, well aware Catharine was but a few steps behind him. As he drew closer to the trio of investigators, already working the scene a strange mix of rage and fear filled him as he took note of the second body in the room.

A woman with short cropped brown hair and lifeless brown eyes stared unseeing, horror written on her face, at the bed. Her eyes taped open. She was held in place by the shackle described in Heart of Clay that Davrik had been held captive by as he was forced to witness the death of Serenity and rebirth of Nivali. The rage was due to theunder standing she was supposed to be Dana. The Killer was adding a new layer to his hunt to further taunt and torment him.

The fear stemmed from the fact that he'd dreamt only a few hours earlier that he was in that spot and Catharine was the victim sprawled out on the bed. Now he wondered had it merely been a dream or was he somehow witness to the terrifying act that had taken place here last night as the rest of the world slumbered.

Catharine tensed behind him at the sight of her and drew a sharp breath. He felt her stir to touch him in an offer of comfort and stepped beyond her reach. She understood the significance of the woman though not the meaning connected to it. She'd seen the photo and he had no doubt now, that more questions were swimming round in that sharp brain of hers but he had no intention of discussing them or her with the nosey writer.

Lance cursed she wasn't nosey and he knew it, curious yes, but she'd not invaded his privacy. He re-directed his temper in the correct direction, the killer was the one he should be annoyed with. He'd crossed the line here and was airing his private life for all to see. The sight of a lifeless Dana cut him to the quick, a harsh reminder of what he'd lost to the sick son of bitch. He wasn't about to lose anything more if Catharine's suspicion proved false he would get her the hell out of LA.

She'd object but he'd see to it that it was done. Lance had no doubt that if he told Bryan to get her out of there the other man would do so. Sure she had a script to finish but she could always fax James Hardagen the pages. While her work was important to Bryan and her publishing house Lance figured keeping her safe was more pressing for her publicist. Though he distrusted the other man the one thing he was sure of was that Bryan had her best interests in mind. It would sting his pride a little but he would leave her to her friend's care, until the killer was caught to ensure she lived through this nightmare.

If she was right... and she wasn't Lance assured himself, but if she was then he'd make sure she was never out of his sight while Sam hunted for the monster that was after her. Again it would cost him a little to leave the hunt to Sam, he had a large score to settle with the beast that was stalking these women, one he'd prefer to settle himself but not at the cost of his pretty faerie.

Lance groaned mentally at the image. Catharine was not his nor was she a faerie. She was flesh and blood a mortal. Fragile and venerable able to be killed the same as him. This wasn't one of her books or his movies he indulged in; this was reality and in this world a life could end without a moment's notice, he knew that better than most.

As he turned his focus from the silenced witness to the victim herself, the new Fury, he wondered what made Catharine think any of this could be about her. She hadn't even been in DC when the man started hunting. She'd said so herself. So, why the fear it was tied to her.

Something he'd heard once nagged at the back of his mind. Writers to some degree wrote what they knew. If that were really the case then what did that say about C.J. Nichols. Dark Heart or at least what he'd read of it so far was nightmarish. She told a tale of an innocent girl barely a woman being wooed, bedded, and hunted by monsters. Only to eventually become one to save someone dear to her. Catharine was nothing like Serenity and yet he reasoned that the frail woman could be like another personality in a split, only in C.J.'s case her alter ego was on a printed page.

Lance rejected the notion as soon as it entered into his head. He was reading too much into it and the book. Despite his dismissal of the thought, he still wondered if there was any truth hidden within the pages of the fiction and if there was, what that meant for his case.

83

Catharine stared with unblinking eyes at the woman garbed in red sprawled out upon the ornate set piece, which was designed as the vampire lord Syvarin's bed. She swallowed thickly as she realized just how little of the detail of the beds appearance she'd changed from the real one. Only the figure of death in the head board was different.

The one she'd slept in for eight years had two angels instead. She felt her stomach roll at the bed in front of her, aware it was bringing back memories she'd have preferred to remain buried.

"Catharine are you all right?" Lance questioned.

She nodded unable to speak and forced herself to look beyond the bed to the body lying in it.

The young woman lay sprawled on the bed her pose mocked that of a woman in the throes of passion but the face was one filled with pain and terror. Her eyes were wide with fear and several cuts ran down her cheek making it look as if she cried blood. A crown of serpents encircled her brow their fangs sunk into her flesh drawing blood. The hair under the crown had been shorn off cut at varying lengths sharp and spiky. Red peaked out at the roots the blonde tainted but not gone. "This woman is not a natural blond she has red hair it was dyed blonde and the killer tried to return it to its natural state, but doesn't know how."

"Why do you say that?" Agent Kessler asked.

"I used to dye my hair blonde when I was younger. When I decided to go back to red I didn't really know what I was doing the first time I tried it looked like that. That's why my hair is short now. I damaged it, had to cut most of it off."

"Is there anything more you can tell us?" Gail Blackwood asked.

"Yes, the girl, I know her she was one of the actresses that came in for the screen test for Serenity."

"You're sure?" the local detective questioned.

Catharine nodded. "Mr. Hardagen will be able to confirm it."

"Anything else?"

"No," Catharine lied, terrified by the truth staring back at her. There were aspects here that were right out of Dark Heart, bits and pieces, things that she'd never even published.

"Do you still think this is about you?" Lance asked.

"Yes," she stated now with certainty. Whoever was behind this, knew things about her book that few had seen. This was definitely about her.

Lance muttered a curse under his breath that she heard over the ear piece he'd given her.

"What was that?" Gail questioned.

"I said I'll go get Mr. Hardagen," Lance lied. "Don't let her out of your sight." He commanded before he turned and left.

Catharine sighed aware that whatever mental plans he'd been making she'd just dashed to pieces, she just hoped he didn't get mad when she revealed later she'd held something back.

84

Pamela slid out of James Hardagen's embrace as Hermes' mind nudged against hers, bidding her move. Detective Roman was coming back for the man and if he found them together any chance she had of gaining a hold of her former lover would vanish like a puff of smoke.

"The knowledge I asked," James demanded.

"The answers you seek are hidden within the pages of the fiction she wrote. Read between the lines to gain the knowledge you seek," Pamela murmured.

"I want direct answers," James snapped.

"You'll get them later, after I get mine," She challenged.

"A woman was murdered on the sound stage sometime last night. She was lain out on the bed in a gown of red a crown of serpents rest upon her brow."

"Thank you, we'll talk further tonight. There is more you wish to know and more you'll have to share. Hermes has blessed our liaison. There are things that we can yet gain from each other. Truth's about the past and now we can share."

"And our tryst?" James questioned; the voice within him making it clear they didn't like to share their women.

"He deems it a fair trade for your allegiance in the war to come," Pamela purred as she raked her nails over his skin with the promise of future pleasure to be had.

"Farewell then Lady, until we meet again," James breathed as his body stirred with desire anew. He kissed her briefly before she withdrew.

James watched as she slipped out the door opposite the sound stage and vanished. He drew a breath before fixing his clothes recalling the reason for her hasty departure. He'd just set himself to rights when the other car door opened to reveal Detective Roman.

"We need you inside."

James nodded before he slipped out of the car to follow the detective over to the sedan. He realized it was now his turn to suit up before he looked the dead woman directly in the eye.

85

Lance led a now properly suited Mr. Hardagen past the yellow crime scene tape and back into the soundstage. Across the floor over to where the victim lay sprawled.

"Mr. Hardagen, Miss Nichols has indicated that the woman in the bed was one of the girls present during the recent screen test of the Serenity roll do you agree?" Agent Kessler asked.

Lance watched as James turned his eyes to the dead woman's face and saw the spark of recognition. "Yes. If you'll give me time I can get you her name," James offered despite turning a little green.

"I know that wasn't easy, so thank you, now can you do me a favor," Lance questioned.

"Of course."

"Get Miss Nichols out of here. Take her back to the house and keep her there." Lance demanded.

James nodded before moving to Catharine's side. "Come on CJ we should leave this to the detective." He stated.

"Right," Catharine agreed without hesitation allowing the actor to lead her away.

"Do you think you can trust him?" Gail Blackwood asked with curiosity.

"I know where he was last night, besides Emily will be there with her," Lance stated.

"You sure you don't want to go with her?" Agent Kessler asked.

"I need to trust that my host is who he appears to be or I'm on my own until help comes and if she's right about this, that's more than I can handle."

"You're too close to this detective," the local cop stated.

"Yeah, probably. I'll stay on the outside of the investigation for now but I won't be shut out. The killer won't allow it."

"He's right," Gail confirmed.

"What makes you so sure?" Agent Kessler asked her.

"The second victim is aimed at him she looks like his old partner. Detective Murphy, the killer wants him here." Gail explained.

Lance felt rage well up inside him. That the killer was making this personal made the game far more dangerous, if he lost perspective then the game would end badly and this was one hunt he didn't want to lose.

86

James watched with amusement as his guest and charge slid into the backseat of the limo and slipped into sleep almost immediately. Whatever truth she was hiding, within her fiction, the sight of the killer's victim had drained her considerably. Her mind was weary and the voice within his head whispered to him promises of a dark intent. When she woke next, Catharine Nichols would be more than ready for him.

James worried for a moment about Emily and how she would react to his desire for the lovely writer and his recent encounter with Hermes slut, but the voice assured him that after his next union with Emily she would never question his actions again. Her will would be his own. James re-assured and pleased, poured himself another glass of wine and drank, imagining the taste of Pamela's power filled blood as he sipped, savoring the flavor of it, as the woman across from him began to stir in her sleep, as her mind was captured in a dream..

87

"Catharine," A voice both foreign and familiar called to her through the distance. She grumbled in resistance not yet ready to wake up.

"Come on, wake up pretty girl," the voice murmured with a hint of amusement.

"Five more minutes," she mumbled her eyes still shut as she requested permission to rest a little while longer.

"Very well," the voice conceded with a light laugh.

She smiled before muttering a thank you. He answered her with an indulgent you're welcome. Her mind was just beginning to slip back into unconsciousness when a hot hungry mouth wrapped around her ear, teeth pulled gently sending a surge of fire to her belly. "Hmm," she moaned with delight at the pleasant assault. "I thought you said I could have five minutes," she teased.

His teeth released the sensitized flesh. "You can and you will rest your eyes, while I prepare you for when I do wake you," he breathed before she felt his face withdraw as he moved on in his efforts to make her crazy for him. His breath brushed against her mouth before his lips locked with hers, claiming hers in a wild kiss that curled her toes and set her flesh burning with the need for him to touch her.

"Ah the beauty begins to stir," he whispered with satisfaction. Talented fingers pushed down the sheet wrapped about her to tempt more excitable parts of her body. Warm hands caressed her eager breasts tormenting the sensitive tips into sharp points waiting for him. She arched up into his touch urging him on even as the fog around her mind began to lift.

Where were her clothes? She never slept naked. Before her mind could question the matter further he attacked her system with a jolt that had her crying out with wanton need as his hungry mouth latched onto her aroused peak. Her hands fisted in his hair drawing him down to her silently pleading for more as the driving center of her lust prepared itself for him.

Catharine's lashes began to flutter as the need to see him became pressing.

"No you don't, naughty girl your five minutes isn't up yet," he teased before he lowered his head to treat the other breast to the same pleasure.

Catharine gasped as his hands ran lower peeling away the rest of her blanket to tease the part of her he desired most. Finger tips danced over her belly button, one pressed inside it mimicking what it would do but a bit lower. She groaned overwhelmed by the mix of sensations. Her hands slid out of his hair, to fist in the discarded sheet as she began to come undone.

Nails raked over and through rough curls as he reached for the part of her that now wept for his touch. "So ready," he said with awe before he gave her what she longed for. As his index finger sank into her hidden depths her eyes flew open and she froze.

"James?" she questioned with disbelief.

He smiled with amusement even as he used his hand to draw a pleasured cry from her as he drove her closer to fulfillment.

"Stop, I thought…"

"It doesn't matter what you thought Catharine you're body responded to me as easily as Serenity's did to Syvarin. You want this as she wanted him, let me give you ease," he whispered before nipping her other ear.

"No, this isn't right, what about Emily," she questioned as she sat up and reached for the blanket trying to separate herself from him and the insane hunger she felt clawing inside her.

"Emily need never know," James stated as he tempted her further, refusing to release his hold on her body just yet.

Catharine gasped as she struggled to resist him. Guilt weighed heavy on her mind as her flesh clamored for him to finish what he'd started. Spirit, mind and body warred for control.

"I'd know," she finally stated when she was able to speak. She took hold of his hand in her own and drew it away from her. She felt her body protest the loss of his touch even as she wrapped the blanket about her.

"Catharine," he whispered the name a desperate plea.

"You need to go," she stated her voice weakened a little, but she held on to her resolve.

"But you want… we want this," James protested.

"It doesn't matter, this is wrong," she said it again before he withdrew and she slipped back into a fitful sleep as her flesh begged for the ease he'd offered.

88

Catharine woke with a jolt as the limo came to a stop. She looked up to see James resting across from her and was relieved. She was mortified at the thought of what she'd been dreaming about. There was a distinct possibility that if her host had been awake he'd have heard first hand just what she was dreaming.

Catharine squirmed in her seat as she became aware the dream had not left her unaffected. She was more aroused than she could ever recall being and felt sick about it because she liked Emily and had no business fantasizing about her fiancé.

Why was she?

She'd thought at first she'd been dreaming about Lance, the last thing she'd been thinking about before she dosed off was how to write the scene between her and him as he suited her up for her book.

That simple kiss between them, she'd wanted it to be so much more. Until she opened her eyes she'd thought her lover to be Lance. It had been a shock to find it was James.

What was the deal with all that talk about Serenity and Syvarin? Why was her subconscious mind being crowded by the two?

"CJ are you coming?" James questioned as he opened the door. Catharine nodded wondering when he'd woken.

She slid out of the limo and followed him into the house. As soon as she got to her room she was going to soak in a hot tub and forget everything that had happened since waking, at least until Lance got back.

"How are you holding up?" James questioned as they walked in the door.

"Okay I guess. I can't believe that a girl we met a few days ago is dead," Catharine stated turning her focus to why she was back here and not at the studio working on her script.

"I know. It's tragic; can I get you anything?" James questioned.

Unbidden the image of him kissing her as he had in the dream flashed before her eyes and she blinked. What was wrong with her? "No, I just want to get some rest," she stated hoping to withdraw before whatever madness had taken hold of her had her acting upon her dreams and doing something she would regret.

"You look pretty shaken let me get you a drink. It will help you take the edge off," James offered.

"No thanks," Catharine replied politely as she made her way upstairs in the direction of her room.

"Suit yourself," James relented and he allowed her to retreat to the privacy of her own room.

Once inside Catharine drew a calming breath she looked to the bathroom and knew that a soak wasn't going to help her. She turned on the laptop and set to work creating the scene she'd been thinking of before dosing off in the limo; hoping that getting the source of the fantasy out of her head would quiet her raging hormones.

89

Sam sat trying once more to read the book of Greek myth he'd picked up during the rainstorm but his attention kept getting pulled to Anna. There was something in her face he couldn't quite figure out but she was definitely lost in thought.

"Where are you at Dr. Gallagher?" he asked her using her last name to draw her out of her own world.

"I was thinking about the candle. I don't think Ian has it."

"Why not," Sam asked curious.

"If he did he'd have used it on you by now," Anna said as a matter of fact.

"Right. If Hermes could tap into that power he'd eliminate me in order to get to you quicker," Sam said in agreement.

"Either that or Artemis would have used it back there to slow our escape," Anna reasoned.

"Okay, let's say you're right and he doesn't have it. Then who does? Who else knows about the dig?"

"His employer," Anna stated.

"What do you know about him?" Sam questioned.

"Not much only that he's the one who put that thug on my tail." Anna said with irritation.

"He put Kadar Handle on your tail?" Sam asked with disquiet.

"Yes," Anna confirmed.

"I see," Sam muttered as his jaw tightened, he now had a pretty good idea who Ian Broody had been taking marching orders from and he didn't much care for it. If Anna was right it meant that someone far more dangerous than Ian had their hands on a Mantle and if Mr. York figured out what it was capable of, there was no telling just how much danger they were all in.

90 SOMEWHERE IN THE BERMUDA TRIANGLE, ATLANTIS

Russell York stood beside his employer in the underground passage, beneath the feasting hall in the temple of the gods. He handed the candle that his team had captured, from the transport headed to the Smithsonian, and watched with baited breath.

The dark figure, who he answered to, set the pewter candle holder encrusted with emeralds in the hands of the image of the god of the underworld, per the instructions of the voice with whom he'd been answering to in his mind, for as long as he could remember.

"Russell!"

"Yes Mr. Halden?" Russell York squeaked, knowing that tone and aware that it could lead to his early demise.

"I thought I told you to get me the candle recovered here," His employer hissed.

"It is sir." Russell York assured him.

"Something here is a fake because nothing happened," Mr. Halden snapped. The voice in his mind assured him that his man was correct, he had the right candle, it was the statue that was a fake. Outraged the man drew his gun and shot the false images. "They are all fakes."

"I don't understand sir none of the statues have been moved since they were brought down here," Mr. York assured him.

"Get me Ian Broody now!" His employer shouted before he turned and left. As he went on his way the voice in his mind told him that Hermes was making his move to assume the seat as King of the gods. "We'll see who gets there first Mr. Broody."

Lance cursed as they finished the examination of the two victims, the killer was escalating at an alarming rate. The amount of torment the two women had endured in the short period of time was horrific and the anger directed particularly at the second woman led Lance to believe that he'd done something to piss the guy off.

He wished he knew what, but figured that it could be as simple as turning up in LA and agreeing to stay at Mr. Hardagen's home. If Catharine was right and this was about her then her stalker wouldn't take too kindly to her having a full time body guard.

She wasn't right, couldn't be, Lance argued though deep down he knew it was a lie. Just as he knew that somehow it was connected to Dark Heart.

"Do you need anything else from me?" Lance questioned the trio of investigators he was working with. He was pleased to see they were all solid, none of them missing a trick.

"Not really, why don't you go, we can handle the rest," Gail assured him.

"Thanks."

"You believe her don't you?" Agent Kessler asked in regard to her suggestion that she was at the center of the investigation.

"Yeah unfortunately I do," Lance finally admitted.

"If she is then she's not telling us everything," Gail stated.

"Yeah I know. I'll see what I can find out," he vowed.

"Good in the meantime I'll start looking from my end as well," the local cop commented.

"Jade Lawson," Lance muttered.

"What?"

"That was the name on the DC ID Jade Lawson. Start there."

The detective nodded before moving off to get started.

"Are you going to be okay?" Gail questioned.

"I'll be fine as soon as we get this creep." Lance replied before he turned to go.

"Do you think we can trust him?" he heard Kessler question as he walked away.

"I don't know. He's walking the razors edge on this," Blackwood stated, before he moved out of range to hear the rest.

Lance didn't like that his objectivity was in question but he understood the reason. If their roles were reversed he'd have the same concerns. But he'd walked this line before, in the past, and stepped away; it had ended up costing Dana her life and him everything he held dear. He wasn't about to make the same mistake twice.

92

Catharine hit the save button, having finished out the scene she'd set to write. She was aware that if Bryan or the house found it or any of her notes for the new book idea she'd have a lot of explaining to do. She was told to work on Dark Heart. It was what she should be doing but her mind wasn't in it. She'd meant what she said to her fans, she didn't see where the thing could go. While she had some interesting concepts she still had no way of giving Serenity the happy ending to her tale; both the public and her publishing house demanded.

Given the world she'd created, Serenity was beyond saving. She was the villain now. Unless there was a way for her to restore her humanity, Serenity was a damned creature beyond hope enslaved by Nivali. As she contemplated the quandary a knock sounded, shaking her out of her musings.

Relieved to be drawn away from the frustrating matter she rose from her seat and crossed the floor to answer the door. Opening it she found her host standing outside with a bottle of red wine in one hand and a pair of glasses in the other.

"I know you said no earlier, but I thought maybe you might have changed your mind about that drink," James explained with a playful smile.

She blinked as she considered the offer caught off guard by his apparent concern for her well-being. "Well, maybe, a drink would be what the doctor ordered," Catharine admitted figuring that the least it would do was free her mind of all the chaos raging within for a little while.

"A good answer after all you must have had quite a scare earlier," James speculated.

"Yeah, it was unnerving seeing her like that. I mean she was only one of hundreds that tried out for the part. Why did he choose her?" Catharine asked.

"You said something to Lance about thinking this is about you." James questioned.

Catharine nodded uneasy, taking another sip of the alcohol she meant to self-medicate with.

"Why?"

"She wasn't much different than I am," Catharine replied without explanation. She felt the effect of the wine hit her like a fist to the gut, it left her more than just a little tipsy. She felt her blood warm pleasantly and her mind recede.

Man I must be more tired than I thought, Catharine reasoned as the cause for her low tolerance, right then.

"Do you still think you're connected to what happened to that woman last night?" James questioned.

"Yes, and it scares me," she confessed, the alcohol causing her to reveal more of herself than she normally would.

James set his glass of wine along with the bottle down on her desk and drew her into his arms. His hands rubbed her back in what she supposed was meant to be a soothing gesture but for some reason it just felt wrong to her.

"Shh, it'll be okay, your detective will take care of you," he murmured in assurance to comfort her.

Catharine told herself her discomfort came from the dream earlier and was irrational but she couldn't ignore it. She pushed him away gently. "This is really sweet of you to fuss Mr. Hardagen but I think you should go. I need to get some rest," she said politely as she reached for his glass.

As soon as she touched it she felt a spark of something dark and then the pleasant feeling of intoxication strengthened. A wave of lust washed so violently through her, it nearly had her passing out. Catharine grabbed hold of the back of her chair to maintain her balance, aware that if she went down James would pick her up and lay her down on the bed like in some sappy romance novel and a dream, that shouldn't have been, might just become reality.

"Are you sure you're okay?" James questioned alarmed as he moved to her aid.

Catharine handed him the cup. "Fine just tired. You should go."

James nodded then turned to go. Catharine closed her eyes as her body screamed in protest, to her denial of it.

When the door was closed and he was gone. She locked it before crawling into bed.

What the hell just happened to me? Catharine wondered as she closed her eyes. She found no relief from the strange madness that had seized her. As soon as her eye lids were lowered pictures from her dream danced before her eyes tormenting her further.

God what was this? She didn't want it," Catharine's mind screamed. Her eyes flew open a moment later as her stomach churned violently.

Catharine lunged from the bed to the bathroom and cried out in agony as her body violently expelled the contents of her stomach. She looked down at the water and felt ill all over again. The color of the wine was such she looked like she'd thrown up blood. Flushing the toilet she rinsed out her mouth and then crawled back into bed. She felt the sensation of drunkenness and desire ease and Catharine muttered her thanks to the heavens.

Her quiet was interrupted by another knock and she uttered a silent curse. Maybe if she didn't respond they'd go away.

"Catharine?" Lance's voice called with concern from the other side of the door.

"Lance," she breathed the name with relief before rising from the bed to answer the door.

"Are you okay?" He asked. She figured he saw something in her appearance that troubled him.

"Yeah, just tired," Catharine paused for a moment and licked her lips nervously unable to just forget the odd events that just occurred. "I've had a strange encounter with our host." She admitted and then regretted it, if he asked for details she'd have to tell him about the crazed note of lust for their host. She didn't want to admit it, wasn't sure how he'd react.

"What does that mean?" Lance demanded. She saw in his face he was berating himself for leaving her alone with the other man.

"It's a little complicated," she began trying to decide how much to reveal now.

"Tell me everything," Lance ordered.

Catharine nodded and began to re-count the bizarre events that had just transpired.

93

Lance listened to Catharine's strange tale with a growing sense of disappointment and disquiet. He sensed she was holding something back, years of police work told him she was not saying something. He stopped her.

"Look I don't know what your hiding but don't Catharine. Whatever the reason you feel you need to, forget it. I need to know everything," Lance stated.

Catharine swallowed and nodded. "I felt an intense irrational desire to give myself to him," Catharine whispered. Her blue eyes lowered and she refused to look at him ashamed.

Lance blinked dumbfounded by the confession. Anger boiled inside him and an intense jealousy, he immediately squashed. There were things as a cop he was aware of that might cause such erratic behavior; things that made his heart go cold. He'd left her with this man and if any of his suspicions were accurate it meant that until Sam got into town he was indeed alone in his efforts to protect her.

"You're sure it was touching the cup that triggered the strengthening of the reaction?" Lance questioned.

"Yes."

"What did it look like? Was it clay?" Lance asked playing a long shot.

"No, it was gold. Why, do you think it's the one Anna is looking for."

"It can't be, the one that was stolen was made of clay," Lance said both confused and disappointed, it was really a shot in the dark he told himself. "Did the wine taste off, is it possible he slipped you a mickey?" Lance suggested.

"No, I'm positive it was the cup. The second I touched it I thought I was going to die if I didn't give into the compulsions I felt, I nearly collapsed trying to get it and him out of here."

"And now?"

"I'm just tired," she murmured.

Lance nodded. Part of him was disgusted at the notion she'd thought even for a minute about giving herself to their host after he'd kissed her as they had the night before. But he could see in her eyes the genuine fear and shame at her bizarre reaction to the other man. She'd tried to spare him the details but he'd not allowed it.

Lance wasn't sure if he believed that the cup itself was the cause of her odd reaction, if it had been made of clay then maybe… but… it was just too absurd, all this stuff about gods and their artifacts.

"Get some sleep, no one will disrupt you again," Lance assured her as he sat down in front of the desk.

"Thank you. I'm s…" she began.

"Don't, this isn't your fault," Lance told her. He figured the jealousy and disappointment would pass, right now he was just glad she was okay.

Catharine nodded and laid back down closing her eyes. Lance struggled with the implications of what had happened. He found himself wishing Sam was there already. He set his gun on the desk bumping the mouse and noted the open file. The top line on the page caught his attention recognizing it as a rendering of earlier between them. Curious, he scrolled back up to the top unable to resist the chance to see just how she'd reacted to the way he'd handled preparing her for entering the crime scene.

It was unorthodox and unprofessional, he'd normally have talked her through it but he'd needed the extra time to prepare for taking her in there. He hadn't counted on Bryan turning up and he'd certainly not planned on kissing her but he hadn't been able to stop himself. He'd needed to remind her that the situation was not just business as usual for him.

As Catharine rested, he read what she'd worked on since leaving the sound stage.

94

James walked into his bedroom, his mood dark, he silently argued with the voice in his mind which had assured him that upon her waking CJ Nichols would be his. He'd just carried out the voice's instructions to the letter and Catharine Nichols had sent him away rather than accept his embrace. He was not pleased. No woman had ever resisted his charms.

The voice assured him that Catharine would be his and soon. He'd simply miscalculated the strength of her spirit. She was weakening and with but a little more of his influence upon her she would fall. James told the voice she'd better and then lamented his current state of arousal with no outlet. His complaint died as his blue eyes settled upon his pretty fiancé sitting at her vanity putting on her makeup for the day. While she was not the flavor he currently craved she would more than satisfy his appetite for now.

He studied her in silence, watching as she drew a green line along the edge of her eyelid and then brushed a bronze powder on. James allowed his thoughts to wander over his previous encounters with the brunette and felt his hunger shift. He watched with interest as her eyes popped open to lock with his in the mirror.

"James. You startled me I thought you'd left for the film shoot. I didn't expect to see you again until late tonight."

"The shoot got canceled." James stated.

"What? Why?" Emily questioned alarmed.

"We found a body at the sound stage."

"Oh no, the killer; Catharine," Emily exclaimed alarmed as she moved to get up.

James smiled, he loved that his lady was so fond of their guest, it would make it all the easier to keep Catharine around. "She's resting," James assured her.

"Good I'll check on her later. Is she okay," Emily murmured.

"I don't know, she's convinced the killer is after her," James admitted.

"How dreadful, are we safe?" Emily questioned.

"Yeah, her detective is here and I've increased security. We're safe," James assured Emily as he drew her into his arms. He kissed her brow and then her cheek to comfort her. Emily melted into his embrace and welcomed the gentle stroking of his hands down her back to sooth her. "When do you have to be at the shoot?" James asked.

"In an hour," Emily answered as his actions moved from comforting to seductive.

"An hour, do you think it could be canceled?" James asked as he rested his forehead against hers. He kissed her deeply, drawing an aroused purr from her.

"James," she murmured both in acceptance and protest.

"I think we need to be here for CJ, both of us," James stated before he kissed her again.

She drew a calming breath as his mouth moved on down her throat. "You taste like wine," she whispered shocked. James was not prone to drinking so early in the day.

"I had a glass with Catharine to calm our nerves." James explained. "Will you stay?" James asked as his hands enticed her to stay with him.

"All right," Emily agreed. No sooner than the words left her lips, James had her in his arms and on their bed. His hands and mouth were everywhere leaving a fire through her system in their wake. His mouth latched onto her neck and Emily cried out both with need and in pain as his teeth pierced her skin drawing blood. Emily's eyes glazed over with pleasure and her mind receded as James bedded her.

As his body was stated the voice within his head assured him that Emily was his alone and would never again desire to be free of him. Her will would now match his own.

95

Anna sat in a chair beside Sam on CJ Nichols private plane bound back for the United States. She was resting her eyes when sleep overcame her. Not long after, she drifted into slumber, her mind was troubled by strange dreams.

As the dream began Anna saw herself standing on a hill top in Jordan overlooking the Dead Sea and the ruined city of Sodom.

"What am I doing back here?" She questioned startled to find herself looking down on the darkness that had begun the bizarre war she was now caught in the middle of.

"There are things here you must see and understand," A familiar voice answered. Anna turned and was surprised to find that standing beside her on the hill was the angel of the Lord that God had sent to save her from Hermes in her dreams when she called for aid over a week ago. "Come," he commanded as he held out his hand for her to take.

Anna studied him with question and doubt. Aware from what she'd been learning in her Bible reading sessions that evil spirits could change their forms as they liked imitating an angel of light if they wished. Hermes, after all had appeared beautiful to her at first in her dream at first glance. "Who are you and whom do you serve?" Anna questioned.

She was surprised when the angel rather than look annoyed or hurt by her mistrust, smiled. "My name does not matter child only my masters does and he is Jesus Christ the Risen Lord and savior of men," he answered. "You are wise to test the spirits you meet Anna. I see you have learned much since last we met, he said pleased.

"I've barely begun to learn anything," Anna stated as she took his offered hand. When she touched him they descended from the hill and in the blink of an eye were in the temple in the king's palace dedicated to the Fallen. "Why have you brought me here?"

"Look and See," the angel commanded as he lit the hall. Anna's gaze moved to the carved image of the gods and goddesses and noted the order had changed, Zeus was missing. In his place in the center, Hermes stood his eyes open roaming watching them. Anna gasped with horror thinking she'd be exposed. "Do not be afraid he cannot see you, the almighty one has hidden you from his eyes, none of them can see you.

Anna nodded her understanding and her gaze moved from her tormentor to the goddess he embraced. The sight before her drew a startled gasp. "Her face it's Pamela's," Anna whispered with disbelief.

"Yes, Hermes has chosen a queen."

"Is there nothing we can do for her?" Anna asked feeling pity for the other woman, though she was a rival for Sam, she knew what it was to be courted by the fallen.

"Her fate I do not know. The Creator has not told me. For now all you can do is pray for her," the angel answered sadly.

Anna fell silent as her eyes moved over the rest of the image. Erebus clung to Pamela, the new Hera and the next change she noted was the image of Dionysus, his eyes were now open but were not yet moving about. He clung to a woman she did not recognize but the face and image altered to show Dionysus holding fast to the woman by one arm trying to draw her into his embrace while Ares pulled her from the opposite side, his eyes fixed only on the woman. When the image shifted back to the woman Anna didn't know, she noted the image of Ares shifted as well to depict him holding the woman she knew, taking that which he'd desired as his own as she fought to escape the War god. The face there chilled Anna's blood.

"Catharine," she exclaimed with alarm as she turned from the image to look to her guide for answers.

"Your friend is in grave danger and her protector does not yet believe in the events transpiring around you. Until he does, it will be up to you to warn her of the storm she is caught in or her fate will be sealed," the angel explained with regret.

When Anna turned her head to look back at the image she saw a veil between herself and the carving. "I don't understand where is Zeus why does his daughter serve the god of knowledge and not him? What is in the stone tablets that Hermes possesses?" Anna said confused.

"Come," the angel ordered once more and Anna reluctantly took his hand. When she did they were whisked away in a brilliant flash of light. Anna closed her eyes to guard against it and when they opened again she found herself standing beside him in Atlantis as it had been in its glory. The angel led her down a gilded street and into Hermes palace.

"Why here?" Anna asked.

"Look and See," the angel answered and he pointed to the door that led into the bed chamber. Anna walked into the room ill at ease recalling her dream when Hermes had tried to seduce her in this city by giving her the knowledge she sought. To her surprise what she found waiting in the room was not the fallen one but a beautiful young girl; barely a woman. She sat on the bed of the would- be god and wept bitter tears in private.

Her long golden hair was tied back in a braid and she wore a white toga with golden sandals set upon her feet. A circlet of golden leaves upon her brow. As the girl cried another of the fallen entered the room behind her.

"Why does such beauty weep?" he questioned as he drew near to her.

The girl lifted her head from the pillow where she wept to face the intruder. "I do not wish to be here my lord."

"Why not, most count themselves blessed to dwell among us," he informed her as he sat down beside her.

"My heart belongs to another," the girl confessed.

"A mortal who will die young, here you are among gods," the fallen boasted as he lifted her chin to look her directly in the eye.

"I did not consent to come here, your servant stole me from my people," the girl lamented.

"He does not need your consent, your people know the cost of his gift to them, you are that sacrifice," the other god reminded his voice growing harsh now at her continued refusal of their laws.

"I will not surrender to his will," the girl hissed with rage.

"Then you will break under mine," the fallen roared before he threw her down on the bed and ravished her. As he bedded her stealing her innocence for himself; Hermes returned from the errand on which he'd been sent to the sight of Zeus defiling his new bride. His blue eyes glowed with fury at the insult.

"Come," the angel's voice demanded and she turned taking his hand. They left Hermes palace behind and when they emerged once more from the light Anna found they were in Zeus's throne room. She looked on in silence as Hermes with the war god's sword struck down the mighty Zeus.

"The debt you owe me for what you've done to my bride," Hermes hissed in fury. When he turned and left, he took with him a small boy with golden hair and blue eyes. A few moments later a young girl with the same blonde hair and stunning blue eyes entered the throne room to discover the king of the gods dead. She wept at the loss of her father and those blue eyes gleamed with a rage of her own.

"Artemis," Anna said with understanding.

The angel nodded then turned to leave the palace. "Come," he instructed once more and as Anna stood and watched the girl for a moment longer a veil descended between her and Artemis blocking her sight. Anna turned and went after the angel.

"What about the tablets?"

"That is not for you to know," he answered simply before holding out his hand for her to take.

Anna nodded and taking the offered hand, she was swept away once more.

"Remember what you have seen," the angel instructed before he and the dream slipped away and all around her became the still darkness of dreamless sleep.

96

Sam looked over at his sleeping companion and an uneasiness began to wash over him. He wondered if it was wise to take her with him to hunt the killer Lance now pursued. She fit the profile of the killer's desired prey in every detail. By taking her with him to LA he may be placing her life in more danger than even Hermes could bring against her.

The idea didn't sit well. He knew the fate of any woman taken by the Fury Killer, he'd seen it first hand and he had no interest in letting that sick monster get his hands on Anna. The thought of her enduring such suffering turned his stomach and made it hard to breath. No he wasn't about to expose her to this particular demon from his past. Best to leave her someplace safe, Sam reasoned.

He was just about to get up and instruct the pilot to change their destination to Colorado so he could drop her off when Anna woke. She blinked a couple times as if trying to recover from a shock and Sam hoped she'd not argue with him about being left behind.

"How long till we reach LA?" Anna asked.

"There's going to be another delay," Sam stated.

"Why?"

"Because you're not going to LA I'm going to have the pilot drop you off in Denver."

"What? Why? No you can't," Anna said with alarm.

"I don' want you in the same town with the Fury Killer Anna you fit his MO."

"Listen to me Sam I have to go there. Catharine is in more danger than Lance can possibly understand or believe."

"What does that mean?"

"I had a visit from our winged friend, he showed me some things that are in motion now and if I don't do something fast

Catharine will be lost to us," Anna exclaimed.

"What?"

"There's too much to explain now but trust me when I say that the least of Catharine's concerns should be this killer of yours. Dionysus and Ares are both courting her right now," Anna stated.

"Ah hell, Lance isn't going to like this," Sam muttered.

"I understand that you don't want me in harm's way, If I were you I'd want me as far away from the crazed killer as I could get you, but I can't walk away from this or her." Anna stated as she pleaded with him to listen to her.

"All right I won't leave you behind but once we land you don't go anywhere without me or Lance you got me," Sam ordered.

Anna nodded her understanding and Sam drew her into his arms. He brushed a kiss on her head. "Stubborn fool woman you'll get us both killed if you're not careful," he grumbled before he bent his head and kissed her.

Anna smiled as she kissed him back; touched that he cared enough to worry about her, but relieved he'd listened. Aware that if he'd not, she'd of had to find her own way to LA and deal with the fallout of going out there against his wishes.

"Did our annoying winged friend mention anything else when you spoke?" Sam questioned after drawing back from their kiss knowing not to let himself get too lost in it.

"Yeah, there was more but it can wait for now," Anna stated. She didn't know how to tell him that his ex-wife was the new chosen of Hermes and for now the would- be Queen of the gods.

"If you say so," Sam said satisfied.

"So, how long till we get to LA?" Anna asked again.

"We'll be there in about an hour, so long as the weather holds," Sam stated as he rested his chin on the top of her head.

"Do you think Artemis will send a storm to slow us down?" Anna questioned.

"I don't know. I hope not but I lost my cell phone at the castle it's possible she could have found it," Sam stated.

Anna nodded. "She's working for Hermes because her father is dead and her twin taken." Anna stated.

"I take it you got that from your dream too," Sam said amused.

"Yeah but I bet she was lied to about who was responsible," Anna added.

"Why do you say that?"

"Because it was Hermes who did it and if she knew that she'd be trying to kill him not help him."

"Right. So, any idea why the messenger god killed the king of the gods?" Sam asked.

"The same reason a lot of people wanted him dead."

"Wait let's see from the reading you did the other night that would be…" Sam closed his eyes and tried to recall the myths she'd been reading before he kissed her. "Oh yeah, Zeus slept with his wife," Sam exclaimed pleased with himself for actually knowing the answer.

Anna giggled amused by his playful mood despite the circumstances. "That's the one," Anna confirmed.

"You saw Pamela there didn't you?" Sam asked unexpectedly.

Anna blinked startled by his abrupt mood shift. "Why do you ask?"

"You said her name in your sleep. What is it?"

"She's Hermes queen and for now the new Hera." Anna muttered.

"Damn."

"I'm sorry Sam, I know you tried…"

"Nothing for it. She always was driven by knowledge and power, I bet Hermes didn't have to try very hard to seduce her," Sam said bitterly.

"She may not be beyond help," Anna offered.

"Maybe. I can't help but wonder if I'd not married her a year ago if she'd have never met Br… Hermes."

"Don't, this is not your fault, for all you know if you hadn't married her, then maybe we would never have met and I'm the one lost to him," Anna argued.

Sam blinked, he'd seen what would have been if he hadn't have gone with her to Atlantis. She'd have been lost to the monster on the other side of the door. He'd thought at the time it was Hermes but now he wasn't so sure, maybe something else, something worse had awaited her on the other side. The thought of her enslaved to Hermes or the dark figure's will, made his blood run cold and he let the guilt go.

"Point taken," Sam stated as he wrapped his arms more tightly around her. Though he hadn't known her long the idea of her lost to one of the fallen was one he didn't want to consider again.

97

Catharine sat at her laptop struggling to put together her book. She was just cursing the whole damn project when a pair of warm hands took hold of her shoulders and began to massage away the stress. Turning she found herself faced yet again with the vampire lord Syvarin.

"Don't touch me," Catharine ordered outraged.

"Relax my dear I'm here not to hurt you but to help you. Don't you see Serenity the mask you wear as the writer weighs heavy on you and wears you out? Put it down and come back to me. I will ensure you want for nothing. No other will ever love you as I do," he murmured as he brushed her hair away from her neck to caress the pale skin. Running his fingers over the sensitive skin where he'd marked Serenity in the book, with his first mark, to claim her as his life's mate.

"That's not true Lance cares for me," Catharine argued.

"He cares yes, but he can't love you. You said it yourself he loves another. A dead woman you can't compete with that," Syvarin reminded as he turned her to look at him.

"He could learn to love me," Catharine protested.

"Ah, but will he be worth the effort, every man you've ever loved has wound up turning into a monster. Do you really believe he's any different?" Syvarin challenged.

"Lance is no monster, he'd not hurt me," Catharine argued weakly.

"You don't believe that. If you did then how can you explain what you wrote earlier after he scared you at the crime scene? You saw it in him, then the temper, banging things and slamming doors that's how it always starts and his kiss last night was hardly a safe one. The same beast you've faced before lies in wait beneath the surface. You'll see," Syvarin taunted as his hands ran down her arms to latch with her fingers drawing her up out of the chair. He led her over to the vanity mirror.

"I got scared that's all it doesn't mean he will hurt me."

"His temper didn't scare you Catharine, it excited you, because deep down inside you is a truth you struggle to hide, one that I know well. You are my Serenity and the truth is you desire to be wanted by a monster. There is a part of you that craves that darkness because it is what you know. A violent cycle perpetuated by your family. It's in your blood. Just as I am in Serenity's blood," Syvarin whispered. "Look at yourself really look and see," he commanded.

Catharine opened her eyes to stare at her reflection and gasped to watch as her own image faded and the blonde image with the haunted hazel eyes, skin pierced at the neck from his bite stared back at her, wrapped in a thin gauzy gown of black that revealed every inch of her body below it.

"That's not who I am," Catharine argued. "You and she are not real. You're but the shadow of a monster I once knew and want nothing more to do with and she is no more." Catharine snapped outraged.

"I'm more real than your Catharine is Serenity and you know me. Your cop you know not. You watched another like him become a beast; better to stick with the demon you know than to ally yourself with one you don't and find out too late it's worse," Syvarin reasoned. His hands slid down her scantily clad figure teasing and arousing, tempting her to surrender herself to him once more.

Catharine closed her eyes and struggled to rebuff his words. Her body stirred with desire and she cursed herself a fool. The image in the glass was a lie. He did not have the access to her he now claimed to have, Catharine assured herself even as she felt the heat of his skin against her own.

It wasn't real none of it was, she told herself willing her mind to believe it.

"You know my power Serenity, if you desire it I can be him for you," he breathed and Catharine's eyes flew open with shock as Syvarin's voice became like Lance's. The image in the mirror was no longer Serenity and Syvarin but Catharine and Lance only an unnatural glow within the icy depths told her it was not him.

"NO! I won't let you play me as easily as you played Serenity. You are not him and you can never be him. You know nothing about him."

Syvarin returned to his true form and laughed at her. "Foolish Serenity I know your Lance as well as I knew Davrik. You are right to say he is emotionally unavailable, the woman he loves he planned to marry. He will never get over her," Syvarin hissed.

"You're lying," Catharine said her voice shook with her uncertainty and she felt her heart sink as his words lodged themselves deep in her mind.

"No my dear on this I speak truth, the box you opened that night that he took from you held her few meager belongings he still possessed along with the ring he gave her." Syvarin revealed.

"Even if that's true you can't know he'll never get over her," Catharine reasoned.

"I can just as I know that there are places in you that when touched will always answer to me," he breathed and to prove it he lowered his mouth to her throat and licked the flesh where his mark was left upon Serenity drawing a startled and aroused cry from Catharine.

"You see you are my Serenity, only she could know the delicious sensation that now swims through you at the feel of my mouth near my mark the anticipation it brings as she waits for me to sink my fangs once more into the tender flesh to begin the ritual of mating," he said with a thrill.

"I will never be your Serenity as I will never give into this. Be gone from me demon or by God I will…"

"YOU'LL WHAT GIRL, YOU'VE NOT BELIEVED IN YOUR GOD FOR AS LONG AS I'VE KNOWN YOU, DON'T YOU GET IT YET, I AM YOUR GOD NOW," Syvarin hissed before he sank his fangs into her neck.

"God No," Catharine screamed in terror and rage as the vampire lord tore the thin fabric about her to claim what he felt was his. No sooner had the words left her mouth, the dream split apart. The vampire lord cried out in rage at the loss of her as she fell into the gentle and peaceful embrace of a dreamless sleep.

98 Unknown

Russell York moved into his office and sat down behind the desk. His nerves were shot. He'd had one job to do since they lost Kadar and it was simple, obtain the candle for Mr. Halden and take him to the dig site in the Bermuda Triangle. He'd done both successfully and still nearly got himself killed because the statue of Hades turned out to be a fake.

How was that his fault? He was glad that whatever it was that drove his employer had caused him to see reason in the end. Beyond relieved that Mr. Halden's considerable temper was no longer directed at him but Ian Broody. As he punched in the good doctor's number Russell wondered just what it was he'd gotten caught in the middle of.

What was it that Magnus Halden was seeking? As the phone rang he figured he was better off not knowing.

"Come on Ian pick up the damn phone," Russell muttered with annoyance as the phone rang for a fourth time.

How was it that the statue in the cave were fakes and how did Mr. Halden know it? Russell's mind wondered and again he scolded himself reasoning it was none of his business.

"Hello?" Ian Broody's voice questioned with a hint of irritation.

"Mr. Broody we need to talk." Russell stated using his most intimidating voice.

"Mr. York how can I help you?" Ian questioned his voice now calm and polite.

"I was out at the dig site today with the boss and he has some concerns," Russell stated.

"Such as?" Ian inquired with interest.

"The statues in the throne room are fakes!" Russell snapped.

"Yes we had replicas made," Ian explained,

"Where are the real ones?" Mr. York hissed.

"I believe they are being prepped for shipment back to the Smithsonian," Ian said quickly.

"Dr. Broody you were told that nothing in the Atlantis site was to be removed. My employer is not pleased to learn that his instructions have been disobeyed. I'm sure I don't have to tell you that it's not wise to anger Mr. Halden."

"No of course not. What do you need?"

"I need a complete list of pieces that have been shipped out of the site as well as those that are being prepped to ship. If they are still on site see that they are put back."

"Of course Mr. York I will get that list together and fax it over," Ian assured him.

"Good. Thank you Ian I'm sure that we won't need to bring in any of our own people to monitor the dig," Russell said politely before he hung up.

"Well?" Magnus Halden questioned as he looked over at his right hand man.

"He says it's being prepped to ship to the museum but I don't believe him. I'm going to put my best man on him, find out where those statues are sir and I believe it would be in your best interest to place someone on site to reign Broody in; he's hiding something." Russell stated.

"See to it. I want that statue," Magnus barked before he turned and walked out of the room.

Russell York swore before he picked up his phone to make the calls needed in order to carry out his plans. Whatever Ian Broody was up to he'd soon find out.

99 ATHENS, GREECE

The man who was once known as Ian Broody hung up his phone and the god raged throwing the offending object across the room putting a hole in the wall. He cursed as he eyed the ten statues he'd taken from the site at Atlantis. "You will not slip free of my hold," he roared at his brethren trapped within the graven images. They hissed and writhed within their prisons and cursed his name vowing that he would never be their king.

"DO YOU THINK YOUR PUPPET YORK SCARES ME HADES; HE MAY HAVE YOUR SCALE BUT SO LONG AS I HAVE YOU HERE, YOU WILL NEVER BE FREE!" Hermes raged.

"YOU CAN'T HOLD US FOREVER!" Ares voice challenged as clearly as if he stood there and Hermes trembled.

The God of War had grown too strong. His influence on his pet mortal was a powerful one. He needed to find the human connected to the Ares Mantle and kill him before he found a way to lead his disciple to the statue and could seize control, for himself.

Hermes cursed the holes in his memory if he could just recall what the other mantles looked like or where the Zeus Mantle was then he could seal his hold upon the others and ensure he alone became the new king of the gods.

Hermes sighed; it bothered him that he'd had to share his lady with another but if it gained him an ally to stand against the others then he was more than willing to share the lovely Pamela for a short time. Besides it wasn't like the other man could sire an heir with her. Though his pretty wife didn't know it yet his seed within her had already taken root.

The time of the old gods return had begun and it seemed that the war for the crown was soon to follow. Not if he had anything to say about it. If things went according to his design there would be no war. He would cement his claim to the throne first. He was well on his way. He alone of his brethren was free, he had a companion and her belly swelled with his heir all he lacked was Zeus' Mantle.

With Zaharrah's help interpreting the woman Anna's notes he'd have it as well and soon then he'd make the foolish mortal woman regret her refusal of him, he'd see her punished until she renounced her faith in that upstart savior of hers and when she did he'd make her a slave to his will, she would be his bride in time , Hermes vowed.

His temper rose dangerously at the thought of the woman Anna as the mortal's soul imprisoned within stone raged at her refusal of them both. Hermes smiled as he fed off the mortal's fury; his own power strengthening.

"YES I KNOW, I'D HAVE SET HER AS THE QUEEN OF THE GODS BUT SHE SPURNED US AND I PROMISE YOU SHE WILL PAY FOR IT," Hermes whispered to the mortal assuring him that Anna's rejection would not go forgotten.

"What will you do to her?" the spirit asked with interest.

"I WILL MAKE HER GROVEL AT MY FEET."

"Her companion who interfered, he must suffer as well. Make him the first to die on the old alter," Ian hissed.

"NO, I HAVE A BETTER USE FOR THAT MAN," Hermes said with a wicked glee as an idea formed in his mind.

"Tell me," Ian requested.

"I'LL USE THE MAN TO BREAK THE WOMAN. SHE'LL BEG FOR HIS LIFE AND WHEN I ASK HER WHAT SHE WOULD GIVE FOR IT SHE'LL PAY ME ANY PRICE." Hermes said amused. He felt his power swell further as the man thrilled in the idea, fantasizing about it, seeing the woman who'd left; groveling, pleading for the life of the man Sam.

"What will you demand for payment?" Ian asked fascinated, wanting to build upon the sick dream to see it all, his mind hungry for whatever bit of his old life he could latch onto unaware that the more he indulged in Hermes dark desires the more of himself faded away.

"THE PRICE OF HIS LIFE WILL BE A HIGH ONE. WHEN I FINALLY DO BED HER ON THE STONE ALTER SHE WILL BE A WILLING PARTICIPANT; IF ONLY TO SPARE HER PROTECTOR A HORRIBLE DEATH," Hermes stated. He laughed as Ian's mind grabbed hold of the idea and ran with it picturing the act clearly, putting himself in the place of the god.

That's right mortal give yourself over to your hate and rage forget any light you ever knew, feed me the power I need so that I can reign in this realm as the new king of the gods. Hermes urged silently aware that the darker the mortals soul became the easier it would be for him to devour.

"You'll let the man live?" Ian questioned with disbelief.

"NO WHEN HER WILL WAS NO MORE, THE MAN SAM WILL DIE." Hermes declared before he turned his attention from his puppet back to his brethren who raged to see his power grow.

"NONE OF YOU WILL CHALLENGE ME I WILL BECOME THE KING OF THE GODS."

100

Lance came to the end of the sequence Catharine had written; based on their encounter before entering the crime scene and felt a strange mix of distaste and lust run through him together. He was ashamed by the hunger he felt stirring in him after reading the final scene; while steamy it was hardly what he'd call romantic. A bit of hurt joined with the other mixed emotions at the idea she thought he would behave so.

"Did you like it?" Catharine's voice questioned from behind him and he cursed realizing he'd just gotten caught snooping through her things.

"I'm sorry I shouldn't have…" Lance began.

"No need to apologize detective I was foolish enough to leave it open I imagine you couldn't resist. I know if it were me I wouldn't be able to," Catharine said dismissively.

"It was…"

"Yeah."

"Do you really think I'd behave that way?" Lance asked.

"No," she admitted with a measure of faith in his character she wasn't sure she felt.

"Then why did you write it like that?" Lance snapped with irritation.

"You scared me earlier," she confessed.

"What do you mean? When? How?" Lance asked shocked.

"At the crime scene you were angry with me. "

"I wasn't angry."

"Yes, you were. You were banging that box around and you slammed the trunk. It spooked me a little. It felt a little too familiar."

"What does that mean?" Lance asked with interest.

"Nothing," she answered not ready to get into this discussion just yet.

"Bull Shit. You don't get to tell me I scared you by slamming doors and banging box lids and then say it's nothing," Lance snapped. "Not after those couple things have you writing a scene where my proxy all but rapes you," he added with disgust. He watched as she shrank back from him and mentally cursed. "Damn it Catharine I'm not mad at you. Annoyed maybe but even still I'm sure as hell not going to hurt you," he stated working to draw his temper back in line because it was obvious she couldn't handle it.

"You don't have to curse at me detective. I understand you don't like my answer but I'm not ready to discuss this matter with you. I hardly know you." She stated.

"I can respect that as the man who kissed you last night, but you need to understand I'm not just asking as that guy. I'm asking as the cop involved in a homicide investigation and your bodyguard until that killer is caught. You said earlier you think he's after you and I need to know why? What makes you think that? "

"Fair enough," Catharine said with understanding.

"I heard once that writers write about what they know. If that's the case, then I want to know where Dark Heart came from. That is some seriously dark shit. I've read Heart of Glass and most of Heart of Clay, both books are about an innocent young girl barely a woman who is hunted and eventually bedded by monsters. How much of the fiction translates to fact?" Lance asked. The man who kissed her the night before didn't want to know but the cop had to.

To his disbelief, rather than speak she laughed. Not her normal sweet laugh that sounded like bells ringing but a low humorless laugh that had the hair on the back of his neck standing on end. "You find this amusing; because frankly I don't think there's anything funny about that question." Lance said with irritation.

"It is funny to me."

"Then you've got a sick sense of humor Miss Nichols."

"Not funny hah, hah, funny odd. Do you know you're the first person to read the series and ask me that question?" Catharine asked.

Lance blinked stunned. "Nobody?" He asked with disbelief.

"That's right. Everyone else gets so caught up in the beautiful and tragic Serenity they don't even see how dark it is." Catharine said with disgust.

"Not even Bryan?" Lance asked still finding it hard to believe no one had considered the possibility that the author's words were some reflection of her own life.

"Nope. He's as over the moon about Serenity as the rest of my fans," Catharine said with a shrug.

"Well, I'm asking and as the cop I need answers."

"And the man?" she asked curious.

"Doesn't really want to know," Lance admitted.

"Why?" Catharine questioned.

"I don't like the idea of someone hurting you like that," Lance stated.

Catharine nodded. "I'm not going to get into all the details detective, so please don't ask for them, but you are right there is some truth folded within the pages of the fiction," she confirmed.

Lance swallowed, the man feeling sick. A giant ball of fear settled in the pit of his stomach, it chilled him to the bone and cut at him like ice. He felt a need to draw her into his arms and comfort her in an effort to chase the nightmares of her past but the cop stayed his hands. He had to look at her as a witness or suspect on a case. He had to ask the questions that would shed light on the mystery at hand.

"When I asked you if your ex-husband could be responsible for this you said he couldn't; why?"

"Tom isn't the sort to make a public spectacle of his feelings," Catharine stated. "If he killed someone no one would ever hear about it."

"He's like Syvarin," Lance stated with understanding.

Catharine blinked with surprise. "Yes, impressive detective," she stated with a hint of annoyance. "Tom was not the type to use brute strength to get what he wanted he preferred..."

"To play with your head and to manipulate you to his ends," the cop finished seeing her ex's character clearly through the pages of her book. "Did he really kidnap you?" The man asked unable to hold back the question.

"No, the kidnapping is an exaggeration. Tom and I met in New York He was a hotshot attorney with a big name law-firm, don't ask which because I won't say. I came on to staff as a paralegal working to get my law degree. We met and eventually I fell for him. We split for a time; for reasons I won't get into but he tracked me down and convinced me to come back. He asked me to marry him and the idiot that I am; I said yes. After he got his ring on my finger we moved from New York to DC for his career. I quit school and he started to show his true colors. Hell if it wasn't for him and his mother; Dark Heart would have never seen the light of day."

Catharine explained.

"You weren't going to publish it?"

"No, Heart of Glass was supposed to be a coping tool. His Mother read it then passed it on to an editor at the publishing house without talking to me about it and he'd worked the contract; that's why I'm now stuck writing a fourth book. "

"Damn."

"Yeah, real bombshell right? CJ Nichols never wanted to see Dark heart in print," she said with a chuckle.

It was; but he couldn't let her distract him from what he had to do. "Who was before Tom?" The cop questioned.

"Kurt," as she said the name he could see her visibly shake.

"He's the one you think could be our killer. Why?"

"He told me once that if I ever left him he'd kill me. It's not too far of a stretch to see him venting his frustration at losing my trail and killing other women that look like me," Catharine said with disgust.

"You believe him capable of killing you?"

"Yes."

"Why?"

"I'm not going to discuss him any further with you Lance. I'm not ready and neither are you. I'll say one last thing on this matter and then we're going to put Dark Heart and the men they are about away for awhile. I may be wrong about Kurt being the killer because he doesn't know anything about Dark Heart."

"What does that mean?"

"There were aspects at the crime scene staging that reflect things about Serenity and the books creation that I never printed but were in my notes."

"Who had access to your notes?"

"Tom, My in-laws, my editor, a couple of the staff at the publishing house and maybe the cover artist."

"What about Bryan?" Lance questioned.

"Sorry to disappoint you detective but no, Bryan was not privy to that meeting."

"Could anyone else have gained access to them?"

"Maybe, but not likely," Catharine admitted.

"What sort of things?"

"The cover for Heart of Clay almost looked exactly like that. In the end the house decided the readers would like it better if Serenity maintained the torn innocence that my readers fell in love with."

"Shit."

"Yeah, I don't think this is about me detective; I know it is," Catharine stated with regret to have to burst his bubble but knowing he was right the cop needed to know.

"Why didn't you say any of this at the crime scene?"

"And run the risk of the world finding out the Fury Killer is mislabeled and should be Dark Heart Stalker or some other such name. Do you know the media circus that would create? It would require a press meet and I hate public appearances for reasons I'm sure you're beginning to understand. I know you've probably got to share this with agent Blackwood but do me a favor and try to keep this as need to know as possible."

"I'll do what I can," Lance assured her.

"Thanks."

The cop satisfied for now let the rest go as she asked. After all he had parts of his life he wasn't ready to share with her yet either. "You're welcome."

"I'm sorry about the scene I wrote. I'm not planning to keep it that way," she told him.

"I'm glad. I'm sorry if for a minute I made you believe I could become another one of your monsters," Lance whispered. He drew her into his arms to offer her whatever comfort she would allow. He kissed her forehead and ran his hands down her arms.

"I'm scared," she breathed for only him to hear before she buried her face in his shoulder.

"I'm not going to let anything happen to you Catharine," he vowed as he held her tight.

"I feel surrounded by enemies," she confessed, "and some of them are only in my mind," she said.

"Why do you say that?" Lance questioned alarmed.

"I keep having nightmares about Syvarin trying to convince me I'm Serenity," Catharine explained.

Lance felt that ball of icy fear in his gut begin to melt and writhe like serpents. "I'm sure it's just the stress of having to write another book and the film," Lance stated in a bid to ease her mind, even as his own fear grew.

Something Sam said to him before in his favorite bar flitted into his mind. Unbidden the conversation played out in his head again.

"Anna and I have been charged with the task of locating and

protecting ten mantles of the old gods. The cup is one of them."
Sam had revealed to him. Lance had thought it was the alcohol
talking and called him on it.

"Oh hell! Old gods? You've got to be kidding!" Lance had
responded with disbelief.

"I wish I were," Sam answered with a sigh.

"You know how that sounds right?" Lance suggested.

"Yeah, it sounds even more insane when you say that the one
who gave you the task is an angel of God." Sam stated with a
laugh.

"Shit. You are serious. Okay, let's pretend for a moment I
believe you. Anything I should be aware of if I find this cup?"

"Yeah don't touch it. Also if you start having dreams about
gods be afraid," were Sam's parting words of warning on the
matter.

Dreams Sam had warned against them, Syvarin was far from a
god but something about the comment set his thoughts back to that
discussion.

"I hope you're right, I feel like I'm losing my mind," Catharine
said alarmed.

"It'll be okay," he told her, though part of him was beginning to
wonder if the killer hunting her was her only threat.

"I want to believe you," she confessed as she lifted her head to
meet his gaze.

"You can," he assured her before he kissed her. He felt the
tension in her body ease as she lost herself in his kiss. Relieved to
see her spirit lighten once more he told himself he'd help her find
something to do to draw her mind away from all her stress. But
when Sam and Anna got in he was going to ask Anna a little bit
more about the cup and its particular god

101

Sam walked down the steps of the private plane and into the hanger at LAX. When he said they owed Catharine, he hadn't been kidding, if it weren't for the generous writer, he had no doubt that Hermes would have found them by now. Anna's passport was being monitored, had been since she left the dig site. Being able to come and go without passing through security made it possible for them to move about off the grid.

How long this good fortune would continue he didn't know? Sam reasoned that sooner or later with Pamela involved he'd learn of the connection and even the plane would be tracked. He sighed, no point in borrowing trouble now. For the moment they were able to travel undetected. He still wondered if Artemis was going to turn up here on their trail due to his cell phone; if Lance had left anything in his message about where he was there was a good chance she would.

While he had his messages pass coded, he understood that Artemis was working for a man... no a fallen one, who could obtain information out there, so long as it was known to another. Beyond that, Pamela had already proven she could break his passwords; that was clearly how she'd known to find him in Israel. She'd been able to track him via the credit card he'd used in the gift shop. He'd known better than to do that but had figured his identity was yet unknown. He didn't expect his ex to try and follow him. He wished now he hadn't bought the damn aspirin then maybe she never would have crossed paths with Hermes

Sam shook his head, Anna was right wasting time on what if was pointless; changing one thing might change more than that. Deciding it was time to get the show on the road Sam loaded their belongings into the car waiting in the hanger. He made a quick visual sweep of the area. Finding it clear Sam signaled Anna with the go ahead nod and watched as she made her way off the plane.

Her blonde hair was pulled up into a tight bun. Sam pulled a ball cap out of the car along with a pair of sun glasses. He set the cap on her head careful to tuck all her hair inside. And then gave her the shades to cover her eyes. Sam was taking no chances. They were in the same city as the Fury Killer and he wasn't about to let the sick son of a bitch see that Anna was to his particular taste.

When he was sure she was as well disguised as he could make her on the move, Sam opened the car door and let her in. He then pulled out her phone and punched in Lance's number.

102

Lance felt Catharine ease back from his kiss and cursed; there she went again. Every time he got a little too close she spooked. He blinked as he reminded himself she had good reason to. He didn't know the full extent of what she'd been through but given what he'd read he knew it was bad.

"Sorry, I shouldn't have done that you're not ready and honestly neither am I," he admitted.

Catharine nodded. "Thank you for understanding," she said sheepishly.

"I don't at least not fully but I've seen enough to know I've got no business adding even unintentional pressure or stress. If we do take the next step forward into whatever this is between us it will be when you're ready," he assured her.

Catharine smiled and wrapped her arms around him. Lance held her close to him for a moment but the sound of his phone ringing brought an abrupt end to the peaceful moment. Lance reluctantly let go of Catharine and answered the phone.

"Hello."

"We're in the neighborhood; where are you?" Sam's voice asked with impatience.

"James Hardagen's home," Lance replied he rattled off the address and then said, "Sam step on it things are worse than I originally thought."

"We're on our way, hold tight for a little bit longer," Sam answered before he ended the call on his side.

Lance hung up his phone and drew a breath, he'd never been more relieved to hear the cavalry was coming. He just wished he'd had a chance to talk to Anna before Sam hung up. Lance reminded himself he could always call her back but reasoned their chat could wait a few more minutes.

"They're here?" Catharine asked surprised.

"Yeah, they're on their way, now we won't be on our own for too much longer," Lance assured her.

"But Anna..."

"I'm sure Sam has it covered." Lance stated. He didn't even want to think about the possibility of the mad man setting his eye on Anna and seizing the opportunity presented to claim another convenient target.

"If it gets too dangerous for her we could always send her out," Catharine suggested.

"Same goes for you," Lance muttered.

"I can't run from this guy Lance and you know it. If I do innocent people will suffer for it." Catharine argued.

"I'm not going to sit back and watch while this guy hunts you Catharine. If I think it's too dangerous you're gone!"

"Whatever you say detective," she muttered with irritation.

"How is it I always seem to say the wrong thing where you're concerned when I'm trying to look out for you?" Lance snapped exasperated.

"It's not what you're saying Lance it's how you say it. I'm not one of your rookies, or even a black and white beat cop, you can order around, so stop trying."

"Don't you get that what I'm telling you is for your own good?" Lance questioned with disbelief.

"I've spent more years than I care to admit doing what other people told me because they had my best interest at heart. I don't take orders from anyone anymore." Catharine snapped.

"You are the most infuriating woman I've ever met," Lance muttered. "I can understand your reluctance to listen but you need to understand; I'm not them."

"I know."

"No, you don't. Not really. You have a reasonable mistrust of men and a general dislike of anyone that dares to try and tell you how to run your life. That's normal given what's happened to you, but you can't let fear run your life. What I'm saying isn't to control or hurt you it's to help you." Lance stated calmly trying to reason with her.

"I get that but Lance if I'm right and this is about me then the only way we're going to stop this guy is if I..." Catharine began.

"No. Not another word. I know what you're going to say Catharine and I won't hear it. So put that idea out of your head."

Lance snapped before he turned away from her.

"Ah! You're behaving like such a cave man, why do I always bring that trait out in men," Catharine grumbled as she crossed her arms over her chest and stared at his back.

"I don't want to see anything bad happen to you Catharine."

"And I can't sit by and let innocent people die in my place," Catharine countered.

Lance opened his mouth to argue further but a knock sounded at the door.

"Lance, CJ are you expecting guests?" Emily questioned with interest.

"Yeah, sorry I didn't mention it when I got home. I called an old friend in to help with handling security around here for you and CJ as well as to assist with the hunt. He was bringing a friend. They're names are Sam Abrams and Anna Gallagher." Lance explained.

"Oh, well your guests are here," Emily's voice said pleasantly from the other side of the door. "I'll go let them in."

"We'll finish this discussion later," Lance muttered.

"It is finished," Catharine snapped before she moved to leave. Lance grabbed her by the arm to stop her and she shrugged him off. He cursed mentally knowing he'd made a mess of that but aware it couldn't have gone any other way. He wasn't about to let her attempt what she was thinking; if he lost her... Lance brushed the image aside unable to face it. Not sure if he could face the death of another person he cared about at that mad man's hands.

103

Sam stood in the main hall of Mr. Hardagen's home, Anna was to his right and a little behind him. He held their bags, his eyes moving over his surroundings. He noted the various cameras and the top end security system and could see the reason for their destination. The place was a veritable fortress. If the Fury Killer was indeed out there watching, waiting for a chance to strike; James Hardagen's home was a secure place to keep Miss Nichol's.

"They're on their way down, you'll have to excuse James he's upstairs resting after his scare earlier today," Emily stated as she re-entered the hall. The pretty brunette woman had only opened the door to them after confirming that Lance was expecting them and learning their names.

"That's fine I'm sure we'll meet him later. Sorry for the intrusion," Anna stated before she took off her sunglasses. The brunette gasped at the sight of her hazel eyes.

"Oh my you have amazing eyes, do they change with what you wear?" Emily asked with interest.

"Yes," Anna replied as she hung the shades from the collar of her shirt. "I'd take off the hat but I'm not allowed until I'm clear of the windows," Anna stated.

Emily nodded. "So, what is it you do for a living Mr. Abrams?" Emily asked wondering how Lance knew him.

Sam tensed not caring for the awkward meet and greet with their hostess. He was going to give Lance a piece of his mind for the lack of notice to their hosts to his coming. He was there to pay back a favor not on a social visit and Lance knew him well enough to know he hated to walk into the middle of a lot of chitchat and questions about who he was. He was about to answer her having little choice when Lance and Catharine came down the steps. Sam stopped his mental tirade in its tracks at the sight of the detective.

To the casual observer the other man seemed fine but Sam was not the average man. He saw the worry lines in the cop's brow, the start of dark smudges under the eyes. Ice blue that was normally calm and emotionless, were near wild. A mix of fear and temper just below the surface, his smile was a forced one, jaw tight. Lance Roman was on edge. It seemed that whatever had shifted before they landed was worse than Sam had figured on.

"Sam thank you for dropping everything and coming out here," Lance said. Sam noted the other man visibly relaxed at the sight of him. "Anna I see he's got you taking steps to ensure you don't draw unwanted attention."

"I tried to get her to stay behind," Sam stated with a hint of irritation.

"That might have been better," Catharine said as she eyed the other woman with concern.

"I'll go if you do," Anna challenged as she studied the pretty writer.

"Lance tried to get me to but I told him if I leave this guy will just follow me or other innocent people will suffer at his hand," Catharine stated.

"If she's staying then I do too," Anna declared.

"You don't have to," Catharine assured her.

"Um tell you what we can finish this discussion in the lounge. I wasn't expecting anyone so I'll need to prepare a room..." Emily began. Sam's back stiffened at the comment. "Or two," she amended aware she'd made a bad assumption. "Catharine why don't you show Anna to your room she can put her things in there for now and freshen up if she wants."

Catharine nodded and Anna took her bag from Sam. The two moved up the stairs out of sight leaving Sam and Lance alone with their hostess.

"Lance, show Mr. Abrams into the lounge. I'll go get James and then see about those rooms," Emily stated before she too retreated from the hall.

"You look like shit Lance," Sam stated once their hostess was out of ear shot.

"Gee thanks."

"What gives?" Sam asked with concern.

"I'll explain it all later, part of it I'll get into once our host joins us." Lance stated.

Sam nodded. "I was going to slug you for not telling your host we were coming," Sam muttered.

"I deserve it," Lance stated "why aren't you now."

"Can't bring myself to kick a friend when he's down," Sam stated before he turned to follow the detective into the lounge to wait for their host.

104

Catharine opened the door to her room and flipped on the light; Anna whistled at the sight of the room. "Nice digs," she said with appreciation.

"Thanks our host's idea of a guest room is more like a grand suite," Catharine said amused.

"How are you dealing with everything going on?" Anna asked as she set her bag on the floor.

"I've been better. Lance and I are butting heads over the whole thing."

"Why?"

"He's trying to boss me around."

"It's because he cares. Sam tried to muscle me out of here as well," Anna stated with a sigh.

"Cave men," Catharine muttered.

"No, that's not how they behave. They behave like knights of old or cops. Not sure why Sam does, he was a reporter and is an MMA fighter. Something strange there I haven't figured it out yet. If they were cave men we'd have been popped over the head by now and dragged off for our own good," Anna corrected.

Catharine smiled amused. "Okay I stand corrected."

"The question isn't his behavior here, because his desire to get you out of harm's way is understandable. The real issue is why does it bother you so much that he is behaving so?" Anna reasoned.

"I…" Catharine began in her defense.

"You don't have to answer me just think about it. Now enough of that I'm here for a reason. I had a dream that you were in grave danger."

Catharine froze. "What kind of dream?"

"In it I saw the graven images at the dig, three were moving, one is Hermes which I was aware of, the other two are Dionysus and Ares."

"The War god and the god of Wine?"

"Right. Here's where it gets weird so bear with me?" Anna requested.

Catharine nodded as the two sat down on the lounger. "Okay, talk me through it."

"First I'll tell you about the images themselves. The real one depicts the gods marching in a set order. Some of the gods embracing their wives, for example Zeus is holding Hera and Demeter is clinging to him. Hades holds Persephone."

"Okay I'm with you."

"In the dream Hermes had taken the position of Zeus in the image, he's now in control of the pantheon. In his embrace was the new Hera—Pamela. She's his bride. "

"Got it."

"Okay now here's where it gets rough. Dionysus's bride is not set, the first face I didn't know until I got here, but the second one is yours. Have you been having any weird dreams lately?" Anna questioned.

"Yeah one of my character's, he's been tormenting me lately," Catharine replied.

"Who?"

"Syvarin."

"It's not Syvarin it's Dionysus, it makes perfect sense in Roman myth he's called Baucus and some myths have him as the origin of the vampire. He must love playing the role."

"Okay, still following you."

"When the image is you, Dionysus's embrace changes he has you by one arm trying to draw you in, and Ares has you by the other, his eyes are only fixed on you. When it's the other woman Emily, Ares has you in his grasp. Catharine the dreams you're having are not natural you are being courted by the fallen."

"This is all too much," Catharine muttered with disbelief and yet she'd felt the effect of Dionysus's influence earlier that day.

"I know, believe me I thought it was madness when Hermes pursued me, but there is nothing safe about what is happening to you and it is real."

"What can I expect? How can I protect myself against them?" Catharine questioned.

"This spirit will try to get hold of you and bend you to its will. It will make you think and feel that you want it. It will play upon your weaknesses and try to convince you to embrace it and if that doesn't work, then it will try to buy your consent with promises of things you desire most. If you anger him he will take what he desires at least in your mind by force. He has a connection to you."

"Such as?"

"Your tie to Dionysus is easy to see; storytelling, theatre began with his followers and beyond that the vampire is prominent in your own work. That he's appeared to you as Syvarin speaks volumes, he wants you to think he's part of your mind, it makes it easier for him to manipulate you. As for Ares I'm not sure but he too feels he has a right; maybe even a stronger claim to you."

"I have an idea what that might be. So what do I do about it?"

"They will use that foothold to try and strengthen their influence over you. You can't let either one get to you. Your only defense is crying out to God for aid. Don't speak with them. "

"God?" Catharine questioned with disbelief. Anna was the last person she'd have ever thought would bring up God.

"Yes. I know…"

"God is not anyone I can turn to… I walked away from him a long time ago when he abandoned me," Catharine hissed.

Anna blinked, stunned by the ferocity of the other woman's voice.

"Catharine, I understand…"

"You can't possibly understand how I feel about this, so don't patronize me Miss Gallagher. Quite frankly I'm dumbfounded you'd even bring him up; you're an anthropologist and an intellectual. How can you believe in a loving God when you've seen firsthand the atrocities that happen in this world," Catharine raged.

"You're right I can't understand how you feel. I'm sorry I shouldn't have said that; each of us bares our own troubles, but if you can believe me that there are fallen ones, old gods as they like to pretend; then why the refusal to believe in a divine creator?"

"I don't deny there is a creator but I can't swallow that crap they told me growing up about how he loves us always and never forsakes us. If that were so then why does it feel like he lost sight of me," Catharine said with frustration.

"He hasn't, he sent one of his angels to me in a dream to warn you of the storm you're caught in. I'm here now because he does love you and doesn't want to see you fall as Serenity did," Anna whispered.

"Nice, well it's too little too late," Catharine stated before she rose from the couch and left.

Anna cursed, well now she could see Ares influence on the other woman, she'd never been witness to such rage in another before and Anna wondered at the cause of it. She drew a breath and whispered a prayer to the heavens for aid; it seemed that performing the task she'd been given was going to prove harder than she initially believed.

105

Emily stepped into the room she shared with James and found he was no longer resting in their bed. She walked over to his desk and found him sitting in his chair in front of the computer. He was flipping through a stack of head shots. Looking for the girl who had been murdered Emily figured as she joined him.

"So, who was at the door then?" James questioned.

"It seems Lance invited a friend to lend a hand with security. He forgot to mention it earlier." Emily stated a bit exasperated.

"I see and who are they?"

"The woman's name is Anna Gallagher. I don't know a whole lot about her yet. Haven't even really gotten a feel for what she looks like. The man is Sam Abrams, I was just asking him what it was he did for a living when Lance and Catharine emerged from their rooms."

"Sam Abrams?"

"Yeah that's right do you know him?" Emily asked surprised.

"Man where is he?" James asked like a kid at Christmas.

"In the lounge waiting; who is he?"

"He is one of the guys I saw fight in Vegas while I was out there," James said excited.

"Oh, well then why don't you head downstairs and introduce yourself. I'll see about getting a couple rooms ready." Emily said with a smile aware that Sam and Anna would indeed be staying on as house guests.

"Put them in the rooms across from Miss Nichols and the detective," James instructed.

Emily nodded and then departed. James pulled the head shot for the dead girl to give it to Lance then got up from his chair and headed for the lounge to meet Mr. Abrams and feel out Miss Gallagher.

106

Lance looked up from his seat as James Hardagen entered the room. His blue eyes watched him with mistrust. The bizarre encounter Catharine had described having with the other man made him jealous, angry and unsure. A war was stirring inside him; one that told him to strike out and defend but his rational mind told him that to do so was wrong.

"Sam Abrams, meet James Hardagen our host," Lance stated as he indicated the blond haired blue eyed actor who'd taken on the task of directing the Dark Heart films.

"Mr. Hardagen," Sam said with a nod.

"Mr. Abrams I saw your fight in Vegas, it was impressive. I'm surprised you're not in the gym gearing up for the next one," James said with amusement.

"I would be, but unfortunately that elbow to the face broke my orbital bone. I'm out for at least eight weeks." Sam explained.

"A shame," James said.

"I'll get back in the ring in time," Sam stated.

"I'm sure. Detective here is the photo of the girl found earlier today," James supplied as he handed over the head shot."

"Thanks, I'll be sure agent Blackwood gets it. Since we're alone I feel I should inform you both of the latest development in the case. After speaking with Catharine earlier it has become abundantly clear to me that she is in the center of this."

"What's changed?" James questioned.

"What I'm about to say goes no further than this room. Mr. Hardagen. It's being shared with you because you've allowed Catharine to stay here and the man chasing her is an opportunist, he may turn and take Emily simply because she's near CJ."

"Understood."

"The sight you saw this morning James and the one with which you are familiar Sam, the way the victims are posed is connected to Dark Heart. The victims are not Furies as we originally believed...."

"They are Serenity," James gasped with understanding.

"Yes. Apparently the picture we see is an alternate cover image for Heart of Clay."

"Shit." Sam cursed with displeasure.

"What is wrong Mr. Abrams?" James asked startled by the other man's sudden mood shift.

"My friend, she's a perfect look alike for Serenity," Sam muttered.

"I see."

"She won't leave?" Lance asked with displeasure.

"Afraid not," Sam confirmed.

"Then we keep her hidden. She doesn't go anywhere alone, none of them do?" Lance said in a tone that made it clear that the order would be carried out.

"Agreed," Sam answered his mood returning to the cool control that he possessed upon first meeting his host.

"Right, so you feel Emily is in danger as well then?" James asked surprised.

"No one near CJ Nichols is safe. So consider carefully James if you still want her staying here." Lance warned.

"I appreciate your candor with me detective but it will not change my offer of invitation. CJ is safer here than on her own and I owe her a great deal, her books have likely saved my career and reputation as an actor." James stated.

"Okay then, I have to update Agent Blackwood on all of this. For now I don't want the case discussed in front of the ladies. I won't have them involved." Lance ordered.

"Done," Sam answered without a second's hesitation. He was in agreement with the detective the less Anna knew about the case and his connection to it the better.

After a moment of doubt James nodded his agreement.

"Good. We'll discuss the matter further when the opportunity rises. For now, I suggest we table the discussion as the women could come in at any moment," Lance stated.

"Emily is upstairs preparing rooms for you and Miss Gallagher. You'll be directly across the hall from CJ and the detective. Mr. Abram's room has the same access as yours detective. I trust you'll explain later," James stated.

"Right," Lance answered assuring his host it would be handled.

"Excellent, if there is nothing else you gentlemen require I have business to attend to," James stated.

"We're square," Lance assured the other man. He then sat and watched as their host left. Once James was gone Lance drew a breath to steady his nerves.

"I take it there's something more," Sam said knowingly.

"Yeah, I'm not sure how much our host can be trusted," Lance revealed.

"I see," Sam said his voice hinted, he didn't care for where this was headed.

"A new wrinkle has surfaced and it's left me troubled."

"If you're not sure he's safe then why are we staying here?" Sam demanded.

"Security here is better than at a hotel. It's a private residence less public endangerment this way. Harder for anyone to bug the place you know the drill."

"What kind of wrinkle?" Sam questioned seeing the detective's point.

Lance checked to make sure no one was coming before he began to relate the events that had transpired earlier according to Catharine.

"Damn, it seems Anna was right she needed to come," Sam muttered.

"What does that mean?" Lance asked.

"I'm not sure I can explain it effectively, you'll need to talk with her when she comes down. For now I suggest you take this time to make your calls and finish up business," Sam stated.

Lance nodded. He turned his attention from his associate to his phone and stepped out of the lounge into the privacy of the empty hallway. Punching in the number for Gail he waited for the FBI agent to pick up. As the phone rang he considered his words carefully, aware that if he said too much Agent Blackwood and Kessler would have no choice but to pull him off the team.

107 LAX

Artemis stepped off the plane which Hermes had given her for hunting the woman. Behind her the sun began to set in the distance. A westerly wind brushed against her skin in greeting and the news it carried made her eyes glow bright with fury.

HE was here. Hermes messages had said nothing of the War god's beginning to move. She'd worked long and hard over the years to ensure that Ares never rose from the ashes of the disaster that had befallen the gods. That he had managed to slip through her grasp made her blood boil. The sky above began to stir clouds, gathering lightening crashed and she blinked.

Now was not the time to lose her grip of the heavens. To create a storm now where none had been would only alert the War god to her presence and she did not want him to know she was there. The woman Anna could wait. From here on in Artemis's hunt was for Ares. This time she would see to it her Father's murderer paid for his crimes. Ares would never rise to power again. His puppet would fall and no other would ever possess his mantle again.

108

Zaharrah made her way down the dark corridors of the old god's temple toward the library where she'd been at work for months now, sifting through ancient scrolls and texts. She took a seat at her work space and once more began the task of sifting through Anna's research. Though she knew the meaning behind it she had to maintain the guise of doing the work which Broody had assigned her.

She struggled to focus her mind, buzzed with concern for the safety of Darrian and all those involved here at the dig. Her meet with the elders of the 'Black Hand' troubled her. There was something more going on here than what they were saying. They were to wound up over the assignment being completed. She cursed them and their damn secrets she'd spent her whole life doing their bidding blindly. Unaware of why or what was really happening.

She'd once been as blindly loyal to the order as Darrian but something had changed for her in Ithaca. What it had been even she couldn't explain fully but being there crossing paths with Anna and Broody had shaken her from slumber. She'd begun to seek answers and had not cared for what she discovered. Something inside her had told her that the cause she fought for was a fool's war and she'd walked away.

In doing so she'd given up her most valued possession but it had been worth it.

Zaharrah turned her thoughts from the dangerous path it was wandering down and back to the notes in front of her. She had to stay focused on the task at hand. Get the work done and get Darrian out of there.

"Dr. Lynch so good to see you back, I trust your trip was a success?" Ian Broody's voice questioned from behind her.

Zaharrah turned to face the man her instincts warning her not to let him have any advantage over her. The simple, and harmless, if not glory hungry, scientist she'd met in Ithaca was not whom she now stood before. No this man was a threat to her and to any who opposed him. Whatever Anna was up to, going after these mantles, she'd walked into a hornets nest, if she was challenging him.

Zaharrah felt a foreign power press against her mind seeking to enter and tightened her protective measures. "Yes, the matter has been handled."

"Back at it already, that's good to see have you uncovered anything new?" Ian questioned his eyes locked with hers and a faint blue glow came from the irises. Zaharrah blinked and felt her mind's defenses begin to weaken. She realized that if she lied in that moment he would see it. He would see the lie and in its discovery see all the secrets she kept so carefully hidden.

Unwilling to let that happen Zaharrah made a dangerous choice. "As a matter of fact I was just noting that there is a difference between the statues here in Atlantis and the ones in Sodom and Gomorrah." Zaharrah revealed.

"There is?" Dr. broody questioned with fascination.

"Yes. In the pictures here, the statues stand with nothing in their hands, but in the images from Sodom and Gomorrah they each hold an object. Hermes holds a horn, Hades the scales, Eros a bow, Helios a whip, Ares a sword, Chaos a scroll, Zeus has the crown upon his brow, Poseidon a trident, and Hephaestus wear his gauntlets for forging and Dionysus his cup."

"So then these are the mantles the tablet speaks of," Ian said with excitement.

"It would seem so," Zaharrah confirmed.

"Excellent work Dr. Lynch keep at Anna's notes, perhaps they will hold a clue as to where we will find these mantles," Broody instructed before he turned and left.

Zaharrah turned back to Anna's notes grateful to be free of the man's gaze. As she pulled herself back together Zaharrah was sure of one thing, the man she'd just spoken with was not Dr. Ian Broody.

She wasn't even sure that he was human anymore. Her gut told her that Ian had gotten his hands on one of the mantles already and as the legend she'd read years ago suggested the man was gone and in his place was an old god. If she were a betting woman which she wasn't, she'd lay odds on his being Hermes the god of Knowledge.

109

Hermes made his way from his library into the work space designated for the mortal he'd taken the place of. He let his thoughts wander over the information Zaharrah had delivered him concerning the mantles. He could see them in his mind now. Ten artifacts given to him in a gilded chest, a gift from his bride forged in secret by an unknown hand. Tools meant to speed their efforts in concurring the mortal world.

Each god was to endow the gift with part of his power and present it to a mortal champion. Someone they trusted to concur and rule. The mortal would spread their influence into territories beyond the lands they currently ruled over and spread their religion with others. The mantle would ensure the mortal chosen remained loyal, so long as they wielded it, no rebellion would ever rise to turn against them. In short the gift and power would allow them to succeed in enslaving men where their prince had failed.

He'd taken his with delight, at the treasure and his bride's finally submitting to his authority over her. He'd assured her that the others would be given to his brethren the night of the Solstice feast.

In the gift he'd also seen an opportunity to claim his vengeance upon Zeus and let his enemy take the fall for the act. Knowledge was the thing he treasured above all other things and he understood in a way his brethren did not that knowledge was the most powerful of weapons. If wielded correctly it could slay even the mightiest of warriors. With the knowledge he now held Hermes set his heart and mind to slaying the mighty Zeus the self-appointed king of the gods.

Hermes blinked as the memory faded back into nothingness. Only the image of the mantles remained in his mind burned there like a brand behind his eyes. He smiled aware then of the location of Helios whip, the mortal Broody had held it in his hands some years earlier long before Sodom was discovered. The whip waited for any who could see it in Ithaca, now all he had to do was collect it before Miss Gallagher remembered it.

110

James Hardagen sat at his desk reading over the pages of the second script which Catharine had given him the night before. He was in the midst of noting camera angles and lighting changes when he became aware of another's presence within the room. Turning he smiled at the sight of Pamela Walsh standing on his balcony studying him.

"So you did come I wasn't sure you would," James said amused.

"I told you there is still much we can learn one from the other," Pamela purred as she crossed the floor to his side. She knelt before his feet and kissed his hand in an old display of respect and James laughed.

"I've forgotten how cunning the lord of knowledge truly is, He sends to me one that he knows I cannot turn away," James whispered before he drew her into his arms and nipped her ear.

"You seek information on the mortal Catharine," Pamela stated.

"I do and you wish to know more about the murder; there is much I have learned since last we spoke," James teased as he nipped at her neck.

"Then I believe an exchange is in order," Pamela murmured as her hands played over his body.

"Come, I will show you much," James assured her," he took her by the hand and lead her back out of the house the way she'd come in. Slipping into the limo he ordered the driver take him to the studio before he turned his full passion loose on Hermes slut. Partaking in all the fruits of her bounty that were offered thrilling in the taste of her powered blood growing stronger with every sip.

111

Lance hung up his phone as Catharine walked into the lounge, Anna was a few strides behind her and clearly upset.

"Anna you got a second?" Lance asked.

"Sure, what do you need?" she questioned as she turned her focus from the writer to the cop.

"A couple things, they're kind of related," Lance admitted.

"Okay."

"First, I guess… is that cup you're looking for, could the clay have been hiding something else?" Lance blurted out.

Anna blinked shocked by the question, the last thing she expected to be on his mind right now was the missing goblet.

"Yeah it could have. The cup was unnaturally heavy for being made of only clay. Why do you ask?"

"Catharine had her hands on a cup earlier and it had a strange effect on her. My first thought was maybe it was your mantle thing, but when she told me it wasn't clay I dismissed it as coincidence what happened. Like maybe Mr. Hardagen had drugged her."

"Tell me what happened." Anna instructed.

"Well she said she felt suddenly very drunk though she'd only had a few sips of wine and she…" Lance began trying to put into words, the rest made his temper rise once more. Why couldn't he get his jealousy in check here?

"No need to say it I think I can imagine. It's possible she did have contact with the mantle." Anna stated.

"What can you tell me about Dionysus?" Lance asked.

"Well, he was the god of wine and debauchery to put it bluntly. His followers began the art of the theatre as we know it today. His roman version was a far darker manifestation as the legends go Baucus as he was called was the father of the vampire."

"Son of a bitch," Lance muttered with disgust.

"Yeah. I know you don't believe all this stuff about old gods and people being possessed…"

"It's a little too fantastic to grasp," Lance admitted.

"You're right to worry for her. Catharine is in more danger than you or she can possibly know." Anna warned.

"Sam said you came here for Catharine. Why?"

"I had a dream in it I saw that Catharine was being weighed as a potential bride for two of the fallen."

"Two? If one is Dionysus then who is the other?"

"Ares."

"The War god?" Lance questioned.

"Right."

"Catharine is not one to declare war," Lance said seeing the idea as absurd.

"War is more than battle, its conflict, anger, hate, rage, wrath and strife. The woman I just spoke with is full of these emotions. CJ Nichols is hiding things about herself beneath that calm cool exterior. She's in great pain Lance and it makes her very angry and mistrustful."

"This is ridiculous the whole notion, mantles with power and old gods returning seeking to bed mortals its crazy, Anna."

"I know how it sounds but it's true."

"I don't believe…" Lance began exasperated.

"That's why I'm here," Anna admitted before she moved on.

Lance cursed before moving back into the lounge to join the others.

112

Sam watched as Anna made her way into the lounge from the hall. Her shoulders were stiff, a worry line marred her brow and he wondered what had happened since she left his side. She sank down on the couch next to him but to his disappointment and surprise maintained a respectful distance from him that she'd not bothered with since he'd rescued her in the throne room under Atlantis.

"What's troubling you," Sam questioned with concern at her sudden mood shift.

"The cup is here," Anna muttered in reply.

"You're sure?" Same asked with disquiet, understanding now the avoidance of closeness with him. If she was right that meant they were sitting in the center of the lair of their enemy and revealing too much about themselves left them vulnerable. It also meant she didn't want to draw any extra attention from her host.

"Yes, I think Catharine actually held it just before we got here," Anna admitted.

"Damn."

"I've got to find it and get it away from Mr. Hardagen."

"How do you propose to do that?" Sam inquired his voice hinting at temper; this was not a good idea. Moving to take it, if she got caught, well he wasn't keen on the notion of her angering another of the fallen.

"Not sure yet, I'll think of something," Anna assured him.

"Be careful okay, you've already got one god, fallen whatever you want to call them mad at you I don't want to see you ending up in another one's cross hairs," Sam stated.

"I'll do my best to keep off his radar," she promised him.

"Good," Sam murmured with relief. He wanted to draw her close to him to brush her lips with a gentle kiss but knew it was ill advised. The less insight their host had into the dynamic of their relationship the better. If a fallen was involved here he'd use that connection to his advantage.

"Who are you really Sam?" Anna questioned her hazel eyes studied him with curiosity.

Sam cursed, he'd hoped to avoid this topic for a while yet. He should have known Anna would see the inconsistency in his behavior, the little hints that he was more than what he pretended to be. "What do you mean?" Sam questioned feigning ignorance though part of him wanted to tell her everything where with Pamela he'd never come clean. He wondered why now he needed to be honest when with the woman he'd married and claimed to love he'd been able to lie.

"I mean in the hotel room you fought off a dozen men like it was child's play, now recently you wielded a sword like you'd done it for years. You knew how to treat a bullet wound and you drove to evade a tail like it was as second nature as breathing. A fighter doesn't have those instincts and neither does a reporter. So who are you?"

"Now's not the time for this discussion," Sam warned as the click of Emily's heels echoed down the hall signaling her return.

"Later then," Anna relented as the other woman joined them in the lounge.

"Your rooms are ready now, why don't you go get settled in then join us out by the pool," Emily suggested.

Anna nodded and rose to her feet. Catharine smiled and followed Emily from the room. Sam got up to follow Anna upstairs to their rooms but then turned his attention back to Lance. "What did Mr. Hardagen mean earlier with his comment about the room having the same access as yours?" Sam questioned.

"There's a door that connects your room to Anna's a key will be waiting for you."

Sam blinked not caring for the news. If there was a key for the passage there might be more than one. Which meant their host may just have the power to come and go from their personal space as he pleased. And if that were so Sam could think of a dozen other less pleasant scenarios that were possible as well. As soon as he got unpacked Sam intended to make sure that their fortress was as secure as it appeared.

113

Catharine settled into one of the pool deck chairs and tried to relax, all that talk with Anna about old gods and dreams had shaken her more than she cared to admit. Her anger at the notion of turning to God for aid had stunned her. She'd been unaware of just how upset she was at the lord she'd once loved as a child. Catharine was also hyper aware of the fact that it had only been when she called out to the creator she now railed against, that she'd escaped her nightmares.

Guilt clawed at her insides for the cold defiance she'd shown moments before but she couldn't shake off the way she felt either. The things that had happened to her after her mother died were not the kind of things a loving God would allow to happen to a child of his; her mind raged.

"I think I'll get some drinks going, you look like you could use one after the day you've had," Emily said with compassion.

"Thanks," Catharine answered feeling a new wave of guilt for the things she'd been feeling earlier for this woman's lover and fiancé. Anna's comment about preventing her from falling as Serenity did, played over in her mind and she laughed at the notion.

"You find something amusing about this situation?" Lance questioned.

Catharine opened her eyes and looking up found him standing over her. Those cold, cop, icy blue eyes of his watching her closely trying to read whatever was on her mind. "Not the situation." She assured him.

"Then why are you laughing that god awful laugh that makes my cop senses go crazy," Lance asked.

"It's a private joke detective," she stated her voice a bit testy.

"Care to let me in on it," Lance asked.

He was angry with her again she noted; he understood that this particular laugh was not a good one. How did he know? She wondered, he knew nothing about her and yet he saw things he shouldn't. "Not right now," she replied simply. If she had her way he'd never know the meaning behind this particular laugh. There were some things about her past she wasn't about to share not even with him.

"Whatever, look, there's something I think you should know about your room," Lance stated now that he had a minute alone with her.

"What's that detective," she questioned as she studied him with interest. He was tense, now uneasy about something. She watched as he knelt down beside her chair those icy eyes lit within as temper flared again. He didn't like her being so formal with him; interesting.

"It's connected to mine by a door. Our host gave me a key for the lock."

Catharine blinked at that; her blue eyes widening with fear at the implications. "I see so he just gave you free reign to come and go from my bed as you please unobserved, detective," she said her own temper flaring. She didn't like being maneuvered or manipulated and what Lance was saying sure made it sound like James Hardagen had taken steps to ensure that she and the detective wound up giving into their mutual attraction.

But perhaps more unnerving was the fact that her host may well have had the same ability until he gave the key to Lance or worse yet, James Hardagen may still possess the means to do so as he chose.

"Yes, I have no intention of using that key Catharine but I thought you should know it existed," Lance murmured.

Thank you for the warning detective I appreciate your candor…"

"Stop that." Lance muttered interrupting her.

"Stop what?"

"Stop acting like we've just met and are no more than a couple of strangers, I don't like it," Lance warned.

"But we have only just met detective and in all honesty you're little more than a stranger to me," she reminded.

"You know that's not true," he challenged. She watched as those cool blue eyes of his began to melt as the desire he felt for her began to stir inside him once more.

Catharine bit her lip as the hunger she'd felt earlier for him rose through anger and fear to crowd her thoughts. Unbidden the memory of his kiss flooded her thoughts and made her ache with the desire to feel his wicked mouth hot and wild against her own. Her skin burned with the need of his touch as she mentally undressed him with her eyes.

"Do I detective?" she questioned with amusement as she pushed him a little more. Part of her was waiting for his control to snap, knowing when it did he'd forget his promise to not press her. That delicious mouth of his would press against hers and take what he wanted from her and what she now desired of him. While the other half of her questioned what the hell was wrong with her.

"Catharine," he breathed her name; the word both a plea and a warning.

"Detec…"

She didn't get to finish the taunt as his lips were on hers cutting it off muffling the rest. His kiss was hard and demanding bruising her lips. His fingers fisted in her hair holding her in place for him as he stole her breath away.

Catharine laughed to herself at the victory, as he lost himself in the kiss. Yes this was what she wanted her mind crowed as a hand slid out of her hair to brush over her wanton flesh. She stretched and moaned under his caress encouraging him begging for more. The other half of her cried out in alarm not ready for the leap that her dark side seemed to crave like a drug addict.

Lance's lips drew away from hers breaking the kiss. He licked his lips reveling in the taste of her that still lingered there and she smiled knowing he was lost to her now. His eyes opened to look at her. The pale blue orbs were no longer cool but a blazing fire of lust waiting to combust. They raked over her body with an intensity that told her his mind was now running wild with fantasies of his own but when their eyes met he froze. "I'm sorry," he whispered.

Catharine opened her mouth to ask for what but froze as he lifted a hand to her face and brushed away tears she'd been unaware of that had fallen from her eyes. He set a kiss on her forehead before he turned and walked away.

Catharine drew a breath as the fire died out, half of her cursed him for leaving her unsatisfied while the other half felt a sense of relief wash over her. Whatever madness had seized hold of her in that moment he'd been able to see beyond it and keep his word to her; for that she was grateful.

114

Pamela followed James Hardagen from the limo and past the police line into the sound stage. She watched as he crossed the room to the set, staged to look like the vampire lord's chambers. The bed she noted was missing as was the set piece for where Davrik was to be held captive during the climactic scene where Serenity gives up control of her mind to Nivali to save Davrik.

"She was sprawled out here on the bed the same pose as the victims before her. Detective Roman revealed to me earlier that that image was meant to be the cover of Heart of Clay until the higher ups decided to keep the innocence of Serenity's image for the readers."

"The victim?"

"One of the girls who tried out for the role of Serenity in Kim Frasier's absence."

"So it is about Miss Nichol's then?"

"Yes. What do you know about her?"

"That Catharine is not her given name. She's hiding from something dark and dangerous, has been for years, but it always haunts her." Pamela murmured as she moved about the staging area, she felt a jolt, another power other than his a far more potent one and wondered if he'd noticed it.

"What can you tell me about Anna Gallagher?"

Pamela laughed. "She's turned up has she? The little archeologist is a danger to you. She knows about the mantles and will stop at nothing to get them. Don't trust her. My lord wants her, if you can manage her capture, Hermes will offer a trade. The girl for access to your image; the right to return to your full glory," Pamela whispered.

"Consider her as good as caught then," James assured her before he led her out of the stage, careful to reseal the crime scene so that none would know it had been disturbed.

As she stepped outside Pamela found herself faced with Artemis. "Good eve Mr. Hardagen till we meet again," she murmured before brushing a kiss on his lips.

"Farewell mi lady," he answered, he gave her a parting grope before sliding back into the limo and speeding away into the night.

"Greetings my sister, and well met, you have tracked down our enemies and no doubt are now aware of a far more dangerous adversary on the move." Artemis stated with a bow.

"Ares."

"Yes my old foe is moving to rise, he will fail I swear it," Artemis assured her.

"I have located the lost mantle but Hermes has bid us hold off on collecting it. He means to use the wine lord to capture Miss Gallagher."

"Indeed his methods are well suited to the challenge. You my lady must return to our lord and thy husband, the enemy that moves here now is too great a danger even for you to risk."

Pamela nodded her understanding and moved past the huntress to the car which she had come in. Sliding into the back seat she bid the driver take her back to the airport as Hermes mind pressed against her own calling her back to him with the promise of a great reward for her good work.

115

Artemis watched as her car sped away with Hermes bride safely inside moving beyond Ares reach. She sent her powers before the precious cargo to ensure that no storm bar her escape. With Eros bow strapped to her back and her sword at her hip the goddess summoned the four winds and bid them seek out her prey Ares puppet would not escape her. The War God would never return to walk upon the Earth again.

His hand had slain her father the king of the gods in a bid for power, he would not obtain it so long as she drew breath. Ares would never reign she would ensure that Hermes obtained her Father's crown and took his place as the new king of the gods. Then her debt to him would be paid and he would keep his promise to her and help her to locate her missing twin; Apollo. She'd not seen him since the day her father fell and even the winds could not locate him.

Though the others had told her he was dead she knew otherwise she still felt him. He was trapped somewhere, the winds couldn't reach. Hermes with his gift would be able to learn the location from Ares memories after she stole them. She would get them just before she slayed his puppet. As for his mantle she'd ensure no one ever found it again; Artemis vowed before she turned and walked away from the sound stage.

116

Sam set his bag down on the bed and set to unpacking his things, when he'd handled the basics, clothes and toiletries he pulled out a small device that could have passed for an mp3 player and set it on his hip putting an earphone in, he walked the perimeter of the room as if learning the layout of the space. To his distaste the small device beeped softly indicating the room was not clean. Somewhere within the chamber was either a camera or mike possibly both.

Sam ground his teeth together as he considered his best move. If he messed with the device, whatever it was his host would be aware of the fact, he was on to him or more to the point aware he was not the mere fighter he pretended to be. No his best step was to identify the device and leave it be. However it posed a further complication in that if it was a camera he couldn't just unpack his gear in the open.

Sam jammed the signal long enough to identify the offending invasion and cursed, the worst case scenario was in play, their host was watching them without their knowledge. He had a damn camera pointed right at the bed. The sick bastard gave him a key hoping to get a free show. Well James Hardagen was going to be sorely disappointed because Sam had no intention of bedding Anna anytime soon. He'd rushed things with Pamela and he knew how that had ended, he wasn't about to make the same mistake twice.

Un-jamming the signal Sam moved his bag out of the view of the camera and unpacked his gear. Guns and throwing knives, cuffs, flak jacket, flash grenade and gas, com units and a number of other tools he'd thought to never need again and yet for reasons he couldn't explain even to himself had held on to despite protocol.

He stowed the equipment in the dark recess of his closet and covered it with the mundane to avoid its detection. His stuff unpacked Sam moved out of the room to knock on Anna's door, he intended to check her living quarters for the same intrusion and warn her that not everything here was what it appeared.

117

Anna was just starting to hang up her clothes in the closet when a knock sounded at the door. She crossed the floor to the door and opening it, was faced with Sam. He looked moody and distracted. He had a music player clipped to his hip and one earphone tucked in his ear.

Rather than greet her he simply walked in like he owned the place. He stalked about the space like a jungle cat inspecting its territory and set her nerves on edge. Who was he? What was he? Most of the time he seemed like an ordinary man just the fighter or former reporter he claimed to be but in moments like this she saw something there beneath the surface, something dark, dangerous, lethal even.

"Sam?" she questioned unsure not caring for the almost possessive behavior being displayed at the moment, she wondered how he would have reacted if he'd found her alone in here speaking with their host or even Lance. She brushed the notion aside. It was unimportant what mattered now was that he understood this was not his space it was hers. "What the hell do you think you're doing just barging in here and…"

"The place is bugged," Sam hissed interrupting her having his confirmation.

Anna paled at the news she was sick and tired of being watched. She spent well over a year at the dig having her every move observed and weighed. "Can he hear us?" Anna asked.

"No."

"Good. Then tell me right now who the hell are you?"

"Who I am is an MMA fighter the man you know. Who I was is another story." He stated.

"Care to explain or shall I just have Catharine create a story for me," Anna asked bitterly. She was tired of finding that what she thought she knew to be true was nothing but lies.

"I used to work for the government. I was part of a team put together by Home Land Security, an anti-terrorist unit out of DC. My job at the paper was a cover. It allowed me to travel without a lot of questions and gave us a means to control media leakage." Sam explained.

"A spy?" she asked with shock.

"Sort of I guess," Sam said not comfortable with the term. "More like a soldier," he stated trying to explain it.

"Kadar was a target?" Anna asked.

"Yes."

"I need a minute," she muttered trying to grasp the idea. She'd been followed by a known terrorist assassin. That meant the people the Smithsonian was working with were dangerous. "I've been working for terrorists?"

"Possibly," Sam confirmed.

"Shit," Anna exclaimed with a growing sense of dread. "Terrorists that know about the mantels," she said now feeling sick. The explosion that led to the discovery of Sodom had been planned. She and Broody had been led along like a mule by the nose to unearth the lost cities and in turn Atlantis. "I've been set up from the start. Marked for death even, maybe when I proved to be useless," Anna breathed as fear became a living thing within her clawing to get free.

Sam swallowed struggling to hold back from her, the need to comfort her was tearing at him but he knew if he did their host would see too much. "We don't know that for sure," he offered.

"Don't lie to me Sam. Is that why you've stayed with me to complete some assignment that was left undone?" Anna questioned hurt and angry. Her hazel eyes a stormy grey that darkened as her suspicions grew.

Sam cursed. "No. Of course not. How could you think that? I'm here because I choose to be. I don't want to see you get hurt Anna. I…"

"Don't Anna me Mr. Abrams I' m right about this and we both know it. You think Broody's employer is a person of interest in some old case and you've been using me to solve it."

"You're wrong Anna. I'd never put you in that man's cross hairs or deliberately leave you there for that matter. I'm here because I care about what happens to you. I don't want to see any harm befall you," Sam stated.

"Why did you wait so long to say anything about this?" Anna

asked still skeptical.

"I didn't know how to. Hell, I never even told Pamela and we were married," Sam muttered.

Anna blinked stunned by the confession and oddly pleased by it. He was trusting her with his secrets, things he'd never even shared with his ex. "What do we do now? I mean about the bug and all?" Anna asked relenting.

"Leave it. Let our host think he has the access to us he seems to want. Just be careful what he's allowed to see," Sam replied.

Anna nodded. "Can you give me a couple minutes Sam? I need to clear my head before I join everyone else down by the pool."

"Of course, to be honest I'd prefer it if you stayed out of the open," Sam whispered as he moved to her side as he passed her, he let his fingers brush against hers in the faintest of caresses.

Anna felt the light touch but in it was a wealth of emotions he dared not to convey under the watchful eye of the camera. "I may rest then try to avoid the inevitable jet lag that always seems to catch up with me," she whispered. "See you later?" she questioned.

"Yes, we'll find a private corner and speak further about everything," Sam assured her before he turned and left. Anna sank down on the bed and closed her eyes trying to free her mind of the mix of fear and suspicion running riot through her mind. She wanted to believe Sam when he told her he hadn't been using her to complete some unfinished assignment but she'd been used in the past to advance Broody's career and it was too easy to see Sam in the same light. Simpler to imagine that she meant nothing to him because that was all she knew.

118

Sam cursed as he made his way down the steps and towards the pool. He'd really screwed that up. He should have known that Anna's intelligent mind would put the pieces together surrounding her own situation and see the truth. He'd expected her to see that she'd been working for terrorists for her to truly grasp the gravity of the situation she was in to recognize the fact that she was not as safe as she assumed and to realize she needed him close by. He'd never figured her to conclude he was using her to finish the damn mission.

Nothing could be farther from the truth, the idea of using her as bait to draw out Mr. York sickened him. Anna was not anything he was willing to sacrifice. He'd left his job to protect Pamela's life. With Anna he'd not rest until he was sure that she was beyond the reach of death's hand.

Sam trembled at the image well aware there was a damn good chance that York was by now well on his way to being just that Death. The candle was taken by a yet unknown entity and Sam was willing to bet his gym that York was connected to it. The explosion that she'd mentioned was his doing somehow. Which, meant as she'd reasoned that Mr. York knew about the mantels he sent the construction team out in that exact location to guarantee Sodom was unearthed. He'd been aware it was there, known about Atlantis as well, How? Who was he and what connection did he have to the fallen?

Sam pushed the questions crowding his mind aside as he reached the pool rejoining Catharine and Lance. He noted the other man looked troubled and hated himself for adding more fuel to an already raging fire but he had little choice. The detective needed to be aware of the fact they were not as secure as he believed.

"Where's Anna?" Catharine asked surprised when he returned

alone.

"Resting, trying to avoid a bad case of jet lag," Sam answered.

"Well then it appears that we're two members down for dinner," Emily stated as she returned from the kitchen with a blender of daiquiris.

"Oh?" Sam questioned.

"James stepped out on business. No telling when he'll be back," Emily said with a shrug. She poured a drink for Catharine and handed it over to her. "Here this should help you relax," Emily stated.

"Thanks."

"You want one detective?"

"No thanks I and Mr. Abrams will be working on security," Lance answered.

"Suit yourself come on Catharine I guess it's just you and me for now, if you boys change your mind we'll be in the hot tub," Emily laughed before she took Catharine by the hand and dragged her off.

Lance groaned at the comment. "I hate to darken your mood any further but we've got a problem," Sam muttered.

"We've got a crazed killer on the loose and according to Anna I've got two old gods trying to bed m... Miss Nichols what else could you possibly add to that." Lance snapped.

"Our host is spying on us," Sam whispered.

"Ah hell."

"Here take this go over your room and Catharine's to be sure I found a camera in my room and a couple in Anna's all pointed at the bed."

"That explains the key then," Lance grumbled.

Sam nodded.

"I'll go have a look then. Do me a favor…"

"I've got her covered, let Anna know our host is out and if she still intends to look for the cup now is the time to do so." Sam stated.

Lance nodded before he turned and withdrew from the pool deck. Sam watched him go. The detective's pause in his tirade about the troubles surrounding them had said more than Lance probably wanted to; about how he felt about the pretty writer. To anyone else the slight hesitation in her name would mean nothing but for Sam it meant a world of trouble.

The normally calm, cool and collected detective was anything but where Catharine Nichols was concerned. The words that Lance had not uttered but Sam could hear plain as day were 'my woman'. Lance was too close to this thing that made the hunt to come that much more complicated.

Not that he had any room to comment he knew he was too close to the task of keeping Anna safe.

119

Lance pulled out his cell phone and punched in a text, he sent it to Anna's number before he slipped into his room. He'd claim he came upstairs to change into his trunks; if Emily questioned his absence from the pool area. As he walked the room with Sam's device he cursed at the soft beeping emitted and his jaw tightened. Just as Sam had said the room was bugged.

The hair on the back of Lance's neck stood on end at the revelation. James Hardagen had been watching him since he got there. The likely hood was he'd been watching Catharine as well. That the damn voyeur had been witness to every private moment the two shared within her room. He'd have to check to know for sure.

"Damn it." Lance didn't want to add any more undue stress to Catharine's mind unless it was needed, she was worried enough as it was. He'd just use the key James had given him to take a peek and then if it proved true he'd let her know, if not well she'd never know anything about it.

While he wasn't too keen on the idea of invading her personal space in this way he had to know. He'd leave something in the room to let her know he'd been there and to give a pretense for his presence in the room to their host. His mind made up Lance picked up the key off his night table where he'd left it and crossed to door. Unlocking it he stepped inside the darkened bedroom.

120

Anna heard the soft beep of her phone indicating a text and lifted her head from her pillow. She read the brief message and slipped out of the bed. She crossed the room with a cool calm she didn't feel and walked out. Once in the hall she focused her thoughts on the cup. Searching for its power signature, she found its touch faint but there and followed it. A dim wash of power radiating from within the walls it led her past a number of other guest rooms into a separate wing of the home.

The trail grew stronger at a pair of heavy oak double doors that led no doubt to the master bedroom. She turned the knob and to her shock and disbelief it gave under her touch opening into the room within.

Like the guest rooms James Hardagen's sleeping quarters were an elaborate series of rooms, the one she stood in now was clearly a space used for entertaining guests, the wall to the right was open and in its recess was a dining area. Moving past the secondary room she stepped into the heart of the master suite. The air in the room was warm, moist and heavy. The smell of sex and alcohol hung over her and made her stomach churn with unease. She felt the press of the mantles power grow stronger and knew she was close.

Her eyes ran over the room taking it in. The bed was the central focal point drawing her eye unerring to it. The California king was opulent with crimson silk laid out like a red carpet in invitation, a mirror hung over the bed. The gilded frame was ornately carved with cherubs perched on the four posts. Looking down on its occupants.

The bed was massive taking up nearly the entire central wall, to its left was a passage that led into another corner of the suite and the right was the same. Anna moved past the bed peeking in the left passage she found the master bath. Turning she moved past the bed into the other passage way.

Here she found what could only be described as James Hardagen's private office. In the center was a large glass topped desk where his computer sat with 32" flat screen television for a monitor. "Guess you like a nice big picture of whatever you happen to capture on your little cameras," Anna muttered to herself with distaste as she moved deeper into the room.

The back wall was lined with a sealed case, inside were a number of different earthen goblets but none of them was the one she sought. As she reached the table beneath the case she cursed, there under it lay pieces of crumbled earth they radiated with the latent power of the mantle they had concealed but the cup itself was nowhere to be found.

She had to get out of there before her host got back and she drew unwanted attention to herself.

"Beautiful aren't they?" James Hardagen's voice questioned.

"Yes, you have quite a collection," Anna replied her voice steady despite being caught in his room.

"What are you doing in here Miss Gallagher?"

"I was curious I'm sorry it's a horrible habit of mine. I didn't mean to intrude just wanted to see a bit of the house. My room is so nice I wondered what the rest of it was like. I was mortified when I realized I wound up in your room but when I saw them I had to have a better look," Anna said sheepishly.

"It's quite all right. No harm was done. Those are my grail replicas," James stated.

"You'll have to tell me about them some time," Anna requested as she moved past him to leave.

"Of course, I take it antiquities is a shared passion then?" he questioned.

"Yes, you could say that," Anna admitted.

"Then you must have loved the bed," he said amused.

Anna blinked. "The bed?" she asked confused.

"Yes it's the set piece from Devil's Advocate and a replica of Louise the 14th's bed." James said with amusement as he followed her out of his office and back into the bedroom.

Her eyes strayed to the bed and in that moment she saw herself sprawled out on the red silk staring up at the reflection above as Sam stared down at her naked body. She blinked turning from the image even as her heart began to pound. "It's a lovely piece but my interest leans more to the genuine article," Anna stated as she felt her body strain with need. It clawed in her belly and made her blush under the intensity of it. She had to get out of there now.

"Ah, pretty Anna it's a pity I'd have been happy to give you a closer look at it," James murmured as he moved closer to her.

She saw it then; clutched in his hand a golden goblet with ruby and amethyst adorning it. The grip was the image of a scantily clad woman marked by Bacchus. "James the cup, oh god," she groaned under the intensity of the lust radiating in the room.

"YES THE CUP, DO YOU WANT A DRINK DOCTOR?" he teased even as he lifted it to his own lips. The wine within that poured forth was red as blood and the smell of it hit her system like a sledgehammer.

"No!" she shouted in refusal. Even as just the smell of it began to affect her .His power was growing. Anna stumbled away from him heading for the door.

"RELAX MISS GALLAGHER I'VE NO INTENT TO HARM YOU FOR NOW. WHAT GOOD WOULD THAT DO ME? IF YOU DISAPPEARED THE OTHERS WOULD GROW SUSPICIOUS. NO, YOU AMUSE ME DEAR AND I THINK PERHAPS WE CAN HELP EACH OTHER."

"Not likely," Anna quipped.

"DON'T BE SO HASTY DOCTOR IT DOESN'T BECOME YOU."

"I won't help you in your efforts to woo Catharine or in any other venture you may be plotting," Anna hissed.

"MY DEAR YOU SHOULD BE MORE CAREFUL AFTER ALL HERMES HAS NAMED YOU HIS ENEMY AND IS OFFERING A CONSIDERABLE PRIZE FOR YOUR RETURN. HOWEVER I'D BE WILLING TO FORGET HIS OFFER IF YOU WOULD SHARE WITH ME THE INFORMATION HE SEEKS."

"You'd double cross him then?" Anna asked shocked by his boldness.

"NO, I'D TAKE YOU OUT OF THE EQUATION AND FOR THE INFORMATION HE SEEKS; NO DOUBT HE WILL STILL REWARD ME WELL."

"What would you require of me if I were to accept your offer?" Anna questioned though she had no intention of accepting it, she figured it was best to not anger him further.

"TURN A BLIND EYE TO MY ENDEAVORS WITH THE LOVELY WRITER."

"Your movement in her direction is a fools game Dionysus she is being courted by another whose claim on her is far stronger."

"ARES, YES I'VE PICKED UP ON HIS SCENT BUT UNTIL HE MAKES THAT CLAIM PUBLIC, I HAVE NO INTENTION OF BACKING OFF. MISS NICHOLS IS JUST A BIT OF SPORT, I'VE NO REAL PLANS FOR HER," Dionysus admitted.

"Then let her be," Anna entreated.

"YOU ARE TOO QUICK TO PUSH ME AWAY, BETTER ME TOYING WITH HER THAN ARES. WITH YOUR SHARP MIND YOU MUST HAVE A REASONABLE IDEA JUST WHO HIS PUPPET IS," Dionysus whispered.

"The killer," Anna sighed.

"SEE YOU'RE SO CLEVER, SWEET ANNA. BETTER TO HAVE ME TORMENT HER THAN FOR HIM TO SLIP INTO HER MIND AND TIGHTEN HIS NET," the wine god whispered.

"You're not the harmless spirit you play at being. I…"

"SHH, NO NEED TO ANSWER NOW; YOU'VE GOT FORTY-EIGHT HOURS TO CONSIDER. FOR NOW GO FIND YOUR SAM AND BID HIM EASE THE ACHE THAT'S AWAKENED WITHIN YOU. IF HE WON'T DO SO THEN SEARCH ME OUT. YOU KNOW WHERE TO FIND ME, I'LL BE MORE THAN WILLING TO AID YOU THERE AS WELL."

"That will never happen," Anna muttered.

"SO YOU SAY, BUT WE'LL SEE." Dionysus breathed, he brushed a hand down her arm enflaming her body further; before allowing her to exit his room.

121

Catharine stepped into her room aware that Sam was just outside the door. She wondered where Lance had gone off to and figured that wherever he was, he'd left Sam to keep his eye on her. While the notion of the hot tub was a pleasant one Catharine was not about to borrow one of Emily's suits again. The slender models idea of a suit was a thin wisp of cloth which was barely legal. While daring and reckless were a part of her vocabulary there were just some things she wasn't willing to risk and over exposure to any man's eye was one of them.

As she flipped on the lights Catharine tried to remember where she'd put her suit. She nearly jumped out of her skin to find she was not alone. Lance was standing near her bed looking at something.

"Detective what are you doing in here?" She questioned, relieved she'd not started to shed her clothes before the lights were on as was her habit.

He blinked startled to see her. His mouth opened to answer her and shut again as if he wasn't sure what to say. "I…"

"So much for not using that key, you didn't even make it an hour before breaking your word," she said with annoyance.

"I had something for you and I wanted it to be a surprise. I'm sorry. Here you take the key." Lance said as he held out the object in question.

"I'm sorry I'm just out of sorts," she muttered.

"It's understandable. You walked in to a crime scene. You're under a lot of pressure from your boss, you've got Bryan over-stepping his place in your life. Now it's clear you've got a crazed killer tracking you. I'd be concerned if you weren't a little upset." Lance assured her.

Catharine eyed him with mistrust he wasn't being completely

truthful about his reason for being there. He wasn't saying something but what that was she didn't know. "Well, detective if you don't mind…"

"Yeah, I should probably… just do me a favor," Lance requested, he switched on the radio before he moved closer to her.

"What do you want Lance?" She asked trying to get a clear picture of what he was up to.

He closed the distance between them so that his lips were pressed against her ear. "Don't change out in the open," he breathed so only she would hear him.

Catharine blinked at the request her blue eyes locked with his and silently asked why.

His gaze moved to the radio at his hip. "Listen to this," he requested.

She took the earphone from his ear and put it in her own. Rather than music she heard a repeated beeping similar to the sound emitted by a metal detector. She felt her stomach tighten as realization set in, the room was bugged.

122

Sam stood a silent sentinel outside Catharine's door. He followed her up from the pool not taking his eyes off her. He wondered where Anna was; if she was okay. He didn't like the idea of her hunting for the cup alone. He considered looking for her now, after all he knew Catharine was no longer unguarded. He'd heard her speaking with Lance, but the truth was he didn't even know where to begin and having two people roaming the halls without permission might be a bit much.

Sam was about to move back into his room when he spotted her. She stumbled down the hall not quite running but definitely rushed. "Anna," he called to her concerned.

"Sam," she gasped his name with relief.

"What happened?" He questioned seeing something was wrong.

"James caught me in his room," she blurted out unable to contain her emotions.

"Shit." Sam raked his fingers through his hair and tried to quiet his temper, he never should have let her go alone. He should have had Lance go with her or insisted on her waiting for him. He was supposed to be protecting her. He'd done a bang up job so far. He managed to lose her once already during that time she'd been taken by Hermes and nearly turned into a sacrifice and now she'd been caught snooping by Dionysus's puppet.

Some hero, at the rate he was going he might as well just hand her over to the fallen on a silver platter because he was being too damn careless. Too many things were pulling him in different directions right now. He needed backup for the job at hand and for the first time in his life there was none to tap. Sure he had connections but none he could draw into the midst of this. He had to do a better job, not let her out of his sight again.

If anything happened to her…

Sam shoved the notion aside he couldn't think that way, refused to invite trouble. Thinking like that would push him to the edge of his control. He didn't want to go there, he knew it would dull his instincts and he needed to be sharp, focused more than ever. Lance was already walking the tight rope for control, Sam couldn't afford to go there too. He was all that stood between Anna and disaster.

Sam was at her side with two strides and drew her into his arms. Hazel eyes widened with shock as he enfolded her in his arms. She still wore the cap he set on her head earlier to hide her from the madman that was watching Catharine. As he held her close he found he wanted, no had to see her. To know she was okay. Sam pulled the hat off her head and tossed it aside. He stared at her hair it was tied back restrained and that wouldn't do. He pulled the bun down freeing the long golden locks. Her hair fell down around him and he drew in her scent. His fingers sank into the blonde curtain as he lowered his head to rest against hers. His eyes locked with hers as her breath brushed against his lips.

There, that was better. He could see her now; his Anna. Sam noted the possessive tone but did not bother correcting it. He'd worry about that later. For now he'd enjoy the moment. He watched as those hazel eyes lit with questions as the fear eased. Yes, there was his lady. He didn't want her tamed or caged though part of him argued that was exactly what needed to happen. He needed to lock her away in a room under guard somewhere beyond the enemies reach.

It wasn't an option; he knew it. She was the one called to find the mantles, she could sense them, if she didn't do it the fallen would return. Sam railed against the heavens for putting her in this place even as he wondered if she refused the task if another would be chosen. He understood Anna well enough to know that she would never turn her back on the mission. She'd started the clock ticking when she discovered Sodom, or at least that's how she saw it.

Sam knew better, York had started it. He'd known exactly where the city lay, known what would be unearthed. Used her to get it and now was moving in the shadows to an end he didn't know. Sam could feel the world around him spinning out of his control at a rapid pace. The clock was ticking.

Sam cursed as he clung to her trying to find his footing in the midst of the chaos. Her words from earlier echoed in his mind.

She'd accused him of using her to complete his failed mission and though it wasn't true he was beginning to see that he was going to be pulled back to it. He had to inform his contacts of what he'd learned. When he turned over Kadar he'd promised them answers, they wouldn't wait forever.

Beyond that Sam knew he had to work the case. Somehow it was connected to all this.

Lance had been right he was here now, because of whom he'd been before Pamela. He was with Anna in this fight given that he was the only one qualified to protect her from the storm she was caught in the middle of and he was failing her. He had to put aside the mistakes of the past, let go of the normal life he'd begun to build for himself and embrace the warrior again.

"Are you okay?" he asked her finding his voice once more.

"Yes, he offered me a trade gave me time to think it over," Anna explained.

"What?" Sam asked with disbelief he drew back from her with alarm. "What did he want?"

"The information Hermes is after and for me to step back from Catharine. He claims he's just playing with her no real plans to make her his bride."

"If you agree to his terms?" Sam asked feeling ill.

"Hermes won't need me anymore," Anna said with a shrug.

"So aid one to escape the other, assuming you can trust him." Sam said with disgust.

"Which I can't they're liars and manipulators by nature."

He relaxed closing the distance between them once more. "So, why were you so scared?"

"He has the cup I saw it. It did something to me," she explained.

"What?"

"It started when I tried to leave. I mentioned that it was his artifacts that caught my attention and he commented on the bed as we were walking past it he mentioned its history I looked back curious that's when it started. I saw us in that bed."

"Us?"

"Yes, it stirred me up then I saw the cup, he offered me a drink but I refused. I didn't taste it but I could smell it. I felt drunk almost immediately and the desire the flash from the bed woke, became unbearable. I knew if I didn't get away from him I was going to lose it."

"You seem fine now," Sam assured her.

"The further I got away from the cup the more the effects eased. Either that or he released me I'm not sure."

"You're not going after the cup alone again," he told her. Then because he needed to, he kissed her good night before walking her to her room. "The rooms being watched be mindful of that," he entreated before letting her go.

Anna nodded before slipping into the room. He heard her lock the door and smiled. Good girl. She was learning. Good, but a locked door wasn't enough to keep him satisfied he grabbed a chair from his room and took post by the door. No one was going in that room uninvited. He sighed and stretched, it was going to be a long night.

123

Catharine swallowed with disgust at the idea her privacy had been invaded. She wondered just how much her host had seen but pushed the matter aside. She knew now and he wasn't going to get any more of her. With that in mind she moved to send Lance on his way.

"Nice, I'll see you around de..." she began but the words were cut off as his fingers sank into her hair and his lips met hers. Catharine sank into his embrace unable to resist him.

When his lips parted hers they were at her ear again teeth nipped at tender skin before his voice in a low pitch related to her how the room was bugged cameras and sound both. Not to let on that she knew. The longer their host thought they were unaware of it the better.

Catharine absorbed the information but struggled to focus, his close proximity getting to her. She'd wanted him earlier, still did it seemed the more she tried to deny it the worse the hunger grew.

"Lance," she breathed his name the word a desperate plea.

"It's you on the cover," Lance gasped with disbelief.

"You see too much," she said startled.

"Were you and the artist?"

"We dated."

"Did you pose..." Lance began his mood shifting.

"No, he had a picture of my face he used it to draw her," Catharine explained.

"But he's seen this face this haunted look of desire and fear," Lance said with understanding.

"Lance, please that was a long time ago. He's gone and you're here, you're who I want," she assured him.

"But you're not ready. Until I look at you and there's no fear in your eyes..."

"You're words are generous Lance but misplaced I don't know that I'll ever be able to look at something I lust after without the fear," she admitted before she kissed him.

124 Unknown

HE watched with disgust as the detective, despite good intentions, groaned under the power of HIS sweet Serenity's kiss. The other man's hand took hold of her neck, his fingers fisting in her red hair; taking control of the kiss and her. HE listened with disgust as HIS bride moaned like a whore for his hunter. The cop had graduated from a mere annoyance to full on rival.

Detective Roman was going to pay dearly for daring to try and corrupt her. HE'D stood by and watched as she gave herself to another man once before and she fell for someone who ended up hurting or controlling her and it seemed her taste in men had not improved with LANCE! The seemingly nice guy was already showing signs of possessiveness and a need to dominate her.

HE growled in rage as HE watched the other man mark her ivory skin as the pair got swept away by the intense lust that Dionysus had stirred up within her. The god of wine would soon know he was wasting his time with Serenity; she was HIS. But before HE stepped out of the shadows and into the light to be counted to take HIS place once more among his brethren the detective would have to be dealt with.

Lance Roman would be given one warning to back away from HIS bride before HIS vengeance was dealt out. HE cursed in fury as the cop took liberties with Serenity's body that he had no right to.

Kiss swollen lips parted and she cried the detective's name, her voice desperate as need and fear became unbearable. The detective didn't hear her cry, his mouth simply captured hers once more as hands groped and mouth devoured. Revealing LANCE'S true nature; he was taking now what he desired without hesitation or care for the feelings or needs of the woman in his arms.

The cop would suffer for it. HE vowed before HE turned his

attention to the young woman his lady had lain out for him. "Scream for me beauty," HE murmured before he drew the knife at his hip from it sheath and set to work.

125

Catharine moaned with a fevered hunger at the feel of Lance's hand as it slid beneath her panties to find her more than ready for him. He groaned with the knowledge but drew back.

"Damn it Catharine, I want you I'm not going to lie I want you so much it hurts…" he gasped struggling to ease back as the reality that they were not alone once more filled his mind.

"Then take me," she demanded lost to him.

"This isn't going to happen, not here, not now," he breathed even as he drew her closer so that he could whisper in her ear once more. "Not with him watching us, listening." Lance drew his hands out of her clothes as he pulled back from the wild storm of passion that threatened to consume them both.

He watched as Serenity's haunted look returned to her face as his words sank in past the haze of lust.

"What's happening to me?" she questioned with disbelief and disgust as reality crashed in around her. They were being watched she'd known it when he kissed her and yet had lost track of it and everything in his embrace, she felt drunk with the need that tore through her and it scared her.

She'd never been the type to rush into a man's bed. Love and sex was the one thing she treaded slowly with. It went against her nature to leap here, she'd learned the hard way that men were not to be trusted. Yet here she was standing before him her body trembling with want for his touch and though she knew they were being observed she wanted him naked in her bed.

Catharine bit her lower lip as her mind conjured up images of multiple options of the things they could be doing once she got him there. "Damn it this has to stop," she muttered she stumbled backwards away from him knowing if she didn't get distance she would be lost to the thirst that had a hold of her.

"Catharine are you okay?" Lance asked alarmed, seeing her retreat she seemed disoriented almost as if she were drunk. He cursed as he wondered just how much of that daiquiri she'd drank. He moved to help her but she shrank back.

"Don't touch me Lance I can't... oh God what is this, why doesn't it let up," she said in frustration even as she swiped at her tears.

"How much did you have to drink?"

"Nothing."

"What?"

"Nothing I set my glass down and came up here to change."

"What the hell?" Lance questioned with alarm. If she hadn't had anything to drink then why did she stumble as if drunk?

"God I don't want this not like this," she cried out in fear as the press of lust over her grew thicker. Her stomach boiled in fury at her words and as before she made her way to the bathroom and got sick.

Lance watched dumbstruck as she emptied her stomach of a blood red wine she'd not been drinking. He felt his own stomach roll with fear at the event. Anna's warning rang in his ears and he cursed as he knew the only explanation was that James Hardagen did have the cup of Dionysus and the power she claimed it possessed was real. Whatever its influence was it had hold of Catharine and she couldn't shake it.

Worse yet he didn't know how to protect her and he had the sneaking suspicion that if Anna was right about Dionysus then Ares was out there too and his puppet was a madman killing innocent women to perfect his image of a wanton Serenity before he turned his blade on his chosen bride.

The lady who lay curled on her side, her skin pressed against the cold tile. She shook uncontrollably her body wracked with a fit of soundless sobs for fear of what was happening to her. Grief and shame written upon her beautiful face; that made him want to kill. But there was no foe with which to fight.

Catharine's attackers now were not men but monsters that hid in shadows and used unnatural means to strike at her. They'd used him against her. Lance cursed his lack of control, disgusted he'd let things get so out of hand. He prided himself on his restraint and yet despite his vow earlier to not push her he'd done just that. He'd pressed her for more when she'd meant to retreat and in doing so had caused this torment she now endured.

He felt retched and unworthy of her in that moment. A voice

within him told him to leave her, he couldn't help her. He was too close to her and that connection would only wind up hurting her. He'd nearly bedded her though he knew Dionysus was watching, listening in, waiting for them to surrender to their hunger so that he could look on for his own pleasure.

Lance choked back his own guilt. What had he done to her? God how could he face her again? He knew she was fragile. Saw that on her shoulders she carried a heavy burden of pain brought down upon her by those she should have been able to trust. He'd wanted to protect her and instead had wound up the blade with which Dionysus stabbed her.

"Catharine?" he whispered her name, afraid that after the silence between them, even a conversational tone would startle her. He spoke needing to know he was still welcome in her presence; worried that now desire and friendship would become hate.

Frightened blue eyes turned to meet him. He felt his lungs constrict at the sight of her, she looked like a wounded animal, cornered, wild, and dangerous. The wild hunger raging within him went out like a candles flame as he cursed himself again, he'd known she wasn't ready to be with him.

"Do you want me to leave?" he asked her willing to do so if it would ease her fear.

Her lips parted but no words did she utter as if the ability to speak failed her. Instead she shook her head in answer.

Lance sank down on the floor beside her. He watched as the fear in her eyes subsided a little and the look on her face became tamer. He reached out with a tentative hand wanting to comfort her but he did not touch her yet. Giving her control now where he'd taken it earlier.

When she did not withdraw from him he brushed her hair away from her face and tucked it behind her ear. "Shh, it's over now you're okay, I'm sorry," he murmured as he gathered her into his arms and held her close. Her mind eased as exhaustion took hold of her and she slipped into sleep.

"I've got you, you're safe," he whispered as he rest his brow against her. "Forgive me," he requested. He lifted his head to keep watch over her nothing more would trouble her sleep that night.

126 ATHENS, GREECE

Pamela stepped out of the car which had brought her from the airport to the man Ian Broody's home. She walked up the stone steps and through the ornate front door. Her heels clicked on the marble floor, each step grew faster as it carried her closer to her lord.

As she entered his office, perhaps throne room was a better description for it now, she mused his blue eyes lit with pleasure at the site of her.

"Ah my dearest lady I am pleased to see you have returned," Hermes crooned as he drew her into his arms and kissed her. He replenished the power he'd given her which Dionysus had been feeding off of with his kiss and reasserted his hold upon her.

"My lord, I come with gifts and news," Pamela murmured with a smile.

"Show me this gift, then you shall share this news," Hermes entreated.

Pamela nodded and she drew from her bag the gauntlets she had taken from the workspace at the Vulcan's Forge. Hermes laughed with delight at the mantle, the sight of it bringing back more bits of his memory. He took them from her hands and placed them in the graven images hands. The spirit trapped within roared in rage as its power was ripped from it and endowed to Hermes. When the exchange was complete the statue shattered.

Hermes eyes snapped open the blue hew now lit with an orange fire beneath it. "One has fallen the others will follow," he whispered to his bride before he drew her once more into his embrace. He leaned down and rest his forehead against her brow. "Come now open your mind to me my love, show me all," he entreated as he let his power encircle her.

Pamela did as he bid her and gasped as she felt his power pour through her body and his mind touched her own. They spoke no words as they were not necessary all she knew filled his mind as he kissed her.

"You've done well my lady, better than I even hoped. Artemis was right to send you back, Ares is a beast, he'd harm you to prevent my rise to power, but he is too late. I'll not ever give him access to this place or you." Hermes vowed.

"What is your desire of me now my lord," she questioned.

"Go to Ithaca there is a whip there that was found during a dig bring it to me," he requested.

"As you wish," she answered simply.

"Pamela my darling, when you return the time will be at hand for our union to be made official. We shall be wed."

"Then I wait with impatience until that day rises my lord," she breathed before she kissed him farewell.

Hermes deepened the kiss and reveled in her eagerness for him. Around him his brethren raged at being forced to witness his freedom to claim her.

127

Lance woke to the electronic chirp of his cell phone ringing. He blinked away sleep to find himself sitting on a cold tile bathroom floor. Catharine lay asleep her head resting in his lap. As he reached for his phone he tried to piece together the night before and the vivid image of her expelling a wine she'd not drunk flashed before his eyes. He swallowed as he pressed the talk button.

"Hello."

"Detective Roman, I'm sorry to disturb you but we've got another one," Gail Blackwood stated her voice grim.

"Ah Hell, where?"

"The victims house when we came here to take a look through her place this morning we found the next one, Looks like he started on her around the time we were working the other scene."

"When did you find her?"

"About eight I wasn't going to call you in but there's something here you need to see."

"Where?" Lance asked as dread ran through him. He listened as agent Blackwood rattled off the address. His eyes moved to the sleeping figure in his lap and watched as red lashes fluttered and pale lids lifted, blue eyes met with his full of question. "I'm on my way." Lance stated before he disconnected the call.

"Trouble?" Catharine questioned as she lifted her head and sat up.

"Afraid so," Lance confirmed.

"He's killed someone else hasn't he," Catharine reasoned, feeling ill, aware that whoever the killer was the only way that he would stop was if he had her.

"Yes, I've got to go."

"I understand."

"You stay in here and rest, I don't want you anywhere near our host," Lance ordered.

"Okay," she relented, too tired to argue with him, at being bossed around. "You have to tell me about it when you get back," Catharine countered.

"Why?"

"Because this is about me Lance, whatever he's done it's because of me," She stated.

"Don't you ever say that again, do you hear me," Lance snapped with outrage. "This is not your fault. He's a lunatic and a killer, he's to blame here not you."

"He's after me if…"

"No! I told you get that notion out of your head it's never going to happen," Lance shouted in defiance. He got up from the floor and turned to go; their conversation was over for now, when he got back he was going to make damn sure she didn't bring up the insane idea again. She'd play bait in a trap for the sick bastard over his dead body, Lance swore before he walked out of the bathroom. He stalked through her room and out the door into the hall.

He'd just been contemplating waking Sam to keep an eye on her when his eyes landed on the other man asleep in a chair outside Anna's room. He wondered at it but didn't have time to question it. Sam's eyes snapped open at the sound of his closing the door. "Don't let her go anywhere," Lance muttered.

Sam nodded.

"Another victim's turned up. I'll be back as soon as I can," he stated before he moved down the hall towards the steps and out of James Hardagen's home.

128

Anna woke with her hair tussled, skin flushed and her body slick with sweat. As she threw off the covers, the soft cotton night gown, she pulled on in the dark before climbing into bed, caressed her feminine curves and made her draw a sharp breath as the light touch tore through her system like a hurricane and went straight to her womb. She cursed as once more an intense lust stirred within her.

As she lay there her mind was filled with the images of fevered dreams that had tormented her throughout the night. Intense and erotic bits and pieces played out now in the light of day. Flashes of her and Sam kissing, touching, tasting, images so vivid she could feel them. Anna bit her lower lip to fight back a moan. This was Dionysus's power, the influence of the cup she told herself with disgust even as the images became more explicit.

Well, she knew what to do about the Fallens' attacks now and she didn't have to put up with this, Anna assured herself. Closing her eyes she bowed her head and whispered a prayer to the heavens requesting that God take the intense unnatural hunger from her, release her mind of Dionysus's hold. When she finished, the images abated and the lust she felt inside her receded but it did not depart. While no longer painful her body still clamored with wanting for Sam.

Startled she prayed again asking this time for God to take her desire for Sam from her and nothing happened. What was wrong, why wasn't anything happening? Anna wondered. Was her prayer being blocked somehow? Her spirit troubled and confused Anna opened her bag and pulled out the Bible she'd been given back at the dig site in Israel by a colleague. She hoped it would have the answers she needed.

129

Lance climbed out of his car in front of the bright blue two story cottage rental two blocks away from Venice Beach. He saw the yellow crime scene tape across the way at the street level access and knew he was in the right place. A black and white sat on the drive lights flashing and agent's Kessler's SUV was just two spaces over. It was a nice neighborhood on a quiet street no doubt the neighbors were already watching with trepidation and concern.

He crossed the street and moved up the steps. Ducking under the tape he moved inside and made his way through the sitting area to the back where he saw Agent Blackwood and Kessler, he figured that must be where they'd discovered the body. He steeled his nerves in a bid to prepare for whatever it was that Gail felt he had to see.

"Detective," Agent Kessler said in greeting as he joined them.

"Morning, so what did he leave us this time?" Lance questioned.

"A bloody mess," Kessler answered with disgust.

"What we got for the time line suggests that the victim was most likely taken around the time we were processing the scene yesterday. He tortured her for hours, normal markers but coroner places time of death around 8p.m."

"That's odd he normally keeps them longer," Lance stated.

"From what we can gather it appears he got angry for some reason and he lost it."

"Lost it how?" Lance questioned with disbelief, the guy never lost control he was brutal, vicious and methodical.

"He mutilated her body." Gail said bluntly.

"Damn."

"The series of cuts under her eye grew exponentially. Her face was beyond recognition. The blade was also used on her chest, hips and thighs. It was in this region of her body when he cut her too deep severing her femoral artery. She bled out as he finished the ritual kill." Agent Kessler explained,

"We had to send the black and white out he nearly lost it," Gail added.

"Where is she?"

"We sent her back to the lab for further examination, all early signs suggest that the rape was worse as well. We won't know for sure until the M.E. is done but the escalation isn't why you're here," Agent Kessler stated.

"Then why?" Lance asked.

"He left us this." Gail said as she handed him a stack of pages. "These are copies; you can touch them, I think you need to read them detective."

"What are they?"

"Pages from the movie script with changes from the killer." Gail explained.

Lance nodded, he then looked down to the copies and fell into the scene.

'LANCE closed his eyes as regret and sorrow filled him. She'd made her choice he had to honor it even if it destroyed him to do so. "Serenity, please," he breathed as he drew her against him.

"I am yours no more. Go."

LANCE roared in rage at her denial of his claim, his eye glowed with power. "You will always be mine," he snapped before he kissed her. '

Lance blinked, drawing back from Catharine's words, he knew the scene he'd read it the last time he picked up Heart of Clay. This was the pivotal moment in the plot, the scene that would seal Serenity's fate.

Beneath the dialogue written in red was the first of the killer's changes.

'LANCE'S fingers sink into her red hair grabbing her by the back of the head holding her captive. Forgetting his oaths as a knight and stealing her ability to choose. His mouth presses hers with hunger hard and demanding bruising her lips with his kiss. Serenity struggles in his grasp at first but soon yields to him unable to deny his claim.

LANCE'S kiss destroys her will and she moans in wanton need like a whore. He smiles knowing he has her. His hands slide out of her hair to grope and fondle eager flesh, he's till now only dreamed of. '

Lance swallowed feeling sick as the edit ended. He knew the scene god he'd lived it. The sick bastard was tapped into James Hardagen's video feed. He'd seen everything last night. He was the one who made the killer mad.

"It gets worse," Gail commented seeing he looked ill.

"Did you sleep with Miss Nichol's?" Agent Kessler asked bluntly.

"No, of course not," Lance said with irritation.

"Are you sure because the killer sure seems to think so," Kessler snapped.

Lance's eyes lit with temper. "I said I didn't sleep with her. I don't care what that sick bastard thinks," Lance snapped but he knew that was a lie because if the killer thought he'd slept with Catharine he might hurt her.

His eyes moved back to the page needing to know just how far last night's little episode pushed the man.

'Serenity trembles at the feel of the cool night air on her skin as she feels the filmy black fabric about her fall away. She sighs at the feel of his hands upon her.'

'LANCE'S mouth came away from Serenity's lips moving down her neck, he drew her ivory skin into his warm mouth, teeth scraping it to mark her as his hand ran over belly and lower to touch the part of her he craved most. He groaned with pleasure to find her wet and ready for him.'

'Serenity felt him lay her back in the tall grass and the prick of his fangs as he bit her inner thigh making his final mark of claim in the mating ceremony. Davrik's green eyes turned to the dark shroud wrapped about her.

"I will have her. You will not interfere," he hissed at the spirit that had kept her from him before. The spirit said nothing but in compliance the cloak fell back laying lifeless on the ground. Satisfied Davrik shed his garments and stretched out over her. He kissed her nipping at her lip lightly as he joined their bodies together.'

Lance drew back from the scene skimming ahead. Kessler was right the killer did think he'd slept with her which meant he'd stopped watching after he touched Catharine. It was at that moment the girl's fate had been sealed. Her killer had turned his knife against her skin cutting her where Lance's hand's had been on Catharine.

If he'd had any doubts about Catharine's claim the murders were connected to her they were gone now. The madman was watching her every move and James Hardagen had given him full access to her. Hell that meant he'd been in the house or at least on the property and if that were the case, well, with the key connecting the rooms in the house there was a fair chance that he'd already obtained the means to enter her room.

Lance felt sick and angry, things were slipping out of his control at an alarming rate. He had to get Catharine out of that house and out of LA before it was too late. Lance skipped over the rest of the original text to the next bit written in red he needed to know the enemy's thoughts if he wanted to have any chance of beating him.

"As LANCE and Serenity lay naked together, bodies entwined, basking in the afterglow, drowsy with sleep from their exertions, a SHADOW crept toward them. His steps were soundless his eyes bright with fury. LANCE 'S time had come, he like those before him had crossed the line. Serenity was not his for the taking she belonged to the SHADOW. HE'D seen Serenity's suffering at the hands of Syvarin, he wasn't about to let this one hurt her as well. HE drew the lovers apart in his rage. LANCE stumbled to get to his feet, body still weak from his exertions, his weapon beyond his reach. The SHADOW drew his knife from its sheath and struck. He drove the blade into LANCE'S heart and watched as the spark of life drained from his icy blue eyes.

"For defiling my bride," the SHADOW hissed before he pulled the knife from LANCE'S chest, his rage not yet cooled, the SHADOW turned his blade to the part of his rival he loathed the most and unmanned him. Serenity screamed in horror at the sight. The SHADOW turned, her lover's blood dripping from his knife. HE wiped it clean and put it away. With two strides he stood before her. His eyes glowed with power and hunger as he looked upon her ivory skin. "Now Serenity, at last you are mine," the SHADOW declared before he grabbed her by the arm and drew her against him to claim her as his bride. "

Lance turned away from the rest, he didn't need to read anymore, he got the point, the killer was done targeting look-a-likes he was coming after Catharine and him. He'd gone from adversary on the hunt to a target. He'd pushed the sick bastard too far. Time was running out.

"Like I said the killer seems to think you did. So I'm going to ask you again, did you fuck CJ Nichols?" Kessler asked.

"No," Lance said his voice hard and cold. Not caring for the vulgarity used to describe what had nearly transpired between him and Catharine the night before, if they had slept together he'd never look at it that way.

"Not that I'd blame you if you did. I mean she is a gorgeous piece of tail, if I'd had a chance at her I'd have taken it," Agent Kessler commented; so only Lance could hear him.

Lance understood the reason for the comment, Kessler was pushing him, the way he might a suspect, trying to get him to admit he'd crossed a line; he had no business crossing. Lance should have just said no, he knew it but the last bit had him seeing red and before he knew what he was doing his fist flew hitting the agent in the jaw.

"That's it you're done! You are way too close to this thing. You are officially off the case," Kessler snapped.

Lance cursed mentally. "Fine by me, I never wanted back on it in the first place," Lance said with disgust. While it was the truth, he wasn't about to walk away from it now.

"Good. If I catch you interfering detective I'll have your ass thrown in jail for assault and impeding an investigation."

"I won't get in your way with the case. But I'm not leaving." Lance stated.

"We'll need to speak to Miss Nichol's about the information she gave you," Gail stated.

"Yeah fine, but just you," Lance muttered. He raked his fingers through his hair in a show of nervousness.

"Did you sleep with her to get thrown off the case?" Kessler asked.

"No, I didn't sleep with her. Whatever the killer thinks happened he's mistaken," Lance stated before he turned and walked out.

"Do you believe him?" Kessler asked as he went.

"Yeah, I do." Gail Blackwood answered. "I'm going to go speak to Miss Nichol's. For the record you're right to have pulled him, he's too close to this, but I object to the way you handled that."

"Objection noted," Kessler stated before he turned his attention back to the crime scene

130 Miami, Florida

Zaharrah stepped into her hotel room grateful to get away from the dig and Broody's watchful eye. Things there were getting bad fast. Once inside the relative safety of her room Zaharrah took out a small device and swept it for bugs. She was pleased to find that while Broody was watching her at the dig, he'd yet to try to invade her personal space. He still trusted her at least for now. Drawing the curtains closed she took out the package that had been waiting for her at the front desk.

Unwrapping it she found within it the artifact that had started the hunt for Anna. The disk was approximately 7" in diameter; made of a strange melding of a yet unknown metal and granite. The two had been smelted together in a way that didn't currently exist. This melding made the disk appear to be like molten silver. Zaharrah laughed noting that two of the rings were missing. The key should have varied in color from white to black and been divided into five sections. She knew this from the records of her people.

The central ring had been no bigger than a quarter and inscribed in it in Hebrew and Greek an assortment of letters. According to the legend if it were touched in the correct spot it would change to form coherent words. Apparently Anna had figured it out because the piece was missing.

The inner track had been black; and contained within it were white distinct dotted patterns and lines that made no clear image unless you knew the alignment of the stars in the heavens, then you would note, they were like that of several constellations but did not line up correctly. Touching the North Star would fix it. It too was missing. In their place she could see a strange white crystal unlike any found on earth.

So Anna had begun to unravel the mystery of the key and taken it apart. Zaharrah smiled; her elders would be furious but she didn't care, the key was useless without the rings and she figured dismantling it was the best thing that could happen. She studied the rest of it having only read about it until now.

The outer ring was white. Inscribed in it was a form of strange writing. One not even her people could translate; the language of the gods themselves. The second track was like fine silver. Carved within were four intricate symbols. The signs for the four elements, Earth, Fire, Air and Water, Lines at odd angles came off the symbols. Small leaves extended from them, the branches of the tree of knowledge of good and evil. Legends didn't tell how to open this ring, their ancestor never got that far before death took them.

The third section was like pewter. It depicted the image of various objects and possessed the only bit of color, each image held a small gemstone at its heart. Zaharrah ran her finger over each one. A cup with an emerald, a scepter in amethyst, a scale with a ruby, a horn in black , a whip in Carnelian, gantlets of Lapis and pearl, a bow with an amber, a scroll with a fire opal, sword with a sapphire, and finally the crown of white crystal like that in the center of the disk.

When her finger brushed the gem in the crown the others shifted. The cup held the amethyst, the scepter, the lapis and pearl, the scales the emerald, the horn a sapphire, the whip a fire opal, the gauntlets amber, the bow a ruby, the scroll the strange black crystal like that in the throne room and the sword the carnelian. The ring itself fell loose into the disk. She pulled it free and set it aside to find more of the white crystal below.

What was it? Where did it come from? What was the secret that her elders guarded with such devotion as to be willing to die to keep it? Zaharrah cursed not having the answers. But she knew one thing for certain, whatever the key was for it was evil. She needed to get it away from the dig site as Anna had and ensure that the rings already removed didn't find their way back to it.

Picking up the one she'd freed she studied it closer. So this was how the mantles Anna spoke of were adorned. If that were so then Broody was already moving to collect the whip. She realized recalling the one they'd discovered in Ithaca. The grip had boasted a fire opal in the top making it an unusual find. Broody would remember it as she did. She wrapped up the disk to send it out as she wrote a letter to her contact requesting the whip be obtained. She only hoped it wasn't too late.

131

Lance walked back into James Hardagen's home to find his host and hostess sitting by the pool.

"Ah one of our guests emerges at last," James said amused as he studied the detective. "Did you enjoy your evening?" He questioned.

"We need to talk," Lance snapped his temper still up.

"Of course, forgive me my dear I'll be back in a moment," James said to his pretty fiancé before he brushed a kiss on her lips. He let it deepen for a moment before letting her go and getting to his feet.

Lance turned and headed back into the house, James only a few steps behind him.

"How can I help you detective," James inquired.

"Drop the act Hardagen it's getting old. I know about your surveillance and so does the killer," Lance spat out with disgust.

"Does he now and how do you know that?" James asked with interest.

"He left me a message at the scene this morning pages of your movie script, the scene where Serenity and Davrik seal her fate. He made changes to it that reflect what we both know happened in her room last night. Trouble is he didn't bother to watch everything he thinks I finished the job and he's done playing games with substitutes he's coming after her."

"Good," Catharine stated as she and Anna walked into the room.

"Damn it Catharine get out," Lance snapped as Sam joined them.

"No. I'm not going to sit back and wait for this guy. If he's coming for me then let's have him turn up when we're ready for him. I want to set a trap."

"I told you that's..." Lance began but his protest was interrupted.

"Sounds like a great idea," Gail Blackwood commented as she was shown in by the butler.

"No," Lance countered in defiance.

"Would you rather wait for him to move on his own?" Gail challenged.

"Let me get her out of here," Lance countered.

"You'd only be postponing the inevitable, we both know he isn't going to just let her slip away from those pages, it sounds like he's been watching her a long time." Gail reminded.

"What do you mean?" Catharine asked startled.

"He mentions having waited for Serenity looking on while she endures her mistreatment at Syvarin's hand," Gail explained.

Catharine visibly paled at the news. "Did he threaten you?" she asked with fear.

Lance blinked stunned she'd been able to see it.

"He did," Gail confirmed. "How did you know?"

"I'm a writer it's my job to understand the way a characters mind works. If he were in the book as he seems to want to be that's what I would write," Catharine stated coolly, her eyes conveyed disappointment that Lance had believed he could keep that detail from her.

"Let me get you away from this?" Lance entreated his eyes pleading with her to accept.

"No, I want this over with," Catharine refused.

Lance nodded with regret. He wasn't sure if he could watch her do this. "I suggest you take this discussion outside," Lance muttered.

"Aren't you coming?" Catharine asked with disbelief.

"I'll be along in a minute, first Mr. Hardagen and I have something to attend to," Lance said with resignation.

"Right." James stated, he led Lance upstairs in the direction of his room as Catharine and the others headed for the pool deck.

132

Lance walked into James Hardagen's bedroom past the California king into a room to the right. The private work space had a glass top, desk where a laptop sat with a 32" flat screen above it. The set up infuriated him knowing what the other man watched in here but he said nothing, simply watched as his host killed the video and audio feed coming from the four guest rooms.

Voyeur's tended to think of themselves as harmless, Lance knew better from years of working in homicide. Sooner or later just watching wasn't enough. They eventually crossed the line between silent unobtrusive observer to intruder and with time worse.

"It's done detective," James stated.

"Good. Our hunter doesn't need to see anything more of what Miss Nichol's does behind closed doors," Lance stated with disgust. He turned to leave not wanting to linger here. Aware that if Catharine had any chance of setting the trap she had in mind to, they were going to need Mr. Hardagen's help and Lance's insulting the man or getting into it with him would not help matters.

As he walked past the bed he felt the room grow thick with tension. His eyes skimmed over the bed unable to look away he noted the gilded cherubs on the frame and felt his gut clench aware that this bed would serve the killer for his final scene. His gaze drifted to the mirror on the ceiling and for a moment he saw in the reflection Catharine's lifeless body splayed out, wrapped in the crimson silk toga, a crown of serpents on her brow.

NO!

That wasn't going to happen, he was going to stop it. Lance vowed with determination.

He blinked and the image was gone, the mirror empty. His gaze moved to the bed itself. The crimson silk that lay in the midst of the gilded frame looked like a welcome mat of red carpet, it would be cool and comforting. The mattress soft; his mind whispered.

As he looked at it he pictured Catharine laying in it eyes closed like some sleeping faerie princess waiting to be woken. He imagined himself at her side leaning over her attempting to wake her with a chaste kiss. Her smiling but not opening her eyes, his lips pressing against hers a second time, no longer light or closed but hard, open and demanding tasting hers nipping at her lower lip to demand entrance as he kissed her deeper. His hands playing over her silk wrapped body, peeling it away like wrapping paper to find warm eager flesh.

Lance blinked drawing back from the day-dream what was he doing?

"YOU PUZZLE ME DETECTIVE," James said amused.

"How so?"

"WELL, YOU HAD HER IN YOUR ARMS LAST NIGHT, SHE WAS HOT, EAGER, WILLING, AND READY AND YOU KNEW IT. YOU WANTED HER, I KNOW YOU DID I COULD FEEL IT POURING OFF YOU, RUNNING THROUGH YOU, SO WHY DIDN'T YOU TAKE HER?" the other man asked.

Lance turned to stare at his host outraged the man would dare bring up something so private. As he looked upon the other man his heart skipped a beat. Rather than blue James Hardagen's eyes glowed violet. He swallowed holding back the angry response he'd been about to shout as fear filled him.

Any doubts he had about Anna's claims of old gods possessing mortals died out in that moment as he realized the man who spoke with him now was not James Hardagen but the god, fallen, Dionysus. "As much as I wanted her last night I knew you were watching and I wasn't willing to expose her to you that way," Lance muttered.

He took a step back from the other man wanting to reach the door, needing to get out of that room, the place was pulsing with the gods power. He understood now the reason for the bizarre fantasy and felt sickened by it. This want to be deity was messing with him trying to push him to bed Catharine. Why? What good did his bedding her do this fallen? Didn't Anna tell him Dionysus wanted Catharine for himself? How did pushing them together get him closer to that goal? What was this god playing at? Lance wondered as he reached the door.

Dionysus laughed as Lance reached for the handle but it didn't budge. "DID YOU REALLY IMAGINE YOU COULD SIMPLY LEAVE AT WILL DETECTIVE? YOU ARE AN ARROGANT ONE AREN'T YOU? YOU'LL LEAVE WHEN I ALLOW IT, WE'RE NOT DONE TALKING," The wine god said with a hint of temper.

Lance cursed mentally he figured angering an old god was a bad idea and should be on his list of things not to do but damn it he wanted out of that room and away from the fucking bed. Something about it made his instincts buzz with warning. He could feel the hairs on the back of his neck standing on end.

"SO YOU THINK BY NOT TAKING HER AS YOU DESIRED TO; THAT YOU SPARED HER FROM MY GAZE, YOU MORTALS ARE SO NAIVE. DO YOU HONESTLY THINK I WASN'T IN THAT ROOM WITH YOU LAST NIGHT?" Dionysus said amused.

Lance blinked. Dumbstruck and horrified at the implication as the answer to the questions he'd been asking slipped into place. Each time one of them gave into their lust this fallen got to experience it as well. Lance's eyes settled on the bed and he saw it for what it was, an altar. The worship that Dionysus desired most was intoxication and mindless acts of fornication driven by lust. That was where his power grew.

By picturing himself there he'd unknowingly been offering his worship.

"AH, UNDERSTANDING AWAKENS. YES LANCE I WAS THERE WITH YOU AS YOU TASTED HER LIPS, TOUCHED HER BODY AND MARKED HER SKIN. I FELT HER BODY ACCEPT US AS YOU TOUCHED HER TO SEE IF SHE WAS READY, COULD SMELL HER AROUSAL. YOU KEPT NOTHING OF HER FROM ME," Dionysus whispered.

"That's not true, I kept the part of her you desired most from you," Lance corrected.

"NOT FOR LONG DETECTIVE, EACH HOUR THAT PASSES THE WINE SHE TASTED, ITS INFLUENCE UPON HER GROWS STRONGER. SOON SHE WILL COME TO ME."

"You're wrong. Catharine won't surrender to you; fallen one," Lance stated with more certainty than he felt.

"MAYBE NOT, BUT SHE WILL GIVE HERSELF TO YOU AND THAT WILL SUFFICE," Dionysus said with a smile.

"I won't give into this," Lance challenged.

"YOU WON'T BE ABLE TO RESIST," Dionysus mocked, before he poked Lance in the forehead right between the eyes. At his touch Lance felt the desire that had begun to stir in him with the vision reawaken and grow exponentially before his eyes he watched the dream begin to play itself out it was so real he could taste her.

"No," he groaned in defiance. "God no," he cried out and the door handle under his grasp gave way. Lance stumbled out into the hall. He drew a sigh of relief as the image shattered and the hunger abated. He looked back at the fallen one and noted James Hardagen's eyes were blue once more. The old god was gone, for now.

133

Catharine sat down in one of the deck chairs at the round poolside table where she and her hosts had eaten the first night she stayed with them. Agent Blackwood sat down across from her. Catharine tried not to stare at the other woman but found it difficult. Gail's resemblance to Dana Murphy was uncanny and she couldn't help but wonder what Lance thought of her. Part of her felt threatened by Gail after all she was a living breathing reminder of what Lance had lost and being around her, he might feel things that he couldn't with her.

Catharine shook her head it didn't matter, it couldn't right now; the only thing that mattered was catching the killer after her before he went after Lance. With this in mind Catharine watched as Sam and Anna took a seat at the table as well. She envied them for a moment, they didn't have the kind of obstacles between their affections that she and Lance did. Their romance would be a smooth and easy one by comparison. Drawing a breath, Catharine fought for calm that seemed just beyond her reach.

Temper and lust warred within her, stirring up her emotions and making her crazy. She wished silently that she'd never accepted James's offer for a drink but more so that she'd never touched that damn cup. She hadn't been right since. "Agent Blackwood I'd like to introduce you to detective Roman's friends this is Anna Gallagher an archeologist for the Smithsonian and Sam Abrams, MMA fighter. Sam, Anna this is Gail Blackwood. Lance's partner on the case," Catharine stated.

"Hello," Gail said eyeing the pair with curiosity.

"Lance brought me in to help with security," Sam explained.

"And her? Do you really think it's wise for her to be here?" Gail questioned eyeing Anna with concern.

"I'm here for Catharine," Anna said simply.

Gail nodded, though Catharine could see she questioned the wisdom of the choice.

"Wow, I've never seen such a fine looking but grim bunch of people," Emily said amused as she walked over from her lounge chair.

"We've heard from the killer again," Catharine stated as Emily sank down in the empty chair beside Gail.

"Oh dear," Emily said with alarm as a pair of strong hands grabbed he by the shoulders.

"Relax Em, we're perfectly safe," James assured her. She lifted her head to look at him and he brushed a kiss on her forehead before taking a seat beside her.

Lance sunk down into the empty chair at Catharine's right. She looked over at him and noted he looked weary now, when he hadn't before, she wondered what had happened since he left her side in the lounge but didn't ask. Whatever it was it could wait.

"So, you said you wanted to set a trap," Gail prompted.

"That's right. I figure with the film being interrupted again James will need to reassure his people that the film is still going to be made and on time," Catharine stated.

"Yeah I will," James confirmed.

"That should give us the perfect stage to set a trap." Catharine said with a smile.

"What do you have in mind?" Gail asked with interest.

The group listened with bated breath as Catharine laid out her idea. She hadn't even finished when Lance gave his response.

"This is a horrible idea there are about a hundred ways this thing could go bad," Lance muttered.

"Have you got anything better?" Catharine challenged, hurt he'd not be in favor of the idea.

"No," he admitted.

"Then unless anyone else has any objections," Catharine quipped, waiting for a response and getting none. "That's exactly what we're going to do," she added. A grim look of determination replaced her smile as the others nodded.

"We'll need to be able to gain access to the soundstage, get the actors back together," James pointed out.

"That can be arranged," Gail assured him.

"I better get started on the arrangements," James stated. He rose from the table with Emily at his side to begin putting the party together. "Saturday too soon?" he questioned.

"No, Saturday should be fine," Gail answered. She took out her phone and dialed Agent Kessler's number.

Catharine rose from the table and headed inside. God, Saturday, which was in twenty-four hours, she didn't know if she would be ready that soon. Sure it was her idea and she was the one pushing for a trap but she wasn't as brave as she pretended to be, quite frankly the idea of facing this guy made her want to scream with terror but she was through with running and refused to hide, she'd done both for as long as she could remember and it had done her no good. It was time to face her demons head on.

134

Lance watched as Agent Blackwood hung up her phone. "Where are you on the list of suspects?" Lance questioned.

"Nowhere yet, we're checking the artist a bit deeper but so far they're all clean," Gail revealed.

"Damn. Okay, will you check on one more for me," Lance requested.

"Yeah," Agent Blackwood said.

"Check out her publicist Bryan."

"Do you suspect him?"

"Yeah, no I'm not sure. I just got a bad feeling about the guy it's probably nothing. Every time I've seen them together or over heard them talking they're arguing and he's sticking his nose too far into her personal business." Lance stated.

"I'll look into it," Gail assured him. "For what it's worth I think the way Kessler handled you was a prick thing to do but he's right detective you're way too close to this thing."

"Yeah, I know it." Lance admitted.

"I've got to go I'll let you know if I get anything."

"Thanks," Lance said with a sigh before she rose from the table and left.

"I won't let her out of my sight, once you're off her," Sam assured Lance.

"I know."

"She's right this is the best way to handle this," Sam stated.

"Yeah I get that but I don't like it. How would you feel if it were Anna with her head in his cross hairs," Lance muttered.

"Probably about the same," Sam admitted. "Are you in for the day?"

"Yeah, I sort of got kicked off the case," Lance said with

disgust.

Sam blinked stunned. "How?"

"I don't want to talk about it. It's humiliating," Lance groaned. "Why do you want to know?"

"I need to get a new cell phone." Sam explained.

"Yeah, fine go. I'll keep an eye on Anna," Lance assured him.

"Thanks."

"Hey I am here you know and I can take care of myself," Anna said with exasperation.

"Yeah, I know but this isn't exactly friendly turf," Sam reminded, before he brushed a kiss on her forehead. "I'll be back soon steer clear of our host," Sam requested.

"I will," she assured him before giving him a quick peck on the lips.

Lance watched as the other man left and considered the idea of a drink to calm raw nerves but dismissed it immediately, the last thing he wanted to do right now was give Dionysus any more of a hold on him.

135

Catharine closed her bedroom door and sank down onto her bed. She felt like a nap but knew there was way too much she had to do. She glanced over at her laptop and groaned. How was she supposed to write the rest of the movie script let alone a book, she despised, when right now there was a man out there somewhere waiting for an opportunity to kill her.

She swallowed, thinking like that would drive her crazy, she told herself. She laid down on the bed resting her head on her pillow. Just a few minutes, she thought to herself as she folded down the blankets. She slipped under the soft cool white silk and wrapped it about her protectively. Her lashes fluttered and she began to slip into sleep.

Catharine jumped, startled as the phone in her pocket vibrated and rang jolting her awake once more. Drawing the offending object from her pocket she lifted it to her ear.

"Hello," she said her voice heavy with sleepiness and tinged with temper.

"Catharine did I wake you?" Bryan's voice questioned with concern.

"No, I'm awake what is it?" She asked trying to sound more alert than she felt. The bed beneath her was so comfortable it made it hard to keep her eyes open.

"Are you okay? I heard the shoot was canceled again for the day. Have you heard any news?" he asked.

"I'm all right, just a little tired. The film is still on, they're just not done cleaning up the crime scene yet," Catharine said with yawn.

"Have they found the killer?" Bryn questioned.

"Not yet, he struck again last night."

"I wish you'd let me take you out of here," Bryan stated with discomfort.

"I'm not leaving Bry so just let it go okay. I'll be fine," she assured him.

"Why do you trust this detective so much, you barely know him? Is it because you're sleeping with him?" Bryan questioned.

"Damn it Bryan, I don't want to have this argument again. I'm not sleeping with the detective and even if I were it's not your concern," she snapped.

"I'm sorry, you're right I just don't want to see you get hurt again," Bryan muttered.

"I'll be fine," she murmured, the phone slipped from her grasp as sleep drew her under once more.

"I'm sure you will," Bryan answered before the call was disconnected.

136

Anna felt the silence around her become uncomfortable. Lance was lost in his thoughts and Sam's absence was hitting her in a way she'd not anticipated, her mind was trying to wander once more to where Dionysus had led it, when he caught her in James Hardagen's room. She could feel her body stirring and hated it.

Her attempts earlier to quiet the wants awake inside her, had failed miserably and her reading had not shed any light on the reason or given any comfort. She'd read about Paul asking for a thorn in his flesh to be removed and being refused as she was now. She'd also read more passages than she could count about how a man would leave his home to be with his wife. Or how two become one flesh, she didn't get the reference at all she and Sam weren't married. It was maddening.

"Lance," she said needing a distraction.

"Yeah."

"Um what do you need to prove the cup James has is the one stolen from the museum?" She asked.

"Well aside from your testimony which is of little use given the fact the cup here looks nothing like the one that was taken I'd need some sort of evidence that connects him to the thief," Lance answered. His eyes, she noted held questions as to why she'd brought that up and hints of fear. "Did he mess with you earlier?" Anna questioned with alarm.

Lance blinked stunned by the question.

"He did. Are you okay?" She asked.

"Yeah I guess and no. I… he said things that unnerved me."

"What things?"

"That when we give into our lusts he's in the midst of the act," Lance said with disgust.

Anna cursed. Now she saw what he was playing at. She'd been right he wasn't the harmless spirit he pretended to be. Dionysus was far more dangerous than Hermes had been. He'd gotten each of them alone set them up to fall one by one, only Sam remained untouched and she was going to make damn sure he stayed that way. "He's been playing us since he invited us in his house," Anna said with disgust.

"Yeah, so it seems," Lance muttered. "What do we do?"

"Prove James stole that cup and get it out of his hands," Anna muttered. "Tell me about your thief," Anna requested.

"I can do one better I've got a photo," Lance stated. He drew it out of his wallet where he'd stuck it in Vegas and handed it to her.

Anna studied the image and gasped.

"What is it?"

"I've seen this guy," she said with excitement.

"What? Where?"

"I'm not sure maybe while we were in Vegas. Let me look through my pictures, see what I can find. If I'm right, I know James was there. I saw him at the bank remember?" Anna stated.

"Yeah but until I can put them together it's just a coincidence he could have been there for the contest," Lance argued.

"He wasn't on the guest list for the ad."

"It doesn't matter he can claim he was invited," Lance argued playing devil's advocate.

"Right, I'll go see about those photos then, for now just hang in there," she muttered before she rose from the table and left him alone. "

137

Lance growled at being left alone with his thoughts, there was too much in his head right now crowding him with a mix of emotions that would slowly drive him mad. He wondered how Anna knew what the fallen had done to him but hadn't been able to ask. He'd seen how Dionysus's influence had affected Catharine and was aware Anna had been told about the first bizarre incident.

He recalled the image of Catharine, head hanging over the toilet expelling a blood red wine she'd not drunk that day and felt his stomach churn with disgust. Would he now endure the same fate? Could he trust himself to be alone with her? He didn't know and that scared him. But more than the uncertainty of what the old god had done to him and how it would affect him; he worried about the killer.

He was out there, watching, waiting, lurking nearby and the fact that he'd lost his free pass to see her without her knowledge no doubt would anger him. This plan of hers was madness, all those people all the rooms it would be too easy for the killer to get to her and slip out unnoticed. Not to mention the fact they'd only be strengthening Dionysus's hold on James. The fallen was probably thrilling in the idea of a vampire themed party. There would be wine, women and music if they weren't careful it might just turn into a full out orgy of old. Lance cursed as he got to his feet. He had to go see Catharine despite the danger that might be in it. He had to make her call this damn thing off.

138

Sam stood by the register, new phone in hand waiting for the sym-card to be updated with his old data. He'd had the previous phone memory stored in back up incase anything happened to it. Years of covering his ass had led to certain habits and right now he was glad of it. Wherever Artemis was; if she had his phone in a matter of seconds it would be no better than a paper weight.

"All right Mr. Abrams it should be all set." The clerk stated.

No sooner had the words been spoken but the phone rang.

"Hello," Sam said as he connected the call.

"Abrams where in the hell have you been. We picked up Kadar where you instructed but you promised us an explanation, it's been well over 24 hours," a familiar voice shouted from the other end.

Sam cursed he'd known it wouldn't be long before he heard from them but he'd not counted on it being immediate. They weren't exactly patient people, he reminded himself and for good reason.

"Yeah sorry about that I lost my phone in the UK. Just got in to grab a new one. I've been busy," Sam muttered as he walked out of the store.

"No shit you've been busy, our records show you've been back to Israel, then taken a hop to Miami, from there out to Colorado and then England and we've got you out in LA somewhere, what the devil is going on. You know you're not supposed to leave Vegas unless we clear it first."

"I didn't have any choice. A civilian walked into my gym with Kadar on her tail, I've been trying to get her clear since," Sam stated, it was true enough.

"Why'd she come to you?"

"Lance Roman sent her. Look I haven't got a lot of time to get into this right now and I'm not exactly in a secure location. I've got a lot on my plate, I'll get you everything I have as soon as I get a free moment," Sam assured him.

"What kind of shit storm did the DC cop drag you into this time Abrams?"

"Same one, his killers back," Sam muttered before he disconnected the call. Sam got into the rental car and started back for James Hardagen's home. He pressed the button to mute the incoming call, he'd deal with the agency once he had more to give them. He realized that meant speaking to Anna about what she knew. He hoped she didn't come back at him with a wounded I told you so and then an angry not so polite request that he get lost because if she did, she was going to be sorely disappointed. Sam had no intention of going anywhere. He was going to stick by her through this thing to the end.

139

Catharine sat at her laptop staring at the blinking screen. The last line of her outline stared back at her waiting for her to complete it but nothing sprang to mind. She was stuck and she knew it. Serenity had sought cover in the woods where no mortal dared enter and yet the one who pursued her had followed her in.

Who was he, why was he following her? She didn't know she couldn't see his face and it was starting to scare her. Catharine always knew where her story was taking her. It was what had made writing Dark Heart so easy she'd seen the end from the beginning. Now she was writing blind she didn't know where to go. Damn it who are you? She snapped at the shadowed image in her mind in frustration and he still refused to speak.

Catharine growled with annoyance and a dark male laugh rumbled out of the corner behind her. She turned startled and the room faded.

She found herself once more in the woods near the water's edge where she'd left Serenity in the outline, looking down at the water she found her hair was long silken strands of the palest gold. About her body was wrapped the white Grecian gown Serenity was famous for. She snarled at the sight.

"I am not Serenity," she shouted in defiance, aware that once more she'd been drawn into an unnatural dream. "Stop wasting your time with this charade Dionysus, it won't work. I know myself and I know who you are as well, you can't convince me you're Syvarin," she snapped.

"Oh you are a vision when you're angry," The man murmured as he stepped out of the shadows. The form he wore was not the vampire lords but Kovrin's. The sight of him ruggedly tan with that dark hair and those predatory eyes stole her breath.

"Switching faces won't get to me either," she lied, seeing the werewolf prince shook her to her core, he was the epitome of everything she feared most in the world. As he moved closer to her his lips curled into a smile to reveal his wolf like teeth.

"We both know you don't mean that Catharine I can smell your fear," he boasted.

"You're not him," she whispered as she shut her eyes trying to drive the image from her mind. It proved to be a terrible mistake. His hand brushed against her skin and she gasped at the touch, she knew it, knew him. God she was wrong it was him. Somehow the nightmare she'd created had slipped out of his cage in her mind and he was here now invading her dreams. "You're dead," she challenged trying to make the nightmare before her go away.

"I'm not dead you killed me on the written page but the man I represent still lives. Therefore I live," he murmured as his hands came to rest on her shoulders, clawed fingers meeting just above her breasts.

"Don't touch me," she hissed with dread as her eyes flew open.

"Shh, come now my dear you know that when I touch you so, you like it," he teased as he drew her back against his chest to grind his erection against her ass.

"I never wanted you," she snapped in defiance even as her body too used to the act, responded pressing back against him giving him more friction.

"She never welcomed you, the vampire lord challenged as he emerged from the shadows. She chose me instead, used me as her sword to defeat you." He stated as he took her hand in his to draw her free of the werewolf's grasp.

Catharine screamed with horror as reality crashed in on her the beast that held her now was not Dionysus as she'd originally believed. "I am not your Serenity," she cried out in desperation as she crumbled to her knees.

"Ah, but you are," the werewolf snarled.

"No, she isn't she's mine," Dionysus argued. "You've made no open claim to her."

"I am now, my hold on her reaches deeper than yours, cupbearer," the werewolf growled as his nails swiped at the vampire lord's face.

Syvarin hissed in rage at the blow as the cuts sealed themselves. "My hold on her is older," he argued.

"That's a lie and you know it," the wolf roared.

Catharine watched as the two men, monsters, gods, demons, she didn't know what to call them really, postured for the right to claim her in stunned disbelief for a moment before shaking free of her stupor. While they were busy with each other she should be running, she told herself. No, not running, that would draw their attention, instead she took the opportunity to slip away. Crawling through dirt, leaf litter, and briars searching for a way out of the woods and the dream.

"Enough! We waste time with this she's getting away," the vampire lord snapped.

"Indeed. Tell you what, a hunt then. Whoever finds her first here shall have first taste until the dispute can be settled," the were-wolf suggested.

"Agreed," Dionysus stated before he turned to pursue the mortal woman.

"Fool. This is one hunt he can't win," the wolf mocked before he lifted his head and drew in a breath, he picked up her scent instantly, and he knew it well. It made it easier, she'd drawn blood. Kovrin took off following her scent. Hot on the trail of his prey.

Catharine was aware of the moment their argument ended, could hear them moving about in the wood searching her out. She stayed low to the ground careful not to draw attention to herself, she had to find a place to hide. As she crawled she came to a familiar spot and cursed knowing the fallen chasing her were altering the dream world around her to their own ends.

"Now I have you," he breathed with pleasure, his predatory eyes gleamed with a strange orange glow. Catharine turned to face him and trembled with fear and damn him anticipation, she cursed the man he'd been based upon for leaving her so vulnerable to this monsters hunger.

"Ares," she whispered the name acknowledging his true form and he laughed as he closed the distance between them.

"I TOLD HIM YOU KNEW ME BETTER," he crowed loud enough for Dionysus to hear. He wanted his brother who'd dared to try and touch her to know she'd seen him immediately for who he was unlike the cup bearer who'd been the vampire lord to her until this time.

"Leave me be please," Catharine requested.

"NO SERENITY, IT'S TIME FOR THIS COURTSHIP TO END. YOU'RE MINE. YOU KNOW IT TO BE TRUE I'VE BEEN STIRRING INSIDE OF YOU FOR YEARS WAITING FOR YOU TO EMBRACE ME, NOW AT LAST YOU KNOW ME. YOU WANT ME. I WON'T LET YOUR FEAR TURN ME

AWAY FROM YOU," he whispered as he came to kneel at her side.

"I don't want you, I never have," she muttered in defiance as she sat up. Her eyes moved past him to see the vampire lord lingering in the distance. "Help me," she entreated desperate to be free of Kovrin.

"I CANNOT GIRL I MADE A DEAL HE FOUND YOU HE GETS THE FIRST TASTE," Dionysus hissed with rage. "YOU CHEATED BROTHER."

"YOU DELUDED YOURSELF, CUP BEARER," Ares corrected before he tipped his head down to capture her lips.

"Doesn't what I want here have any weight. It's my dream after all," Catharine argued desperate, trying to reason with them.

"I KNOW WHAT YOU WANT SERENITY, I'VE ALWAYS KNOWN, I CAN SMELL IT ON YOU," He assured her before his mouth covered hers tasting lips he'd dreamt of longer than he cared to admit. He'd taken other brides over the years but none had eluded him as long as her. She was his Hestia and he was going to make her scream his name with such pleasure, Dionysus turned back to his pretty model.

Catharine struggled in his grasp to not give in, he disgusted her and yet he was right, her body was preparing itself for him It was HIS fault. HE'D done this to her. It didn't matter how much time had passed or how she'd changed, the fact remained that whether she wanted a man or not her body was conditioned to respond to their hunger for her. It betrayed her now yielding to the war god's advances though she wanted nothing to do with him. She was helpless before him, powerless to stop him. As his lips parted hers, tears tracked down her face, her eyes held that haunted look of fear and desire, the cover of her novels had made famous.

She trembled with shame as his hands and mouth fell upon her flesh inflaming her with lust.

"Let me go. I don't want you!" she shouted with all her will.

"YOU HAVE NO SAY HERE," the War god hissed as his hands moved lower to seize hold of her hips, he turned her over on her belly preparing her to mate as Kovrin would. Blending dream, fiction, and her reality together in a way that she was certain would drive her mad.

"NO! Do you hear me? I said no damn you!" Catharine shouted in rage and he laughed with pleasure.

140

Lance lifted his hand to the door prepared to knock trying to find the words to explain to Catharine why she couldn't go through with setting her trap. All thought left his head at the sound of her angry voice thick with fear. He didn't think, didn't hesitate. He simply stuck the key James had given him in the lock and prayed it worked on the main door as well.

The door swung open to reveal her laying on the bed eyes closed thrashing in sleep caught in some messed up nightmare. He was across the room and at her side with only a couple strides. He drew her into his arms and tried to wake her. But she did not respond to his touch nor did she stir when he called to her. He didn't know what she was dreaming of for sure but he could guess and he wanted her to snap out of it.

"Come on Catharine open your eyes," he commanded. But nothing happened.

"Please, no let me go," she whimpered as she curled in on herself trying to get away from whatever monster tormented her.

"Damn it Catharine, come on honey wake up I don't know how to help you," he muttered with frustration. He wasn't sure how it was possible but this was worse than dealing with a killer hunting her at least a killer he could confront, whatever tormented her now was beyond his reach. "God help her," he snapped in fury as he watched bruises like finger prints begin to appear on her skin. "Please," he entreated desperate for her nightmare to end.

141

Ares ripped her gown to shreds leaving her bare before him as he managed to gain control of her legs. The hell cat had been kicking and screaming since her last denial of him. She wasted her time, her energy and her breath; in but a moment it would be over she would be his here in the dream world and it wouldn't be long after till he had her in the flesh.

She thought her fight would dissuade him but she was so wrong every bit of anger and each attempt to fight back only made him want her more; only strengthened his hold upon her. She'd yet to notice it, but her arousal which she denied so adamantly had only intensified, she was more than ready for him now and he was finally ready for her.

"YOU'RE GOING NOWHERE, YOU WILL BEARWITNESS," he growled at Dionysus forbidding the god the right to leave and sulk.

"I WILL STAY BUT WHEN YOU'RE DONE I GET MY TASTE," the cup bearer challenged.

"AS YOU LIKE BUT KNOW THIS IT WILL BE THE ONLY TASTE YOU EVER HAVE," Ares stated before he untied his breaches to expose his aroused flesh to the cool night air. He pressed his need against her lifted rear letting her feel the heat of him against her. Burning her with his touch; she cried out in fear, protest and hunger all at once. "THAT'S RIGHT, I'M HERE," he taunted as he drew her back against him. Thrilling in the feel of her heat and the press of her against him tightening his groin, it had been too long since he had a woman so, millennia since he warred with one here.

"God no, this isn't going to happen."

Ares hissed in rage at the mention of the name and to punish her he slapped the curve of her ass allowing nails to sink into tender flesh. She cried out in pain and pleasure at the sensation. "DON'T YOU DARE UTTER THAT NAME BEFORE ME. YOU HAVE NO LOVE FOR HIM, YOU TOLD THAT MEDDLER SO," he hissed before he hit her again.

"I lied to her, to both of you, and most of all myself," Catharine cried out in confession. "God forgive me I'm sorry, please help me," she breathed in desperation.

Ares roared in rage as his desires were left thwarted and Dionysus laughed mocking his brother for taking too long as Catharine fell out of the dream.

142

Catharine's eyes shot open and she found herself wrapped in the silk sheet of the bed she'd dosed off in. Warm arms were wrapped about her cradling her, fingers trying to sooth. Lance. She stared up at him with wonder and disbelief. How? She noted the door left open and figured he'd let himself in. She didn't know if she should be furious or grateful.

She studied him with curiosity and noted his eyes were closed his lips moved but no sound did he utter. His face was twisted with fear and grief and she wanted to make it go away. Reaching out she wrapped her arms around his neck drawing him to her. She watched as his eyes flew open and relief filled them.

"Thank God," he breathed before his lips crashed into hers kissing her with an intensity that stole her breath away. When his lips parted hers, he rest his forehead against her brow and drew a couple deep cleansing breaths. When he found some level of calm he spoke again. "Are you okay?"

"Yeah, bad dream that's all," she assured him.

"Don't lie to me Catharine, I know it was him," Lance snapped angry, she'd try to make light of it.

"Lance, please I don't want to talk about it," Catharine said as she let him go looking to retreat now. He'd seen too much and yet nothing. "I've got other things to worry about."

"No, this takes priority even over the damn trap," Lance muttered.

"Why are you so against it?" Catharine asked.

"Why are you so hell bent on putting yourself out for him to take? Do you want to be caught? Do you want him?" Lance asked mortified recalling what she'd written of Serenity. She was torn and conflicted, despised both the monsters who chased her and yet needed them.

"No. God why would you say that?" she asked hurt.

"You wrote it," Lance muttered.

"Damn it I wish you'd never touched that damn book," she cursed with rage as she pushed at him trying to get away.

Lance held her fast not about to let her walk away from this now. He'd seen too much to let her run. "Part of me does as well. I liked you better when I could believe the lie you wrapped about yourself. I liked Catharine but that's not who you are. Is it, Serenity? " he muttered.

"Don't call me that," Catharine hissed.

"It is your name isn't it?" he said with understanding.

"Not anymore," she murmured. "How did you figure it out?" she asked with curiosity as she studied him. How did he do that? How did he see through her lies?

"It's in the pages of Heart of Clay when Ashella reveals her history it's like a confession, she tells the reader she was born Serenity. It's you telling your reader the truth."

"You see too much Lance."

"Tell me?" he requested.

"What?" she questioned, fear churning within her. She felt him wrapping her to him in threads that she knew could destroy her.

"Everything." He answered before he brushed a strand of her fiery hair away from her eyes wanting to stare into those blue pools that held the truth.

"Lance," she said frightened not wanting to face it not with him. She wanted him to be able to believe the lie.

"Talk to me Catharine, the not knowing, the speculation of it may drive me mad. I can't protect you from things I don't know or understand, he wants you dead, someone from your past that knows you're Serenity. " Lance stated.

Catharine nodded he was right. By remaining silent she was endangering his life as well as her own. He needed to understand why she was setting the trap, then maybe he'd help her instead of fight with her. "You're right, my silence will only hurt you and me but my words will not give your mind any comfort," Catharine warned. She reached into the bed side table and pulled a pack of cigarettes out of the drawer.

Lance blinked. He'd not seen her light up once since they met. How was that possible?

"I don' smoke anymore, but I keep a pack to remind me of a time when I did. My name is Serenity, Jade, Catharine, Collins. I was an only child my father was a drunk, he beat my mother and occasionally me. He died when I was young at my Mother's hand. Self-defense but she was never whole again. I left shortly after I turned eighteen. I started college and was doing fine until someone broke into my apartment. Nothing appeared to be missing but it scared me, I called the police." Catharine began. She broke from the telling to lick dry lips, her fingers wrapped around the cigarettes and picked them up.

143

Lance brushed his fingers through her hair and tried to ease her discomfort. The man didn't want to push her, he wanted to protect her from whatever it was she'd endured but the cop knew she had to face it. She'd reinvented herself at least twice to hide from whatever nightmare she'd endured and that was dangerous. He'd seen others do that, heard stories of them losing their grip on reality. Their personality splitting to cope with the world they couldn't face themselves. He didn't want to see that happen to her.

He watched as her fist clenched the old worn pack like a life line. "The cop that turned up was named Kurt Dryden. He took the case seriously when no one had ever taken my complaints as valid before. He checked the place thoroughly, it turned out something was missing…"

"A pair of panties, or a bra, maybe some kind of nightgown," Lance reasoned seeing it in his mind.

"Right, Kurt was very worried he insisted on staying with me until he caught the one responsible for the theft." Catharine stated.

"Did they catch him?" Lance asked.

"No. He poured me a drink said it would take the edge off. I was still too young and naive to understand the danger of the wine. One glass led to two or three and then to his kissing me, kissing to touching and from there a lot more. I swear I said no but I was too drunk to remember. He told me I wanted him. That I'd come on to him. I eventually accepted it as truth. Part of me wonders if he was the thief."

"No I'm willing to bet whoever the killer is, he was the thief," Lance muttered,

"At any rate this went on for a while I got used to him. Convinced myself I was in love with him. I was even ready to marry him, until he turned violent." Catharine muttered.

"What set him off?" Lance asked.

"I pushed him away one night because I was tired and didn't feel good. I was pregnant and didn't have a clue. He beat me bloody and then had me anyway. When he left I went to the hospital. Was told I miscarried, they asked who'd hurt me but I didn't say anything. I knew they'd never believe me. I went home. Made up my mind to leave him, I'd seen what happened to my mother. I wasn't about to let that happen to me. He caught me packing. We fought he told me if I left he'd kill me. It was in that moment I knew I could never use the name Serenity again." She stated.

"So you left home which was?"

"Doesn't matter. I moved to New York and became Jade," She said in dismissal.

"You said before that you left Tom for a time. Why?"

"I received a letter warning me away from him. I thought that Kurt had found me and I left, but it was the killer I guess. I wish I'd listened to him and not gone back to Tom."

"Why?"

"Because I never saw Tom for whom he really was until we were married. But the killer knew. Tom revealed his true nature on our wedding night. I endured him for several years until I found out he was cheating on me, then I filed for divorce," Catharine explained.

Lance said nothing he simply drew her closer. "Why do you let me near you?" Lance questioned with curiosity.

"I don't know, I shouldn't want to be, you're right you should remind me of Kurt but you don't." She whispered.

"So you want to set the trap to face the killer instead of run," Lance stated.

"Exactly," she whispered as she snuggled in closer to him.

"Okay fair enough but I need you to understand why I'm against it," Lance stated with impatience.

She nodded and waited for what he would say.

Lance drew a breath to steady his nerves, he didn't know if he was ready to tell her about Dana but understood he had to. She shared with him a part of herself she wasn't ready to and now for her to understand his objections, he'd have to tell her about what happened to Dana. "When I worked in homicide I was partnered with the woman you saw in that photo. Her name was Dana Murphy. We pulled the first Fury Killer victim. When the others started turning up it became our case. We were three deep in it. Officially working a serial when things went to hell; I lost everything that mattered to me to this case."

"How did he kill her?"

"No. It would be easier if he had," Lance muttered.

Catharine blinked her blue eyes held questions she didn't dare utter. He smiled amused, somehow they understood each other though they'd barely met. She saw that if she spoke now he'd not say any more.

"Dana and I were a week away from getting married when the Fury Killer took her best friend. Dana took it hard. The killer was watching her, he took one look at Heather and struck. She was his ideal target young, blonde, beautiful with those bewitching hazel eyes he seems obsessed with. Where does that fit in?"

"As Jade I wore contacts."

Lance nodded. "Dana didn't handle it losing Heather; broke her. She became obsessed with the case. I knew something was wrong at the funeral I hadn't seen her in days, she was pale, too pale and thin. She'd probably lost at least five pounds. She withdrew, called the wedding off. I watched from the outside as her inability to let it go took her heart, her mind, her body and eventually her life," Lance stated with regret.

"What happened?"

"She shut me out wouldn't let me back in. I left homicide I couldn't watch her tear herself apart like that. I came home from work to find her at the apartment. She'd killed herself in her despair at not being able to find Heather's killer. I think she blamed herself for what happened."

"I'm sorry," Catharine whispered.

"I don't want you trying to draw this guy out because if something goes wrong and he gets you I don't know if I could survive it," Lance said.

"I can understand where you're coming from Lance but even seeing where your objection comes from I can't walk away from this. I've been running from the monsters that scare me for as long as I can remember. If I do it now I'll be doing it for the rest of my life and I can't live like that anymore. I won't. I've portrayed myself as so weak, I can't even stand my own name."

"You're not as weak as the Serenity you've written yourself," Lance argued.

"How can you say that? I told you..."

"Yes, you did and you've exaggerated your own faults within

the pages as you've overdramatized their cruelty. You said it yourself, you walked away from Kurt and you left Tom some women never leave. You went on your own. In the books Serenity never does. She only leaves when someone else takes care of her problems for her," Lance stated.

Catharine blinked shocked by the observation. She'd never thought of it that way.

"You're not a monster and you're not looking for someone to hurt or control you if you were you'd let me tell you what to do. I see the frightened girl and I understand the vampire image but that's not who you are. I see the faerie," He whispered.

"Faerie, you see me as a faerie, Lancelot?" she asked amused.

Lance blinked he couldn't believe he'd said that aloud but as he saw her eyes dance with amusement he knew she needed to hear it. "Yeah, I see you as a smart, spirited, and dazzling faerie princess who isn't afraid to use her magic to get what she wants," Lance admitted.

He watched as she bit her lip holding back a grin. Both embarrassed and flattered by the description. "You're full of surprises detective," she said amused.

"I'm going to stand by you through this but understand if I think it gets too dangerous I will not hesitate to get you out of here," Lance muttered changing the subject.

"Fair enough, but understand that if you do, I'm going to protest the action."

"I won't like it but I'll understand it," Lance assured her as he rested his chin on the crown of her head.

"Are we okay now?" Catharine asked him.

"Yeah, we're okay Serenity." he assured her.

"Good I like you Lance, I don't want us to fight," she murmured.

"Neither do I," he assured her as he eased his hold on her.

Catharine curled up closer to him. "Thank you," she whispered.

"For what?" he asked.

"Everything," she answered not knowing where to begin.

"You're welcome," he answered.

"Stay with me?" she requested.

He said nothing simply nodded. He kicked off his shoes and sank down on the bed beside her. She sank back down beside him and he drew her back against him holding her close. He kept his eyes on the door in case Anna emerged from across the hall.

144

Anna sat at her desk flipping through the photos stored on her camera looking for an image of the thief that Lance had shown her. She cursed as she found nothing. Where was it? She knew she'd seen him, was certain, it was while they were in Vegas.

Anna set her camera down and reached in her bag she drew out the jewelry Catharine had gifted her from the ball and let her mind drift back to that night. She went over the crowd in her thoughts trying to recall if he'd been there and groaned to realize he hadn't. Damn it where then?

The memory was there just out of reach and it gnawed at her mind like a dog with a bone. She swore again as the image of the necklace in her hand made her thoughts wander to that night on the elevator.

She felt Sam pressed against her once more as he held her close shielding her from her enemies. She felt the desire she'd known that night stir inside her, felt his hand on her face as he lifted her chin so their eyes met. Saw first surprise and then that spark of hunger that had startled her and thrilled her all at once. That awkward first moment of awareness that there was something between them, he hadn't kissed her then but he told her he wanted to. He wouldn't kiss her until much later in the hotel in Israel but she wanted him too. As she thought about the moment, memory became fantasy as she pictured his head lowering to capture her lips.

Anna blinked no, she wasn't going there not now.

"I just need to stay busy until he gets back and it'll be easier," she assured herself. Since her efforts to find the place she'd seen the thief had come up empty, she'd turn her attention to other matters. Picking up one of her books of legends she flipped open the cover and turned over to the last page she'd read. She'd try to find the tale connected to the crown or the scepter. Anna's eyes skimmed over the text turning to her work to ignore the hunger beginning to rise up within her once more.

145

James sat behind his desk putting together a list of calls to make in order to arrange the party Catharine was proposing. He was excited at the prospect, the voice within him whispered possibilities of things they could do. He thrilled at the images that danced before his eyes. His mouth watered at the promise of pleasure to be had. Reaching over he drew his bottle of wine from the drawer and poured himself a glass. He stared at it within the cup and noted it was redder in the cup than the one in the bottle.

As he sipped it he was jolted by the taste since he'd tasted Pamela's blood and sipped Emily's the wine within the goblet tasted of it, a taste that he was beginning to crave. As he drank his thoughts turned to Emily. He wanted her now at least until Catharine came around. As if she heard him, she walked into his office to rest her hands on his shoulders.

"How are the arrangements coming?" She asked.

"Good, I've got the list together just waiting on the green light," James stated. The phone on his desk rang and James picked it up.

"Hello."

"Mr. Hardagen, the set is clear for use," Gail Blackwood stated.

"Thank you," James said pleased.

"You're all set," Gail stated before she hung up.

James laughed as he set the phone down.

"What is it?" Emily asked with curiosity, she'd never seen James in such a good mood.

"We're good to go. I'll just make those calls and all the pieces will be in place, filming starts again tomorrow."

"Perfect."

"No one thing will make it perfect Em," he whispered.

"What?"

"You," James breathed before he drew her down in the chair with him and kissed her. He nipped her lip drawing blood getting a taste of what he desired, then let her go and swatted her butt. "Go on I'll be along in a few," he assured her before he picked up the phone to make his calls. He watched with satisfaction as she did as she was told, just like the voice had promised she would.

146

Lance lifted his head from the pillow beside Catharine at the sound of footsteps in the hall, he brushed a kiss on her brow before he rose from the bed. Gun in hand he moved out into the hall to see Sam.

"You're on edge," Sam muttered at the sight of the gun.

"I've got a killer who wants my head, and to hurt the woman I'm protecting, a freaking god or two tormenting her sleep, the wine god messing with me yeah I'm edgy." Lance snapped.

"Well, I'm afraid my news is only going to compound things," Sam stated.

"And that would be?" Lance prompted.

"I don't have a lot of time here, the agency is calling, they'll be pressing for a meeting." Sam explained.

"Perfect, well, at least we both know this shouldn't take too much longer," Lance stated.

"You're still not comfortable with setting a trap are you?"

"No, I'm not but I'm in," Lance assured him.

"Good. I'll hold off a meet as long as I can. How is she?" Sam questioned.

"Catharine is resting, Anna's been in her room since you left doing some kind of research, no one's come or gone from the room," Lance replied not sure who Sam was referring to."

"Good. I've got Anna for now get some rest," Sam instructed.

Lance nodded, put the gun away and moved back into Catharine's room. He closed the door behind him before he laid back down beside her and let sleep take him.

147

Pamela stepped off the chopper Hermes had loaded her into after their passionate embrace. She studied the ring on her finger and trembled with the knowledge, when next they met they would be wed. She would be the new queen of the gods. Hermes had entrusted her with the task of collecting yet another mantle for him.

When she gave him the whip that would give him three so far and two others were in LA, one was missing and she had to wonder if Magnus was behind it but she kept this suspicion to herself. If he was she'd not dare to cross him even unknowingly. Magnus Halden was far too dangerous even under the protection of a god; especially if he was being fed power by another one.

Pamela made her way up the steps of the museum to speak to the curator, aware that the letter she carried was not going to make the man happy.

"Can I help you Miss?" the older man at the desk questioned. He eyed her with puzzlement, she wasn't the type that typically frequented the place Pamela imagined.

"Yes I'm here at Dr. Broody's request," Pamela stated.

"And you are?"

"His new partner," Pamela replied simply before she handed over the letter.

"I see," the man muttered. His gray eyes turned to the page and putting on his glasses he read it over. "Ian assured us we could keep the whip on display for the foreseeable future it is one of our most prized pieces." The curator stated with objection.

"The whip it turns out may be one part of a much grander collection, he wants to verify his belief and if it proves right, well let's just say, you'll be getting back the whip and additional pieces to go with it," Pamela stated with a smile.

"I see, well in that case I think we can accommodate Mr. Broody," the older man said with delight. He came out from behind the counter and led Pamela to the case where the whip was out on display. "Wait here I'll see about a case for transport," the curator offered before he slipped away.

Pamela studied the whip with interest and thrilled at the sensation of the power she could feel radiating from it. She heard Helios's voice whisper to her, offer her gifts beyond that which Hermes had given her if she would but give the whip to another.

"It's beautiful isn't it Miss Walsh," A familiar voice muttered behind her.

"Yes, indeed it is, Mr. York." Pamela agreed keeping her voice neutral though fear stirred in her blood. She moved to turn and look at him.

"Eyes front Pamela, no need to draw attention to each other. Magnus is pleased to learn you're in Broody's inner circle."

"Does he want the whip?" Pamela questioned.

"No, let the good doctor have his prize, do nothing to make him question your loyalty."

"What does Mr. Halden want?" Pamela asked.

"For now nothing, but if Broody gets close to the crown Magnus will want to know of it," Mr. York stated.

"Of course," Pamela assured him.

"Good, you always were a smart woman Miss Walsh," York said amused before he walked away.

Pamela drew a shaky breath. Things were getting out of hand fast. The sooner Hermes had the whip the better. Magnus Halden was one man she didn't want anywhere near her life again. She watched as the curator took the whip from the case and sealed it in a travel case before handing it over to her.

"Give Ian our regards and our thanks." The man requested.

"I will," Pamela assured him before she stepped back outside and got back on the chopper. "Pilot watch for other air traffic we don't want anyone following us," Pamela muttered.

"Of course Miss Walsh," the man answered before he lifted the chopper into the air and took to the skies.

148 Los Angels, California

Anna woke from sleep with a jolt to the sound of a knock at the door. She cursed to find she'd dosed off, her efforts to keep from dreaming had been pointless, in the end she'd fallen asleep and done nothing but dream. Fevered images played through her mind, bits of dreams that left her hot and bothered.

She cursed herself a fool for ever thinking it wise to look for the cup without Sam. She'd left herself open to the fallen one's attack. She'd walked right into his trap and now she couldn't shake free of his spell. More disturbing; was the knowledge of what Lance had said, the more she let her lust get the better of her, the more access to herself she gave the god of wine.

The knock, that woke her, repeated, and was followed by Sam's voice calling her name. She groaned mentally; now was not the time for her to face him. Not when her body was screaming for his touch. "I'm busy Mr. Abrams, what do you want?" she questioned through the door hoping to get him to go.

"I've got something I need to tell you," he said patiently. She heard him shift outside and pictured him leaning against the door.

"Can't it wait?" she asked crisply. She pressed her cheek against the door and sighed at the feel of the cool wood against her heated skin. The sound of his voice was doing nothing to ease the ache building within her.

She could picture him in her mind, stepping through the door and pressing her against it as he kissed her senseless. No stop thinking like that, Anna commanded herself but her will was not strong enough to make it stop. Once more she prayed for the lust to be taken from her and as before it eased but was not gone.

"No, there are things happening around me you need to know about, and you need to hear them now before things get too far along." Sam stated.

"Fine," Anna relented she lifted her face from the door and unlocked it to let him in.

"Are you okay?" Sam asked his blue eyes were troubled.

He probably was confused by her hesitation to let him in. She hadn't shut him out since the incident with Pamela. "Yes you just woke me, I'm a little cranky," she stated.

"Sorry, Lance mentioned you were working on research," Sam stated.

"Yes, Lance showed me a photo of the thief that took the cup from the museum, I recognized him and was trying to place where from, but I can't quite find the answer. I switched to reading the legends looking for possible reference to the crown and scepter, I must have dosed off."

"Did you…" Sam began but his phone rang. He cursed checked the number and seeing it wasn't the agency but his MMA trainer. "I'm sorry, I've got to take this," Sam said in apology, before connecting the call. "Hello."

Anna stood silent listening to the one sided conversation.

"Yeah I'm doing better the bone is healing nicely but I'm not clear to be back in the gym just yet," Sam stated.

Anna blinked realizing the call must be related to his fight. The thought of that night flashed the memory she was trying to shake loose. It was no wonder she'd had trouble locating it she'd been shot earlier that night. "Sam did you tape your fight?" Anna questioned.

Sam covered the phone to answer her. "Yeah why?"

"Because I need that tape I know where I saw the thief and I can place him with James Hardagen," Anna stated.

"Coach the tape of the fight night can you send it to me?" Sam requested. He listened to the reply and then gave thanks, before rattling off the address. He then hung up the phone. "You realize that even if you're right that unless we can place them at the same bank or something concrete even the tape won't be enough to arrest him."

"I know but I know which bank to check too," Anna reminded.

"Okay, as soon as I get the tape we'll pass it and the bank onto Lance to follow up on." Sam assured her.

149

Sam studied Anna with a growing sense of disquiet. She was behaving strangely. From her refusal to open the door at first to using his last name to ask him to wait, to her silence now in response to his giving her what she'd asked for. He noted she was careful to keep her distance from him.

Sam reached out to touch her and her eyes widened with fright. "Don't touch me," she snapped with panic.

"What's wrong?" Sam questioned as his hand dropped to his side.

"I don't know. I can't shake off whatever Dionysus did to me," Anna admitted.

"Have you prayed about it?" Sam asked feeling his gut clench at her confession. He'd hoped that whatever Dionysus had done to her would have no lasting effect, to hear her admit it was, made him uneasy.

"Yes, that's the most frustrating thing, it eases but it won't leave me completely."

"Why?" Sam asked confused, so far anything a fallen threw at them, a prayer could defeat and now it wasn't working.

"I don't know. I read on and off for hours but I got no clear answers."

"I'll kill him," Sam muttered his temper flaring dangerously at the news. He didn't care for the implications or the manipulation, he wanted Anna, but not if what she felt for him wasn't real.

"No. You can't! If you do, the cup will take you and I'll be lost," she said with fear.

"What does that mean?" Sam asked.

"It means this fallen picks his target wisely," a familiar voice answered from everywhere and yet nowhere.

Sam turned to see the angel that had aided them so far at his side. "Thank God you're here, help her. Take his curse away."

"Is that what you really want, for her to no longer desire you? For her eye to fall upon another," the angel asked.

Sam blinked. Why was it his choice? If it meant she'd have peace yes, his mind answered but a part of him deep down cried out in protest.

"That's what I thought. No, this is not something that can be taken away." The Angel stated.

"I didn't say anything," Sam objected.

"Yes, you did," the angel corrected.

"What do I do then?" Anna asked.

"Pray for strength to endure."

"Why can't it be taken away?" Sam asked.

"Because the spirit knows better than the will what a person needs," the angel replied cryptically.

"Can you just once give us a straight answer," Sam said annoyed.

"I did if you have ears to hear," the angel explained before he touched Anna. She relaxed visibly as the lust running through her eased.

"Why are you here?" Anna asked.

"To warn you the road ahead will be hard and fraught with danger. Do not give up hope or give into the influence of the fallen," the angel said before he vanished.

"Great what the hell does that mean?" Sam asked not caring for the words said or the implication they made.

"I don't know but promise me you won't go after Dionysus," she requested.

"Anna..."

"Promise me!"

"I promise," Sam relented before he drew her into his arms.

150

Catharine woke to find herself still wrapped in Lance's arms on the bed. She wondered how long they'd been resting there but figured it didn't matter. Her stomach rumbled with hunger and she moved to get up. The arm about her middle tightened pulling her back.

"Where are you going?" Lance asked.

"I'm hungry detective I was going to get something to eat," Catharine answered.

"Stay here I'll get it. What do you want?" Lance asked.

"Something salty," she replied.

"How's popcorn sound?" Lance asked.

"Perfect," she replied.

"I'll get a bowl and we can spend the rest of the evening watching a movie," Lance offered.

"Sounds like a plan."

"Stay put and don't let anyone in," Lance requested.

"Okay," she assured him, she watched as he rose from the bed and slipped out the door. She set her cigarettes back in the night table before picking up the T.V. remote, she was ready to start looking for something to watch when she heard the door open and shut once more. "Did you forget something detective?" Catharine asked as she looked up at the door with a grin. "Bryan... what are you doing here?"

Bryan crossed the room to sit down on the bed beside her. He took her hand in his. "I came to convince you to leave town with me, if there is a killer loose in the city then let's get out of here," he requested.

"I can't Bryan I need to stay and face this."

"You're playing with your life," Bryan warned as he let her go.

"I trust in detective Roman's ability to protect me," Catharine stated.

"You don't know this Lance of yours. For all you know he could be the killer," Bryan snapped with anger.

"That's just ridiculous Lance is not dangerous," Catharine said with outrage.

"Damn it Catharine you're judgment where men is concerned is not sound. Your trust in the detective is misplaced. Is your faith in him so unshakable because you're sleeping with him?" Bryan asked his brown eyes lit with temper.

"I don't see how that's any of your business, one way or the other," Lance muttered as he stepped back in the room. His ice blue eyes looked at the scene, Catharine noted his temper and sighed. These two really didn't like each other.

"Lance I know you mean well, but butt out I can handle Bryan," Catharine stated calmly.

"Catharine I don't like this, every time I see you two together you're fighting," Lance said with objection.

"I said I've got this, back off detective, go get the popcorn, please," she requested.

"Fine," Lance relented, he withdrew from the room. Catharine waited until she was sure he was out of earshot.

"Does that look like a man who wants to hurt me?" Catharine asked.

"Tom didn't look dangerous either," Bryan reminded.

"You don't either, should I stay away from you?" Catharine countered.

"That's not fair CJ," Bryan said wounded.

"I'm not leaving Bry I've got to finish this."

"Okay, but promise me you'll be careful." Bryan requested.

"I will but you have to promise me you'll give detective Roman a chance," Catharine requested.

"All right, I will for you."

"Thank you." Catharine said with a smile.

"You're welcome CJ," he answered before he brushed a kiss on her cheek, he then turned and left.

151

As Lance waited for the popcorn to finish popping his phone rang.

"Hello," he said annoyed.

"Detective Roman I looked into the publicist for you," Gail Blackwood stated.

"And?" Lance prompted.

"No red flags, we're still looking but he looks clean," Gail answered.

Lance sighed with relief. "Thanks," he disconnected the call and blew out a breath, it looked like he owed the other man an apology. Lance pulled the popcorn out of the microwave and poured it into a bowl. Picking it up he left the kitchen and headed back to Catharine's room, as he was headed up the stairs Bryan was coming down.

"Look, Bryan, I don't like the way you push CJ around but I get it. You care about her and you don't want to see her get hurt. Steps are being taken to stop the killer hunting her. I won't get into the details but if things go bad I'll want you to take Catharine and get her out of here."

"I will," Bryan assured him.

"Thanks. Do me a favor go easy on CJ she's not as strong as she appears." Lance said.

"What does that mean?"

"It's not my place to answer that; just know she's had it rough."

"I'll try. Did you sleep with her Lance?"

"Like I said before it's not really your business, but no. The trouble is the killer thinks I did. He wants me dead and if he gets it you'll have to protect her," Lance stated.

Bryan nodded. "Maybe I had you figured wrong detective," he

murmured.

"Yeah, I think maybe we both were reading the other wrong," Lance admitted.

"Good night, Lance," Bryan said before he left. Lance moved up the steps to rejoin Catharine.

152

Anna lifted her head from Sam's chest where it rested as she recalled he'd had something he needed to say to her, it was why she let him in. Hazel met with blue and she asked. "What was it you needed to tell me?"

Sam blinked, between her hunt for the thief, his phone call and then learning about Dionysus's spell on her he'd nearly forgotten the reason he'd gone to see her. Part of him wanted to let the matter go for the moment but she needed to know about the phone call he'd received while out earlier in the day. It would change their working relationship and if left unsaid might just ruin the closeness she felt for him.

"I told you yesterday a little bit about my old job remember," Sam prompted hoping that by bringing up the subject again she wouldn't draw away from him.

"Yes, you said you were some kind of soldier," Anna replied, as she remembered he'd preferred that word to spy. She also recalled she'd accused him of using her to complete some old case. Her conclusion had been totally unfounded and irrational. She'd acted poorly and she figured she owed him an apology. After what Ian had done to her at Ithaca she didn't trust easily.

"You were right about Kadar having been a sort of target of mine," Sam admitted.

Anna drew away from him her body rigid as anger and hurt ran through her. He had been using her and she'd been all set to apologize, damn him. Anna opened her mouth ready to let him have it.

"It's not what you think, please just hear me out," Sam requested. Anna nodded, she owed him that much, at least, she figured. "Thank you. When you walked into my gym one of the guys mentioned a leggy blonde was looking for me. That was the last thing I wanted to see right then, because I'd just had a brush with Pamela earlier."

"That's why you were being so uncooperative?" Anna said with understanding.

"Yeah, she really messed me up. I was going to send you away but then Hanna mentioned someone was asking for you up front and I saw that look in your eyes, the spooked one that said you were in trouble. I dragged you into my office and when I saw Kadar, well I knew immediately you were in a lot more trouble than you could understand. I agreed to help you because Lance sent you to me, but more, I knew Kadar; what he was capable of. If anything had happened to you I'd have felt responsible. I didn't want to see you get hurt." Sam explained.

"If I'd gotten hurt, really hurt, it would be on me. I chose to leave the dig in Israel though I knew I was being watched. I took that risk." Anna reminded.

"Yeah, but you didn't understand how big a risk it was. I knew if he did come after you, he'd kill you. For all my best efforts I still managed to get you shot."

"You took care of me," she reminded.

"Yeah, I did. Then you asked me to go with you to Israel and I hesitated unsure. I had that vision that I told you about and I stayed with you. "

Anna relaxed a little recalling what he'd told her. "Okay, I believe you. You weren't using me." She relented. "I'm sorry I said those things before. I said them because of what Ian did to me, but I know you're not like Ian," Anna whispered before she settled back into his embrace.

"You've been hurt before, it's understandable that you would expect it to happen again. Just like part of me figures you'll leave when things get rough," Sam confessed.

"I told you, I'm not going anywhere Sam," she reminded.

He nodded. "You remember that day when the room was hit and Pamela took you in the confusion?"

"How can I forget? It led to me waking up in the throne room to witness Ian's becoming Hermes," Anna said with disgust.

"When I took Kadar down that day I contacted the agency to collect him, not to complete the mission but to ensure he didn't come after us again. To keep Mr. York from learning about the mantles," Sam explained.

"What was your assignment originally or can you say?" Anna

asked curious.

"I was supposed to apprehend Kadar, in order to take his place for a test mission for Mr. York, upon completing the task I was to infiltrate York's cell and take it down."

"What happened?"

"I got Kadar but Mr. York got Pamela, I had to trade his safe passage for her safe return," Sam said.

"You gave him up for her?"

"Yeah, I loved her. My choice ended up costing me my job and then, isn't it grand, Pamela left me because I was a danger to her precious career." Sam said with disgust.

"I'm sorry, I know how it feels to lose everything for the wrong person," Anna whispered.

"It didn't end up being everything, just what I knew, then it opened the way for the gym and my fighting career. I like it better, but the old job is coming back." Sam admitted.

"What does that mean?"

"I promised the agency an explanation when I turned over Kadar, they called today looking for the information. They'll want a meet but I'm holding it off as long as I can because of the killer but I can't hold them back indefinitely." Sam muttered.

"What do you need from me to satisfy them until you can get in for a meet?" Anna asked.

"Anything pertaining to Kadar, who he was working with or for," Sam stated.

"I've got a lot then, including a tip your people don't know. Mr. York isn't the one in charge. He answers to some guy named Halden. I've got photos of the men who were following me and York. You can have all of it," she assured him.

Sam let her go and looked at her again dumbfounded at the news. "No wonder Kadar tried to kill you," Sam breathed, with disbelief.

"I'll put it together for you," Anna said with a smile. Pleased she'd managed to impress him.

"Thanks, that should get them off my back at least for a little while," Sam said gratefully.

"You're welcome, think of it as my way of returning the favor," she said with a shrug.

"You don't need to pay me back Anna," he assured her.

"I know, Sam," she replied before she closed the last few inches between them and pressed her lips to his. His mouth came alive at the feel of hers against it. Sam held her close to him savoring her kiss, relieved to have gotten through the discussion without hurting each other. He didn't want Anna hurt by anything or anyone especially him.

As he felt their kiss grow more desperate, he broke it, aware it was time for him to go. "Night Anna," he whispered before he brushed a kiss on her forehead then turned to leave.

"Night Sam," she answered and watched as he went. Once the door was closed she turned her focus to gathering everything she had from the dig pertaining to Mr. York and the men he'd set to watching her.

153 SATURDAY 9AN

James Hardagen watched as both the cast and crew for Heart of Clay gathered on the sound stage. He was pleased to see no one missing. CJ stood to his right, the detective just behind her keeping watch. Her publicist was at her side, everyone was in place.

"I want to thank you all for coming today on such short notice. I know the past few days have been trying for all of us. But I don't want this recent tragedy to slow down production and to help get everyone reinvested and excited about the project again I'm throwing a party tomorrow night at my place. Each of you should come as your favorite character from the series. It's my understanding CJ will be making a huge announcement that night and you'll be the first to hear it." James said with excitement.

Catharine watched as the crowd began to react, every eye there settled on her and she swallowed uneasy. "That's right, it's big. I'll be signing books that night as well so it should be a fun night," Catharine stated with a smile and prayed they didn't ask her a million questions.

James smiled as the crowd began to buzz with speculation. Everyone there would be attending and he had no doubt other celebrities would turn out as well. It would be a great party. Maybe even the party of the year. His star that had begun to crash was rising quickly now. Connecting his name to the Dark heart Trilogy was the best choice he'd ever made. He'd have to thank Emily properly for it.

Perhaps he'd add extra fuel to the media fire by announcing his engagement to the lovely model tomorrow night as well. She'd more than earned her place at his side and he knew now that there wasn't anyone else he'd rather share his life with. She'd learn to accept his occasional indiscretions in the future, it was a part of the image after all but she'd share his name and everything that came with it.

154

Catharine felt the eyes of the crowd and grew uneasy. She spent a lot of years staying out of the spotlight, drawing everyone's attention, felt weird. The press of the crowd on her soon became too much. She slipped away and headed back to the office. She still needed to finish the script.

She was sitting at the workspace Mr. Hardagen had provided her that passed as a desk waiting for her laptop to boot up when the door behind her squeaked open and then slammed shut. She turned to see Lance, his ice blue eyes were cold and angry.

"Detective?"

"Are you insane? A masked party, special announcements, there's a man trying to kill you. You shouldn't be drawing extra attention to yourself," Lance snapped.

"If I let this guy dictate my every move I'd never go out again. I have a career that requires me to be in the public eye every once and a while. If I'm not the career dies out."

"Is the damn book worth your life?"

"Whether I like it or not that book is my life until I can make a name apart from Dark Heart," Catharine snapped.

"If you want to die fine but I'm not going to sit by and watch, I'm out Catharine," he warned.

"That's fine detective I've always been better off without a man looking over my shoulder telling me what to do," Catharine snapped.

"I thought we were…" Lance began hurt.

"You thought wrong," she said simply before she turned her attention back to her laptop.

Lance cursed with disgust before he turned and left slamming the door behind him. Catharine drew a breath trying to ease the ache around her heart. She'd done the right thing she assured herself, she couldn't risk getting that close to a man again.

155

Lance stormed through the hall temper driving him, hurt and disbelief on his face as he walked past Bryan, he muttered a cold retort. "Good luck with that ice queen," he muttered with disgust before he moved on.

He watched as Agent Kessler moved to take position outside Catharine's door before moving outside into the daylight. He heard the sound of heels and turned to see Agent Blackwood.

"Detective, I thought you might be interested to know our prime suspect at the moment is the artist, he's been in three of the locations the killer has struck in the last year. We're still looking to connect him to the others."

"What's your take?"

"Honestly, I don't see him as our guy. He's a fall guy."

"Keep an eye on the publicist," Lance muttered.

"We looked into him he's clean," Gail stated.

"I know watch him anyway. There's something about the guy I just don't trust," Lance muttered.

"You got it," Gail replied.

"Do you think he bought it?"

"If your right and the killers watching her yeah he bought it hell I did." Gail admitted. "Go I've got my eye on Miss Nichols," she assured him.

Lance nodded before he turned and left.

156

Anna rose from her desk taking the various information she'd gathered the night before with her. She'd put everything together in her black leather portfolio in a logical order. She made sure there were names dates and anything else she thought might be of importance to Sam.

With everything together she rose from her desk and crossed the floor to the door connecting her room to his and knocked. The door opened and Sam studied her with concern. "You look tired," he commented.

"I didn't sleep much," she admitted. "Here's everything as promised," she stated as she handed him the leather book. Sam took it and set it down on the dresser by the door.

"Thank you. Is there anything I can do for you?" Sam asked.

"No, I'm fine for now," she replied.

"This came for us a little while ago," Sam said as he produced a DVD.

"Why didn't you get me?"

"I didn't want to wake you," Sam said with a shrug.

"That's sweet of you. Shall we see if I'm right?" she asked.

Sam nodded, he stepped aside to let her in before turning and following her into the sitting room. He popped the DVD into the player and flipped on the T.V. Fast-forwarding to his fight they watched as the camera moved to the crowd and there clear as day was James Hardagen and Mr. Smith.

"You were right," Sam muttered. He moved back to the dresser, opened the leather book and flipped through the Intel she'd put together. She was good, thorough. "Ever thought about a job gathering intelligence information," Sam questioned.

"Not interested I prefer dealing with lost civilizations, it's generally safer," she murmured.

"Except for the occasional job that leaves you fighting old gods," Sam reminded.

"That's normally not part of my job description," Anna countered.

"Right, but having men like this follow you is just part of a normal day," Sam muttered.

"Maybe," she admitted.

"Is this the first time you've encountered these people?" Sam asked.

"No. Mr. York was Broody's backer at the Ithaca dig," Anna admitted.

"Shit."

"What is it?"

"You were already on York's radar, he'll be coming after you once he realizes you're a threat to him," Sam explained.

"I've got fallen chasing me, I think Mr. York is a minor problem in comparison," Anna stated.

"Not if he took the candle," Sam muttered.

Anna blinked. Her hazel eyes turned green, she'd not thought of that possibility.

"As soon as we're done here I'm getting you into hiding. I'm not leaving you out in the open for him to get hold of," Sam muttered.

"What about the other mantles?" Anna asked.

"You keep doing the research, I'll find them," Sam assured her.

"But you can't touch them," Anna reminded.

"Once I've located them, I'll bring you in," Sam reasoned.

"That won't work Sam and you know it, we either do this together or not at all," Anna challenged.

Sam nodded, knowing she was right but not liking the idea of her being in the line of fire. He had to find a way to keep her safe.

"I'm going to give this to Lance, hopefully it, plus the info on the bank will give him enough to confiscate the cup," Anna stated as she got to her feet.

"I'll take care of it," Sam stated.

"No, this is my mess to clean up, I've got it. You get that information to your people," Anna instructed. She pulled the DVD from the player and turned to go.

"Anna,"

"Relax Sam I'll be fine," she assured him before she turned and left.

157

Sam picked up the leather book and noted a data chip. He slid it into his phone and smiled. She really did think of everything. Dialing an all too familiar number he pressed talk. The phone rang once before the other end was picked up.

"Mr. Abrams it's about time, we've been trying to reach you since you hung up yesterday."

"I have the information you requested. I'm sending the file now. I can't get into where it's from yet, I'll be done with my business here soon, and then we can talk directly. What I'm sending should keep you busy till then," Sam stated.

"Are you still in contact with Miss Walsh?"

"No, that's over."

"We may just bring you back in on this."

"I don't know if I want back in," Sam stated.

"We'll talk further on it after you get clear of LA."

"Can't wait," Sam muttered before he hung up. Under normal circumstances he might just take the job being offered, but he wasn't on his own, there was Anna to think of and she was already in this thing too deep. He didn't want to see her end up where he'd found Pamela after letting Kadar slip out of the country or worse.

He needed to get Anna clear of all this before it got too hot.

158

Lance was in his room packing when Anna knocked.

"Detective Roman, I take it the plan is in full swing," she commented.

He nodded.

"I've got the proof you need that James and the thief met in Vegas," Anna said holding out a disk.

"What is it?"

"Sam's fight during the broadcast, there is a shot of Mr. Hardagen speaking with your thief, as for the bank you know which one it is you took me there before we left for the airport," Anna reminded.

"I'll look into it," Lance assured her.

"Where will you go?"

"It's better if nobody knows," Lance stated as he shoved the last of his things back into his duffle bag.

"Fair enough," Anna relented. "Thank you for everything, Lance," Anna said before she gave him a hug and walked out.

Lance nodded before he shouldered his bag and left.

159

Catharine sighed with relief as she finished the script for Heart of Clay, everything was now complete. Reading the story again made her realize she'd left some things unresolved. A big one was what had happened to Davrik. He'd vowed vengeance on his sire but had never come back to claim it. He'd left believing Serenity was gone and only Nivali remained. What if he learned he was wrong?

Would he come back for her? Just because the man in her life he'd represented was out of it didn't mean the character had to do the same. Maybe it was time he came back, wouldn't the time that had passed have changed him? Maybe he was the yet unknown shadowy figure chasing after Serenity; maybe Lance was right and she was more than what she seemed to be, perhaps she needed to face her demons one last time and overcome them at last.

Catharine opened her notes for book four and typed these musings on the page, it would mean making changes to book three, drastic changes to it and the end of book one as well but just maybe if she made those changes Serenity would be set free and the readers would finally get what they wanted a happy ending for Serenity.

She started to type up notes on the changes to be made.

'The first of which was it would be Davrik to drive off Kovrin not Syvarin. Serenity would not make any deal with the devil in book one. Syvarin would intrude as intended but Serenity would go to his castle on her own to finish some task yet undone. When her daughter entered the scene to slay Syvarin to rescue her love it would be with Davrik's aid, mother and daughter would face off but Serenity would be set free.

Davrik would face his sire, strip him of his power but the rat would escape, one of his servants would see to it. She'd need to include some scene with Kovrin in it so that the readers knew he was still alive, maybe a scene where Syvarin hires Kovrin to hunt down Davrik, he can't have his rogue prince returning to take Nivali or to kill him and take his throne. As payment Kovrin is given the right to mate Nivali.

While he's out taking care of the hunt Syvarin begins his raids in the were-wolf territory, he captures several warriors and enslaves them, uses them to begin concurring other vampire lord's lands. While at the end of book three Rachel and Derrick have brought a stop to Syvarin's reign in his own land, he can slip away to some other territory he's since claimed. Kovrin can return to find his people in shambles and swear vengeance against Syvarin setting the stage for the fourth book and the final show down between the three men who seek Serenity and bring end to the treaty between vampire and were-wolf, reopening the blood wars.'

As she finished typing the last line Catharine smiled, at last she had an answer to the riddle, how could she give Serenity a happy ending when she was a monster. She made her less the monster than the others. She still didn't know if Nivali could go back to being the Serenity Davrik had loved and her fans were crazy over but she'd cross that bridge when she got to it.

"Looks like you got past your block," Bryan said amused as he read over her shoulder.

"You know I hate it when you do that," Catharine muttered.

"I know, sorry. I couldn't resist. I like it, sounds good. Are you really going to bring them all back for the final act?" Bryan questioned.

"Yeah, I think so, I'm not sure yet how I'm going to set it up but I think it'll work. I just have to make some tweaks."

"What about the movie? Heart of Glass is already done, it shows Syvarin killing Kovrin."

"I'll just talk to James see if we can shoot an alternate ending for the DVD. When it plays on the air include that ending instead. I'll add the new scenes for book two to the script now so it will line up, just a few page re-writes not too bad."

"If you think he'll let you I'd say go for it. What happened between you and the detective earlier?" Bryan asked.

"He wasn't happy about the party tomorrow night or my big announcement. He told me it wasn't the right time to put myself in the spotlight. I told him I had a career to think about and he got mad. He wanted to tell me how to run my life, I wasn't having any of it," Catharine explained.

"I'm sorry to hear it CJ but given the circumstances do you think it was wise to let him leave, I mean he was your best defense against whoever this mad man is," Bryan stated.

"I've got agent Blackwood and Agent Kessler watching me I'll be fine Bry," Catharine assured him. "Do you mind I really should head back to the house, I've got a lot to do to prepare for the party tomorrow and not a lot of time to do it in," Catharine stated.

"Of course, if you want I'll talk to Hardagen about the alternate ending scene," Bryan offered.

"That would be great. Thanks Bry, you're a life saver," she murmured before she saved her work. She turned off her laptop and packed it up to go.

"You're welcome CJ, I hope you know I'm always here for you," he whispered.

She nodded as she shouldered her bag and walked out of the office.

"Miss Nichols," agent Kessler said as she stepped into the hall.

"I'm heading back to the house," Catharine stated.

"Agent Blackwood will accompany you," the man stated.

Catharine nodded before she headed for the door. She looked back to see Bryan approach James and watched as the actors eyes gleamed with excitement, she smiled knowing the alternate ending would get filmed. Dark Heart was about to get a major re-write.

160

Lance watched from a distance as Catharine walked out of the sound stage followed by Gail, she wasn't scheduled to leave for hours but it seemed something had set her into motion early. He followed her car at a safe distance, careful to stay out of her sight as well as anyone watching her. For the trap she'd set to work, the killer had to believe that he'd really left her.

Seeing she was headed back to the house, he turned off the road he was on, down a side-street and pulled into the drive of a small home hidden within the wooded area behind James Hardagen's property. The old guest house had proved to be the perfect place for Lance to set up shop. Not only was it virtually unknown to outsiders due to its lack of use in years, but it provided the perfect view of the manor itself. He mentally thanked Emily for the suggestion as he watched Catharine and Gail from a distance.

He noted Catharine chose to sit out on the pool deck to work today and wondered why. She was normally so private about her work, maybe she was giving the killer more access to watch her or maybe the sunlight was calling to her today because her world was surrounded by so much darkness, whatever it was he could see she was working at a fevered pace. She'd hit on something since last they spoke, she actually looked happy and excited. He knew she was working on Dark Heart, it was all she was allowed to touch. She'd said she hated the series so why the enthusiasm? He wished he could ask her but knew it was impossible at least for now.

As Catharine wrapped up whatever she was working on Emily joined her on the deck.

161

"Catharine, are you busy?" Emily questioned.

"No, I actually just finished the changes to the script I'll be giving the final draft to James tonight," Catharine said pleased.

"Are you really going to kill Serenity in Heart of Clay?" Emily asked.

"Not anymore," Catharine assured her.

"Book four, how is that coming?"

"I haven't got it all figured out yet but I think I'm getting there, the readers will get what they've been asking for," Catharine revealed.

"Really? Wow that's amazing. I won't ask how, I'm sure you won't say. I came out here to see if you wanted to come with me to get a dress for tonight," Emily explained.

"Yeah, I don't have the one from the Serenity Ball or the bash here the other week in honor of Heart of Glass's success. So I think a new dress will be in order," Catharine admitted.

"Great, I'll just grab my purse and we can go," Emily said pleased.

"While you do that I'll put my laptop in the room."

"Gail you should probably pick out a dress too, we don't want you standing out tomorrow night," Emily suggested.

"What about Anna," Gail muttered.

"I'll see if she wants to join us," Catharine stated.

"All right then let's get this over with," Gail grumbled.

Catharine nodded and packed up her work before heading back in the house. As she made her way up the stairs she figured she owed Anna an apology, the other woman had come here to warn her against the danger her mind was in and rather than take her advice she'd yelled at her and mocked her.

Catharine knocked on the other woman's door and waited.

"Catharine, I didn't think you'd be home for a while yet," Anna said with surprise.

"I had a brainstorm and had to get away from all those people. Emily and I are going to go out and get a dress for the party tonight, did you want to join us?"

"I appreciate the invite but I've got my dress from the Serenity Ball," Anna stated.

"Okay." Catharine paused, not wanting to say what she needed to in front of the agent following her. She didn't know how much Gail knew about the other things going on around her and she wasn't about to reveal them if she was in the dark.

"Gail can you give us minute?" Catharine requested.

The agent nodded and moved off back toward the steps.

"Anna I'm sorry about what I said the other day. You were just trying to help me and I repaid your kindness with hostility. You didn't deserve that. I want you to know that I made my peace with God and to thank you for coming here, I know what you've risked by coming."

"No need to thank me, you helped to save my life from Hermes. I couldn't leave you unprotected. I know Lance doesn't really believe in all this stuff about the mantels it's not who he is."

"Are you sure you don't want to come with us?" Catharine asked.

"Yes, I got some work I need to get caught up on, but thanks."

"You're welcome," Catharine stated before she drew Anna into her arms and gave her a hug.

Anna returned the embrace and then drew back. "So are you ready to face the beast tomorrow?"

"As ready as I'll ever be," Catharine muttered, "See you later Anna," she said in parting before she turned and put her laptop in her room. When she reemerged Anna had disappeared into her room once more. Catharine moved back down the steps rejoining Gail and Emily.

"Ready to go," her hostess asked.

"Yep, Anna is staying here but I know her size if I see anything I'll pick it up for her," Catharine stated before the trio left the house.

162

Lance followed the trio from a distance, watched as they shopped for the perfect dress for the party and unbidden memories of the past raced through his mind. Dana and Heather had done the same thing the day the killer took note of the pretty blonde.

Was he watching Catharine now, laughing at the irony of it all? Lance had lost Dana because of a dress shopping trip, would the sick bastard see history repeating itself here as Lance did? Did he view the current task as his Serenity picking out her wedding gown in preparation for their big night? Lance swallowed with disgust, he didn't want to go there; to wander too far into the crazed killers mind.

Ares would definitely see it that way. After her last nightmare, he had no doubt the vessel the War God had chosen was the killer. It explained why the killer's acts had escalated so rapidly of late. Based on the time line Gail had given him it coincided with Anna's discovery of Atlantis. Somehow the killer had come in contact with the War God's sword.

Lance shook his head at the notion running through his head. It was crazy, to anyone else it would be complete lunacy but Lance had seen and experienced enough to know as insane as it sounded it was all true. His enemy here was not just flesh and blood that could be killed, he was warring with an old god.

How did you kill a fallen? Lance wondered. Could you? Were they like vampire's you drive a stake through their heart or cut off their head and they die? Or were they eternal like Hollywood claimed in movies like "FALLEN? He didn't know and the not knowing worried him. He knew how to set a trap for a killer and in truth Catharine's plan was a good one, but he wasn't dealing with a normal man. He worried that the god would slip through the net of her trap and get to her anyway.

Lance turned from his musings as the ladies emerged from the store, each one carried a garment bag. He hoped they were done shopping, he preferred it when Catharine was at the house, at least then he knew she was secure. Too many people were dragged off the street in broad daylight and never seen again.

He watched as the trio got back in the car and headed down the strip, it seemed they weren't quite done yet and he'd just have to wait out this impromptu shopping trip.

163

Pamela unfastened her harness and looked to the pilot.

"We weren't followed?" She questioned.

"No ma'am, not another plane in sight," he assured her.

Pamela blinked, she'd thought for sure Mr. York would follow her back to Ian, after all, he had the statues of the gods, the lock, which held the others captive. If Magnus Halden had any of the keys he'd need to come here. He would come here. The thing was no one except her and Zaharrah knew the location of Ian Broody's private residence, not even Anna. He built it after she left him.

Satisfied that the secret was still safe Pamela stepped off the chopper and made her way up the steps into the dwelling of the former Dr. Ian Broody. She figured now it would be more appropriate to call it the Palace of Hermes. Whip in hand she passed through the door and headed straight for his office knowing that was where she'd find him.

Hermes smiled at the sight of her. He stepped around his desk and crossed the floor to greet her with a kiss. "My goddess you are a sight for weary eyes. I've missed you my lady and after tonight we'll not be apart from one another again. Come show me all that you have done since last we parted," he entreated as he rest his brow against her forehead.

Pamela gave him access to her mind as he requested wanting to keep nothing from him. She waited for the rebuke but none came.

"I see you had a bit of difficulty with Hades servant, no matter, let him believe you have betrayed me. We shall proceed according to plan. The whip my dear?" he requested.

Pamela handed it to him and watched as he set it within Helios grip. The Earth beneath them trembled and the god of the sun roared in fury as his power was stolen from him. The image of the fallen one shattered and Hermes power grew.

"Go make yourself beautiful my love. I shall prepare for later, tonight we shall wed," he whispered before he kissed her once more. Pamela felt the power he'd bestowed upon her stir and swell. Her own power growing with his as need awoke within her, she kissed him back hungry, greedy and his eyes gleamed with delight; even as he drew back denying her the pleasure she craved. "Not now my sweet, I cannot touch you so again till tonight," he whispered with regret before he let her go.

"Why not?" Pamela asked with frustration and disbelief.

"For the rite to be valid I cannot have you this day until we are wed. When the ceremony is done you will truly be my goddess, all my power will be yours to wield and your mind shall be open to me permanently," he murmured. "Now, go," he entreated her again.

Pamela turned and walked out of his work room to the sound of the other gods hissing and raging behind her. She smiled, soon she would be free of everything that bound mankind in this life. She would be immortal.

164 <small>Los Angeles, California</small>

Anna woke to the sound of a knock at her door. Lifting her head she cursed, she'd managed to fall asleep again while trying to work. She'd been dreaming of Sam again and muttered a prayer for strength as she noted the time. She figured everyone must be back from the film set and sighed, so much for peace and quiet, she knew the forty-eight hours Dionysus had given her were drawing to a close. He'd be expecting her answer to his offer soon.

She rose from her desk and crossed the floor to open the door. To her displeasure she found not Catharine or Sam on the other side of her door but James. He held a garment bag in one hand and a bag in the other.

"Miss Gallagher," he said with amusement

"Mr. Hardagen," she said coolly.

"Miss Nichols and Em asked me to see you got these," James said as he stepped past her into the room. He lay the packages on her bed and turned to study her.

"Thank you, now if you don't mind I'd like..." Anna began wanting him out of her room.

"RELAX, PRETTY ANNA I DIDN'T COME HERE TOCOLLECT MY ANSWER, I CAME WITH GIFTS, BESIDES WHAT THE GIRLS BID ME PRESENT YOU WITH, I WANTED YOU TO KNOW I'D DECIDED SINCE WE'RE ALL SO DISTRACTED BY THE PARTY TONIGHT THAT I WAS GOING TO GIVE YOU A REPRIEVE," Dionysus said with a smile.

"A reprieve?" she questioned surprised.

"YES, I'LL GIVE YOU UNTIL THE END OF THE NIGHT TO MAKE YOUR DECISION," the wine god told her.

"Thank you. I've not had much time to think about anything," she admitted.

"I THOUGHT AS MUCH, I CAN MAKE IT EASIER FOR YOU IF YOU LIKE."

"Meaning?" Anna asked uneasy.

James crossed the floor closing the distance between them so that he was close enough to touch her. "RATHER THAN WAIT ON YOUR SAM TO SCRATCH YOUR ITCH, I CAN EASE IT FOR YOU NOW," he murmured as he reached out to grab her chin. His thumb brushed against her lower lip. She turned from his touch with disgust, even as it enflamed her with hunger.

"No thank you," she snapped.

"CONSIDER CAREFULLY MISS GALLAGHER, IF YOU LET ME DO SO, I'LL REMOVE ONE DISTRACTION THAT IS MAKING IT HARDER FOR YOU TO THINK," he whispered as he tapped her forehead between the eyes.

"In God's name be silent fallen one! I'll have no dealing with you," she snapped. Anna watched as violet eyes returned to their natural blue as the spirit retreated and the mortal returned.

"Good night Anna," James said before he turned and left.

Anna drew a calming breath as she prayed against the power the spirit had tried to wrap around her. She was just starting to level out when Sam stepped into the room.

"Are you okay?"

"Yes, he's gone and his influence is broken," she assured him.

"Good. You have no idea how hard it was not to burst in here and interrupt," Sam said struggling to reign in his temper.

"I'm sorry."

"Did he mean what he said, do you think?" Sam asked.

"Yes he gave me more time though I think it was more so he'd have a better hold on my body," Anna admitted. "He doesn't know the way Hermes did, that I've a means to defend against him," Anna added.

"I'm getting you out of this house before tonight ends. I'm not about to risk a double cross or leaving you out for the killer to take as well," Sam said his voice broaching no argument.

Anna nodded. "I'll go with you when the time comes Sam but you can't hide me from our enemies forever or keep me from my task," she told him.

"I know. I don't want you anywhere near this place tomorrow night. You'll make a brief appearance and then you're gone." Sam said before he moved back into his own room.

Anna crossed to the bed and opened the drawstring shopping

bag. She pulled out a card with CJ's insignia and read it, "For tomorrow night, thanks again." Anna unzipped the garment bag and gasped at the sight before her. A vibrant green and blue silk Grecian gown lay within. Its sleeves and square neckline were beaded in sapphire, emerald and aquamarine. It must have cost a fortune, Anna mused as she pulled out golden shoes with matching beadwork set down the center and matching jewelry. She considered objecting, giving it back; it was too much but another note was tucked in with the gown. "You can't refuse."

Anna blinked as tears fell from her eyes. She'd never had anyone she could count as a friend, she realized that had changed through a strange turn of events, she could now call Catharine her friend, and a good one at that.

165 ATHENS, GREECE

Hermes led Pamela through the gardens around his palace. They moved off the land Broody had purchased as his property. Two silent pilgrims on a journey, none had made in over 2000 years. His bride was a vision in her white silken toga. Golden sandals adorned her feet as she traveled beside him up a hill to the Parthenon. He smiled pleased to have a cloudless night.

The moon hung in the sky above them at its brightest. As they moved through the ruins he noted that one stone lay in the center of the roofless structure, the perfect size to replace the alter that had shattered the night they were imprisoned. He could picture it now. He'd led his new bride here to make their union official, despite Zeus's spoiling her. His brethren had been in attendance to bless the union and he'd given them each their mantle; before the ceremony began.

"I Hermes lord of Knowledge and servant of the great prince come this the night of the full moon to the temple of the gods to ask my lord's blessing upon my union with this mortal woman. I have passed this day as you decreed abstaining from her and the wine of Dionysus that your right to my bride is known. Now I present her here, on your alter; I dedicate her to your name great prince, a living sacrifice as I unite our flesh now unite the rest of us, make her my goddess, fill her with my power and make our minds one," Hermes shouted to the heavens the earth and the sea below.

He knew not where the great prince had gone but he let his voice carry throughout the earth before he threw Pamela down upon the stone table. As he tore the gown from her body and stirred her with a hunger more intense than any she'd ever known Hermes spoke in a language not uttered on the earth in two millennia. As their bodies joined he allowed her for a moment to see his true form. A vial beast, not a dragon or any other found in myth or nature. He was not fully animal but was not human either.

He was cursed, one of the fallen. He and the other nine had once been great generals in their prince's army they'd been beings of light that rose against the creator. They'd been thrown from the heavens and now were twisted and black. Darkness shrouded them, consumed them.

He laughed as his bride moaned with pleasure as he took her. Pamela trembled beneath him in both fear and need, she was his now, nothing his brethren would do to claim her would succeed. He let the illusion settle before her eyes again easing her fear, it was easier to complete the rite he'd begun if she was a willing eager participant but he was required to reveal his true face to her here so that she understood which great prince it was he served. Who it was she was being given over to, he roared as he felt his power run out of him and watched with delight as her eyes went black as it filled her for a moment then crashed back into him.

He smiled as his mind entered hers. Her thoughts becoming his own, he whispered to his goddess without speaking a word and told her of the child growing within her belly. Before he drew her close to him and with a thought, they vanished from that sacred ground returning to his palace.

166

Hermes left his bride as the sun began to rise. With his claim cemented, he made his way to his work room, he still had tasks to complete. Most importantly finding the crown before any of the others did. Turning his mind towards Anna he found the shield about it, it was not nearly as strong as it had been when last they met. He smiled it seemed Dionysus was up to his old tricks. Pushing through the cracks he probed her thoughts for information on the mantles.

"How are you hunting for them?" He questioned.

While the response not as immediate as he'd like the whisper came back "Old legends," Hermes laughed it made sense.

"Where is the key?" He inquired but no reply came. Worse a moment later he was forced out of her mind. Hermes raged as his brethren laughed at him, aware how taxing it was on his power to be expelled so.

"Laugh while you can brothers, soon I will have the crown and you will be utterly defeated," he hissed.

Hermes picked up the phone and punched in the number for the mortal woman Zaharrah. "Hello?"

"Dr. Lynch I think I know where Dr. Gallagher is looking for information to locate the mantels."

"Where?" Zaharrah asked curious.

"Old legends, if the mantles are out there, stories would have been written around them," James explained.

"Right, if that's the case then I can think of where one might be now," Zaharrah reasoned.

"Which one?" Hermes questioned.

"The sword, Arthurian legend is centered on his sword," Zaharrah said.

"Indeed, look into it, I'll see what I can find on the others," Hermes stated. He was aware the sword had been recovered but perhaps Zaharrah could sort out by whom and give him a name and face for Artemis to hunt.

167

Catharine stood on the second floor next to the rail staring down at the crowd. Behind her Gail stood in her black silk gown watching the people around her. Bryan stood at her left and Anna to her right. Sam was at her side, the two seemingly inseparable. She felt Lance watching her somewhere from the distance and it eased her nerves. The party had been in full swing now for an hour. It was time for her to say her piece and leave.

"As James promised the other night I have big news pertaining to the project. First we're going to shoot an alternate ending for Heart of Glass. I'm not going to get into the details just now but you'll be getting your pages soon. The second is that Heart of Stone will not conclude the series. I am in the process of writing a fourth book in which everything that has come before will be brought together and Serenity will finally find her happy ending as the fans have been asking," Catharine announced.

She watched as the room exploded with the news, everyone speculating on what would happen, how the three books could be brought together. Deciding she'd had all she could stand she retreated back to her room to work.

"You did a great job CJ the house will be thrilled," Bryan enthused.

"Thanks let them know I'm making changes to the first three books to prepare for the fourth novel. I want to be left alone to work. I'll send you the changes as I complete them."

"Of course," Bryan assured her.

"I mean it Bryan, I'm staying out here in LA to work I want no interruptions."

"You'll have it," he assured her.

"Good," she said before she stepped into her room and shut the door closing him and the rest of the party out.

She drew a breath as soon as the door closed, the killer was out there she could feel him watching her. She'd told Lance she wanted to face this head on but the pressure was getting to her. She had to slip away at least for a little while.

Sitting down in front of her laptop she began the task of editing Heart of Glass to include the new material she had in mind. It didn't take long. A few new scenes and the major change to the finale were quickly made but something was missing. If she was going to have Syvarin come after her in book two she needed to establish here that his eye was on her. Catharine set to the task of writing a new scene with the vampire lord watching her but as she worked her fear caught up to her and sleep overtook her.

168

James watched the crowds' enthusiasm over CJ Nichols' big announcement and smiled. Her idea had worked brilliantly, the people were reinvested in the film and looking forward to getting back to work on the project come Monday morning, he knew the new scene was done as well as the script, he couldn't wait to get his hands on the new pages. While she'd cut the vampire lord from part of the first movie, he figured that things were about to get far more interesting for his character.

He was planning on going up to see CJ in a bit and find out what he could about the overall changes to the series, maybe get a feel for what script three would reflect and what to expect for book four. If he had a feel for the series as a whole it would make it easier for him to get the filming of it right.

As the crowd danced and drank, he found himself wondering if one of them in the crowd was the killer. He'd not picked up on Ares presence but the War God had always been good at repressing his true power. Ares work was always subtle to begin with. So many harbored strife and stress in their day to day life it was hard to sense whom it was that was influenced by War. James figured he was there after the dream he'd had with the rival turning up for Serenity's hand, he had no doubt the killer had come to make his claim here as well. James reasoned that if he wanted to get his taste of Miss Nichols before Ares got to her he'd have to do it tonight. Her and Miss Gallagher were both ripe for the plucking and he intended to have them both before the night was out but first he had his own moment in the spotlight to take.

James drew Emily to his side. She smiled up at him her brown eyes glowed with adoration.

"I think your party is a great success," she whispered over the din.

"That it is Em, and only one thing would make this night perfect," he murmured.

"What's that my love," she asked.

"If you would agree to be mine," he answered as he handed her a black velvet box.

Her eyes widened with excitement and joy at the sight of it and the request, she flipped open the lid and stared at the diamond set in gold and threw her arms around his neck. "Yes, of course, I love you so much James," she shouted.

"I love you to Em, so much," he assured her as he put the ring on her finger. He kissed her then asked for quiet in the room.

"Friends, fellows, I have an announcement to make. I've just asked Emily to marry me and she has accepted, so tonight is not just a celebration for the film but for us as well, we are getting married." James declared. He thrilled as the crowd fawned over them and the buzz in the room shifted from the film to him and his pretty bride to be.

"Thank you for your support of our vision to make the Dark Heart series come alive on the big screen, it means the world to both of us. I don't know how many of you are aware but it was my sweet Emily's suggestion that I make Dark Heart into a film series. It was her vision that brought us here and I hope she will be satisfied with it when we are done. For tonight, eat, drink, dance and indulge as you desire in honor of both her vision and our union to come." James requested before he kissed his new fiancé to thunderous applause and the occasional cat call.

Dionysus reveled in the worship about him and felt his power grow, if he was going to make his move it would have to be soon his influence over his guests would be stronger tonight thanks to the party. He smiled as he became aware of Miss Nichols mind, it had once more slipped into the dream-world, it was time to face her without the mask after all she knew him now by name.

169

Catharine sat near the water's edge in the wood that had so often of late crowded her mind. She was staring down at her reflection and noted that the image of Serenity and herself had blended, long blond hair, now it's natural red. Hazel eyes her blue, the gown she wore was of red and orange like that of a flame from the evening's party. She knew the choice to wear that gown was a dangerous one; it was a silent challenge, a declaration that she was ready to face him.

"YOUR GOWN WOULD BE BETTER IN PURPLE," Dionysus quipped and before her eyes the reflection changed, the modest red turning a vibrant purple that left her all but bare before him. "IT'S NOT TOO LATE FOR YOU CATHARINE, TAKE MY HAND ACCEPT MY EMBRACE THIS NIGHT AND I CAN PROTECT YOU FROM THE WAR GOD," he whispered as he drew her back against his chest. His hands took hold of her body in much the same way Syvarin was often depicted holding Serenity.

"Surrender my will to the embrace of one fallen to protect me from another," she questioned with disbelief.

"YES, TURN IN MY ARMS LET ME HAVE YOU AS IDESIRE, LET ME COOL THE FIRE I'VE STIRRED INSIDE OF YOU AND GIVE YOU A PLEASURE UNLIKE ANY YOU'VE EVER KNOWN IN THIS WORLD AND HE CANNOT TOUCH YOU, CANNOT KILL YOU," Dionysus assured her.

"YOU KNOW HE'S LYING," Ares voice thundered from somewhere in the shadows. "YOU KNOW NOTHING HE DOES CAN SPARE YOU FROM ME. I'VE HELD YOU FOR SO LONG, I DON'T EVEN HAVE TO TOUCH YOU TO MAKE YOU ACHE FOR ME," he breathed and to prove it he spoke one word in a tongue she didn't know and felt her flesh tremble with the promise of his touch.

"DON'T LISTEN TO HIM, TAKE THE CUP I OFFER, DRINK DEEP AND FREE YOURSELF OF HIS GRASP," Dionysus argued as he held out his cup to her. The potent smell of the wine made her desire it and him.

"YOU'LL NEVER BE FREE OF ME," Ares reminded as he stepped into the moonlit clearing, he took her by the arm and pulled her free of Dionysus grasp.

The wine god raged at his interruption as Ares took his place pressing himself against her from behind hands imitating Kovrin's tearing at the gown which was once more her own. "DO YOU REMEMBER HOW YOU FELT AS I BENT YOU OVER TO MATE? THE THRILL OF IT, THE HUNGER FOR IT. YOU WANT ME AS YOU ALWAYS HAVE, YOU FLIRT WITH THE WINE GOD AND I FORGIVE YOU THAT, BUT IT IS ME TO WHOM YOU TRULY BELONG. WE HAVE BEEN BATTLING FOR YEARS MY LOVE AND OUR WAR WILL END THIS NIGHT AS IT WAS ALWAYS MEANT TO WITH ME CLAIMING YOU." He breathed the words as he ground the proof of his desire against her ass letting her feel him. She cried out with both fear and need as she recalled all too well the last time they'd met here, she'd been all but powerless to stop him. "YOU DO REMEMBER, SEE IT COMES BACK SO EASY TO YOU. TONIGHT YOU SHALL WEAR MY CROWN," he growled as he held it out for her to see the golden wring of serpents fangs poised to bite her flesh.

"SHE IS NOT YOURS YET BROTHER AND I WILL NOT GIVE UP MY RIGHT TO HER WITHOUT A FIGHT," Dionysus hissed. "MY HOLD ON HER IS AS OLD AS YOURS AND I'VE AS MUCH RIGHT TO HER AS YOU. AFTER ALL WE WERE BOTH THERE WHEN IT BEGAN FOR HER. I DULLED HER SENSES AND TOGETHER WE HAD A TASTE OF HER," Dionysus reminded as he drew the two apart. His touch upon her made her thirst for the cup he offered and the sight of the crown left her shaking with fear.

"SO BE IT," Ares snarled and he drew his sword to defend his right. Dionysus produced a weapon of his own and Catharine looked on with disbelief as the two gods began to battle. Seeing her chance she rose to her feet and fled into the woods. Let them kill each other she'd have neither one, she vowed.

Sparks flew behind her as the two swords clashed. To her dismay the road under her feet always seemed to lead her back to the water's edge where the two waged war. Dionysus was surprisingly good with the blade but he proved no match for the War god.

"SHE'S YOURS, HERE BROTHER, BUT THE RACE IS ON NOW FOR WHO SHALL GET TO HER FIRST IN THE MORTAL WORLD," Dionysus stated before he vanished. Catharine turned and ran once more and Ares gave chase. As she ran Catharine whispered a cry for aid to the creator. A blinding light shown around her and Ares roared in rage. When the light became bearable Catharine found that a great tawny and gold lion stood before her, he roared in challenge to a smaller orange, red and black lion without teeth. The smaller lion roared back in fury at the interloper.

"She Is MINE I've Had HER…" Ares began in challenge.

"**SILENCE! SHE IS MY CHILD I'VE HAD HER SINCE THE DAY SHE WAS FORMED IN HER MOTHER'S WOMB. SHE CALLED TO ME AS A CHILD AND SHE HAS RETURNED TO ME NOW, BE GONE FROM HERE FALLEN AND TORMENT HER NO MORE**," The lion ordered and as she watched the toothless beast turned and vanished.

Catharine trembled before the one who protected her and fell to her knees. "Thank you," she breathed as she wept. "I am so sorry," she said with shame.

The lion drew her into its paws and held her close. "**IT IS FORGIVEN DAUGHTER. NEVER FORGET WHO YOU ARE. YOU ARE MINE, A PRINCESS IN A KINGDOM GREATER THAN ANY OTHER IN THIS DREAM-SCAPE OR THE ONE YOU LIVE. FEAR NOT THE BEAST THAT COMES TO DEVOUR HE HAS NO POWER OVER YOU, BUT BE ON GUARD, THE TIME FOR YOU TO FACE YOUR GREAT FOE DRAWS NEAR. REMEMBER I AM WITH YOU ALWAYS**," the lion whispered before he breathed on her and the dream faded away.

170

Lance sat in James Hardagen's office watching the house through the various camera's, so far he'd seen nothing to lead him to believe the killer was there lurking but yet his instincts were screaming at him that the time had come, the killer would make his move tonight. He was there lurking in the shadows hidden by a mask so that none could see him. Lance turned his attention back to the screen watching Catharine's room and he noted with disquiet she'd fallen asleep.

He wondered if she dreamt now and if those dreams were a torment to her. He wished he had some kind of aid against the foe he now battled because for the first time in years he felt powerless to stop what was planned to happen that night. His gaze moved from her room to the hall and he cursed.

"Gail you're not going to believe this but our artist is here and headed your way," Lance said over a com unit Sam had given him in preparation for the night.

"I'm on it," she assured him and Lance watched with satisfaction as Agent Kessler escorted the man, who'd drawn the image the killer was obsessed with, out of the house.

He noted that James was on the move and didn't like it but figured their host wouldn't risk being exposed. He watched as the wine god bypassed Catharine's room at the sight of the agent by the door and made his way toward him. Great just what he didn't want another brush with a fallen. "God save me," he muttered under his breath and he heard the lock in the door click shut.

"He'll do that and more if you mean what you say," a voice said, it came from nowhere and yet everywhere. Lance blinked as the hair on the back of his neck stood on end.

"What the hell?" he questioned as he turned to see where the voice had come from. To his disbelief he found himself faced with a man robed in white his eyes were a brilliant blue his hair a dark earthy brown a light shown about him that was nearly blinding to look upon. Lance swallowed as a peace he couldn't explain washed over him. He swallowed mouth dry. "You're Sam's Angel aren't you," Lance whispered.

"I'm not his, no, but I am the one with which he's spoken."

"Why are you here?"

"You asked for aid, I was sent."

"Why?"

"Because the foe you face is not flesh and blood as you know. Her mind is safe now but you must get her out of here now without delay, the danger you feel stirring is a real one. The killer is indeed here this night and not alone. You've seen he keeps in his company another. The one he will send to take her is one her guard is not looking for, go," the angel said before he vanished, the door unlocked and Lance slipped out of the office.

"Gail don't trust anyone," he warned as he went on the move. When he stepped into James Hardagen's room he figured for sure he'd pass him on the way out but there was no sign of the actor. When the agent gave no response he cursed and switched com channels. "Sam I can't reach Gail," he said with frustration.

"What's up?"

"I had a visit from your winged friend. The killer has an accomplice, she can't trust anyone who wants to see Catharine man or woman."

"Damn."

"Also the wine god has done a disappearing act, thought he was headed here, haven't crossed his path. You might want to get Anna out of here I've got a feeling things are about to be blown to hell," Lance muttered.

"Son of a bitch," Sam cursed. "Thank for the heads up, I'll get your warning to agent Blackwood," Sam assured him.

"Thanks," Lance said with a bit of relief as he moved closer toward the guest wing. He wondered how he and James hadn't crossed paths but dismissed it. Right now he had to get to Serenity.

171

Gail stepped into Catharine's room to find her asleep at her desk. She heard the click of Lance's line opening but whatever it was he was saying was static. She moved to leave as Catharine lifted her head.

"Gail is something wrong?" she asked with alarm.

"No, you just have a visitor, sorry if I woke you," agent Blackwood whispered.

"You didn't, who's out there?"

"The woman playing Serenity," Gail replied.

"I'm not really in the mood for visitors right now, will you send her away?" Catharine requested.

"Of course, try to relax. Agent Kessler escorted the artist off the premises, not sure how he got in. he'll be questioning him now."

"Do you think it's him?" Catharine questioned shocked.

"Honestly no, but it's possible," Gail said with a shrug.

Catharine nodded. "Keep me posted?"

"Of course," Gail assured her. Catharine watched as the agent turned to go.

"You can't send me away, you have to tell me about the script," a familiar voice objected. Catharine's gaze looked to the sitting room to the actress playing Serenity moving toward them.

"I'm sorry she must have crept in while we were talking," Gail said.

"It's okay."

"We'll talk Monday," Catharine assured the actress. What was her name? Catharine found she couldn't remember.

"Monday won't due silly, I want to discuss it now," the girl said her eyes darkened as she spoke, hazel becoming green then blue, grey and finally black.

"You?" Catharine questioned with disbelief watching as those eyes began to glow with an unnatural light. Gail moved to defend her and the unimposing actress struck her. Gail crumbled like a rag doll.

"My lord bid me bring you too him, he's waiting. He's thrilled you've dressed for him and can't wait to finally meet you Serenity. He's waited a long time for this night," the woman murmured as she closed the distance between them.

"Who are you?"

The blonde laughed. "You know me Catharine. I am the essence of your Serenity it's my story you've written and I'll be the one to finish it," she hissed before she knocked out the writer as well. With an inhuman strength she lifted both women from the floor so that they stood on their feet and led them from the room down a secret corridor and out of the house.

172

James laughed, as he made his way along the secret passage from his quarters to the guest suites. The detective thought he was so clever, that by sitting in his office looking over the place he could keep him from Catharine. He was a fool. When he'd built the house he'd made certain adjustments to it to accommodate his indulgences.

His image was not as a bad boy for nothing, he'd had many a girl before Emily and all had claimed he was cheating on them but none had been able to prove it. They'd not been able to catch him at it. He'd invite crowds over for parties such as this one and loaned out guest rooms to his lovers, then he'd slip into bed with them while the crowds reveled. No one saw him come or go because he never entered from the main hall into a room.

James clicked off the surveillance cameras within, before he slipped into Catharine's room through the secret passage. To his disappointment, he found her room empty; the door ajar. There were signs of a struggle and he cursed, it seemed somehow Ares had managed to get here first as well. No matter, there was still one more fruit to be plucked this night and he intended to have it. Miss Gallagher was about to learn her time was up. She either told him what he wanted to know or he would be turning her over to Hermes. After this night one way or the other He would be restored to his full power. His cup would be set in the hands of the statue in which his spirit and true power dwelt, the man James Hardagen would be no more, Dionysus thought, amused as he moved to reopen the passage the detective burst in the room.

"Where is she?" Lance demanded.

"GONE, IT SEEMS YOUR KILLER GOT TO HER DESPITE YOUR EFFORTS," Dionysus mocked.

"How the hell did you get in here? Forget it, I can guess and I can see that your little secret is probably how the killer got her out. When I get back you'll pay for this," Lance raged before he turned to head back to the office, he had to know who had taken her and figure out who they were working with.

173

Sam spotted Lance, head back down the hall toward their host's room in a sprint.

"Lance what's going on?" he questioned over the mike.

"Catharine and agent Blackwood are gone, the killer got to her."

"Shit. What do you need?"

"Get Anna out of here, the son of a bitch has secret passages through the house, direct access," Lance snapped before falling silent.

Sam froze. Shocked by the revelation and outraged. The place was like a damn Trojan Horse, you felt safe but were anything but.

Turning he threw open Anna's bedroom door, he put her inside when Catharine left the party. She blinked startled. "Pack up Doc, time to go," he commanded.

"But…"

"No arguments it's not safe here," Sam stated as he drew her up out of her chair. He threw open the closet and dragged her things out of it.

"What about Catharine?"

"She's gone, killer got to her everything's gone wrong. Lance is working on trying to figure out who and how, when I leave to help him I don't want you anywhere near this place," Sam stated.

Anna nodded and he drew a relieved breath as she set in motion gathering her things. With her bags packed, she came along beside him quietly. The pair loaded up into an SUV and waited for Lance to emerge with the party still in full swing. .

174

Lance sat down behind James Hardagen's desk and tapped on the touch pad for the laptop. He watched as the screen lit up and then clicked on the file for the video feed on Catharine's room.

Pulling it up he backed up the footage to when he left the office and watched it play out. He saw when Gail came in the room, noted the time, then watched with disbelief as the new actress playing Serenity stepped into the room. She took down Agent Blackwood with an ease that gave him chills, then Catharine as well, she picked them up and slipped into the hidden passage.

His killer's accomplice had been right under their nose. He'd met her yesterday and nothing had given her away. She wasn't human, he reasoned as he watched the video again. He was still reeling from the implications when his phone rang.

"Hello," Lance said as he connected the call via speaker phone.

"Detective, I was trying to reach Agent Blackwood but I got her voice mail."

"She and Miss Nichols were taken," Lance stated.

"What?"

"The killer had an accomplice, she got past Agent Blackwood due to the fact she had a reason to be there, she's the new star of the damn movie," Lance muttered. "We were so busy looking for him it never occurred to me to look…" Lance began.

"He played us all of us. You were right we shouldn't have done this," Agent Kessler admitted.

"No need for apologies this was Miss Nichols choice, she wanted to face this. We need to work together now to find them and bring them back." Lance stated.

"Right. Do you think there is any way we'll find them before it's too late?"

"Yes. Because we know more about this now than before. This started with her, it will end where it began," Lance stated.

"Meaning?"

"The answers are in the pages of Dark Heart. What did you find out from the artist?" Lance asked.

"The artist claims he was invited by Bryan Jamison."

"Son of…" Lance began to curse but pushed it aside, his anger was not going to find Catharine, he needed to keep a level head, the anger could wait. "Do you still have him?"

"Yeah."

"Can I speak with him?" Lance asked.

"Why?"

"He was involved with Miss Nichols, he has information about her I don't know."

"Fine."

Lance listened as the phone was passed off. "Hello."

"David, I need to ask you a little bit about Dark Heart," Lance stated.

"Okay."

"The bird on the back in place of her photo, do you know what it is?"

"Yeah it's an Eastern Blue Bird."

"Did she ever tell you why she chose that bird?"

"Said it reminded her of home, is she okay?"

"No, but I'll find her," Lance assured him.

"You think that will help you?"

"Yes, I do was there anything else she ever had you draw, a landscape piece or something pertaining to the series she was fond of said was like home?"

"Yeah I drew a sketch with Serenity in the river near the falls when Davrik saw her for the first time face to face she said the scene was like home," David replied.

"Thanks."

"Bring her back safe detective," David requested.

"I'll do my best," Lance assured him.

"What now?" Kessler asked.

"I'm going to give these clues to my researcher and see if she can figure out what they mean," Lance stated.

"What if you're wrong about this?"

"I'm not, she is Serenity," Lance revealed. Look for a birth certificate for a Serenity, Jade, Catharine, Collins."

"I'm on it."

"Oh one more thing; look for a police report for a break in filed by Serenity age 18."

"Will do. For what it's worth I'm sorry for what I said before," Agent Kessler stated.

"Don't be you were right I am too close to this. Too close to her, I just hope I understand her enough to put together where he's having her taken."

"Do you want me to follow the publicist?"

"It'll be a waste of time, he knows were watching," Lance muttered.

"Agent Blackwood is smart she'll find a way to reach us," Kessler stated.

"So is Miss Nichols, but if what I see coming together here is what it is, she's not going to be ready for this. It'll come as a blow."

"You thought it was him, why?"

"He was too pushy about her personal affairs. Always arguing with her like a lover or spouse might. He felt he had a right to."

"But he came up clear," Kessler said confused.

"I know I actually apologized to him. Look I'm going to get things moving on this end you get started on that end, we don't have time to speculate." Lance stated before he hung up. Picking up the phone he dialed Anna's number.

"Hello?"

"Anna do me a favor look up anything you can get on the Eastern Bluebird. Native locations and then once you have that look for a place in the area with a waterfall." Lance requested.

"Will do," Anna assured him.

"Call me the minute you have something."

"Of course, we'll find her," Anna assured him before she hung up.

Lance put his phone away and noted Bryan was still downstairs speaking with one of the other guests. He rose from his seat and moved to go speak with the clever bastard.

175

James stepped out of the secret passage into Miss Gallagher's room and found that she and her things were gone, it looked as if she'd packed in haste, the closet was still a jar and bathroom drawers hung open.

He cursed, it seemed Lance had warned her Sam of his access to the rooms and the other man had gotten her clear. No matter. He'd track her down easily enough. He figured she'd made her choice and it was to refuse his offer, well that was fine, it just meant she'd be in Hermes hands a bit sooner than he'd intended but it was just as well.

Ares hold was growing too strong in the area, until he cemented his power he was vulnerable. If Hermes wanted the pretty archeologist then he'd get her and when he did Dionysus would be restored to his former glory once more. LA would be his new kingdom, this city suited him nicely, from here he could gather more power than he'd ever possessed in the past. With Emily as his bride he'd be in place to compete for Zeus's crown. All he'd need is a clue where to seek it. With this thought in mind James left Anna's room and moved to find his fiancé, the sooner they wed the better. As for Anna, well he'd just wait for her to call Lance or her Sam or for her to slip once more into the dream realm, one way or the other he'd discover where she was being hidden.

176

Lance started down the steps his ice blue eyes cold as morning frost as they settled upon Catharine's publicist.

"Detective?"

"Bryan, where did she go?"

"Where did who go?" Bryan asked.

"Don't play dumb with me I know you invited David to distract us. You wanted us focused on him while she slipped in and took her out. Tell me where she's taking them and I'll let you live," Lance hissed.

"I don't care for the threat or your tone detective. Tell me how CJ is holding up?" he asked,

"You know damn well she's gone," Lance snapped.

"Gone? What do you mean? Did she leave?"

"No, your pet stooge took her and agent Blackwood to an as of yet unknown location."

"The killer got her?" Bryan asked with alarm.

"No, your accomplice." Lance stared at the other man and noted the slight flicker of fear in his eyes. "I know who you are Ares so let's drop the masks tell me where she is and you're puppet will survive this," Lance bargained.

"You've lost your mind," Bryan said with alarm.

"No, I haven't, you're scared, it's kind of thrilling to see a god sweat," Lance mocked. "Offers off the table I will find her and when I do you're done," Lance warned before he moved on. As he stepped outside he slipped into the back seat of the Sedan.

"Lance the Eastern Bluebird is found from the Eastern Rockies to the gulf of Mexico."

"Okay waterfalls in the north then near New York," Lance suggested.

"I've got a dozen I need something else."

"An island," Lance said.

"Or Rhode Island I've got a town Central Falls Rhode Island about 150 miles from New York."

"Nice work Anna."

"It's not an exact location," Anna reminded.

"No, but it's a start. A destination for a pilot to go to. In the meantime go back to Heart of Clay, the part when Serenity is telling the reader about herself, find me something solid for a location," Lance requested as Sam pulled away from the house..

"I'll see what I can find," Anna assured him before she pulled up her e-book files and began a search of the requested text.

"Back to the airport then," Sam said as he turned the sedan in the direction of LAX.

"Yeah," Lance answered as Sam pulled into traffic. As they went Lance kicked himself for doubting his instincts.

Bryan Jamison was his killer.

177 Loch Ness, Scottish Highlands

Zaharrah stood at the edge of the infamous loch and stared out at it. The rocky hills in the distance her destination. People here were so fixated on the beast in the water they'd missed the true wonder of the site. Her people knew its true secret. These grounds had once boasted the lost city of Arthur and his knights.

Camelot had stood not far from here, the lake was the place Hollywood claimed the sword of the king had been cast. She knew different. The sword had slept deep within a cave in the hills but standing here she felt no latent power. The sword was gone. When it was removed the spirit they'd sealed there was also set free. A thing her people had always feared. She wondered how anyone had gotten past the watchmen but reasoned it didn't matter the damage was already done, Ares Mantle was on the move and SHE was loose. The discovery was unsettling. Zaharrah knew of the mantles due to her reading of the forbidden archives, she wasn't familiar with what they were exactly as there was no real mention of what each was, only that they were cursed objects not meant for man. The only one that her people knew of intimately was the sword. It had been given to her people to keep hidden.

Of all the mantles it was the most dangerous. In its edges was the blood of a god. It more than the others radiated evil, it's influence was far more potent than any other. Whoever possessed it by now was lost to the War god's influence. Things were worse than the elders realized, if the sword had taken a wielder then the time of destruction was fast approaching, she had to slow it down. Not because it was her duty any more, the holy mission of her people was of little import to her any more but there were things she'd given up to protect them from the war coming and she wasn't about to let them get caught in the cross fire. Getting back in her car she flipped open her laptop and ran a search for brutal killings involving a knife with a Greek theme.

She swallowed with disgust as she hit a series of reports on a serial killer in the USA that was on the loose. Reading the latest report, she studied a photo and cursed as she recognized a familiar face. "Sam Abrams. She'd seen him at the dig site of course but she'd known him from before then though he didn't know her. It seemed that if she had any hope of slowing this nightmare down, she was going to have to admit that she wasn't as clueless in regard to the mantles as she'd acted. It was time for the order of the 'Black Hand' to be drawn out of the shadows.

178 U<small>NKNOWN</small>

HE looked upon the sleeping forms of his prey as his accomplice prepared them for HIM. She tied SERENITY up, facing the bed, where she laid out the lovely Gail Blackwood. As HE looked at the woman whom LANCE had entrusted to protect Catharine, he smiled, so like DANA she would serve as a fitting punishment for the DETECTIVE. When he did find this place he'd be too late to save her. She would remind him of his beloved DANA and HE'D be sure to leave a taunt of some kind about the pretty brunette getting her final wish being his last victim.

The message would push LANCE over the edge, he'd succumb to grief and guilt, either end himself to be with DANA in hell or go mad. Either way the DETECTIVE would be out of his hair. HE was going to enjoy preparing Agent Blackwood for LANCE'S arrival, he'd take his time with her after all the DETECTIVE would need ample time to get here.

"Catharine must see what we do now and embrace it, if you want her to become your bride Ares, she must accept the gift I offer her," HIS lady purred as she ruffled his hair.

"She will. I can smell Dionysus wine on her. When she sees ME for who I am she will not be able to resist. She will surrender to me, to US she will become MY SERENITY." He assured her with pleasure.

"Good, our time draws near, the others are closing in, we must finish this before HERMES pet has a chance to pick up your scent." The woman whispered as she bound the agent's wrists to the headboard. She moved on to her feet securing her spread eagle for HIS purposes.

HE stared at the brunette as he drew his knife from its sheath and trembled with anticipation this was a kill he'd waited a long time for. HE knew HE'D not enjoy this as much as the others, she wasn't his preferred flavor of prey but HE knew if he could get through this, find the pleasure in it that HE'D found with the others before her then HE and SERENITY could be ONE FOREVER.

179

Catharine woke to the sound of music playing. The song was both foreign and yet hauntingly familiar. As the fog of unconsciousness began to lift from her mind she recalled being taken by the woman playing Serenity, being aware that she was not human.

"Ah, the sleeper wakes," the woman purred with delight.

"Just in time, I was just explaining to Gail here what I have in store for her," a familiar voice said with amusement.

Catharine blinked and turning she saw a man standing by a huge ornately carved bed, the headboard and footboard both carved with an angel and a warrior who brings death. Candles adorned the walls, stood on stands they were everywhere in white, red, black and some more the color of blood. Thin wisps of gauzy fabric in the same colors draped about the bed like a veil separating her from the area giving it a dream like feel but this was no dream, or nightmare, she couldn't wakeup now and find herself safe wrapped in her bed or in Lance's arms, this was real.

She was in the War God's chambers and she was about to be witness to his latest kill before he made her his bride or she met the same fate.

"You don't have to kill her, I'm here let her go," Catharine entreated. She didn't want anyone else to suffer because of her.

"She knows who I am besides she's the best farewell message I can think to leave for LANCE." The man hissed.

"Bryan? Is that you?" she asked with disbelief.

"Yes, I've waited a long time for you to really see me," he said his voice growing deeper with his excitement.

Catharine swallowed realizing he was pleased she'd known him that whatever he was about to do, he'd now enjoy more. "You don't have to hurt her Bry…Nothing happened between Lance and I. We didn't…"

"He TOUCHED you SERENITY. Your DETECTIVE made you ache with want of him, I won't let HIM become you're DAVRIK. Don't you understand this is not just about you, it's about DARK HEART, it must end right with us together," Bryan raved.

"You're not a part of the series Bry… you never were, Please just let Gail go, I'll write the book however you want," Catharine offered.

"I told you if you ever left me I'd kill you and I meant it. When you ran from me, I hunted you. My hunt led nowhere so I traveled back to the land of my ancestors to seek answers in the family line. I found the Dryden land near Loch Ness and in the high hills, I found this," he said.

Bryan held his knife out for her to see and she noted the grip was encrusted with vivid orange Carnelian that danced along the grip, the pommel and the hilt like flames. The sword of Ares. "Beautiful isn't it? When I found it the knife was a sword imbedded in stone. It whispered to me in the darkness, promised me it would help me find you and take my vengeance. I drew it from the ground and as I did, I felt its power. I knew the men it had slain, the wars it had waged. I knew that with it I could finally have what I wanted. I was like Arthur drawing Excalibur and the world lay at my feet if I only took it. "

She could feel the darkness radiating from it as she felt it in the disk Lance had shown her but this was far stronger. "Bryan listen to me that sword is evil," Catharine breathed hoping to draw him back from his madness.

The knife made her heart pound with a fear she'd not known since her mother died. It was as that fear began to settle over her that what he'd said began to sink in.

Catharine swallowed ill at ease she knew the name Dryden she hadn't heard it in years. "No, you can't be, I'd have seen it. I'd have known," Catharine said with disbelief. She wondered how he was speaking words no other save her and Lance had ever heard. Ares was revealing her secrets, trying to confuse her, she reasoned.

"When I got back I read Heart of Glass and my anger cooled I saw within its pages' that you still loved me though you were wed to another I saw that if I could find a way to burn out my rage that we could be ONE again," he whispered.

"That book wasn't about you Bry… I didn't know you yet."

She reminded, unwilling to accept the notion that he'd played her so well.

"You know me SERENITY, I know you do. When I saw your notes that you were bringing Kovrin back, I knew you'd forgiven me. I didn't mean to hurt you love, if I'd known you were pregnant I'd have never hurt you that way," he assured her.

"No, it's not possible," she said with horror and disbelief.

"Why not you reinvented yourself, why is it so hard to believe I might do the same. I love you SERENITY it's time to come home," he whispered.

"Kurt?" she asked unsure.

"Yes my love," he answered.

"How can you speak of love so? You've been killing me," Catharine said with outrage.

"No, I would never hurt you SERENITY. They are just a means to quiet my temper, after Gail there will be no more. I'll be free of the rage," he assured her, before he turned his focus back to the woman bound on the bed before him.

"Do you think I'll just accept you then, that I'll ever be able to forget what you've done or what you will do to her? I've seen the photos and worse. You've kidnapped, tortured, raped and murdered innocent people. You've really become a monster," Catharine snapped.

"No I've become powerful," he corrected before he moved closer to the frightened woman bound to the bed. With a cool precision he slid the knife between her shoulder and black silk. With a flick of his wrist, he tore the delicate fabric cutting it free of her body he circled the bed to repeat the process with the other sleeve. The fabric fell off her now exposed shoulders, leaving creamy skin revealed to his hungry eyes.

"You are flawless Agent Blackwood, my marks will stand out like paint on a canvas. I'll create my masterpiece tonight, the one no one will ever forget," he whispered with awe before the knife was used to cut the dress from her body leaving her in only her under garments.

"Kurt, please stop this, I'll go with you, I'll finish the book however you want. I'll walk away from everything forever if you want but only if you let her go," Catharine shouted.

"You know I can't do that, SERENITY."

"I can't love a killer," Catharine countered.

"You are a killer SERENITY you just don't know it yet, you'll learn it tonight. You'll see as you watch me at my craft, you'll find your desire for me grow as it did when we made love, you'll soon crave the taste of blood and when it's over and I take you it will be the best you've ever had," he assured her before he handed the knife to his accomplice.

Catharine watched as Kurt knelt by the bed and pulled out from under the white silk sheets a small wooden chest as the woman stripped Gail Blackwood naked for him in preparation for the act to follow. From within the chest he drew the golden serpents that were the Fury Killer's signature mark. He started a blaze in the fireplace to prepare for the torture he would inflict before taking the knife back from his helper.

"SHE IS READY FOR YOU MY LORD," the woman whispered, her hazel eyes beginning to glow with the excitement of what would follow. She thrilled in the madness that shown in Kurt's eyes, in the lust turned violent that stirred within him. In the promise of destruction that he held.

"Thank you my lady, go keep SERENITY company while I work don't let her look away I want her to see the depths of my love for her. I want her to understand. I want her to be set free of the spell that holds her captive. I want her to remember the hunger I taught her long ago," he stated before he advanced to the bed.

"Gail, now you will see the meaning behind my marks," he murmured before he dragged his blade under her eye making the first cut to form her bloody tears.

The FBI agent hissed with the pain as her captor used his power to light the candles around them. "The first tear falls and with it comes the first pain," he whispered and he dragged the bloodied blade over her skin in a twisted caress. Waking her body's sense of touch the cold metal and warm blood swept over her flesh making her squirm as it touched her in places no one was meant to touch without her invitation. Each time she moved resulted in pain as it caused his knife to nick her drawing blood.

"Shh, be still pretty, it's better if you don't fight," he whispered as he brushed the knife over her belly and moved lower. She cried out in protest as his blade brushed over her feminine center before moving on down her inner thighs and down her legs. "Now you're awake and the second tear will fall," he said with amusement before the blade cut under her eye once more.

"Kurt; stop this," Catharine shouted in disgust.

"No. You will see," he hissed. He took hold of one of the snakes and he drove the sharpened fangs into her ankle and bent the metal around her flesh.

Catharine looked on feeling sick as the man she'd trusted as a friend put down the knife and his hands replaced the blade as his instrument of torment. When she tried to close her eyes to shut out the image Kurt's accomplice slapped her.

"YOU DON'T GET TO ESCAPE THIS; YOUR SELFISHNESS HAS BROUGHT THIS UPON HER. IF YOU WANT IT TO END WITH HER THEN YOU BETTER EMBRACE HIM WHEN HE ASKS FOR YOU OTHERWISE YOU'LL SHARE IN HER FATE. "

"I don't care," Catharine breathed. Gail cried out in protest as his touch crossed the line between merely groping to full on rape.

"YOU KNOW THAT HELPLESSNESS, THAT FEAR, THE PAIN AND SHAME DO YOU THINK YOU CAN BARE IT ONCE MORE," the woman asked.

"It doesn't matter," Catharine stated.

"I can get you through it. Ask me to and I will," the woman offered. Catharine said nothing, simply watched in silence as Kurt added another cut under Gail's eye before adding another golden band to her body, this one at her wrist marking the start of the next form of torments.

180

Sam sat beside Anna, Lance was a seat behind them on a plane east bound from California to Rhode Island. He was trying not to worry about the other man. The detective was losing his grip on the little control that he still held. Not that he could blame him, if it were Anna in danger he'd be in the same state. Lance was probably beating himself up for doubting his instincts and for leaving Catharine alone. But none of them had ever suspected the killer might have an accomplice.

Sam opened his mouth to reassure his friend when his phone rang.

"Hello."

"Mr. Abrams can you speak freely?" A familiar voice asked.

"Yes."

"Good. I need your help Sam," she stated.

"I'm a little busy right now Miss Lynch so what is it you need and make it quick," Sam requested with irritation.

"I figure right about now you're chasing after a killer with a cursed blade, so I'll be brief," Zaharrah began.

"How do you know that?" Sam asked with shock.

"I know a good deal about that sword. Your killer is with a woman. She is the more dangerous of the two. She will be the one in control. Whatever she's up to, you have to stop her."

"Why? Who is she?"

"She has many names, to some she is Pandora, to others Hecate, her true name, none know. All that is told of her is that she is the Queen of Hell and the only one she answers to is the prince of the pit," Zaharrah explained.

"Wait I thought the only true goddesses were the daughters of Zeus. Are you telling me that is not so?" Sam asked with alarm. Up until then they'd been operating under the assumption that they were only up against the fallen but if Hecate was out there, couldn't the other goddesses be so as well.

"No she is unique. Her history, I do not have time to get into but she is damned. No longer human but not one of the fallen, she was imprisoned during the time of Arthur the one legend records as Morgana Le-fay. When your killer took the sword he released her and she's been spreading her curse ever since. Whatever she wants Ares is but a puppet in her schemes. Stop her."

"What makes you think I can help you?" Sam questioned irritated.

"Gunnar told me once if anything ever happened to him, I could go to you for aid," she revealed.

"Gunnar, who are you to him Zaharrah?" Sam questioned with disbelief Gunnar Dayan would never tell just anyone about him.

"I am nothing to Gunnar anymore but a ghost," Zaharrah answered before she hung up.

"What is it?" Anna asked seeing the worried look on Sam's face.

"Bryan may not be the one pulling the strings," Sam muttered.

"The woman?"

"Yeah I just got a tip that she's not mortal."

"A fallen?"

"No something else but she'll be after a host," Sam stated.

"Catharine," Lance muttered.

"Or agent Blackwood whichever is a better fit," Sam answered.

"Great just what I didn't need, another damn spirit looking to hurt her," Lance muttered.

"We'll get there in time." Sam assured him as he offered his support.

Lance nodded but said nothing more. Sam sank back in his chair and took Anna's hand in his own, when they landed, the first thing he was doing was making damn sure she was safe before they started looking for clues where Catharine might have been taken.

181

Zaharrah contemplated the ramifications of what she'd just done, what she'd said but didn't care, if that demon queen was allowed to obtain whatever it was she was up to Gunnar would be in danger anyway. She sighed, she'd made hard choices after Ithaca. Now she questioned if she'd taken the best steps after all. It had never occurred to her then that the order would fail in their mandate. That someone would slip past their net of protections to both find the sword or that the lost city would ever be unearthed.

She'd heard the rumors about the explosion that led to the discovery of Sodom and she'd looked into them but so far she'd found nothing to indicate for her that the explosion was planned to find the old city. Now she had to wonder, was someone within the order working against them to free the fallen. If so who and why? As she contemplated the matter her phone rang.

"Hello."

"Dr. Lynch it's me. Please inform Dr. Gallagher that things here are at boiling point they've cracked IT."

"Understood, she'll be told. Watch your back Doc," Zaharrah warned before she hung up the phone. It was time she got back to the Lost City and got Darrian out of there before it boiled over.

182

Sam pulled the sedan into a parking spot out front of building three. He led Anna up the sidewalk and up the stairs to the second floor landing. He walked down the outdoor hall to room 312 and put the key in the lock. Sam opened the door and after switching on the light stepped into the room. He set her bags on the floor next to the door and secured the lock.

Blue eyes studied her with regret. She looked amazing in her dress and he wished he could stay with her. Leaving her alone and unguarded felt wrong but he had little choice, Lance needed his help to find Catharine.

"I can't stay long, Lance will want to get started fast," Sam stated with a sigh.

"I understand, go find Catharine," Anna whispered.

"I don't like leaving you behind," he confessed as he drew her into his arms, he rested his forehead against her brow. Blue met with hazel as he worried over her.

"I'll be fine," she assured him, with a smile.

"Take this," Sam instructed as he held out his gun to her.

"Sam…" she began in protest.

"Don't argue with me Doc take it," he demanded.

Anna nodded before taking the 9mm berretta and the holster. Sam kissed her for a moment needing the contact to calm his nerves. He was supposed to protect her it was why they were put together but now she was on her own at least until he got back.

Her mouth came alive under his and he groaned at the taste of her. She was a shock to the system every time. How such a quiet and reserved woman could get to him this way he'd never know, but she did. Sam drew back as he felt his body begin to stir; now wasn't the time. If he was leaving her unguarded he wasn't going to leave her defenseless. "A gun does you no good if you can't use it. I'm going to teach you before I go," Sam stated as he let her go.

"Okay."

"Take it out of the holster," he instructed. Sam watched as she unhooked the clasp and pulled the black berretta out. "Okay now take the grip in your predominate hand and steady it with the other."

He watched as she did so lifting the weapon, pointing it across the room. Sam moved to stand behind her and had her adjust her stance.

"Good now to sight it you're going to want to look down the barrel, close one eye when your target is lined up with the site here, you squeeze the trigger, go easy, don't pull or jerk or the line will move."

Sam moved closer to her taking her hand in his own, pressing it lightly against the trigger, bringing his face alongside hers to help her sight.

"Like this?" she questioned as she targeted the pillow on the bed.

Sam stepped back, giving her room. "When you're not using it keep the safety on, you don't want to accidently shoot anything or yourself," Sam stated. He pointed out the safety and walked her through the other parts of the gun she should be aware of. "You've got nine shots so make them count."

Anna nodded before putting the weapon back in its holster.

"After I go don't let anyone in but me," he instructed. Sam drew her back into his arms once more.

"I won't," she told him.

"Good, I'll be back as soon as I can," he promised.

"I know you will," she assured him before she kissed him. It was short and quick. Merely a peck compared to the first one and not nearly enough to satisfy him, but he didn't push her, aware that she was still struggling with whatever Dionysus had done to her. "Be careful out there," she requested.

"I will," he assured her and unable to resist, he kissed her again, his hands sinking into her hair pulling lightly to get a better angle. She gasped startled by the silent demand. He took full advantage of her lips parting; tasting deeply of the mouth that seemed to have bewitched him.

He wanted her maybe more than he'd ever wanted anyone. But he didn't want to hurt her. As much as he desired her, he knew if he gave into that hunger now he'd end up doing just that. They may even wind up resenting each other. No this, whatever it was needed to wait.

Sam eased back and his eyes locked with hers once more. "I love you," he murmured before he turned and left. His mind whispered it was too soon, they'd just met but he couldn't take the words back nor did he want to though he barely knew her, he knew it was true.

He loved Annalynn Darcy Gallagher.

183

Once Sam was gone she set up her laptop again, Lance was counting on her to figure out whatever Catharine had written within the pages of her novels to tell them where she was from. Opening the file she began to reread the passage Lance had asked her to and groaned.

He was right there was something here but she wasn't seeing it. Anna blinked as her eyes began to cross. Picking up the phone she was ready to dial Lance when the phone rang.

"Hello."

"Annalynn I've news from Dr. Silvers, she said they've cracked IT," Zaharrah stated.

"Great as if we haven't got enough crap to deal with now I've got to worry about being swept down on by a dragon."

"You sound stressed Dr. Annalynn Darcy Gallagher," Zaharrah quipped.

"Stressed you try reading the same damn passage a dozen times looking for clues about an actual location," Anna snapped.

"Annalynn, such language I'm beginning to wonder if Mr. Abrams is a bad influence," Zaharrah teased.

"Sorry, my friends are counting on me to figure this out so they can save someone. Some crazed killer took our friend."

"Maybe I can help," Zaharrah offered.

"Sure why not? I'll email it to you. If you solve it contact Sam," Anna muttered.

"Will do," Zaharrah assured her before she hung up.

Anna typed up the text and sent it to Zaharrah via e-mail before she turned her attention back to the text but her eyes soon grew heavy and she slipped into sleep.

184

Catharine turned away from the bed as Kurt burned the last of the golden serpents into agent Blackwood's flesh. She'd been forced to watch as a man she'd once loved and trusted beat, tortured and raped her body guard in almost every way imaginable. There wasn't a part of Gail's body he hadn't defiled in one way or another.

"The final cut. You've held up well miss Blackwood but I knew you would, you're not a weak willed actress or even a cheap street whore who tried to convince me she was enjoying herself, no you're strong willed, a fighter. It's been a pleasure transforming you into my final bride. I know you must be tired from our exertions but don't worry after this there's no more torment the marking will be over, then there will be only what you can endure." He breathed

"Damn you Kurt let her go she's endured enough," Catharine shouted in rage.

Kurt laughed. "Look you are blessed, Serenity weeps for you perhaps you're time as my bride will be short indeed."

"No more," Gail begged through split and bleeding lips.

"Soon my love soon," he assured her. He dragged his knife once more beneath her eye creating the tenth and final tear.

"Stop this," Catharine demanded of the woman who had done nothing but watch and keep her from turning away.

"IF YOU WANT TO SEE HER SUFFERING END THEN YOU MUST END IT. TAKE THE KNIFE ON THE TABLE AND SET HER FREE," the woman told her.

"No I won't help you kill her," Catharine hissed.

"I'm sorry Gail, Serenity will not free you, you're suffering will go on until you are no more," Kurt whispered before he drove the first of several small needles into her flesh, she screamed as pain shot through her body.

"Yes, I know it hurt baby, see it's on a pressure point, it will cause the most pain possible, it's okay to cry Gail I won't think less of you," he whispered before he stuck the next one in her. She endured each one without tears but she screamed herself hoarse. Once the metal bits were in place he ran his hand over the un-effected skin with a tender caress.

"Shh, first parts done, relax I won't start the next part until you're heart rates a little more steady, I don't want you passing out for any of it, You're so strong Gail, you're the only one whose made it this far without having to be brought back," he murmured with delight.

She whimpered as his hand danced over flesh sorely abused by him.

"Oh there, that's the way Gail let it all go," he coaxed as his touch became rougher, the promise of her tears exciting him, her screams having already gone a long way towards preparing him for her. "I know you're hurting, no need to hide it from me," he assured her as his hand raked over her belly.

"Kurt please she's had enough," Catharine shouted and she struggled against her own bonds.

"I know she has Serenity but the way this game works, only you can set her free. Take the knife my accomplice showed you and give it to Gail, become my right hand," he whispered as he finished molesting the agent and turned to get the next implement from his box.

"Never I won't be your bride Ares I won't help you kill people," Catharine roared in defiance.

"So be it," Kurt roared in fury. He connected a pair of electric pads to agent Blackwood's skin and then turned on the power. Gail screamed in agony, an earth-shattering sound that shook the room and made Catharine sick.

Tears unbidden fell from Gail's eyes as a searing white hot pain tore through her breaking her at last. Kurt trembled with need at the smell of her tears and the sound of her cry, at last he'd reached her, and Agent Blackwood was now his. He turned off the power and tore the pins that would be in his way from her flesh. He then tore her free of her bindings and flipped her over like a rag doll.

"Kurt!"

"YOU CAN STOP THIS NOW SIMPLY TAKE YOUR PLACE AT HIS SIDE," the woman whispered.

"Never! I'd rather die than go back to him," Catharine snapped.

"A SHAME, I'D HAD SUCH PLANS FOR YOU SERENITY, TOGETHER WE COULD HAVE RISEN IN POWER HIGHER THAN ANY OF THE GODS BUT YOU HAVE CHOSEN TO BE DESTROYED," the woman hissed. She hit Catharine knocking her out cold as Kurt finished with Gail.

"What have you done to her?" he raged seeing Catharine out cold.

"SHE HAS REFUSED US MY LORD, SHE WILL BE YOUR LAST FURY. LEAVE THE WOMAN I'LL SEE TO HER INJURIES SO THAT YOU MIGHT ENJOY HER A WHILE LONGER, MAYBE EVEN THE TWO TOGETHER," the woman whispered.

Kurt rose from the bed and moved to Catharine's side. "Why Serenity, you and I were to be one forever," he said with regret as his accomplice turned Gail over and began tending to her battered body. "Put her in her dress I'll finish it later," he said with disgust before he moved out of the room.

"GAIL," the woman breathed.

"No more," she muttered again through split and bloodied lips.

"SHH, I KNOW HE'S MISUSED YOU GREATLY BUT YOU NEED NOT ENDURE ANYMORE I CAN HELP YOU, JUST ASK IT AND I'LL GIVE YOU THE STRENGTH TO SURVIVE HIM, I'LL GIVE YOU THE POWER TO DESTROY HIM AND ANY OTHER WHO DARES HARM YOU," the woman whispered as she ran a moist cool cloth over her brow and then down her neck.

"Make it stop," Gail hissed in rage and the woman smiled.

Her hazel eyes sparked and glowed with an unnatural light becoming almost red. "I WILL GAIL, ALL YOU HAVE TO DO IS ASK ME BY NAME," the woman murmured as she tended to burned flesh.

"I don't know you," Gail reminded.

"YOU KNOW MY NAME GAIL AS YOU KNOW YOUR OWN," the woman assured her.

Gail nodded. "Help me Hecate I don't want to die here, not like this," she said weakly.

"YOU WON'T," Hecate assured her before she vacated the body she'd been inhabiting and slid into Gail's through the various injuries she'd endured. The agent's eyes widened with shock and fear. Going completely black before she blinked and when her lashes lifted they were the same shifting colors the blondes had been. The woman she'd left, fell to the ground by the bed lifeless.

"THIS BODY IS SO MUCH STRONGER THAN THE OLD ONE, LET'S SEE, FIRST THINGS FIRST," Hecate said with amusement before she used her powers to heal the physical damage done to Gail's body. "NOW, I THINK A PHONE CALL IS IN ORDER, IF ARES THINKS FOR A MINUTE I'M GOING TO HELP HIM OBTAIN HIS POWER IN THIS CRAZED MAN HE'S SADLY MISTAKEN." Hecate muttered before she pulled out Gail's phone.

She dialed the Detective's number and left the line open to create a trace, besides she was going to enjoy breaking the woman's protector by making him listen as Ares tortured and abused her. She was well aware of Hermes hold on the gods at the moment but she'd soon make sure the game changed. The god of Knowledge would not get his way as long as she had anything to say about it.

With her steps taken to prepare for Ares fall made, Hecate slipped on the red gown Kurt had requested she be wearing before lifting the unconscious Serenity from the floor and splaying her out on the bed to prepare her for Ares blade. She was just waking her prisoner when Kurt returned from wherever he'd gone.

"HECATE?" Ares questioned at the site of Gail Blackwood moving about, the blonde dead.

"YES MISS BLACKWOOD WAS MORE THAN WILLING TO ACCEPT MY OFFER OF AID WHEN YOUR SERENITY WOULD NOT, COME IT'S TIME YOUR BRIDE PAYS FOR HER TRESPASSES AGAINST YOU." Hecate prompted as she held his knife out to him.

"INDEED, I'D HOPED IT WOULD BE HER AT MY SIDE BUT GAIL WILL DO, INDEED EVEN NOW MY SEED MAY BE TAKING ROOT WITHIN HER," Ares mocked.

"IT MAY BE," Hecate admitted. "COME CLOSE THE BOOK ON YOUR SERENITY, SHE OFTEN WISHED FOR HER DEATH, NOW WE SHALL GRANT THAT WISH," Hecate said nudging Kurt along. She watched with satisfaction and amusement as Kurt used his knife to cut her dress from her body as he'd done hours earlier with Gail.

He didn't give the knife to Hecate to cut off her undergarments as he had with the others. He knew Serenity intimately, there was no need for courtesy this time. Hecate watched with delight as the man Ares had picked crossed the first of the lines he'd created when they began their game. This kill would not be controlled or calculated as the others before, it would be chaos, and her lord would be pleased.

185

Lance listened to the open line with a growing sense of despair. Gail Blackwood was gone and now nothing stood between Bryan and Catharine. Sam had called Agent Kessler to track Gail's phone and they were closing in on the signal but it would take time. Time Catharine didn't have.

"Serenity, I tried so hard to prevent this but you just can't stay faithful. You're nothing more that the weak little whore you've written yourself as, so disappointing, I did love you baby if you'd just stayed," Bryan said.

"I could never love a killer Kurt," she muttered.

Lance's blood went cold at the mention of the name, Bryan was the cop she'd told him about. It seemed that Bryan and Kurt were one in the same. He'd been under her nose for years playing with her. Biding his time waiting, the son of a bitch had been the one to break into her place, he'd used it as a way to meet her. He wondered if the stalker had done anything more than just break in her place but pushed such notions aside, he'd worry about the implications later for now he needed to focus on finding her.

"The first tear falls and with it comes the first pain," Lance heard the killer declare before a strange silence hung over the line. He cursed as it stretched out. What was the bastard doing to her? The unknown was excruciating.

The silence shattered as Catharine hissed in protest. "You'll pay for this Kurt do you think you'll just get away with abducting a famous writer and federal agent?"

"OH THERE'S MY SERENITY, ALWAYS FIGHTING," HE SAID WITH DELIGHT. "I'M GOING TO ENJOY BREAKING YOU. THAT SPIRIT SO LIKE MY SWEET HESTIA, SHE

RESISTED ME FOR A TIME BUT IN THE END SHE SURRENDERED TO MY DESIRES AS WILL YOU BEFORE YOUR FIRE GOES OUT. IF YOU PROVE PLEASING ENOUGH THEN PERHAPS I'LL SPARE YOU TO BE ONE OF MYHARLOTS." Ares taunted with amusement.

"You won't break me," Catharine said defiantly after a sharp intake of breath.

What the hell was happening? "Tell me we've got something," Lance demanded not sure how much more he could listen to.

"Another five minutes," Kessler's voice answered over the speaker phone.

"Great who knows what that monster will do to her by then?" Lance raged.

"I know detective. We're trying but there's some kind of interference," Kessler stated.

"Find me something," Lance demanded before disconnecting the call.

As soon as the phone was hung up it rang again. "Hello."

"Sam, its Dr. Lynch, Annalynn sent me a copy of that text. I figured out what it means. You're looking for Castle and oak in Central Falls. Gated home, maybe even a beware of dog sign posted," Zaharrah stated.

"Thanks. Do me a favor let Anna know you figured it out."

"Will do, good luck Mr. Abrams and remember the woman is the threat here not Ares." Zaharrah stated before she broke the connection.

"Castle and Oak," Sam stated.

"I hope we're not too late," Lance muttered as he turned the car in the direction of the road indicated.

186

Zaharrah hung up her phone and punched in Anna's number.

"Hello," Anna's voice came across the line grogginess and frustration in her tone.

"Anna, you can relax I figured it out, your Mr. Abrams has been informed."

"Oh thank goodness," Anna breathed with relief. "Thank you Zaharrah I just wasn't seeing it," Anna muttered.

"You're welcome, get some rest Dr. Gallagher you sound beat," Zaharrah suggested.

"I will. Zaharrah be careful out there, Broody…"

"Isn't Broody, I know. You don't have to try to explain I've noticed. I've got one thing left to finish up at the dig and I'll be out as well."

"Good, I think that's wise. I hope whatever it is you need to finish up goes smoothly," Anna said before she hung up.

Zaharrah tucked her phone away before she entered the security line at the airport. She was heading back to Miami and from there the dig site. She was going to find Darrian and even if she had to knock him senseless and drag him out of there, she was getting her brother as far away from the lost city before things got any worse.

187

As Sam drove past the Victorian three story home in white with black trim Lance's stomach clenched, it was nearly identical to the one Catharine had described in Dark Heart. The heavy, iron, gate was complete with a worn out sign that warned to beware of dog.

"Stop the car Sam, we're here," Lance muttered.

Sam pulled the SUV up along a curb around the corner Lance notified Agent Kessler they'd identified the house and were heading in.

"Back up is about ten minutes out, be careful gentlemen and good luck," Kessler said before falling silent.

"You're sure this is it?" Sam questioned.

"Positive I can feel the hair on the back of my neck standing on end. It's exactly like the one she describes in her book," Lance stated.

"Okay then we'll go in quiet, where do you want to start?"

"Start at bottom work our way up," Lance stated.

Sam nodded.

As Lance opened the door he heard Catharine curse.

"The first mark is made now comes the second tear," Kurt stated before Lance slammed the door and started down the street beside Sam. They had to move.

188

Artemis watched as the two mortals slipped past the gate and made their way up the stairs into the three story dwelling. She drew the wind to her and smiled, Ares was here. She'd followed his trail in LA to Dionysus's doorstep but had lost him at the airport. She'd been furious until she spotted the woman Anna.

Artemis had taken a risk following the woman and her companions, figuring they were on the trail of the mantle. Her hunch had not proved fruitless, the War God waited within. The wind shifted bringing with it another power and Artemis cursed. The meddling whore Hecate was here as well. No matter, if she tried to interfere Artemis would take her down as well.

No one was going to save Ares from her wrath today. At last the War God would be brought to justice for his crime against her and her kin.

189

Lance and Sam finished their scan of the ground floor. They found a door that led from the kitchen into the basement. Opening the door the pair moved down the stairs weapons drawn the smell of a fire burning confirmed that what waited below was indeed the lair of their killer.

Lance's heart pounded the need to run pressed heavy on his mind as the killers last words rang in his mind the second tear would fall. He wondered what that meant. Realized that the cuts under the eye were a marking of different torments that his victims were enduring; a score card of sorts.

Hang in there Catharine, his mind whispered as they came to the end of the stairs. The passage was narrow and ended at a sound proof door. Lance pushed it open and found another narrow passage on the other side. The sound of voices carried through the dim corridor, an open doorway loomed in the distance but nothing was yet visible.

"Does this seem too easy?" Lance questioned.

"Yeah, almost like someone is letting us get here," Sam muttered.

"A trap," Lance asked?

"No doesn't feel like a trap, more like a double cross," Sam whispered.

"Do you think Hecate wants us to take out Ares?" Lance questioned.

"Maybe, though, why I'm not sure, "Sam admitted.

"Your tipster, give you any insight into her?"

"Yeah, said Hecate would be looking for a host that was a kindred spirit," Sam replied.

"Maybe she doesn't want him to become the War God," Lance

suggested.

"Damn. No matter what you do, what happens don't kill him," Sam warned.

"Why?"

"If you do the knife will take you for its new wielder. This is a trap just not a conventional one," Sam explained.

Lance nodded his understanding before they moved deeper into Hecate's web.

190

Ares watched as Catharine bit her lip to fight the pain he created as he sliced the skin beneath her eye creating the second bloody tear. Blood stained her lips as her teeth broke her flesh. The War God licked his lips at the sight. He saw now why the man craved her so, his Serenity was indeed a fighter. She excited him in a way the others before her had not been able to.

He'd created the ritual pattern in his killings out of necessity, he needed his victims pained cries, the smell of blood to prepare him for sex. War and battle were what thrilled him, it was where he found his pleasure. But for the second time he found himself unable to resist breaking his own rules. The War God bid his puppet lean over the woman Serenity and his lips wrapped about hers taking his first taste of her lips early.

Unable to resist the forbidden indulgence in the bloody kiss, he found the metallic taste was laced with a potent draught of rage and groaned. She was the embodiment of the old images of the ladies of Fury and he felt his blood begin to burn with want of her. His mouth came alive upon hers, teeth scraping, drawing more of her blood for him to sip. "YOU ARE A WICKED ONE SERENITY," He breathed as he drew back. "YOU DISTRACT ME TOO EASILY FROM MY WORK," he muttered before he returned his focus to his punishment of her. His fingers skimmed over her face, the pad of his thumb brushed her lips capturing a drop of blood, he raised his finger to his lips and sucked it clean, his eyes closing involuntarily at the taste.

He was getting lost in her, the man Kurt's mind pressed urging him to skip the games and take the bitch but Ares was not relenting. He'd lingered on the first tear running his knife over her body in places he'd never bothered with before. Little nicks and cuts marked her ivory skin from her discomfort at the feel of the cold steel against her flesh and as his fingers began to trace down her neck, he knew he'd not be able to stop himself from tasting the blood he'd drawn there.

In the dream realm he'd rushed to claim her and saw now he'd been a fool to do so, Serenity was not a wine to be swallowed in one fast gulp she was meant to be sipped slowly so that you enjoy her to her fullest. He was grateful now that he'd not gotten her in the dream, when before he'd cursed. The not knowing made it easier for him to indulge this way though the man pressed for speed.

As his fingers brushed over the first crimson drop along her throat, he lifted his fingers to taste it. The intoxicating taste made the War God smile. His eyes moved to her flesh and disappointment filled him to find the cut had already closed. He considered biting her but told himself it could wait. His fingers returned to her flesh; skimming lightly over the rest of her throat but rather than move down to feel more intimate flesh, he changed his normal path dragging his touch up bound arms, nails raking skin, marking it. Every inch of her would be subject to his touch. Thanks to Dionysus's work, her body's response to touch was heightened and he intended to drive her mad both with fear and want, before he took her, by the time her fourth tear fell, Serenity would be begging him to take her. .

191

Lance rounded the next corner in the winding passages under the Victorian three story house that had once been Serenity's home. The room was lit within by hundreds of candles, the light was harsh after wandering the dim corridors of the basement. He blinked trying to adjust his sight. Angels and demons alike adorned the décor, their gaze fixed on the center of the room.

Thin wisps of silken fabric hung from the ceiling where the graven images looked in hues of red, orange and yellows. The blending of which looked like a circle of flame. Lance crept toward it and noted beyond, a huge ornately carved bed. Laying upon it naked and bleeding was Catharine. Her arms bound to the head board, her legs spread eagle, feet bound to the foot board.

Lance bit back a roar at the sight as his eyes settled on her captor. Kurt stood over her his fingers skimmed lightly down an arm, along her neck, over her collar bone. Catharine trembled under the touch and pulled at her restraints as she tried to get away from him.

"YOU'RE SO WILLFUL SERENITY, YOU MAKE IT HARD FOR ME TO NOT TREAT MYSELF TO A REAL TASTE OF YOU. I'VE NOT HAD A BRIDE THAT PLEASED ME SO COMPLETELY IN OVER TWO THOUSAND YEARS AND I WANT TO TAKE MY TIME WITH YOU BUT THE MORTAL WHOM I'M SHARING THIS BODY WITH WANTS ALL OF YOU NOW AND IN THE WORST SORT OF WAYS IMAGINABLE, " Ares whispered as his fingers slid down into the valley between her breasts.

"Don't touch me," Catharine roared with disgust as she pulled at her bonds.

"Get your hands off her," Lance hissed as he moved out of the shadows, he shoved the barrel of his gun into the man's back.

"Lance," Catharine gasped with relief as Ares hand stilled.

"DETECTIVE YOU CONTINUE TO SURPRISE ME, HOWEVER DID YOU FIND THE PLACE SO QUICKLY?" Kurt asked amused.

"It was in the pages," Lance muttered. "I said take your grubby paws off her," Lance snapped as he prodded the man again.

"OH, SUCH ANGER, DOES IT BOTHER YOU THAT HE GOT TO TOUCH HER BEFORE YOU DID?" Ares taunted.

"No it disgusts me that you're hurting her," Lance answered. He felt the urge to pull the trigger claw at him. But ignored it recalling Sam's warning.

His eyes moved to Catharine, he hated seeing her like that exposed, helpless that damn haunted look in her eyes the mix of fear and hunger the man David had captured for the series. The one that made her weak version of Serenity famous; it turned his stomach to understand that the wine she'd tasted from Dionysus cup could make her burn with desire for a man she despised.

"LIAR," Ares whispered amused. "YOU WANT TO KILL HIM DON'T YOU? YOU'RE MUSCLES ARE TIGHTWAITING FOR YOU TO GIVE INTO THE IMPULSE TO SQUEEZE THE TRIGGER. YOU'D BE JUSTIFIED IN THE ACT AFTER ALL HE'S A KILLER; BARELY HUMAN. HE MADE SERENITY WATCH AS HE TORTURED AND RAPED AGENT BLACKWOOD," Ares stated as his fingers slithered up the side of her left breast to feel her heart pounding under his touch.

Catharine hissed at his touch.

"That's enough," Lance warned as he clicked off the safety.

Ares laughed as the rage within the other man strengthened his power. "NO, IT WOULD SEEM NOT AS YOU'VE NOT FIRED. SERENITY WOULD DISAGREE AS WELL SINCE ITS BUT A TEASE COMPARED TO WHAT HAS NOWAWAKENED WITHIN HER."

"WHY DO YOU HESITATE LANCE DO YOU WANT TO SEE HIM TORMENT HER?" Hecate questioned.

"Of course not," Lance said with outrage. Where the hell was Sam he was supposed to take this post while he set Catharine loose? Right now he felt as though he were facing the twisted duo on his own.

192

Sam cursed as he shielded himself against the heat of the flames that blazed between him and Lance. He'd watched as the detective slipped past the filmy veil that surrounded the bed where Catharine was held captive by the killer. The moment he tried to follow the curtain became a blazing ring of flames that barred his passage.

The trap here was worse than he'd imagined, the game here for keeps. If Lance gave into the anger driving him and killed Kurt Dryden then he would become the War God but worse still Catharine would fall with him as the influence of Dionysus over her would have her surrendering to Lance's desires and Ares would indeed have a willing bride and he was powerless to stop it.

He was trapped on the outside; looking in as the game played out before him. It seemed Ares saw what Hecate had been playing at and saw something in Lance he liked because he was pushing the detective to kill his current host. Using Catharine as his sword, against the mortal, in the fight for his soul.

"THEN WHY DON'T YOU STRIKE HIM DOWN HE'SMOLESTING YOUR WOMAN." Hecate said with revulsion.

Lance tensed at the words. He shut his eyes to block out the image of Kurt's hands on Catharine.

Sam felt fury stirring in him at the sight of what was happening and wondered how long Lance could resist the need to kill. He figured if it were Anna there, he wouldn't last much longer. "A little help would be nice about now," Sam muttered to the heavens.

"SHE WANTS HIM DEAD," Hecate assured Lance as she tempted him further.

"NOT AS MUCH AS I WANT ARES DEAD," A familiar voice roared as Artemis raced into the room. She took one look at the flames and her eyes glowed with her power as she summoned a storm. Rain poured within the basement putting out the flames as the wind tore the curtains down.

"ARTEMIS," Hecate hissed the name before she grabbed the War Gods mantle and fled the room.

Sam didn't blink, didn't hesitate. He moved across the line that had barred his passage and grabbed Kurt by the arm twisting it behind his back separating him from Catharine before putting his weapon on the man.

He watched as Lance freed Catharine, covered her with his shirt and carried her out of there.

"RELEASE THE WAR GOD'S PUPPET MORTAL OR FACE MY WRATH," Artemis hissed as she advanced.

Sam let go of Kurt, he wasn't about to get in the middle of a battle between a pair of fallen besides, Hecate was getting away and he needed to try and catch her before the knife slipped beyond his reach.

193

Artemis's eyes gleamed red as she drew Eros bow from her back and aimed one of the bronze arrows at her foe. "DO YOU HAVE ANYTHING TO SAY FOR YOURSELF ARES BEFORE I END YOU?" she asked the string taunt, arrow notched ready to be loosed.

"IT WASN'T ME," Ares cried in desperation, but his words fell on deaf ears. The arrow flew piercing his heart. The mortal he inhabited slipped away and the War God's Spirit was sent back to its stone prison.

"FOR YOU FATHER," Artemis whispered before she pulled the arrow free of the dead man. She cleaned the blade and stuck it and the bow back over her shoulder. She made her way out of the dwelling that reeked of The War God's stench and once outside with a bolt of lightning set the house ablaze. Nothing would remain here to draw Ares back to this place. When she found Hecate, Artemis would recover the sword and see to it Ares never came back again. Hermes would not get his hands on that mantle either as long as she lived, no man would ever bear the name Ares again.

As she walked her gaze fell upon the mortal who protected the woman Anna. He turned his gun to point at her. "STAY YOUR HAND MORTAL, OUR BATTLE WILL WAIT. MY BUSINESS FOR NOW IS WITH HECATE," Artemis said before she walked off.

194

Lance laid Catharine across the backseat of the SUV and did his best to make her comfortable. He needed to take care of her. Wanted to tend to her injuries, hold her close to him and comfort her as she faced whatever she'd endured at Kurt or Ares hands. But he couldn't yet, not till they were away from this place. He looked up at the crash of thunder and watched as fire began to consume the house.

The driver's side door opened and Sam slipped behind the wheel.

"What took you so long?" Lance asked as he settled into the passenger side-seat., beside her. He brushed his fingers through her hair needing to touch her just to assure himself she was real.

"Damn curtains became flames they slowed me down. Artemis showed up just at the right moment to help me."

"Man did she seem mad," Lance muttered as Sam pulled away from the curb and started toward the motel.

"Yeah I'm pretty sure she killed him. Told me as she was leaving she's not after us for now, more interested in Hecate.

"Glad she's not after me," Lance said. Catharine's eyes opened she looked at him and she visibly relaxed. "You okay?" he asked her.

"Yeah he didn't…" Catharine began unable to finish the sentence.

"Good. We'll talk later about what happened…"

"Kurt…"

"He's gone, you're safe now" Lance assured her. Catharine sank down on the seat resting her head on his lap.

"Hecate?"

"She's gone, but Artemis is tracking her," Sam supplied as he drove away from the blazing house

"What's our next move?" Catharine questioned.

"For now the only thing I want you to do is rest," Lance replied.

"But the mantle…"

"Lance is right after what you've been through you should be resting maybe even taken to a hospital…"

"No ER not here!" Catharine snapped her voice adamant.

"Easy Serenity, a visit to a doctor can wait, yet" Lance assured her. "Just get some sleep."

"But…"

"We're all going to rest just as soon as we get back to the motel," Sam stated.

"Is that wise Artemis is still out there?" Lance muttered.

"Which is why when we get back to the motel we're packing up and skipping town while she may not be on us she works for Hermes and he'll know soon enough where we are. The sooner we get out of here the better." Sam answered.

"See, nothing more to discuss now, just close your eyes and try to rest," Lance entreated as he brushed a kiss on her forehead.

195

Sam watched as Catharine's eyes closed and she surrendered to sleep with relief but he knew in truth the battle they were fighting was far from over. Hermes was still out there waiting for his chance to get a hold of Zeus's crown. Dionysus was free to roam and continue in his twisted games.

A yet unknown figure had begun to take steps down the path to becoming Hades and Ares while temporarily thwarted would rise again Sam had no doubt. Now there was Hecate to consider as well. The numbers mounting against them were growing by the minute and Sam didn't like it. Their best move was to get the damn crown before any of the fallen did only trouble was none of them knew where to start.

As he made his way back to the motel, back to Anna, he found himself wishing she were with them so they could go straight to the airport and get the hell out of this town, but he'd not been willing to risk her safety by taking her anywhere near the madman. Now he was second guessing the decision and he didn't like it. The one thing he knew after working for the agency was that you couldn't afford to question your choices if you were it meant you were compromised.

Damn the agency...

As soon as he had Anna back he'd have to deal with them before they pulled him in. With this thought in mind he poured on more speed. He hoped the next leg of their journey would be less rough, but he figured it wouldn't as the angels words from before echoed in his mind.

"Why are you here?" Anna asked.

"To warn you the road ahead will be hard and fraught with danger. Do not give up hope or give into the influence of the fallen," the angel said before he vanished.

"You might want to buckle up back there I got a feeling we're in for a bumpy ride," Sam muttered before he whispered a prayer that Anna would be safe until he got back to her.

THE END

THE

MANTLE OF THE GODS

ADVENTURE CONTINUES

WITH...

TRUTH REVEALED

BY TRICIA SPARKS

Always remember that the wicked never rests…

With one woman safe, Sam Abrams returns to find archeologist Annalynn Gallagher gone. Who has taken her is unclear yet Sam is certain of her ultimate destination: into the possession of a would-be messenger of the gods.

…so don't let down your guard.

When Anna had left her dig site, she had left Zaharrah Lynch in charge. The site has become more dangerous, and, worse, the security is becoming lax. Zaharrah, with her sleep haunted by malevolent darkness, knows she can't stay much longer – no matter that her sibling and cohort hasn't completed his task at the dig.

Death waits for everyone…

Zaharrah will wait as long as she can for her brother, but her window of escape is closing fast. Yet leaving will take her deep into the heart of the Jordan desert, to a place she sees in her dreams – and a deity who would claim the world as his own.

…no matter how far you run.

As the hunt for the remaining mantles draws to a close, Sam, Zaharrah, and the others must prepare for a battle that will reveal the hidden, ancient truths – and have unforeseen consequences for one of their number.

Victory or defeat, each will exact its price.

READ ON FOR A SAMPLE

OR

BUY NOW AT

WWW.AMAZON.COM

1

Anna groaned as she rose from her work space yet again. She had been unable to concentrate since Sam left. Her mind was troubled. She was worried for him and Lance and feared for Catharine's safety. As she walked past the end of the bed, her gaze shifted to the night table where the gun Sam had given her earlier lay concealed. She felt a shiver run down her spine as she remembered the feel of the cool metal in her hands and the weight of it.

Ann blinked how had she gotten here? She wasn't a fighter. She was a scientist. Until a few weeks ago the most dangerous thing she'd ever faced was her parents' disappointment in a choice she made. Since her discovery at the dig site in Israel she'd been followed, had her home broken into and even been shot. The injury was healed but she'd bear the scar as a reminder.

She swallowed, aware she was in well over her head. Anna sat down on the end of her bed as reality began to sink in. Catharine was the prisoner of a serial killer; a man who would systematically torture and destroy her. Lance and Sam were on the move to save her. But the man they faced was no ordinary man. He like James Hardagen and Ian Broody were each possessed by the spirit of a fallen one.

She was being hunted by figures that had once been worshiped as gods. The thought of it left her exhausted. Anna lay her head down on the bed.

"I just need a few minutes," she told herself as she closed her eyes .

2

Sam and Lance moving down an old stair case by flash light. Once on flat ground again, they switched off the dim light as they moved through a dark corridor.

"Maybe he's got her in the attic," Sam muttered as they moved on. The dark passage seemed to go on forever.

"He's down here; I can feel him," Lance whispered as they rounded another corner.

The darkness came to an abrupt end as the room that opened up before them was lit by hundreds of candles.

Anna's heart pounded with terror at the sight before her and unable to face it she turned and ran. Whatever they were facing now she didn't want to see it. She couldn't.

Anna slammed the door separating dark corridor form candle filled chamber and locked it. She leaned against the hard oak and trembled. Her breathing heavy and labored as she fought to keep the door shut.

Dionysus who lurked in the shadows smiled. He'd known if he waited that Anna would reveal herself. He moved from the edge of the dream realm where he'd lurked in wait for her return. With a precision that came from centuries of practice, he slipped into her nightmare without touching her mind and alerting her to his presence.

He watched from the shadows in the dark hall as Anna pressed a hand against the door she'd created to close out what lay on the other side. She drew it back as if burned and for a moment the door and the passageway were replaced by the candlelit room. A bed sat in the center of the room, on it lay a naked, bound and bloodied Catharine. Her kidnapper stood over her watching her. A hand brushed over her bare flesh. Lance stood gun at the ready poised to shoot and Sam's path barred by a ring of burning fire.

Anna turned from the image once more and the dark corridor with the door returned. Dionysus noted that oak had become like a vault door, his prey he noted was fighting hard to keep the image of that room and what was happening there from her thoughts. She was agitated and eager for anything else to latch onto. It would make influencing her that much easier.

Dionysus crept closer to his target.

"What are you afraid of Anna?" he whispered gently, probing her mind for the source of her distress.

He watched as the image of the room resurfaced once more. Now only Sam and the killer remained in the room. The two men stood locked in battle, the struggle ending with Ares blade piercing the man Sam's flesh. Once more the image faded and the door reappeared.

Dionysus closed the distance between them with excitement. He was just a few steps away from his goal. Anna's mind was not yet aware of him, if he could just keep her busy he'd be able to pinpoint her location. Okay so the pretty doctor was worried about her Sam. He could work with that. Fear could be a great lever for pushing a mind to surrender to their lusts, he just needed the right hook to draw her in.

As the god of wine and excess dug deeper into the woman Anna's mind, searching for the right button to press, the man he possessed James Hardagen sat aboard a plane bound for the east coast and his prize.

3

Sam cursed as he was forced to stop at yet another light. He'd caught every one wrong since they left the house. He could feel time slipping away from him and it made him angry. His instincts were screaming for him to get back to Anna. He was aware that none of their enemies were there in the city but still he couldn't shake the sense she was in danger.

With each minute that passed the worse it grew. As he made his way toward the hotel the last words the angel had spoken circled round in his mind.

"I'm here to warn you the road ahead will be hard and fraught with danger. Do not give up hope or give into the influence of the fallen."

As he made his way to Anna, Sam wondered what the angel had meant when he said the road ahead would be hard. Hard for who? Was the message for him or for her?

Sam snarled as he was forced to stop for yet another light.

"You okay man?" Lance questioned from the back seat.

"No, this is taking too long."

"We're almost there."

"I know but I can't shake this feeling that Anna's in trouble."

Dionysus gave Anna's mind a nudge back toward the nightmare she was reluctant to face. He watched as the pretty doctor moved deeper into the room where Sam and the killer had been fighting. The man Sam lay on the cool stone floor in a pool of his own blood, his life slipping away. Anna ran to him falling to her knees beside him. With care she lifted his head into her lap.

"Sam, no. don't leave me," she whispered tears fell from her eyes as she kissed his forehead.

"Anna?" he asked his voice weak.

"Yes, it's me," she assured him. She watched as he opened his eyes and let out a breath she'd been holding. "You're going to be okay," she whispered trying to convince herself of it.

"He's dying Anna and it's your fault," Dionysus whispered to her troubled mind. He watched with delight as the lie was accepted.

"I'm sorry," she whispered before she kissed the dying man's lips. As her lips met his a flash of a memory flitted into Dionysus awareness.

The moment before Sam had left to go face the monster Anna now feared would kill him. Once more the room faded and the door separating it from the hall she hid in returned.

"FORGET THIS DARKNESS ANNA AND SHOW ME WHAT HAPPENED. REMEMBER WHAT CAME BEFORE," Dionysus murmured.

He watched with pleasure as Anna turned away from the door to her nightmare to face what lay back down the dark corridor. The hall twisted and turned like a maze and Dionysus followed her every step with care not to get too close. When they came to the end of the winding stairs he found he was no longer in the house but a hotel room.

Dionysus lurked in the dark corridor careful to remain unseen he watched her memory play out like a scene in a movie withfascination. As it neared the end he moved in closer to hear what was being said.

"After I go don't let anyone in but me, not even Lance," the man Sam instructed. Dionysus watched as Sam drew Anna into his arms for a second time.

"I won't," she told him.

"Good, I'll be back as soon as I can," he promised.

"I know you will," she assured him before she kissed him. It was a short and quick meeting of their lips, but Dionysus felt the desire there for more and smiled.

"Yes that's it enjoy the memory," he whispered as he pressed his power against her mind a little, not wanting to startle her from the memory but wanting her to focus on it completely; needing her to build, dream upon it so that he could enter without her sensing it. If he could get inside her mind then he could locate her.

The nightmare began to recede as her mind slipped back into the memory.

"Be careful out there," she requested.

"I will," Sam assured her and unable to resist he kissed her again his hands sinking into her hair pulling lightly to get a better angle. She gasped startled by the silent demand. He took full advantage of her lips parting; drinking deeply.

Anna moaned as the taste of him hit her like a drug and made her flesh clamor with a need that left her weak in the knees and frightened her. How did he get to her so fast? She'd never had another man's kiss affect her so.

She burned for him and if she didn't have him soon she felt she'd die of it. Her arms wrapped around his neck holding him close not wanting him to let go. Sam eased back and his eyes locked with hers. "I love you," he murmured tenderly. She felt his hold on her ease and knew he meant to go.

Dionysus cursed. "Not as much of a memory as I'd hoped for." he muttered to himself. "Oh well so much for subtle," the wine god groused. Desperate to keep Anna there in that moment he pushed at her with a tidal wave of his power.

As it swept over her and sank into her, Dionysus crossed from the dream world into her mind. He laughed as he felt his power crash through her, making a pleasant feeling of desire become a fierce painful hunger, whose teeth had her body aching for her Sam.

"Don't leave me like this Sam, I need you," she pleaded as she pressed herself against him, bringing memory and dream together, blurring the lines between truth and fantasy. Dionysus latched hold of the dream thread and built the lie about her wrapping her further in it.

"Anna," the dream Sam groaned her name at the feel of her pressed against him. His mouth crashed against hers in a bruising kiss that stole her breath away.

Dionysus thrilled in the feel of her lust stirring but knew not to linger in it, she was on guard against his influence and he'd risked as much as he dare. He needed to finish the job here before he played with her. Dionysus looked about the room created from memory and smiled as he noted the hotel name on the phone by the bed as well as the room number. "Got you," he whispered with excitement. The fallen let part of his own mind return to his servant, it whispered the location of the hotel to the man who for now he shared a body with. Having gotten what he came for the wine god turned back to the woman's fantasy.

He noted with satisfaction her mind was running riot with the memory he'd pushed her to indulge in. Fear drove her now, to take, when before she'd hesitated. "That's right pretty Anna, give yourself over to the hunger. Take greedily what you long for now let me in deeper," he crooned tempting her to give into her desire.

Dionysus approached the sleeper boldly now and with the barest of touch he ran his index finger down her cheek.

Goose flesh rose under his caress and she tore Sam's clothes with frustration, she wanted his skin against hers. She wanted to touch him, to feel him.

As Dionysus finger skimmed lower tracing the line of her neck he reveled in the ease with which her mind was responding to his power. He fed her images of things she could do here with her Sam and her mind latched onto them like a starving beast. He cupped her chin much the way Sam had, blending his touch with the fantasy.

"Yes, that's the way Anna, lose yourself in the dream it'll make it that much easier to get to you when I reach you," Dionysus's mind whispered. The pretty doctor moaned as she found her dream lover's flesh.

5

Anna shivered as Sam brushed the thin silk straps of her gown from her shoulders and the blue green fell off her leaving her in nothing but her stockings and underwear. His hands were everywhere at once, it seemed and it was destroying her mind. She felt the pad of his finger brush against her kiss swollen lips and she imagined drawing it in her mouth biting lightly teasing making him groan, the finger became something more and she blinked startled.

What was wrong with her? She'd never thought of such things before. She'd never had any interest in such acts. She'd always been unsure, when it came to this sort of thing.

So why would she think it now? Opening her eyes she found Sam's blue ones staring back at her with question, pain, and need were written on his face, but acceptance. She knew that if she decided to bring an end to it now he'd respect her wish.

He panted, his breathing heavy as he waited for her to decide. She moaned as she felt his fingers play over her throat though he wasn't touching her. The phantom caress moved lower tormenting her breasts through the thin wisp of cloth that passed for her bra. She pictured his mouth latching there through the lace driving her wild and she felt the jolt of pleasure the image brought her, shoot right to the center of her need.

"Sam," she breathed his name trying to find her control as that phantom caress moved lower playing over her belly. She pictured his mouth there tasting, tongue pressing into her navel teasing her with the promise of what he would do if she allowed him to put his mouth lower. She licked her lips her mouth having gone dry.

"What do you want from me Anna?" He whispered as he brushed a strand of her golden hair out of her face. She felt the fingers playing over her body, slide over her hips to squeeze her backside and she jumped startled by the roughness of the touch here. She pictured Sam pressing his need against her here, bending her over teasing her...

FOR MORE,

GET *TRUTH REVEALED* AT

WWW.AMAZON.COM

WANT TO SEE WHERE IT ALL BEGAN?

THEN CHECK OUT

Available at www.amazon.com

A mysterious discovery leads one woman to stumble upon a startling secret of the ancient world...

Annalynn Gallagher is an archeologist working the find of the century with the last person she ever wanted to see again: Dr. Ian Broody, the man who'd ruined her life. Now trouble is brewing at the dig and Anna is determined to prevent the past from repeating itself.

Some secrets should stay in the dark...

As she delves for the answers about the rising turmoil she finds only more danger. From her dig site to her home back in the States, she encounters sabotage, ominous tails, and threats to her safety and sanity. Seeking help, she turns to a man with a history darker than her own.

...or they will drive you over the edge.

Sam Abrams left the blackness of his past behind a long time ago. With his career as a professional fighter on the rise, he has little interest in aiding a prim and proper archeologist with her issues – especially when he has enough of his own. Then he catches sight of what's followed Anna and can't turn away.

Some things have to be fought...

At Anna's dig site, an ancient evil stirs awake. As it reaches back into the world, Ann and Sam land in the heart of a dark storm that could mean the end of them.

...others have to be survived.

The clock has started ticking and the world may never be the same